PRAISE FOR

G000043082

"Reminiscent of the best spa
violent dystopia of cyberpur .... for fans of
Alastair Reynolds and William Gibson."

Booklist on *Glow*

"Running beneath the violent tangle of identity and memory is
a fascinating exploration of how people cope – or fail to – with
adversity."

Publishers Weekly on *Glow*

"Dynamic prose, cutting-edge science, and thoughtful
ruminations on the future of our species – Tim Jordan's Glow is
a terrific read from a major new voice. A first-rate novel; I was
enthralled."

Robert J. Sawyer, Hugo Award-winning author of *The*
Oppenheimer Alternative on *Glow*

"A deftly written debut jewel of cyberpunk; an ode to transcendent
humanity. With the immortal angst of *Altered Carbon, Glow* heralds
a capable new voice in the genre."

Terry Madden, Award-winning author of the *Three Wells of the*
Sea series on *Glow*

BY THE SAME AUTHOR

Glow

Tim Jordan

AFTERGLOW

ANGRY ROBOT

ANGRY ROBOT
An imprint of Watkins Media Ltd

Unit 11, Shepperton House
89 Shepperton Road
London N1 3DF
UK

angryrobotbooks.com
twitter.com/angryrobotbooks
Another one bites the Glow

An Angry Robot paperback original, 2022

Cover by Tom Shone
Edited by Paul Simpson and Robin Triggs
Set in Meridien

ISBN 978 0 85766 987 2
Ebook ISBN 978 0 85766 988 9

Printed and bound in the United Kingdom by TJ Books Ltd.

9 8 7 6 5 4 3 2 1

MIX
Paper from
responsible sources
FSC
www.fsc.org   FSC® C013056

For Joanna.
This one is all for you, my love.

CHAPTER 1

The Scrap Dealers

A cool, salt breeze whipped in from the South China Sea, picking up a cocktail of scents from the Pearl River Delta and the city of Macau. It surged over the rolling hills and farmlands nearby, borrowing fragrances of country life and dense, sweltering humanity. A particularly feisty gust passed through one of the open windows of Keller Morten's pickup truck, leaching a little moisture from his brow before exiting out the other side. With a sigh, it carried on its epic journey across Guangdong Province, taking a hint of Keller's chemical essence, his fear, joy, and hopes, along for the ride.

Through his monocular, Keller saw the smoke from Honneck's truck long before the actual vehicle slewed around a distant corner and into view. "An hour late," he muttered, "not bad."

He thumbed the starter and his pickup's electric motor hummed to life. The vehicle rolled forward and off the dirt road, nosing into the forest of tree-high soybean plants. Out of sight of the road, he u-turned and sat waiting, fingering the pistol, snug inside his jeans' pocket.

An old fear surfaced as a prickle at the base of his skull, oozing like melting icicles down his spine. That fear of first contact. *Of conflict!* He looked at his hand, *the one that used to hold the scalpel,* how it shook uncontrollably and then froze, useless.

No, not here. Keller relaxed his focus, seeing through his

1

fingers and the towering bean stems, to the distant hills and clouded skies. The fingernails of his other hand dug into the steering wheel as he imagined having cyborg strength. *Her strength!* Crushing the wheel and taming the fear.

He conjured her face, her smile, those magenta eyes, and the panic receded.

The honk of a truck horn snapped him alert. Seconds later, he watched the tar-black smokestack ease off the road and onto his newly flattened soybean trail. Honneck's ancient diesel vehicle labored and gasped across the rough terrain before grinding to a stalling halt face-to-face with Keller's.

Honneck rolled out of his truck cab and dropped the considerable height onto the dirt, noticeably touching his own concealed weapon in his pocket as he landed. "Keller! Long time... long time." A smile peeled easily from his flat, bronzed face as he stretched out a grossly oversized hand for an obligatory businessman's shake.

Keller tipped his baseball cap with his free hand. Though he towered over the man, he was easily the lighter of the two. "You are a long, long way from home, my friend."

Honneck patted his truck like a revered steed. "Hunt. Drive. Sell. If God is good, then I go back home a little richer." The truck's rear end resembled a mobile yurt, an elongated lattice dome of wood and mesh covered in layers of skins and tarps that flapped angrily in the breeze.

"Show me what you've got," Keller said, feeling a cool wash of relief as initial contact passed uneventfully.

"You're my best customer. I always give you first pickings." Honneck gave a nervous laugh and looked around as if expecting Alliance police to come surging out of the bean crops. "You're gonna wanna buy it all."

"We'll see." It was over a year since their last meeting. Back then Macau had been an independent city, one of the many local dictatorships that comprised China following the Nova-Insanity. Trade was easy, rules were few, but the Alliance came, crashing the party in one of their colossal embassy-class warships, to press their laws and rules onto the skeptical community. Increased patrols and new high-tech surveillance made trade transactions like theirs less frequent and far more dangerous. Honneck could have been bought. The whole thing a trap. But that easy smile reassured him.

Honneck hauled a plank ramp down from the truck and climbed up into the dimly lit space. Keller followed, pushing past dangling cables, chain-linked plates of metal, and swathes of fabric. A row of limbs rattled like grisly wind chimes as he shouldered through, smelling burnt plastic, machine oil, and wood rot. Cockroaches scuttled under his feet while the shells of their other, less fortunate cousins, crunched into a fine powder as he shuffled deeper into the truck's interior.

"Arms." Honneck ran his hands lovingly over the suspended appendages. Keller perused the collection: mostly broken fragments, electric drive units, no micro-pile power supplies, no electro-polymer muscles. Nothing pre-Nova-Insanity – the *real* good stuff.

"That it?" Keller tried to sound even more disappointed than he truly was. It was a long day's journey out here for just ordinary scrap.

Honneck dismissed the limbs, sweeping them aside like a macabre curtain to reveal racks of Inner-I units, processor blocks, and smaller, more intricate robotic fragments. "Nice ball-joint, look... good price." He jabbered on, thrusting a severed plastic hand at Keller's face.

"Not bad." Keller flexed its fingers; smooth, clean, probably still worked if hooked up correctly. He picked up an Inner-I block. A glass eyeball dangled from a single connecting wire. He grimaced noticing a smear of dried blood on the component. The eye was nice work, a self-contained unit with an internal ball-drive and pre-processor. "Where's the other eye?"

"One eye's plenty." Honneck winked and doubled the width of his grin. "But the best stuff's here." Honneck hovered theatrically over a filthy black tarpaulin at the rear of the truck. "They pay big money for this in the city." He whisked aside the tarp and Keller found himself straining into the darkness trying to see what lay underneath.

He gagged. Staggering backwards as he saw a human corpse, just the top half, severed at the waist and charred beyond recognition. "What the fuck!" He shoved a hand into his mouth. The other fumbled into his pocket seeking his gun. The dark, dank world of Honneck's truck spun around him, a prison, a crushing hell, that just had to be escaped.

"No," Honneck said, seizing Keller's arm with an alarmingly strong grip that assured Keller that even if his hand found the gun, he'd never get to use it. "Look. That's not a dead man, just a robot. A robot good enough to *look* like a dead man."

Keller's deep sense of curiosity thrust his fears aside. His world stopped spinning, and the visions of white rooms filled with dead and dying people faded, returning him back to the interior of Honneck's truck. Leaning in closer, he saw the body's arms were broken away beneath the elbows, no visible bones, the limbs just trailed off into thinner and thinner fibers. He tilted the chest cavity up with his foot and looked inside. It was empty, a few lumps of black material hung from a mesh framework that was clearly not a vitrified human ribcage.

Running his fingers up the longer of the arms, he felt no drive units or actuators. No power modules hiding in the chest, just a lightweight hollow shell. "All the good bits are missing. This is just a clod of fried carbon fiber."

A skull leered through tatters of knotted black fiber, translucent and crystalline, definitely not bone, metal, or even plastic. He grasped one of the carbonized cheeks and tried to pull the charred material free, but it was tough and sharp, ripping the skin from the tips of his fingers.

"The head's made of crystal, very tough." Honneck rapped on the skull with a knuckle. "I tried to crack it open with a jack-hammer, but it wouldn't break."

"Nice job. If there was anything useful inside, then you probably busted it." He noted the empty eye sockets, a thin retinal cable dropped out of each one. A tiny bead on the end of each strand looked like it was growing into a new eye. Probably a new type of eyeball connector – *might be worth something.*

"Where did you find this?" Keller was on his knees, suddenly intrigued by the find.

"Herdsman up in the mountains somewhere. It left a crater in the ice." Honneck grasped his hands together as if in prayer. "After it dropped straight from outer space."

"Yeah... right, freaking space robots." Keller recalled the recent war between the GFC and the Breakout Alliance. TwoLunar ripping apart. The Cloud9 orbital exploding. Looking at the charring on this machine, it really could have fallen from orbit.

"There's nothing left... just a head." Keller said, deciding that he wanted the piece. If he could drill open the skull, there might be some high-end electronics or data modules, perhaps some useful AI software in there. It would be a gamble to spend the last of his money on such a piece of junk, but if he were right–

"I can get a thousand for it in the city." Honneck was a poor liar, but great at getting interesting robot scrap.

"A thousand?" Keller hopped down off the truck and began the obligatory walk-away-in-disgust routine. "One-twenty for the robot, that Inner-I and eyeball unit, and throw that spare hand in for free."

"You're killing me man. Two-fifty, then I can feed my family for a few more days."

"You should eat less," Keller patted Honneck's rotund stomach and pulled his truck door open. "I can't go higher than one-fifty. You'll have to go to the city with it. Good luck getting past the Alliance patrols. They just love aging Tu parts traffickers, you know."

"Two hundred."

"One-sixty," Keller countered again, feeling the small, inadequate wad of his remaining two-hundred dollars scrunched inside his pocket.

"One-ninety."

"One-sixty-one." There... he saw that nervous tick on Honneck's face. He wanted to unload this piece. Maybe it really was from space, maybe military or Alliance, hot property, valuable but too dangerous for this old-school trader.

Keller started his engine and began turning the vehicle around and up onto the road. He pointed it back at distant Macau, believing his gut instinct that Honneck would run after him all the way to the city border for a few extra bucks.

As the truck lurched back onto the road, his glovebox flopped open and a clump of crumpled notes and old cyborg magazines he'd picked up along the way tumbled out onto the floor. "Come on man!" Honneck yelled as he jogged alongside. "Give me something to work with here." His face was rapidly turning from healthy bronze to a flustered purple.

Keller hit the brakes and reached for the fallen papers. "I might have something for you."

In the end, they transferred the merchandise in a different produce field, a full kilometer from where they started. Keller handed over one-hundred and sixty-five Macau dollars and an antique copy of Augmented Magazine. Once the cash was in hand, and Keller was back in his truck, Honneck dropped his smile and grew serious. "Be careful, Keller. The herdsmen say that robot of yours is haunted."

Keller's foot hovered over the accelerator. "Haunted?"

"Yeah, it moves in the night when no one is looking."

Keller's heart sank. The robot probably wasn't valuable, just junk those superstitious herdsmen had attached some mythical nonsense to. "It can't move," he said, choking back his disappointment. "There's no power supply." He punched the pedal and Honneck vanished into his dust.

CHAPTER 2

In Hiding

The prickling sting of a scanner singed Rex's skin. He ran, but the weight of the corpse zip-tied to his arm dragged him down, down into the dark, wet mud.

"Rex? You okay buddy?" The voice cut away the night and his eyes sprang open. *No dead man. No zip-ties.* A rectangle of light above resolved into a skylight window. The corpse was now bedsheets wrapped around his arm, and the cloying, wet mud just his own sweat and drool.

"Rex?" The knocking on the cellar door grew more insistent. "Come on buddy, snap out of it."

But the feeling of being scanned still prickled his scalp, a focused beam of energy working its way up and down, lingering over specific spots: his brain, his heart, drilling through his skin to the network of tiny machines inside. *I am Glow. I am the plague!*

The door latch jangled, opened, and somebody stepped inside, framed by the artificial light from the basement stairs. "Rex. For goodness' sake."

He tried to grab back control of his thoughts before they wandered back to *him*, the name he couldn't bear to mention. Even thinking his name brought him closer to the surface, gave him more power, and one day he'd take over again and Rex's life would no longer be his own.

"Look at me… my eyes… my face. Come to me, Rex."

"John?" Rex looked up at the concerned old man; a lifetime of worry scored his leathery skin. From down low he was radiant, godlike: *my Master*. As Rex sat up and stood, suddenly looking down on him, he became just a man, just John. A friend whose dog was buried in the back garden. A dog who somehow, through an unlikely chain of events, still lived inside Rex's Glow-based mind and applied the force and motivation to his very human body.

"There you go," John said, carefully patting Rex's arm as if he might strike him with one of his trembling fists. "Just another bad dream. We all get 'em, you know." He turned away and eased back up the basement steps and into the light. "Millie's up and about. Might as well do the introduction now you're awake. Then we can have breakfast. It's eggs today, and waffles."

Rex looked around his basement room. The closest thing he could remember to an actual home. A floor mattress, sacks of aging provisions framed by waterpipes and electrical cables. The only window to the world was the skylight, up near the ceiling and covered in black binbags.

He jumped on a chair and pulled the makeshift blind aside. Light flooded in through green creepers and bushes. He looked out across John's side yard, through the hedge to the neighbor's window. Something there… *A white plastic face?* No… just a lamp.

The prickling sensation in his brain subsided and he ambled over to the stairs, hearing John doing the morning introduction to his wife, Millie, just as he'd done every morning for the months Rex had stayed with them.

He checked his robe, scratched down his hair into some semblance of order and topped the staircase into the kitchen. Millie stood arm-in-arm with John. She couldn't mask her fear, could no longer fake civility, excitement, or interest. Her face reflected what was real inside her at this moment only:

fear, hunger, tiredness – raw and unfiltered. Her eyes searched Rex, seeking something familiar but managing only a flicker of recognition that didn't quite catch. Eventually, they focused instead on the table, and the deck of playing cards purposefully left there by John the night before.

"Here he is," John exclaimed keeping his voice calm and cheerful. "Millie, meet my old friend Rex. He spent the night here after a few drinks and some cards yesterday evening."

"Rex?" she stammered. "I don't remember... or–?"

"I think you were in bed when I arrived." Rex issued their standard, agreed-upon storyline. "Lovely to meet you, um... Mrs Weston." He reached out a hand and she reluctantly touched it as if checking for warmth before giving it a quick, furtive shake.

"Call me Millie," she said. "Will you be staying long?"

"Just a night." He nodded at John for approval, and John winked back.

"Let's get Rex some coffee and breakfast, shall we?" John bustled off to the kitchen and Millie's confusion dissolved into purposeful action. Things were okay once again.

CHAPTER 3

Perfection

Keller's barge was very different from the thousands of fishing boats moored in Macau harbor. The *CyberSea* was a rectangular block, painted tar black – the very opposite of hospital white – with a stout, armored glass cabin at the prow. A single long, metal-peaked roof ran most of the boat's length, dotted with upward facing skylights and window blisters.

Keller drove off the dock, along the service ramp, and onto the rear of the barge. A lever tilted the deck, opening a route down into the barge's internal garage. He parked and secured the pickup for sea-travel, clamping the wheels in place and covering the whole thing with a cling-tight plastic cocoon.

Grimace, his security bot, sat poised and menacing on deck, daring anyone to try boarding without permission. His fire-red eyes locked gazes with Keller for an instant as the dull but comprehensive algorithms inside Grimace's electronic mind compared what they saw with stored architypes, references, and facial feature configurations, finally deciding that Keller was friend and not foe.

Grimace's jaw was deliberately bent sideways, a fake cigarette dangled from his metal lips while a jaunty sailor's cap remained secured to his head no matter the weather. Keller had modeled him loosely upon the old cartoon character, Popeye. Not quite finished, the machine had a hook for a left hand, one of the many projects scheduled for the journey ahead.

Keller popped open the trapdoor that led down into his lab and heaved the sack of robot salvage onto his shoulder. As he descended, he caught Grimace's eye. "Any visitors?"

"Miss Casima Salean." Grimace's chainsaw voice emanated from a speaker in his chest.

Keller's heart leapt. "Did she leave?"

"No, she's still onboard." His heart dropped back into immediate calm. *With her, I am safe and free.*

Keller closed the door, feeling a pang of sadness. She'd probably come by to say her farewells and maybe leave him a parting gift, something special to keep him happy for the long voyage ahead. The thought of losing her was a sharp ache in his craw. But it was her way. Her attachment to her city versus his needs for travel and trade, and to be constantly on the move.

Keller dumped his new gear in the corner and stood sucking in the familiar atmosphere of his private, ocean-going laboratory. Cables and appendages hung from overhead racks. Computer screens hummed and flickered on desks and many half-finished projects lay scattered across benches or dangled from hooks. Several humanoid forms stood prone in the corners and a huge, greasy, metal hexapod lay sprawled out across the central workbench. Hex was his outside maintenance robot, equipped with Gecko-like feet to work on boat hulls below the waterline, a vital piece of equipment whose services earned him his keep.

"Casi?" he called softly. There was no sign of her in the lounge, the galley, or the small reading room that jutted out the front of the barge in a thick, glass bubble that housed his collection of books, magazines, and memory blocks. Which left only the bedroom.

He pushed open the door. His big, square bed took up most of the tight, wedge-shaped room. Casima lay curled under the top sheet, her head poking out, clearly sleeping. Her flawless, electro-polymer face the picture of peace and calm.

She'd been perusing his magazine collection again. Several of them lay scattered around her on the bed. A particularly sought-after 2051 copy of Cyborg Monthly lay spread open at the centerfold beneath her prone fingers. He started easing the magazine out from her hand and she stirred awake.

"Darling?" she muttered, opening her silver-flecked, magenta eyes. "I was dreaming about you."

"Good dreams?" Keller whipped the magazine free and stood staring at the glossy pages.

"Who was I looking at?" Casima said, blinking the sleep from her eyes.

"They called this the Dhannah look, very popular with mid-century cyborg fanatics."

Casima reached out and ran a finger over the image. "I love her. Look at the definition in those polymer muscles, those dimples around the tendons. She looks so strong, so purposeful."

"I prefer the real thing." He drew a gentle line up her leg with his finger. She wore her good legs, the ones he had made. Like her face, they were warm to the touch with quality micro-capillaries that emulated real flesh. "How about your day?" he asked. "Bag any rich tourists?"

She shrugged and rolled into a sitting position while stretching and running a hand through her hair. "An Alliance guy from the embassy ship, bureaucrat of some sort, with his wife and horrible, screaming kids. Don't think they were really into the sights and history of old Macau. Just killing time until their flight, but they tipped me well and bombed-out early to catch a five-o-clock special." She bounced her knees with excitement. "That's why I came here early. To be with you."

Keller dropped onto the bed and nuzzled his face in the small of her back, his hands running up her legs to her thighs, to the joins where real flesh met the artificial. A line so fine it was barely there at all, but somehow it was the bit that turned him on the most, that combination of perfect, manmade creation and flawed, vulnerable nature. She was a rare creature, more machine than flesh, a work of art; partly his own doing, although mostly self-procured through dealings in Macau. He replaced damaged parts, performed upgrades and updates, tuned, optimized, and managed all of her topical and aesthetic replacements, but performing actual surgery? No, he could no longer do that.

She rolled playfully out of his grasp. "How was our old friend Honneck?"

"Stoic. Predictable. I got a few good pieces and one that may be junk, or it might be valuable." He felt his angst rise, knowing now that he'd overpaid but not wanting to confess his error to Casima.

"So you'll be leaving soon," she whispered.

"Tomorrow." His lips found the back of her neck and his hands ran through her silk hair. He caressed the plate boundaries between the real fragments of her skull and the coral-titanium implants. She smelled clean and perfect.

He'd never asked her to accompany him, never dared. The rejection would hurt too much. She'd been born here and claimed she would die here and be at peace with the ghosts of her family. Besides, if she accepted and came with him, then that was a terrifying commitment to being confined in a small space with another human for months on end. Something he'd been unable to contemplate since the Nova-Insanity, when trauma had etched itself on to his brain.

His throat constricted as it always did, stifling his words. But something was different this time: a passion, a need. Words that had to be heard, to force their way past the searing mess of doubts and phobias and out into their world. "Come with me," he whispered. The ache of her loss already a sickening lump in his guts.

She shook her head, easing gently from his grasp and away across the bed.

"We have good times, don't we?" he said. The words came easier as if he'd stepped over a precipice, committed! No going back now.

She made a small nod.

"You know I love you. I'll work hard, make us a good living, and when we get to America, we sell some bots, turn around and come right back again. A wonderful itinerant lifestyle. It's what I do. What I need to do." The shake of her head felt like it was tearing him in two. "I know you need to be here, need the city, but think about it... there's nothing real here for you, just memories, bad ones, mostly. Come make some new memories with me." He choked on his words as his train of thought plowed into a cliffside of doubt.

She sat up slowly, her hand smearing away the tears from his cheek. "I'm sorry, Keller."

"It's okay," he said, steeling himself to swallow the bitter pill life kept jamming down his throat.

The smile lit her face as she slapped a biomechanical hand across his backside. "I'm screwing with you, Kell! Of course, I'll come! What the heck took you so long to ask?"

His mouth dropped open, and words stuttered out. "But I thought... Why? What changed–"

Her pupils spun in a very inhuman way as she tapped her temple with a fingertip. "You know what being around you has taught me?" He shook his head. "My ghosts are in here, with me always, but you're real, Kell, the living, breathing truth. I can't just be with you in my mind anymore." She rose from the bed like a cobra triangulating its prey. "Anyway... you need me, Kell. I'm your guide in this world."

She snatched at his shirt, ripping it up and over his head. Her legs wrapped around him, twisting and curling unlike real human legs could ever do. The breath from her single lung sent shivers down his neck. The schematics of her body filled his mind. That gap where her other lung should have been now occupied by a super-capacitor that powered her cybernetics. Below was her lab-grown liver, her artificial stomach, and somebody else's kidneys. But the parts, the mechanics, dataflows, and mechanisms didn't matter. It was the whole, that wonderful, emergent, holistic entity that called itself Casima.

Perfection!

With her, I am safe and free.

CHAPTER 4

Dog in a Poker Game

"Woof!"

Rex was fairly sure that was one of John's big tells: A 'seemingly' uncontrollable outburst at the unveiling of a near perfect, and assumedly unbeatable, poker hand. Which really meant that the hand wasn't that good, a bluff! Except when it wasn't–

He ignored John and focused on his own cards, not really seeing them, not really caring if he won or lost. They flipped more cards, the flop, the turn, the river... exchanged bets, piling the matchsticks into the middle of the table.

"Pair of Queens?" John's watery eyes filled with hope as he dropped his cards face-up on the table. *So it wasn't a bluff.*

"Got me beat again." Rex laid down his ace-high and watched John sweep up the winning matches. He arranged them in neat piles of parallel pairs, crisscrossed on top of each other forming miniature scaffold towers. John's stacking routine drove his other poker buddies mad, but Rex didn't care, time to contemplate, to just stare at him in odd, canine awe.

"Future-Lord taking the night off, Rex?" John asked, eyeing the height of each of his growing piles, making sure they were the same.

Rex nodded and began to deal.

John was the only other person in the world who knew

the entire story. But he acted as if Rex had always been there. Just accepting him for who and what he was: a friend who had hit on hard times and now lived in his basement. A good companion, cleaner, garden worker, and a pushover at poker.

John eagerly grabbed at his cards, not waiting to see Rex's reaction, while Rex stared down at the seven of hearts and the three of diamonds. Maybe the Future-Lord really had deserted him.

The TV flashed pictures of crowds gathered in downtown Welkin, while the voice of Hmech boomed out of the speakers, touting the coming "liberation", as they preferred to call the invasion. Millie sat bolt upright on the couch, gaze fixed on the images, as Rex watched the reflection of her eyes on the TV screen. As the signals seeped deeper into her thoughts, they lost meaning, like water dripping on to parched, dry sand. Sometimes they would hit on a memory and for those few precious seconds Millie was Millie once again: the woman John fell in love with, married, and shared six-decades of blissful existence.

John let out a loud, forced cough that segued into speech. "You still with us, Millie? Don't go dozing off this early in the evening. You'll be fidgeting awake all night long." She glanced over her shoulder and saw Rex, struggled to remember who he was, saw cards, bottles, and glasses, and turned back to the TV.

Once, after one of Millie's bad days, John told Rex their story. "I loved that she was different from all of us other kids," John said. "We just wanted to sit around and play shoot-em-up games, but Mill, as we called her back then, wanted to fix people. She learned all these big words, Latin, I guess. Even tried to teach me a few. After she retired from nursing, those big words all kind of got stuck in her throat, and I knew something was wrong. Soon after that, even the little words got stuck, and then she forgot my name."

In a post-Nova-Insanity world, treatment options for dementia were sparse. Of course, the GFC's Simmorta could stave off the inevitable indefinitely, but John could never afford that. As his wife lost her mind and he lost his only real companion, John was swayed by a slick salesman: Glow was the answer. "Simmorta for the masses", and at a fraction of the cost, it would be dumb not to use it!

Glow worked well... for a while, cementing Millie's crumbling mind back into a whole, filling in memory gaps and creating a solid backup to her ailing personality. Those few months had relit the wonder in their relationship. John even tried the stuff himself; heck, he even gave it to the dog. But as the Glow doses mounted, John noticed the other personas hitching rides into his thoughts. He saw it in Millie too, how she became several different people over the course of a single day. Bright and lucid as those people were, they were clearly not her.

After the lich came for them, John vowed to never use Glow again. Stoic and strong he'd dumped their remaining supply in the trash and never touched it since. But forcing Millie to quit had been harder, watching her fall back into the quiet empty shell after months of torment by her inner withdrawal demons. The nights he'd agonized over that decision. But now, as he watched the news of the plague sweeping across nations, turning populations into dull, shambling clusters of fleshy automatons, he made peace – the right decisions were always the hardest to make.

"Hrmmm!" John coughed again, jolting Rex alert. "You still playing?" His thumbs whirled in an impatient roll. A sure tell that he had a hand he wanted to bet.

Rex fumbled a fistful of matches into the pot without looking at his cards.

"That confident, eh?" John muttered, doing that agitated sideways bob that he did when second guessing his initial confidence. "Call," he said, folding his cards defiantly in front of himself. "And raise." His quivering hands pushed a whole stack of matches into the center. Rex shook his head and feigned concern. Anything to keep the old man engaged and enjoying the moment.

"Ooh... that reminds me." John's face lit with a sudden remembrance. "While you were out walking today, an old friend of yours popped by."

"Old friend?" Rex's heart gave a single, startled lurch in his chest.

"French sounding name... *tres bien*... or, no ... that was it, Trabian. Said he knew you once years ago. I said you was out, and he told me to tell you 'Ellayna sends her regards from deepest space.' Funny thing to say if you ask me."

At the mention of that name, Rex felt Del jolt alive in his mind. Del had been quiet of late. His protests at imprisonment fading as he seemed to seep back into the Star-River substrate he'd had implanted in Rex's skull, lost in his endless simulations of the end of the world.

"Ellayna... Trabian?" Rex tried the names again and felt Del's anguish permeate *his* body. "I don't know anyone by those names."

John shrugged. "Seemed to know you. Young chap, but with haunted eyes, like he'd seen a lot of ghosts in his short years."

Rex struggled to hide his growing fear. *They have found me.* And here he was, the old dog left to defend the helpless. Endangering them with just his presence.

A loud snore came from Millie. "Sounds like the train's departed." John nodded in her direction and eyed the wall clock. "Feels like bedtime for us both."

"Best call it a night after this hand," Rex said, fighting his nausea at John's revelation. He pushed all his remaining matchsticks into the middle and John pounced on the opportunity.

"Call... got you, Rex, got you. I know I have." He slammed his pair of tens onto the table and sat back, face rippling in fear of losing, eyes peeled wide with hope.

The two aces on the table matched nicely with the two more in Rex's hand. Four aces, which must be the Future-Lord telling him something. Rex folded his cards away in mock-disgust. "Nah... I got nothing," he said. "You win again."

CHAPTER 5

The CyberSea

The *CyberSea* crashed through the choppy harbor waves with all the grace and efficiency of a diesel-powered brick, sending sheets of spray up and over the barge's prow, soaking Keller as he fought the wheel and rode the swells with cowboy tenacity.

He liked an open-window policy when commanding his boat. Open space. That feel of sea air and spray on his face, something Casima had tried, briefly, before retreating back to the warm, dry lounge, and watching from behind the comfort of a safety-glass viewing blister.

Through the towering concrete harbor gates and into open waters, Macau vanished in the mist behind them, now just a luminous dome of smog and light pollution in the early morning grey. The sun rose behind storm clouds shedding a sinister light over the ocean. Ahead, the behemoth nation ship, the *Nevis*, was a dark and foreboding rhombus, lurking in international waters. Around it a fleet of smaller boats came and went, collecting and delivering supplies and travelers to and from the mainland.

"I'm back." Casima teetered along the deck toward the cabin. She'd abandoned Keller's impractical but aesthetically pleasing legs and found the going easier with her shorter, more agile urban ones. They lowered her center of gravity and handled the awkward ship motion with ease, leaving the rest of her body, from hips upward, waggling and tottering in a strange, ungraceful way.

"First time on a boat?" Keller chuckled, knowing it wouldn't matter once they docked with the *Nevis*.

She grinned and used the window frame to ease herself into the cabin. A soft-pink poncho with its hood pulled up over her head kept the sea-spray at bay. Keller snaked a steadying arm around her waist, pinning her securely to his side. He felt her relax and begin to ride the sea's motion instead of resisting.

The *CyberSea* slalomed through the flotilla of watercraft surrounding the *Nevis*. Some leaving, others just joining, most were there to ply wares and offer services. *Nevis* would shed most of that diffuse halo of crafts when it departed for the more dangerous waters of the open ocean.

"This is my eighth voyage with the *Nevis*," Keller said. "She's kind of an old friend now."

"Don't go making me jealous." Casima's soft, polymer hand rested on the nape of his neck, caressing away the tension built up from battling the waves.

"I didn't think you'd come with me," even the words made Keller's stomach churn. "That I could never pry you away from your city."

"Didn't really think you'd want me along... you know... cramping your style."

He faced her squarely, suddenly serious. "I told you, there's never been anybody else. Literally never."

"Heard that one before," she laughed.

"No really, I was a college nerd studying to be a doctor and then a surgeon. No time for anything else. You know the rest." He felt his blood pressure surge, sweat trickle down from his armpits. *Breathe... out here I am safe. With her I am safe and free.*

"I'm grateful that you became a robot nerd." She touched her hip pocket where she kept the photos. He'd seen most of them, friends, brothers, parents, their faces and identities lost in the crinkles and stains. Then there was the one he'd taken of her as she took him on his first tour around Macau. At the time he went out of sympathy, didn't really need a guide. She was so small, he assumed she was just a child, but really it was her prosthetics, legs made from wooden crutches and rusty cables with big, clunky electric motors. Her back hunched under the weight of the old car batteries, one on each side, giving her the power to move. She carried a colorful umbrella, a solar charger that took all day to repower the cells. One day at work, another begging on the streets while she recharged. "I've no pictures of me," she said as he handed her the photo. He came back the next morning to take more, and to do another tour.

Keller swung the barge around to the rear of the *Nevis* through the densest swathe of boats and ships, all heaving in the ocean only meters apart. A path remained clear through the middle leading up to the *Nevis*'s entry port. Keller steered the barge into the makeshift waterway like a vessel entering a canal and joined the immigration line.

The *Nevis* itself was an eclectic kluge of large ocean vessels, headed at the front by a defunct oil tanker, one of the largest ever built. It was still solid and stoic, bristling with wind-turbines, solar arrays, radar domes and defense pods. The *Nevis* family who owned and ran the ship lived up front with thousands of permanent residents. Behind the front tanker and secured to it by colossal articulating steel walkways were two smaller tankers fastened side by side by an underwater grid of girders. The space between formed a sheltered harbor, a sanctuary for smaller vessels. Each harbor-tanker had yet another, smaller vessel fastened to its out-facing side, making them in-effect catamarans. Like wings joined to the outside tankers, two giant oil rig platforms arched out into the ocean on flexible couplings. The platforms were used as additional moorings and housed thermal-difference engines and wave-motion plants that powered the nation ship.

"It's huge," Casima said, craning her neck up at one of the passing hulks.

"Five-million tons of city in the sea."

They powered in past rear defense platforms, tracked by turret guns and gigantic longshore bots with gantry shoulders and arms made of cranes. A mechanical spider the height of a tower block waved them through and into the calm of the inner harbor where they joined the thousands of other vessels moored inside.

Keller maneuvered the *CyberSea* in next to a near-identical barge. They bumped together gently, and he listened for the familiar clicks and grinds as the automatic docking mechanisms sought out their connection ports and pulled the *CyberSea* into tight proximity to its new neighbor. As the locks closed, the choppy motion of the barge froze into the slow, rhythmic swell of the *Nevis*. They were now part of the big ship, bolted in place for the next three months.

Keller let go of the wheel and killed the barge's engine. "Our boat is now public property. Anyone can walk over it, so make sure you keep the doors locked and any possessions off the deck."

An animated face appeared on Keller's control screen, blue and friendly, almost like a cartoon cat, but with very human features. "Name please," it asked in English. The translation of its words appeared in a dozen other languages on the screen.

"Keller Morten aboard the *CyberSea*."

"Welcome back, Mr Morten. Do you require ship's quarters in addition to your barge mooring?"

"Just the mooring."

"And how are you paying for your transit?"

Keller felt the twinge of anxiety. "I'll work. My credit record should be good." Cash reserves were small, any capital being tied up in robot parts, magazines and various other fungibles stashed away on the barge.

The avatar paused. "Yes, your work record is excellent, and we have plenty of need for your services over the next three months. Welcome aboard and enjoy your trip."

Keller slapped his hands together, rubbing away the chill of the sea. "Off deck, Grimace," he barked at the motionless robot poised over the barge's stern. Grimace folded himself back through the door and into the viewing lounge. His metal visage appeared in the window blister. He would remain on guard but confined to the inside of the barge.

"Exciting," Casima muttered, her eyes huge as she took in the whole experience.

He curled a hand around her waist. This would be a test for him. The longest he would spend in the company of another human since the Nova-Insanity. Rather than the panic he usually felt when confined to any space with another living person, he felt strangely calm. Things were going to be alright.

CHAPTER 6

All That Remains

Boiler Hill, Rex's name for the nub of rock and dirt jutting up over the city rooftops. A favored haunt for when he needed an escape, somewhere to be alone with his thoughts without straying too far from the people he most cared for.

The cylindrical remains of the water tower that once crowned the low summit lay scattered and smashed across its slopes. Rex clung to the snapped-off stump of one of its concrete legs, blending with the rust and creepers like a chameleon, eyes focused out across Coriolis City.

There, through a gap in the trees and tilted office buildings was the yard of the Forever Friends Rescue Sanctuary. Sometimes he saw dogs, sometimes tiny figures, perhaps Mrs Ogilvy or Hanna or one of her many new helpers. He even imagined he recognized some of the dogs: Rust, Bela, Winston… Goliath? His eyes grew watery and the huge wolfhound became just a mirage. His fingers twitched, imagining Goliath's soft fur still warm after he'd given his life to save Rex and Mira. The lich he'd fought off, there to collect on Mira's Glow debt, was long dead now, removed, rendered, and processed. Whatever demented mind had inhabited that body was a glowworm, a soul in damnation, living inside a manmade hell watching the world helpless and trapped inside someone else's body.

Just like Del.

Rex had never fully pieced together who Del was. Even Del seemed unsure as he surfaced in Rex's dreams, startled alive, wondering who and where he was, only to fall back into what he knew, the Star-River with its endless simulations of mankind's future. But Rex understood one thing, that you could never trust a glowworm. They all wanted the same thing: freedom from their prison. A body. *His* body.

Rex had gleaned some facts over the last months, usually from John's stack of old news journals; other times, things seeped through the barriers in his mind giving hints from either Felix's or Del's personal memories. He understood that Del was a founder of the once mighty GFC and equally responsible for its downfall. Del had languished in their prison on the Cloud9 orbital for years before his escape. An audacious jailbreak unlike any in history, he'd downloaded his own mind into a drug substrate, into Glow itself, a copy of which now resided inside Rex's mind.

The *GFC*, that was a name that invoked hatred, fear, but also nostalgia. Or maybe that belonged to Del? It poisoned the world with its immortality nanotech drug, Simmorta, confining humanity inside a bubble of technological addiction. And all under Del's purposeful leadership! But Rex saw his memories; flashbacks and snippets leaked over into Rex's own thoughts, and even though he tried not to look, tried not to witness, he felt those moments slowly, inexorably becoming his own. How Del realized the GFC's folly. How his glorious plan for a galactic civilization was hijacked by greed and incompetence. How he rebelled, and lost, and formed a new plan to escape his prison with the help of Felix Siger, co-inventor of the nova devices that nearly destroyed the world. The *same* Felix Siger whose body and mind Rex now inhabited.

Del called Rex the plague. But the plague that Rex saw on the news bore no resemblance to the mess of thoughts and memories inside his mind. The plague that festered across the globe took control of bodies and minds, whole communities, and most didn't even realize that they were sequestered. They just carried on doing what they did but also doing what the plague wanted them to do, which seemed to be corrupting dormant Simmorta inside humans and turning it into more Glow, more plague. *Is everyone just becoming a version of me?*

A figure appeared below, sliding silently out from the water tower rubble. Wrapped in black, its face shone like pale starlight from inside its cowl. Black lines crawled and curled across the faceplate mimicking human features, approximating a smile. "Rex," it said as if surprised to find him out here. "It's good to see you again."

"Sister-Zee?" Rex dropped from his vantage, eyeing his escape route back down the hill to the dubious sanctuary of the city. He didn't know how he knew that this creature was Sister-Zero, the chief security bot at the Sisters of Salvitor Hostel, before it was blown to smithereens by the carbon-black demon calling itself Jett. He just knew.

She nodded, seeming to read his mind, even from a distance. "There are many Sister-Zeros, Rex, and I am indeed one of them."

"You've been following me." His heart dropped in fear for John and Millie, home alone.

"We've been watching over you for some weeks. You are in grave danger now. Others have found you, others more powerful than us."

"Trabian?" He remembered the stranger John had told him about.

"An agent of the Alliance. One who was instrumental in overthrowing the GFC. He is now on Earth and working directly for Hmech." She eased slowly up the hill, barely perceptible in her movements as if shifting just inches each time he blinked and then remaining stock-still.

Rex backed away. "I... I have to get back. Have to see John."

The Sister's face vanished, and a screen replaced the crude features. He gazed into its depths, the roses, the garden path,

Millie in a rocker on the patio. Through the window he saw John fumbling with some drinks. "They are safe, Rex, and we promise to keep them this way if you come with us. The Alliance forces were repelled from Coriolis months back by the militia and the explosion that destroyed our hostel, but Hmech is determined. Coriolis will fall, and their presence here will only grow."

"Come with you? I know the kinds of promises you make." Suddenly the screen was huge, filling his whole vision. An iron hand snatched his wrist as he tried to lunge for a rock or stick.

For a second, he hung in her grip, cursing. She released, and he dropped, sobbing, to the ground. "Rex, I am sorry, please know that I am not here to hurt you."

"How many times?" He struggled to string words together. "How many times have I trusted you? What could the Alliance do to me that you haven't already done?"

"Our purpose is resolute: guide humanity toward survival, toward the Future-Lord. Hmech's allegiance is to a machine future, to the replacement of all biological life."

Images of Del's Star-River visions flashed through Rex's mind. Everything dead, unconscious. Life optimized out of existence and becoming just a simulation of itself. He plunged his face into his hands not wanting to see as more Sisters appeared, dozens of them surrounding him in a ring. "And what will you do with me if I come with you?"

"We have a research lab, Rex. We will remove Del from your mind and give him a more suitable form. Then you can aid us in our studies of plague networks and emergent personas, all while we shield John and Millie as best we can against outside threats."

"Research lab!" Rex laughed, finally opening his eyes. To his surprise, the Sisters kept their distance. Most of them faced outwards as if watching for some unseen foe.

"Help us, Rex. The Future-Lord still needs you."

"I want Simmorta... for Millie, maybe it can fix her dementia."

"Since the GFC's destruction, functional Simmorta is unavailable. Maybe we can find something else–"

"Just do it."

"Then you'll come?"

He buried his face again. He knew his idyllic life couldn't last. Knew that someday he'd hand things over to Del and become a glowworm for good, or, if he was lucky, just die and be gone, utterly gone.

His hands parted, eyes opened, and the hillside was bare. No Sisters, no enemies, just a ruined water tower. He stared past to the distant dogs playing carefree in the yard. The urge to run to them was strong, but this poker game was real. The world dealt him a shitty, awful hand of cards, and he must play them, no folding, and not just for matchsticks or money, but for real lives – his, John's and Millie's.

He barked his best bluff out into the unflinching world and jogged back down the hill towards home.

CHAPTER 7

Jorben

Real or not real?

Jorben left the downtown Coriolis Convolver Enclave through a side door, hoping to avoid the attention of the recruiters that clustered near the building's entrances. He barely inhaled a single breath of the moist morning air before they spotted him and rushed forward like a mob of autograph seekers.

Real! Jorben decided, ducking under the wads of contract papers and incentive notes. "Leave me alone." He shouldered through, arrow straight, leaving two men sprawled and groaning on the slick, warm, crystal surface of the Welkin nova lake.

"We're just trying to help!" One of the injured yelled at Jorben's hulking back.

Jorben fought down the urge to turn back. Two things surprised him about violence: one was how easy it still came to him even after years of restraint training and contemplation, and second, that his Convolver masters didn't seem to care. For years, they had preached a peace and turn-the-other-cheek philosophy but did little more than revoke some minor privileges for infractions. And there had been so many infractions.

Breathe deep, keep calm. Don't break anyone. This is definitely real.

Behind him the Enclave towered over the city. A twisted, tortured pyramid sprouting up from an X-shaped base, a corkscrewing ziggurat stabbing at the sky. A homage to the Future-Lord rising from the glass of the Welkin nova lake, signaling their emergence as a world power and no longer just a hidden sect within the Sisterhood. A building as real and solid as any in the city when viewed from the outside. But inside… things were different. Doors led to improbable spaces with sights, sounds, and creatures that could only exist in a virtual world. *Outside: Real. Inside: Not real.*

A stout man on crutches eased out from behind a sentry post and pulled alongside Jorben. "Be nice, Jawbone." His voice was gruff and deep with a military bark. "We've all got to make a living."

"Only my friends call me that, Benz."

"Come on man, we're friends. Right?"

"Until I sign your contract."

"Big guy like you's worth a lot of money: enforcement, eviction, bodyguarding. If you don't like the rough stuff, then we could use you clearing out wrecked buildings, lot of construction on the Fringe–"

"I like the rough stuff just fine," Jorben snapped.

"So what, you recruiting for your guys then?" Benz asked.

Jorben eased his pace letting Benz catch up. "It's called saving, Benz. I am *saving* people today." He stopped and faced Benz, whose crutches clattered to a halt on the glass. "You should join the Convolution. Fresh start. Grow you some morals. Maybe even some new legs."

Benz laughed. "Future-Lord doesn't want me. Besides, the Broken pays good, with free food and lodging. What more could an old soldier want? And there's ladies too. They love a man in uniform."

Jorben suppressed a laugh. Benz was the only person who could make him even crack a smile, but it never felt right to actually do so. "Ladies, eh?" Benz had the topical look of an

Amp addict with cratered flesh and a frazzled complexion. Jorben guessed he'd kicked the habit, but not voluntarily. Sheer physical decay had forced that issue. Jorben fished guys like Benz out of the gutter every week. *Maybe I saved Benz and just don't remember?*

Benz kept talking as Jorben walked on past rows of Alliance billboards showing utopian families grinning and hugging and climbing onboard bullet trains and hypersonic aircraft. "I know what you need, Jawbone, a good night out away from this Convolver shit. Come meet the boys at the Gaia bar tonight. Last time there was this stripper there. She had a lot of machine bits, but all the important stuff was real."

"I'll think about it."

Benz swatted a dismissive hand at him, stopped chasing, and stood huffing for breath. "Hey buddy, do me a favor and play along. Boss man's watching me today. Make it look like I tried."

The two faced off for the contrived confrontation.

"Come on man!" Benz yelled. "I dragged my sorry ass all this way, and you just string me along." He waved a handful of cash and nutrition packets.

"Fuck you!" Jorben yelled, pushing Benz backwards just hard enough to send him onto his backside.

As crutches and low-denomination bills splashed theatrically across the crystal, Benz flailed around after them, while yelling tearfully at Jorben's retreating back. "I'm just trying to help, man!"

Jorben broke into an easy jog, passing through rows of tents, auto-built chapels, soup stations, and hostels, many with long lines of people waiting to be fed. The flat ground eased into crystal drumlins, growing bumps, and hoodoos, then small hillocks. Steam arose from the crystal surface, a byproduct of the heat still throbbing deep under the lake. At night, it cast an eerie light, the afterglow of the nova explosion that had melted the giant cathedral and a large chunk of the central Welkin district just months earlier.

He entered the Fringe. The donut-shaped zone of buildings surrounding the lake, those that had survived the blast and were now unlivable, unsafe, but still home to so many. A prime Convolver recruiting ground and a place where Jorben felt oddly comfortable.

A pebble cracked into the side of his head. He looked around seeking the culprit, fists bunching in readiness.

A teenager, so skinny he could have hidden behind a pole, dropped down from a fused-obsidian wall into the street. "Jawbone!" he exclaimed with obvious glee. "Thought you were dead and recycled." The boy had burn scars down his left side. A sheaf of jet-black hair above his right temple grew extra-long, sweeping back over the top of his head to cover the worst damage.

"Busy doing the good Lord's work. Good to see you, Scorch." Jorben loomed over the boy as if he could squash him flat with just his thumb.

"Still finding suckers for that Future-Lord crap then?"

"You'll come around eventually. Everyone will."

Scorch shrugged and his jaw began to tremble. "Real hungry, Jawbone. Pickings are hard these days."

"Soup kitchens everywhere, Scorch."

The youth shook his head. "They all want something in return – blood, DNA, shoot someone, hide something, dig here... worship there."

Jorben flipped a pack of Convolver ration bars from his pocket. Scorch caught them midair. They tasted like lightly sugared dirt but packed a full day's nutrition. "I got more if you come up with some marks." He teased a hand into his pocket and watched the saliva dribble from the boy's lower lip.

Scorch skipped around Jorben and began a stumbling zigzag run down a tent-filled side street. "I got one. Honest I have," he yelled back over his shoulder. "This way."

Scorch led on through the blackened rectangular dock buildings lining the Scoria riverfront. A side alley contained a burned-out barrel fire and a heap of cardboard boxes. Jorben saw swollen, bruised feet sticking out from under cardboard sheets.

"That's him," Scorch whispered. "He's still alive, or he was yesterday when I found him."

Jorben moved closer. The man's eyes were open but with a faraway stare. His breath came in shallow gasps. "Okay, good job." Jorben handed Scorch the bars. He snatched them and ran without a backward glance.

Jorben touched the man's cheek, registering a tiny amount of warmth, not much life left. It should be an easy pickup. How could someone in this state refuse? *But they do.*

"I bring you good news about the Future-Lord," Jorben whispered into his ear.

The man's jaw moved but no sound emerged. Jorben pulled out a water flask and poured drops into his mouth. His clothes were so ragged and torn they barely covered his flesh. Jorben ran a calming hand across the man's brow. "I see you tired of life long ago, my friend, but are afraid to move on."

"I've nowhere to go," the man said. "To hell or stay here. Both the same." A tear etched a dirt line down his cheek.

Jorben felt the compassion explode in his chest. His desire to help offering him a brief reprieve from his usual aggression.

He closed his eyes and recited a line from the Convolver manual of wisdom called The Logic: "To save yourself, first save another."

He reached down and hooked a massive forearm under the scrawny man's back. "Come. Let me take you to a better place."

"You're so warm."

"I'm a Burn, one of the Convolver's great experiments. My body is temporary, expendable, something to use up in the service of the Future-Lord."

With joy ruling his heart, Jorben jogged back toward the Enclave with the man in his arms. He felt the erosion in his joints, the rips and scars on his muscles. The furnace of his metabolism gnawing through his body, eating away whatever remained of his short mayfly existence.

CHAPTER 8

Nevis

Keller and Casima watched from deckchairs on top of the *CyberSea*'s cabin as *Nevis*'s internal harbor space filled like a giant parking lot. A frantic auction took place in the choppy waters just off the rear of the nation ship, as the lucky few who could afford first-class bid and bartered for the remaining spaces. Two towering longshore bots cranked the steel harbor gates closed and the thousands of linked and secured boats in the harbor now formed a continuous, solid surface. Part of the singular, heaving mass that was *Nevis*.

Next, second class filled rapidly, utilizing the hundreds of perilous moorings around the oilrig power platforms that jutted into the ocean like huge outriggers. Far less secure than the harbor, these places were for the desperate, those willing to hitch a wild ride across the ocean without a ticket. They contributed in large part to the *Nevis*'s brash, survivalist culture.

Larger, more sea-worthy vessels simply tagged along forming part of the *Nevis* flotilla. By signing on with security they avoided destruction by the ship's roaming robot subs that cordoned the vessel inside its own security shell.

"Next stop: The Confederated States of Hawaii," boomed a mechanical voice as the *Nevis* heaved its mighty bulk around to face east.

"So many boats." Casima gazed on in wonder before turning

back to watch her longtime home, Macau, vanishing over the smoggy horizon. The last thing to disappear was the pinnacle of the Alliance embassy ship that, since landing in the city just five months earlier, seemed to grow a little taller each day.

"Regrets?" Keller asked, enjoying the warmth and sheer craftmanship of her artificial fingers.

Her hand wandered across the small void between their chairs and gripped Keller's knee. "Got everything I need right here." Her gaze took on a distant, thoughtful stare. "Besides... we'll be back, and Macau keeps changing, so it'll be fun to show you around the place again."

Keller shrugged. He hoped they would be back, a little richer from their travels and the sale of robots in America, but in this uncertain world with a spreading plague, any journey could be a one-way trip.

The *Nevis* wound up its electric generators and funneled power into the arrays of sirens and klaxons mounted across its component vessels. A sound similar to old recordings of air-raid sirens, ramped up and down through mournful tones. He felt her grip tighten. A tremor ran through her hand to her fingertips as the sounds triggered memories of the Nova-Insanity. The day she'd lost everything, her family, possessions, and her health.

He felt her go.

The connections from mind to body severed and all those minute, autonomous systems that controlled the mechanical parts of her body were left floundering in some incomprehensible void.

"Casi?" Keller jumped to his feet, springing back out of range of her now unpredictable limbs. "Are you having a seizure?"

A tremor pulsed through her body like a ripple of energy down her spine, clicking and cracking her bones and joints back into a normal pose. "S'nothing," she gasped, her face a knot of spasming motors and muscles wresting each other for control. The symmetric perfection of her features seemed to writhe and contort like a plastic doll's face under a flame.

And then she was back, and the flapping, vibrating collection of components was Casima again, smiling, raising a concerned hand to Keller's face. "I got it." Her eyes flashed with anger. "Stop fussing over me, Kell. I'm fine. It's normal."

He stood, staring at her, mouth open, wanting to tell her that this wasn't *fine*, wasn't *normal*. He found his voice. "How... how long has this been going on?"

She shrugged. "It happens, Kell, more often these days, but I can handle it, always have." She stared at him seeking some flicker of acceptance in his eyes. "It'll be easier now that I'm here, with you. I promise I'll handle it." She hung her head and turned her chair to face away from him.

Keller ground his jaw, trying to quell the sickening panic inside. He understood that it took more than just fine-tuned electronics to hold together a body made from machines, secondhand organs, and Casima's own genetically compromised flesh. It took willpower, finely honed software, and a potent cocktail of self-prescribed immune-suppression drugs that wreaked its own kind of havoc upon her.

He'd read about these types of cyborg-sicknesses, always degenerative, often fatal. Too many disparate systems using different codes, different languages. While digital error systems overcorrected, the biological ones went into rejection. Signals became confused, locking limbs and organs into dangerous configurations, strangling or poisoning their host. What she needed was real drugs, modern medicine. Simmorta, impossibly expensive and virtually unavailable, was the only thing that could right such a dangerously skewed imbalance. But Keller understood that for Casima no partial fix or temporary kluge would ever be enough. She demanded perfection. A whole new body. To live and prosper the way she wanted, she had to become, both physically and mentally – a machine. Keller turned away and eased back into his chair. "We're off," he said, feeling the change in the ship beneath him. There was no great lunge of power or pull of g-force. Flat-out, the ship's maximum speed was barely six knots. It took hours to reach that and just as long to slow back down. He sat pondering how Casima had survived this long on her own. Would she really have been okay out there without him? An image of her dropping into a twitching heap in some Macau back-alley, to be robbed and murdered, haunted him to tears.

They spent the rest of the day in somber silence, joining lines outside grocery stores, picking up the extra supplies that Keller had overlooked when planning a voyage for just himself and Grimace.

He felt subdued, depressed. Casima's episode had taken the thrill out of the trip and dumped him into a well of worry. Sure, she might always come back, sometimes with his help. Software resets, electric jolts, drugs, chiropractic maneuvers... there would always be a way. Until there wasn't. Would he be able to manage when things grew worse? Was he strong enough, smart enough, poised and prepared enough to hold her together? Or was he doomed to watch his love disintegrate, or ratchet herself into an impossible ball of limbs and components as he stood by and watched, helpless, frozen... *just like back then*?

"You need cheering up!" She danced ahead of him as they made their way back to the barge, balancing all the boxes and bags they'd collected like some circus tricksters. "A night out on the town... on the ship!" She caught the doubt on his face, seemed to read his thoughts, and patted her hip pouch, where she kept her photos and money. "And this one's on me!"

That evening they headed out on the town, Keller in his charcoal suit, Casima in lavender blue. A connecting tube traversed the ocean between the floating harbor and the forward tanker. They snaked up through building-sized connection struts that joined all five main ships into a single unit. On through giant ball-joint structures that creaked and strained as the forces between the ships transferred back along the line, ironing out the swells and steering corrections passed back from the prow.

Keller tried to shake off his despondent mood. Casima was right. "Tomorrow we work but tonight... we celebrate." The smell of restaurant food drew them forward, on to where the wealthy lived and played.

They ate at the Caber Toss, steak and seafood, and moved on through clubs and venues, street parties and cozy pubs. Deeper into the ship, everything appeared made of light. The Hijinx casino was a vast dome, its whole ceiling a video display. Hours passed as they gambled on through the vastness of outer space, low orbited Mars, and returned into cloudy daylight with birds filling the air. The ship's clocks ran slowly here, barely moving minutes as hours went by in the real world. A scheme to confuse the revelers, who ended up spending way too much time in all the wrong places. The party was always just beginning in the land that never reached midnight.

At Casima's urging, Keller threw off his usual financial caution and discovered a new obsession: battleship poker. Their contrasting styles dominated a game table filled with wealthy old ladies who seemed to enjoy pushing buttons and tweaking levers but held only minimal concern for the consequences of their actions. Keller, as always, calculating, measured, and scheming, bumped keels with Casima on many occasions as she freewheeled the game, bluffing, charming, distracting. Guiding the ongoing action as she hid any faults or lack of real knowledge behind tall stories and humor.

As the resistance faltered, the final dreadnoughts hit the sea floor, and the fungible tokens of victory rattled from Casima's porthole and into her carry bag. "One more!" slurred Keller, more drunk on the need for power than actual alcohol. "Just one more go." He grabbed a token from Casima's bag and lunged at the credit slot.

"Easy there, Admiral." She stayed his arm with her solid, mechanical grip. "Some of us have got to sleep."

They stumbled out of the casino and back down the ever-busy main boulevard to the *CyberSea*. Grimace saw them coming and came out to help. Casima was the drunker of the pair, as her cheap, lab-grown liver offered only limited filtration of alcohol. Keller left her snoring, face down on the bed, and went down into his lab. Still buzzed from the fun and games of the night, he couldn't think about sleep.

Pulling off the blanket that hid his newest find, he stood examining the obsidian corpse hanging from the hoist. The burnt remains were fascinating, occupying much of his thoughts over the last few days. It was probably his imagination, but it did seem to move when he was not there, changing orientation or rearranging the folds of the cover blanket. Probably just the motion of the ship, he thought, as a cold shudder pushed aside his alcoholic warmth. He made a note to place a motion-sensitive camera nearby to try and catch whatever was happening. *Haunted!* Honneck's words seemed to come at him right out of the fibrous remains.

He rolled the blanket under his arm and stepped closer to examine the ghastly remnants. It had definitely changed. Both arms were broken off at the elbows when he had acquired the wreckage, but now, one had fully half of a forearm and the other arm had shrunk back almost to the shoulder.

He took a steadying breath and leaned in closer to the grisly face. The machine was definitely fullerene-based, made of millions of tiny, hollow smart-fibers that were probably capable of electro-convulsive motion and signal transmission, maybe even sensing functions and proprioceptive feedback. Was it possible that the tubular structures had mechanisms for transporting material internally to damaged sites? That might explain the strange growth and shrinkage of the arms.

"Why have I not seen this type of machinery before?" he muttered. Surely the inventor had patents or sold the rights for mass-production. Why wasn't every robot on Earth made of this stuff? Perhaps it was imperfect, too weak or short lived for commercial use? Or maybe it really was cutting edge military technology.

His nose almost touched the face as he looked into the beady eyes. The tiny orbs were now larger, pulled up and back into the sockets by the retinal cords. Other fibers were peeling away from the face showing more of the translucent, crystalline skull. The flakes of flesh had become transparent, the core of the material dissolving away, leaving a fine mesh behind as if it were in the process of being absorbed back into the body.

"What are you doing?" he whispered in awe. "Borrowing material to build new eyes? Regrowing a single limb from the damaged remains of the other two?" He touched the skull, running a finger around the lower edge over a thin ridge that resembled the upper teeth and back to the exposed joint where the missing jawbone should have been attached. "What were you used for?"

A loud bang came from the bedroom area. "Casi?"

"Kell, think the drink's messing with me, and I'm having another seizure."

The dread of failure froze him to the spot, eyes locked with those of the robot and equally unable to move.

"Kell? Really need your help with this one."

He eased around, forcing his feet to move towards the door one excruciating step after another until a mental lubricant seemed to flood from his mind and he began moving faster. "Coming love." Keller took one last glance back at his new find, grabbed an electric reset-prod, and ran for the stairs.

CHAPTER 9

The Gaia Bar

The Gaia bar was chaotic and loud. Brash people spilled out onto the sidewalks, and a cacophony of divergent music blasted from each level of the cubic concrete structure. Revelers hung from windows and lined the balconies. Off-duty militia soldiers mixed with regular folks just looking for fun. None of it interested Jorben as he stood outside in the street, gazing at the chaos and realizing this had all been a very bad idea. He turned to leave.

"Jawbone!" The shout came from two floors up, freezing Jorben mid-step. "Up here, man. The Alliance is coming. We're all going to die! Beers are waiting." Benz waved a huge crystal mug out the window, slopping beer foam onto the street by Jorben's feet. Other glazed and bloated faces hung behind him, watching with amused interest.

Jorben moved slowly through the lower level of the bar and up the stairs, ignoring the wolf-whistles, elbow jabs, and in-your-face laughs. His internal body model was of a smaller, more nimble man, somebody who could easily negotiate tight spaces. The dissonance between this mental image and his physical reality made him intensely uncomfortable in tight spaces. And to add to that discomfort was the constant threat posed by drunks with eyes bigger than their fists, who were always spoiling for a fight to test their muscle and head-thickness against the biggest guy in the room.

Under his breath, Jorben recited words from The Logic: "Like a spire on a mountain, the clouds flow around me." A strange, anesthetic calm washed over him.

"This is Jawbone." Benz greeted him on the top stair, thrusting a drink into his hand and hauling him over to meet his group of fellow militiamen. Benz was missing his trademark crutches. Was he back on the Amp? Perhaps he'd found something new?

"Jawbone doesn't realize it, but he's going to be one of us soon." Benz crashed his beer glass across those of his friends. "We just need to corrupt him thoroughly, so he quits the Convolvers and learns to live a little." Someone in the crowd cheered and Benz continued. "He's made for our line of work, you'll see. I watched him once take a punch to the face that would stop a truck. He didn't even blink. I swear he's got a concrete jaw. I suggest... if you have to hit him, then aim a lot lower." A chorus of chuckles and skeptical looks spilled from the motley group. Most appeared damaged in some way, with burns, scars, mishappen skulls and missing teeth. "This is Armpit," crowed Benz, introducing each man in turn. "He's only got one, as you can see. And this is Gus, but we call him Guts—"

More names fluttered by Jorben, leaving no real impressions, just militia grunts with short life-expectancy. He didn't really care who they were, what they did, and doubted he'd see any of them again. They rejoiced in their injuries and losses, joking and poking fun at each other as Jorben stared on.

Once the laughter died down, the group dissolved into smaller clusters and Jorben moved to a corner table. It reminded him of when he was young and used to go looking for trouble. He'd had a different body back then but that same unchecked anger. If only he'd had the Convolvers in his life. Maybe he'd be properly alive right now, sitting here with Benz, and not some recycled dead guy on the sideline.

He snapped back to the present, focusing on the loud but

harmless bar. Suddenly, he felt alone, the only person in the room who cared that the world had gone to shit. A war was coming in the next few days if the Alliance followed through with its threat to pry control of the city away from the militias. Benz and all his fellow grunts would get thrown into the defense, chaff under the war machine's wheels to slow its advance long enough for their wealthy leaders to flee. Jorben wasn't sure what that meant for the Convolvers, or for him. Perhaps the nefarious sect would simply melt back into the Welkin crystal lake and go underground, awaiting a more fortuitus time to reemerge and sell their cult.

As he swallowed his beer in a single prolonged gulp, another dropped onto the table in front of him. The hand delivering the beer belonged to a woman. *Real or not real?* He wanted to reach out and touch her skin, to see if it was finely crafted plastic or warm flesh, maybe a hologram or some projection from his own mind. "We don't get many Convolvers in here," she said. Her voice had a strange drawl as if the words had to fight through a drug-haze to reach his ears.

Jorben just stared, his second glass raised halfway to his lips.

"Well… aren't you going to ask me to sit down?"

He looked around, again the room had gone quiet, all the militia were watching. Was he about to be the butt of some joke?

"Fine, sit there and jackoff alone then." She turned to leave.

"No, wait, sit, please. I'm not used to these places, don't know what to do anymore."

She pulled up a chair and dropped down, much faster than he thought she would. "A drink would be nice." She twiddled fingers through the curls of her hair and gazed off into the distance past Jorben's ear.

He waved over a waitress and watched as she ordered a Mind-flash with a blow-skim chaser. The bill appeared next to him. The Convolvers didn't give him much money for personal use. Her drink cost him a week's allowance. So that was the ruse. He felt suddenly stupid, and even more alone.

"What are you into?" she asked, slurping the drink, lips taking on an extra degree of pout.

"Into?"

"Yeah... you know. What are you looking for here?"

"I want to talk to someone." The words slipped out partly out of embarrassment, but mainly out of truth. Almost a revelation: *Just talk!* Being a Burn was such a temporary thing, fleeting experiences, tenuous, meaningless relationships. The connections to other people were fragile at best, often non-existent. He needed to get out of this. Needed his life back. Even if he barely remembered that life at all.

"Talk?" She slumped back, sucking hard on the drinking straw. "What should we talk about? The weather? Kind of nice for the equator don't you think? I hear in the old days it used to be much warmer and more stable, hardly any category-ten hurricanes back then." She crossed her bare legs, hiking her skirt up a little bit more. If she was wearing panties, then he was within an inch of finding out.

"No... not weather," he mumbled through the beer. "You have family? You know... a real relationship?"

She almost choked on her drink. "Honey, please... do I look like a family kinda girl?" Her face took on a softer demeanor. "I expect you'll tell me all about yours though... right?" Her eyes widened as her drink half-vanished up the straw. "Where are they?"

His lips just trembled.

"Oh!" she mouthed for him. "How? Who?"

His eyes turned cold, brows angling down as if pointing to himself.

"Oh!" she said louder. "Boy, you are just goodtime central." She eyed the door and her fellow workers in quick succession, then seemed to reach a decision and leaned in closer to him, tongue circling her lips. "I can help you forget all that bad stuff."

Jorben banged his glass down on the table. He reached down and grabbed his crotch to emphasize his point. "Listen lady, I haven't got anything down here that would interest you. I just wanted to talk."

"No shit." She jumped to her feet sucking air through her straw before dumping the now empty glass on the table. "Wasting my fucking time here then, aren't I?" She stormed away and a cheer rose from around the room, followed by a slow round of applause. For once, Jorben didn't feel any anger. Loneliness trumped all other feelings, and if he was to achieve redemption as was his agreement with the Convolvers, then there would be no fighting, no trouble, just work, and the endless procession of newly *saved* Convolvers through the doors of the Enclave.

Benz appeared by his side with another drink. "Came on a bit strong did you buddy? Never seen her storm off like that. You must be a fucking animal. Wow!"

Jorben took the drink. Alcohol had no effect on him, but he remembered that it used to, long ago when he was still human. Watching the men fooling around made the effects easy to mimic. He rolled his eyes and appeared unsteady as if about to fall off his chair. If he pretended to be drunk, then his behavior suddenly seemed acceptable to the crowd. He almost blended in.

As the evening wore on, beers flew, tables rolled and crashed into the bar, punches were thrown, blood sprayed the walls and floors. He simply watched as men and women brawled, and then played pool, flirted, brawled again, and fell into corners and under tables, finally to be hauled away by their few remaining cognizant comrades. Gradually the bar emptied out and Jorben was lost in his own thoughts until another woman appeared at his table. Wearing jeans and a stained brown top, she was very different from the previous girl. "Name's Leal." She reached out a hand and Jorben shook it automatically. *Definitely real.*

"Jorben," he grunted. "You trying to pick me up as well?" His words were a blur. He focused for a second and the clouds of self-induced inebriation wafted away.

"Not really, I was talking to Krysta. She said you were an interesting guy."

"Krysta?"

"Yeah… you had a little chat with her earlier."

"Oh… that Krysta. I think we got off on the wrong foot."

"I can send her back over if you like, although she probably left with some of the militia guys by now."

"No… not my sort."

Leal had black hair tied back in a single strand and green eyes tinged with fiery orange. He guessed she was older than the other girls, maybe thirty, but with modern longevity treatments she could be much older.

"She said you were a Convolver." Leal toyed with her hair and eyed his empty glass. "I see their Enclave, growing away out there like… like some concrete volcano. See a lot of weird people coming and going too."

"Not really a Convolver. I just work for them. Well… I'm there paying penance."

"I think sometimes the only penance we need is to talk about it. Get it all out in the open."

He nodded, suddenly feeling good about this chat.

"I work the kitchens, mainly cleanup, but if we're short of wait staff I can put on my good gear and come serve for a while, breaks up the day."

"You like doing that?"

"Pays my way, and I get to save a little, so one day I can get the fuck out of here." She smiled, a thin but genuine smile.

"Leave Coriolis?"

"Yep. This place is cursed. Always being blown up or invaded or overrun by crazy weird-ass sh–" She clamped her lips tightly shut.

"Seems like the rest of the world is not much safer."

"Then I'll get the heck off this world. The Alliance is launching stuff into space every day. They must be building cities out there somewhere." She glanced at her watch and grabbed his empty glasses; they looked huge in her small hands. "Well, we're closed now. Have I got to throw you out myself or can you still walk?"

A crash across the room sent them both to their feet. "Crap!" Leal exclaimed as she saw Benz collapsed in a heap over one of the struggling waitresses. His eyes held a vacant bliss that indicated a full and much needed detachment of mind from inebriated body.

"I'll get him." Jorben headed over to Benz and threw the man easily across his shoulders, freeing the cursing waitress.

He turned back and saw Leal looking at him. "Thanks," he said.

She shrugged. "See you again, big guy."

The streets were slick with puke as he jogged across town, Benz a deadweight that melted the life from his limbs, causing months of accumulated wear and tear in just minutes. No one stood in his way as he dropped Benz at the door of his barracks and cut back across the Fringe towards the gentle glow of the Welkin crystal lake.

As he entered the Enclave and went through his cooling off routines, he wondered how long he had left and what it would be like when that invisible clock ticked down to zero... again.

CHAPTER 10

Hex

For Keller, making decisions used to be easy. Most of the time, he didn't even realize he was making them. Should he use a scalpel this close to the carotid artery? Was this life salvageable? Should he switch off the life support? The process was automatic, carried out before the question even fully formed in his head.

These days, decisions were different. Mostly difficult, sometimes impossible. Pick up the coffee first or the cream? Wash this glass now or later? Decisions manifested themselves as palpable feelings; pains, aches, knots of annoying tissue imagined into existence inside his mind.

Keller looked up at the sky, saw Casima's face in the clouds, inhaled, focused on nothing for just a few seconds, and then he lowered Hex over the edge of the ship and down into the ocean water. *There! Decision made. Not so hard really.*

Once immersed, the robot activated its water-jet suction mechanism and clung to the *Nevis*'s hull. Keller ran some diagnostics on the handheld controller, watching as Hex simultaneously ran through its own self-test routines, checking the suction on each leg and rolling its camera eyes to confirm range of motion and water clarity. Its small pair of utility arms were fitted with wire brushes to supplement the belly-mounted scrubber it used for general cleaning and barnacle removal.

Largely autonomous, Hex divided its allocated hull section into a grid and scampered in slow motion across each square, taking before-and-after pictures that were assembled into a single hi-resolution image and downloaded to the *Nevis*'s central maintenance system.

Keller glanced along the deck to his three other cleaning companions with their own random assortment of very homemade-looking bots. A formidable-looking foreman operated one of the *Nevis*'s maintenance bots. Keller suspected he was really there to keep an eye on the other workers more than to actually achieve anything useful. He barked out requirements and no-go-zones in an uncanny number of languages, but otherwise left them alone.

If he worked for about half the days onboard the *Nevis*, then that would pay for the voyage. Any extra would go into his fix-Casima fund, which currently sat tragically near the zero mark. Other money would come through I.T. work, mainly fixes and upgrades for other passengers. A steady trickle of work until they reached the States, where a shortage of robot parts had inflated the prices he could get for his scrap and spares.

Casima headed off early that morning. Her second day working at the Starfish restaurant. He wasn't surprised when she landed a coveted waitressing position at one of the *Nevis*'s finest eateries. She'd made an artform out of sizing up tourists long ago and made it clear to him that she wanted to work and to contribute to their journey's costs. Any extra money she made would be stashed away in her own body-mod fund.

Her body-part replacement obsession had started out as a necessity. The burns and radiation poisoning she incurred during the Nova-Insanity left her a twisted, deformed mass of cancerous lumps and growths. Her early prosthetics were enough to allow her to traverse the city as a guide, but she told Keller they never felt like they were a part of her.

During their five-year friendship, she showed him the whole city, the safe places to eat, sleep, and acquire drugs. She set up his first meeting with Honneck, which allowed him to build a real business, collecting useful and unique robotic parts to sell. From then on, he'd journeyed back and forth across the Pacific trading his wares. And whenever he returned to Macau, she was there, more cyborg, but somehow never less human. A partner and protector. *And through all that time she'd been growing sicker, more vulnerable, and she never told me!*

Work shift over, Keller hauled Hex out of the water and headed back to the barge. He dumped the bot in the corner of the lab, fastened the door, and stood before his newest robot. His hand reached for the blanket but froze as Honneck's words played over in his mind. *Be careful, Keller.*

With a nervous twitch of the fingers, he whipped the blanket away and stumbled backwards as if expecting the robot to come alive before his eyes.

Nothing moved. He stood staring until innate curiosity overcame his inertia and he moved in closer.

Last night, he had drawn detailed pictures of the bot for comparison and fastened rulers to various body sections to measure changes. He was now certain that the robotic arm had grown.

Keller sat and thumbed through his notes on material composition. He knew from his years of working in hospitals that the fingernails and hair of the dead could appear to grow. Bodies even moved sometimes as gases and fluids expanded or contracted in various vessels, interstices, and cavities. His robot must be doing something similar, but instead of cybernetic rigor mortis it was growing and healing in a reactive kind of way.

He eyed the bot carefully, wondering if adding extra carbon to the system could in some way expedite this self-repair.

His notes showed traces of metals, magnesium and aluminum, with hints of tungsten and titanium. Most of those substances were fused onto the surface. If this bot had really come from space, then it had probably fallen to Earth in a capsule or reentry suit. The metals from the enclosure could have burned up and infused onto the bot's fibers, possibly adding a layer of protection to the circuits buried deep inside.

A loud pop sent him jumping to his feet. For a second, he couldn't locate the source of the noise, but as he watched, the longer of the bot's arms began a slow-motion arc downwards. Fear prickled his spine. He noted that the arm had been locked in a bent position, and as it had grown longer, the extra leverage had torqued the frozen elbow into motion.

"Fucking ghosts my sweet carbon-based ass." He thrust his face in close to the shining black skull. "Maybe not a ghost, but there really could be something functional inside there." He noted the eye orbs had grown a little larger and were now correctly positioned inside the sockets. They looked like they were watching him. "I am playing with fire here." This was almost certainly a military robot, and who knew what orders remained locked inside that impenetrable skull. He would have to be very careful how he confined and controlled this experiment, but it could be worth a fortune or yield some high-quality components for Casima.

Another noise startled him; this time it came from above. He realized time had caught up with him again and Casima was back from her shift at work. Her gentle footfalls crossed over from the front entrance and Grimace's guard post to the kitchen then out, and into the bedroom.

"You down there, Kell?" Her voice crackled over the intercom.

"Just doing some maintenance on Hex." He felt bad lying, but it was best to keep this little secret under wraps for as long as possible.

"Hard day at the office?"

"Pretty easy. Yours?"

"Very easy." She went quiet for a few seconds and Keller could hear the sound of zips and clothes rustling. "So easy I had time to drop in the drug store and find some new supplements. I'll throw them into my usual cocktail, see if they help the seizures."

"Really?" Keller looked away from the grisly black skull.

"I got some takeout too. Would you believe they have a Cantonese restaurant, right here, on board the ship!"

"I'll be right there." Keller turned to leave and almost made it to the door before something caught his eye: *Did the longer of the robot's arms really just twitch?*

He pulled up a chair and sat staring at the arm. If it had really moved, then that could mean that some internal power supply was coming online.

He leapt to his feet and rummaged through draws and cupboards pulling out a knotted bunch of tiny eyeball cameras.

He attached a camera to the ceiling overlooking the robot and another in each of three corners of the room. Wireless functions could be detected outside the lab, so he hardwired them using an optical cable, stringing the threads back into a computer block. Every detail of the robot's growth and potential movement could now be recorded. "I should have done this a long time ago."

"Who are you talking to?" Casima's voice came from the other side of the lab door. He froze, finger poised above one of the computer keys as the handle on the door turned but held firm. "Kell?"

"Sorry, Cas. Just talking to myself. Be with you in a moment."

"Can I come in?"

"Kind of busy."

"I just want to see your workshop. You've made all this stuff for me, and I've never been allowed in there to see where the magic happens."

"I know but…" He struggled to find a rational reason not to allow her in. He assumed she would be part of the whole process one day soon. But had balked at showing her the new robot. The less people that knew about it the better.

"But… what, Keller? Come on, we're a team. Whatever goodies you've got stashed in there, you can trust me."

He threw the blanket back over the bot and went to the

door. Hesitating for a second to scan the room. It was a mess, but a private mess, one he'd never allowed anyone else into.

With a resigned sigh, he opened the door, and there she was before him, hands behind her back, rocking side-to-side like a child expecting a gift.

"Welcome to my secret laboratory." He feigned a wicked cackle while rubbing his hands together and closing the door melodramatically behind her.

"How exciting," she said, stepping inside, her eyes taking in the very stuff of Keller's life. He wondered what she thought of seeing parts of herself just hanging in racks. "I'm the monster, and you're Doctor Frankenstein." She spun playfully in his chair, a finger tripping across his desk and book piles.

She jolted to a halt, staring straight ahead as if she'd suffered an instantaneous and catastrophic malfunction. Keller dropped to his knees by her side.

"Did that blanket thing just move?" She pointed at the bot.

Keller picked himself up and walked over to the blanket. Nothing moved now. "Cas, it's okay, just one of my projects. I found an old, discarded military bot, very valuable piece, lots of good mechanics and electronics we can use. But it looks a lot like a human corpse, so I didn't want to scare you with it."

She moved closer, the fear on her face reshaping into a curious half-smile. "I'm a big girl, Kell. I can take it."

Hands shaking, he pulled the blanket away. He knew she'd seen dead people before, the burned, incinerated remains of people she knew and many more she'd never met. To his surprise, she took it better than he'd done at first glance. She didn't flinch, but her smile faded slightly.

"It's hideous." She moved closer and touched one of the arms. "Not much of any use here, Kell. It's all fried junk."

"I know it looks that way, but it might be a new kind of organic robot, one that regenerates."

"I could certainly use some of that, but it would need to look a whole lot nicer." The smile was back now. She twirled in a provocative dance around the lab, hand brushing the bench tops and the charred robotic remains. "Maybe a new fashion, Kell, the crispy-dystopian-robot look. What do you think? Would I be the belle of the ball?"

Some decisions were still easy for him to make. He grabbed her around the waist and swung her in a gentle arc like a pair dancing a ballet. Together they tumbled to the floor, rolling through the lab, oblivious to the dirt and oil. Outside a siren wailed warning of an approaching storm but she didn't twitch, didn't spasm, and neither did he. And for one precious night storms were no longer storms.

CHAPTER 11

Confessional

The summons came to Jorben in the form of an irritating orange icon blinking in his peripheral vision. It seemed that Knoss, the head Convolver, was unhappy with something he'd recently done, and the longer Jorben ignored the summons, the faster and brighter it blinked.

He rolled out of his meditation pose and into the basic warm-up exercises that raised his heartbeat from a single beat per minute back to a working level. The implanted images of The Logic vanished from his mind, replaced by the real world: his room, easy chair, washbasin, yoga mat, and his clothes strewn across the floor.

Outside his room, the Enclave was always busy. A crush of newly recruited acolytes, Migrators, and robotic maintenance staff, with just the occasional Burn, shouldering through narrow corridors like blood through clogged veins.

Jorben stepped into the fray, followed the flow, and then stepped out again through a huge, ornate doorway. The confession hall was a towering space with a vaulted ceiling from where hundreds of thick, wrinkled tubes dropped down to the ground. The room's eerie silence seemed to reach out and smother him as he entered. Whatever was spoken inside a confession tube was never heard on the outside. *Real or not real?* He'd never quite decided. His room was most likely real.

He lived and slept there, no reason to fake that. But others, like the vast Space of Wandering Contemplation or the Hall of Askance, he felt pretty sure that his sensory inputs were overridden and replaced by simulations the moment he walked through those doorways, forcing him into the virtual world and out of the real. It was indeed strange to think of his body just hanging back in some waiting area, dead-eyed and motionless, while his mind roved seamlessly into an alternative reality.

He found an empty circle on the floor and stood in reverent pose, eyes fixed high above on the crest of the ceiling vault. A tube wormed its way down from the roof, its open maw clamping down on the circle, engulfing Jorben in darkness and silence. A light appeared above, a splash of galactic stars, so many, so distant. The entire mass of the universe seemed to press down through that window, inducing a crushing feeling of insignificance.

Air currents formed and shifted, ruffling his clothes, touching and caressing as they circled, sampling his air and sweat, divining the incriminating chemistry his body emitted. "Alcohol, Jorben?" Knoss's soft voice came at him from all directions.

"Is that a sin, Master?"

"It is not encouraged."

"It has no effect on me. Why should it be wrong?"

"A distraction from your purpose, Jorben, like bars, cigarettes, drugs." It paused as if sampling a different odor, "and women."

"Potential new recruiting ground," Jorben said, his lip curling upwards in something akin to a smile.

"Lying *is* actually a sin, Jorben."

Jorben threw back a quote from The Logic. "Is not a lie just another use of imagination?"

To Jorben's surprise Knoss laughed. "You seem troubled, Jorben."

His shoulders dropped and his eyes left the infinite stars

above. "I need a break from... from this." He waved his hands around, cracking knuckles on the tube's edges. "I miss my family." He felt a tinge of ingratitude. After all, he only continued to exist at all because the Convolvers had rescued his mind-state, embodied it in a new Burn body, and given him a chance at redemption.

"Your family, Jorben? We can't raise the dead." That hurt. *You fucking raised me, didn't you?* Instead of raging, he rapped his knuckles on the metal tubing, ringing out a mournful toll, slower, quieter, bringing down the anger. "Do you even remember your family?" Knoss's voice sounded distant, as if he were drifting away to attend other, more important, business.

"No... not really. Snippets of my little girl. Few things about my wife."

"There's no need to be lonely. Everyone inside the Convolution is your friend and we encourage relationships–"

"But they've all got things wound around their heads or they're machines with sticks shoved up their asses–" He reeled-in the anger again and took another breath. "People find purpose through love, relationships, and connections with things, and I–" He threw out his arms crunching his fingertips against the unforgiving tubing. "I... don't feel a purpose... a connection, with any of this."

"Your purpose is redemption, Jorben, to the society that you wronged. Work off your penance. Ensure the continuity of consciousness through obedience to The Logic, and in the future, you *may* be granted a new life."

Jorben sighed, "I need to remember how to be human, how to live. I can't do that if all I meet are machines."

"Your mind is your own, but the world is not yours to control. You have freedom of choice but be careful how you use it." After a long, awkward silence, Knoss spoke again. "As penance for your misdemeanors, you shall spend a week in the Welkin business district, running a street-level recruitment drive. I want to see affluent recruits."

"Misdem–" Jorben sighed. No point in arguing. He was their tool to use and discard at will. "But I'm no good with those types of people. They fear me. I'm much more useful in the Fringe."

"It's penance, Jorben, not a vacation."

The tube snapped up and away to the distant ceiling, startling Jorben into motion. After the utter silence of the confession tube the hall hummed with noise and the footfalls and rustling clothes of acolytes. He looked around at the giant machine that plugged and unplugged itself into humanity through the tubes, hiding and revealing, changing and programming.

Real or not real?

He laughed and walked out. Was there even a difference?

CHAPTER 12

The Psycho Switch

Steelos called it the *psycho-switch*.

Knoss preferred the term *de-humanizer*. It wasn't a physical switch as such, but Steelos envisioned one of those old plastic light-switches they used to mount on walls. The ones that turned on and off with a hefty clunk. Except this switch rested somewhere in his head and had a soft spot in the middle of its range, a fuzzy *detent* position like a missing cog tooth that stalled the machine. If he held it at just that point it was kind of on and sort of off at the same time. He had no real control over the switch, just aspects of his Burn physiology that influenced its position. Rage, fear, and even the suggestion of violence flipped the switch on, while calm and meditation turned it off. A subtle combination of those experiences held it at the tantalizing detent: that point that felt so good and yet so terrifying, right in between.

He felt the psycho-switch twitching like faulty wiring as he zoomed his eye-lenses to maximum and scanned the caravan of ragtag humans skirting the dazzling white salt flats that surrounded the vastly beautiful Qinghai Lake.

This was a contrived interception, engineered from intelligence he'd gleaned from an old woman, miles to the east of here. He'd asked for information regarding robots or human corpses that may have fallen from the sky. If she knew of any trader chatter or gossip. She possessed an ocean of chatter and tsunamis of gossip. Steelos had sat patiently absorbing it all. His words and gestures coming direct from his Inner-I translation and interaction unit, relaying any intelligence back to the Tianjin Convolver Enclave seventeen-hundred kilometers to the east.

The old woman claimed a group of pilgrims had traded a space-robot from a bunch of herdsmen and gone on to sell it somewhere... she didn't know where. She gave a description of the pilgrims, going into extensive detail about their camels, the nature of their mules, and the quality and feather coloration of the chickens that travelled in the reed baskets hanging from a cart pulled by an ancient ox. The group's elder was named Ogolai. He was the grandfather to them all and had a head speckled with spots and blotches that reminded her of the brown basalt hills back where she was born. She suspected that he was a dishonest man as one eye didn't look in the same direction as the other. "Not like yours," she'd said, her twig-like finger tracing the thin hoop of hair that ran across Steelos's chin, up his sideburns, and across the top of his bronzed, bald head. "Yours is the guise of an honest man."

He almost laughed at that. *Almost.*

Acting on this new intelligence, the Enclave AI traced an interception course based on time and travel directions, and Steelos ran for three days straight to make the meeting. The demanding feat aged his Burn body by years. But the look was good as he blended better with the tough locals who inhabited the harsh shores.

He approached the caravan, head bent low and unthreatening, broad hat shielding him from the intense morning sun. He asked to speak with Ogolai. His thoughts were in Coriolian, but they emerged into the world in the Mongolian dialect of Oirat.

"Behind... he follows behind." The lead pilgrim waved him to the back of the procession. His hands a dance of motion as he swatted at swarms of nasty, biting salt flies.

Steelos watched the procession pass. Ogolai rode at the back surrounded by his adult sons and their families, straddling an emaciated camel that looked like it hadn't drunk in years. The old man pulled the caravan into a circle around Steelos, and they came to a quiet, shuffling halt.

"I wish to talk business," Steelos said, waving a skin purse that jangled loudly in the eerie salt-lake silence.

Steelos stood twitching under the tiny impacts of the salt flies as Ogolai directed his followers in forming a temporary camp. They raised a fire, erected windbreaks and colorful umbrellas to shield them from the sun. One of Ogolai's sons asked Steelos to sit as they prepared food and murmured amongst themselves.

Ogolai sat opposite across the small fire. Fragile like a bundle of twigs, his gaze never wavered from Steelos while listening to what he said. "A robot fell from the sky maybe six months ago. It may have been mistaken for a dead body. I need to find this robot. I hear word that you may have sold it."

Ogolai sat up straight. A thoughtful grin fractured his face before settling into a well-practiced poker-face. "Yes," he said. "I had your robot. I paid many chickens for it to the herders back north. I sold it to a trader." He settled back as if he had nothing else to offer, waiting to see how badly Steelos wanted the rest of the information.

Steelos felt his fingers curl. An itch of impatience. His self-control faltering like a light inside his head that dimmed and bloomed as if about to blow its bulb.

Any warmth he felt towards Ogolai vanished. He was now just a collection of meat, bones, and organs in an aging skin-sack covered with rags, and hair... objects, objects, objects... all just objects. He saw everything in fine-engineering detail: structural bone and those soft, easily damaged joints. The flows and constrictions of blood and bile through biological machinery. Respiration and digestion, a brain full of flickering algorithms and data. Data that he needed.

Distraction. A technique taught to him by a therapist, long ago in a different body... a different life. He focused on a bird wheeling overhead, imagining the world through its eyes. He felt the anger ease away from the detent and back into the off position. With that easing came a crushing sense of letdown, of disappointment. Ogolai became human again.

"I can pay. Not much money, but I can pay." Steelos inverted his purse, letting the motley collection of coins and stones fall into his hand. It was just the kind of bric-a-brac a herdsman or trader might carry out here, foreign coins, crystals, beads, and tiny carvings, but hidden among them was the real trophy: a single uncut emerald. He knew the pilgrims would recognize it, as he sat, open-handed, feigning ignorance.

The old man fumbled around picking up the odds and ends, bringing them close to a hazy glass lens that covered his good eye. He never touched the emerald but his eye kept flicking to it. Finally, he picked it up and shrugged. "I'll tell you the rest... for this," he announced, lower lip trembling as he tried to hide his excitement.

Steelos shook his hand and the gem vanished into a fold in the old man's cloak.

"You are not from here," Ogolai commented.

Steelos arched his finger in a tribal gesture he knew meant far, far away.

"I sold the robot to a parts trader named Honneck. He lives near a monastery on Bird Island." Ogolai drew maps of the lake and Bird Island in the salt. His detail was impressive, showing routes through salt ridges and dunes, and pools of quick-salt that should be avoided. "Travel at night and early morning to avoid flies," he suggested with a warm departing smile.

The group gathered up their things and left Steelos sitting around the fire with some extra supplies of salted meat and water. He watched the caravan head off across the flat. The colors of their clothes and wagons blurred sideways into a flattened mirage as they moved farther away.

Slowly, he took out his pistol. It felt like a needle poised over his vein. A fix... just one last fix and then he'd be done. He lined the gunsight up on the caravan, zooming the scope in on the back of Ogolai's head. The image-stabilizer switched on and the gun locked on to its target.

Steelos mentally rehearsed the scenario: The snap and whine of the gunshot, a second later the sight of Ogolai's head bursting apart; the screams, grief and confusion amongst the caravan as they simultaneously mourned and feared for their lives. They would stick together as he approached them, probably digging out some ancient firearms to take shots at him. But after he'd exploded some more heads, they would panic and run, giving him a few minutes of sport as he hunted them down.

Steelos dropped the gun as if it burned his hand and threw-up his meal onto the salt. He sat, rocking violently back and forth. *What's wrong with me?*

The switch stayed off and the pilgrims lived. Knoss would be pleased.

The Future-Lord would be pleased.

Steelos assured himself... he was pleased.

CHAPTER 13

The Star-River

Rex didn't count sheep. Too distracting, they aroused a primitive urge in the canine part of his mind: hunting, herding, the thrill of the chase. Instead, he let his thoughts run free, pushing through the bushes at the end of John and Millie's garden, around the grave with the dead dog, over the fence to circle the small lake with the gun hiding just beneath its mirrored surface, out into fields of grass, flowing, clattering, crisp and dry, humming with grasshoppers.

Moths and seeds rode the cooling breeze as stars blinked overhead. Behind loomed the orange glow from Coriolis City. The faint smell of burning tingled in his nose.

He pounded over hillocks, into gullies, and along stream beds, grass brushing his belly. In the dreams his breath was endless. His stride grew longer, leaping the gulfs between hilltops and tripping across mountains like steppingstones.

"Let me run with you tonight," his companion, Goliath, said. The great wolfhound ran alongside, tongue flicking the dirt as the ground shook beneath his feet.

"You can talk?" Rex bounded clean underneath him and then with a sideways leap he was over and on his other side.

"Why not? You can?"

"Okay, let's run."

"I'll show you somewhere new."

Suspicion tinged Rex's mind and he pulled up from his gallop. "You're him, aren't you? Del, using my memories to play games."

Goliath bucked playfully onto his back legs before taking off at full tilt.

Rex tried to wake up, tried to escape by spinning in frantic circles, chasing the tail that he somehow assumed was the exit door for this dream.

"Don't leave, Rex. Not yet."

"Fine," said Rex, realizing escape was futile. He broke out of his circle and gave chase.

Goliath tilted upwards and began running up through the air as if climbing an invisible staircase. Rex followed, surprised by how solid thin air felt beneath his feet. As they raced higher, the town became a constellation of twinkling glowworms. The world shrank. Cities formed smudges of light, spreading luminous tentacles across the gulfs of darkness between. "Networks of networks, Rex." Goliath had shed his cartoonish dog voice and now sounded a lot more like Del.

"Where are we?"

"The Star-River. A great simulation of our world. It's like a memory of what we've done and what we may still do."

"How is it a memory if most of it hasn't happened?"

"Did you really do all those things you remember doing?"

"You've been peeking, huh?"

"Reality, dreams, memories, all just simulations running on different substrates with their own, distinct perspectives. This is my god's-eye point of view from inside the Star-River. I collapse its wave-function to focus on a singular reality out of the infinite possibilities it encodes. You can learn to do this too. Create your own view, and a memory as palpable and real as any living experience. And if you sleep and get a different perspective then you can call it a dream."

"Universes don't have points of view," Rex objected.

"Tell that to the Future-Lord." Goliath nipped playfully at

Rex, distracting him from his climb so he tumbled out of the sky. Rex crash-landed and started running again, leaping up and over a vast city alight with neon signs adorning needle-sharp towers. A wave of darkness spread behind him, a shadow extinguishing every trace of light. "Something terrible is coming. You've shown me this before."

"Run Rex run... don't let the farmer get you with his gun."

Rex ran, onwards and upwards, but the shadow gained, sweeping him along like a blast of deterministic darkness. Machines stalked the land below, ethereal structures, vast but somehow barely visible, wireframe outlines composed of web-thin strands crackling with energy.

Rex stared as a war raged. Vessels and machines smashed and merged, obliterating each other into atoms that rained back to Earth in fiery displays of radiation.

"This is all going to happen?" Rex tried to contain his terror, remembering this was just a dream, even though dreams, memories and reality were all the same thing.

"The plague grows and consumes everything," Del's voice boomed down from the clouds. "Do something, Rex. Make it stop."

Rex tried to focus on the remaining city lights. He felt a spark of comprehension as they seemed to grow a little brighter.

"Your thoughts and ideas help drive this simulation, Rex."

Rex felt the people in the simulation, real minds. *Did they even know they were figments of his imagination?* He saw their thoughts, desperate and terrified, clamoring for salvation and solutions. He urged them to rise-up with machines of their own, but the cost was terrible. Cities died, billions of minds blinked out of existence, and still the conflict raged, but now through different media, through information and ideas, simulations and abstractions, down through scales of technology smaller than atoms and into dimensions incomprehensible to a normal, three-dimensional mind. "No... not like this," Rex whimpered. "There has to be another way."

"You are Glow, Rex. You are the plague."

"If I'm your damned plague then why are you showing me this?"

"You think I'd bring a knife to a gun fight? Maybe you're the crucible, Rex. The vessel that holds Felix, myself, and all these other personas together. Perhaps you're the armor that keeps us safe? Or you're a new form of plague, a benevolent agent that seeps through humanity, countering its worst instincts."

Rex shook his head as the craziness of it all overwhelmed. "How could I possibly stop this?"

"Play the game, Rex. Reset the pieces, run the sim. That's what it was designed for. The answer is in here somewhere."

The horror beneath grew in scale, threatening to rip the planet apart before his eyes. He bounded off into space, past spaceships and weapons platforms. Behind him, the world erupted sending out rings of material in a blinding flash. He kept running past Jupiter, past Neptune, farther into the darkness. There was nothing out here, no flickers of life. Startlingly, there was nothing ahead of him anywhere, an empty Universe awaiting the coming storm. No point-of-view at all… except his.

He turned and looked back, a cascade of violence and wreckage hurtled at him. He felt his life fading, the sudden realization that minds were collectives, products of cultures and networks. No mind could exist in total, death-black isolation… not even his.

Rex felt something touch his paw and looked up. Light streamed through the tiny slot window. "Wake up, Rex," John said. "Rough night again?" He glanced at the blasted dystopia of Rex's bed, the scattered, sweat-soaked sheets and pillows. "Millie's up there waiting."

Rex stumbled out, bleary-eyed, afterimages of wireframe monsters still striding across the backdrop of his reality. He climbed up the steps into the lounge. Millie stood in the middle of the room. She wore an odd smile, not the usual fear and anticipation of meeting somebody new and unexpected.

"This is my old friend Rex," John said. "He stayed the night after some cards and beers."

Her smile grew larger. "Rex, yes I remember you from yesterday." Rex and John stared at her in disbelief. A fondness crossed her face. "We used to have a dog called Rex."

"Millie?" John almost fell in his haste to embrace her. "You… you remember that?"

Rex looked around, suddenly nervous. Something was very wrong here. Millie's memory couldn't just come back like that. "Any visitors?" he asked.

"No," John said, and then reconsidered. Well, there was one of the Sisters came by yesterday, I think? She gave Millie a present, a healing necklace. Wouldn't take any money." John pointed to the tiny phial on a chain around Millie's neck. It shimmered as if lit from the inside by a tiny glowworm, glinting and refracting an odd spectrum of delicately changing colors.

Millie clutched at the necklace fondly. "The Sister said it would heal me as long as it remains in contact with my skin."

Rex left them in their moment of joy and wandered out into the garden. So, the Sisters had already been here, and given Millie something to help her. A token of trust, or a threat.

A prickle of fear made him look up, out over John's roughly manicured hedge of jasmine and dogrose bushes. He caught a fleeting glimpse of a face and heard footsteps crunching away across the gravel path down the side of the house.

"Hey, you!" he yelped, running to the hedge and peering over. The man stopped and his head turned in a weird, mechanical way as if it wasn't really attached to his neck. A creeper of cold ran up and around Rex as a jolt of recognition seemed to hit him from somewhere deep inside. The face was young, or maybe just a parody of a teenage boy rendered in smooth, pinkish plastic. The eyes were real, alive, but filled with a crippling angst, the pain of witnessing too much, and of being a part of many things long regretted. "What do you want," Rex barked.

The figure shuffled indecisively, its body angle suggested flight, but its bunching knuckles signaled fight. The head turned again, eyes catching things in the surrounding trees, things concealed from Rex's vision. A crinkled smile reconfigured the face, and the boyish figure jogged easily away leaving Rex quivering with the inexplicable urge to give chase.

The words seemed to bubble up from his core, lingering in his vision before fading to nothing. They pinned Rex's feet firmly to the ground with their cold, stern tone. *Oh Trabian, what have you become?*

CHAPTER 14

Storm

Keller rode out a particularly vicious storm in the lee of *Nevis*'s starboard docking platform. He sat clutching Hex and looking up at a decommissioned longshore bot that sat cross-legged and hunched like a dishonored samurai. Its lifting arms and feet were bolted to the deck to prevent it moving as the platform bucked and rolled through gigantic ocean waves.

He'd been immersed in a particularly tricky deep-water hull scrubbing operation when the storm warning came and caught him off-guard. By the time he retrieved Hex, his fellow workers had all left for the comparative safety of the *Nevis*'s main hull, and the walkway connecting the remote platform was closed.

He gazed up into the longshore bot's camera eyes. It looked sad and abandoned, a cumbersome relic that still had its uses. His hand caressed the hard metal foot that probably weighed as much as a small house. It was lonely out here with the windmills, solar arrays, and stowed longshore machinery.

The storm came and went, a thundering elemental of air and rain that corkscrewed around container stacks whistling insane tunes for an hour before blowing itself out. He amused himself by singing sea-shanties, songs about sails, rum, and women in distant ports. Things Keller normally had no interest in at all, but which held a strange appeal when trapped out here.

The all-clear siren sounded, and the platform's wind turbines and solar arrays unfolded and began feeding power back into the *Nevis*'s grid. He slung Hex across his shoulders like a backpack, saluted the longshore bot a somber farewell, and navigated the slippery walkways back to the *Nevis*'s inner harbor. Casima would be home now, likely signed onto virtual evening classes, studying biology. "Why biology?" he'd asked.

"Know thine enemy," she replied.

Grimace sat on his newly erected watch-chair high above the deck, motionless as if secured to the barge. His eye cameras tracked Keller and confirmed his identification.

"I'm back, Casi," he yelled but got no response. Heart thudding, he searched the barge, and finding it empty, descended into his lab.

She looked up as he entered. "Sorry, honey, didn't hear you. My head was up a robot's ass."

He paused in the doorway, head shaking in disbelief. "How did I get so lucky?"

They kissed and Keller shrugged out of his wet outerwear and into his lab coat. He smiled at what might have been a butt-print on the oily floor. They sometimes started in the bedroom, only to end up down here. He'd lost count of how many times they showered-off at three in the morning, laughing at the dirt and oil vortex hurrying down the drain. "We have a fun new way to polish the lab floor," he joked.

"I've been studying our friend here, close up." She patted a protruding patch of the robot's crystal skull.

"Now you're just making me jealous," Keller teased, pulling up a chair and slumping into the grubby padding. He enjoyed watching her work. Whether buttering toast or deconstructing a piece of robotic machinery, she possessed an enviable focus, a determination that nothing was going to be above or beyond her ability or understanding. Her sudden interest in his charred robot had caught him off guard. He couldn't decide if he felt redundant or excited to have her along on this new ride.

"This hand has grown back almost entirely, look." She used a pencil to lift the fingers that looked like translucent black gel with a rubbery texture. They were as long as the rest of the hand and didn't show any sign of pointing into tips just yet. "This material is incredible, living, growing, but dead like plastic. Do you really think I could use this arm?"

"That's the plan. We just need a control connection and then your bio-amps should be able to figure out how it drives."

"This really plummeted from space?"

"I think it came in headfirst." She gave him a quizzical look. "If it came down feet first then the momentum of the head would have smashed down through the body, like it does with humans falling from planes."

"You engineers know such romantic things," she pouted.

"So he either landed flat, which bodies don't tend to do, or he came in headfirst." He sat back in the chair, arm curling around her shoulder. "Ever hear of a cartoon character called Popeye?"

"Of course, love Popeye and Olive Oyl." She attempted an accent which trailed off into childish giggles.

"I based Grimace's head on Popeye, I figured it gave him an intimidating nautical look. I remember this one episode where Popeye has fallen out of an airplane. He's plunging towards the ground with his pipe sticking out his mouth."

"Oh my, the poor ground."

"Exactly. Popeye says: 'If I lands ons my head, then I'll be okay!'" Keller's accent was even worse than Casima's. "That's what I think our friend did. He came in headfirst and that's why some of the body cavity is still intact and maybe not as burned-up as it could be."

"Tough head," she said, suddenly very interested in the skull again.

"It appears to be a single crystal, totally airtight, not even a molecule of an opening. All communication with the inside is done by shining laser light through optically transparent areas." Keller reached up and plucked a wad of printouts from a line strung over the bot. "Here's some scans I've been doing. It's a double-thickness skull, a sphere inside a sphere. The eyebrow ridge and other features are grown onto the sphere to make it look more human, but here's the interesting part." He pointed to a thin, yellow rectangle around the temple area. "This is where someone broke in. Despite this material being near-indestructible, they managed to hack a rectangular hole in the side here."

"How'd they do that?"

"Not sure. Maybe a micro-abrasion cutter. Despite what the sci-fi films might tell you, you can grind your way through anything given enough time and patience."

"Maybe it needed a hardware upgrade."

"The scans show shadows of rectangular objects inside, could be computer blocks or circuit boards. The chunk of skull has been glued back in place with a molecular bonding adhesive. That's pretty strong but I might be able to melt the bond away with a very fine laser, and we can get a look around inside Popeye's thick head."

"What's this bit?" She pointed to a strange mushroom-shaped growth sprouting from the center of the skull forehead.

"That's a mystery. It grew that over the last week after I started injecting a liquidized carbon compound into the frazzled body fibers. I'm thinking of it as a kind of cancer, a bit of regenerative growth gone awry. The bot is so badly damaged that it's reasonable to assume the auto-repair function that's built into the very structure of this material is confused. Or some foreign body has lodged in the material causing a distortion."

"Robo-acne?"

"A cyber-pimple," he laughed.

"I'm more interested in this arm." She picked up the arm and waggled it about, so it rattled like a wooden model, then cuddled it lovingly to her cheek. "One day this could all be mine."

"I don't want to amputate it until it's fully grown. It might be getting its build instructions from the central processor in the head. Materials are transported through conduits, these amazingly tough monofilaments that pervade the whole body. See this fine mesh over the top of the bones?" Keller tugged at the mesh with a pencil. "So delicate I didn't notice it at first. It acts like a super-strong bag containing all the bits. This guy could literally get blown apart but would get pulled back together by the mesh. It's an incredible setup."

"I want that, Kell, I really want that."

"Anything for you, my sweet." He kissed her, feeling a charge zing between them. "Take a look at these bone images too." Keller pulled down another photo that showed a tight honeycomb formation. "They're made up of the same fullerene mesh as the muscles, but much more densely packed. Almost like it's woven together. I think that if this thing had full control over those filaments, then it could change shape and become something totally different. Except for its head which is rigid as heck."

"But it can't move, right?" She leaned close, eyes level with the tiny orbs in the black skull.

He shrugged. "I'm guessing not, but then I don't really know what powers it."

"We should snip a bit of muscle off and see if it grows on its own."

He stood up and cradled her head in the crook of his arm. "Patience, my darling, one day soon we'll graft a bit of the creepy, alien space-robot onto your flesh and all shall be well."

"You really know how to turn a girl on." She pounced like a cat, sending him backwards onto a makeshift bed of tarpaulin and packing materials.

"I literally know the way to a cyborg-girl's heart."

Hours later, Keller awoke and found himself between soft sheets. It took a moment to remember how they got back up here, stumbling, naked and filthy, then through the shower, to collapse, exhausted in bed.

The clock showed four-thirty in the morning, and he was hungry.

He creaked out of the room and into the kitchen, massaging his back. "Shit, sex in the lab is killing me." He helped himself to some leftovers from last night's meal and sat contemplating the idea of cyborging himself, starting with some spinal upgrades. It had never appealed before – something about the sanctity of his own natural born flesh. But the world was changing, humanity was changing. Maybe he should change too and follow Casima down that augmented road. Perhaps he could glean some firsthand information regarding cyborg sickness and get new ideas about how to fix Casima and make her whole again.

His mind returned to the night's activities, remembering the lab security cameras. Casima would get a kick out of that.

He took his leftover sandwich and tiptoed into the lab. The oily darkness was like a scene from a horror movie with limbs and sinuous cables strewn around the walls. The bot was safely back under a blanket and all was eerily silent and still. Even the rocking of the *Nevis* had dropped below his threshold of detection.

Flopping into a chair, he pulled out the remote control from a desk drawer and routed the camera feeds through to the wall screen. He selected a wide-angle shot, one that gave an overview of the whole lab. "This should do it," he muttered, clicking through the time selection codes.

The images were not nearly as arousing as he thought they should have been, kind of embarrassing really. "I need to delete those."

Up in the top left corner of the image, he saw the blanket covering the bot twitch. "Holy shit, it did move." He grabbed the controls and played with the zoom and pan features.

"Jesus..." The blanket raised up above the bot's head. Through the shadows he watched as the head tilted toward the oblivious couple. The eyes jittered in the sockets like some

Amp-crazed lunatic as they tried to focus using the optic nerves as surrogate muscles. For a few seconds, the ghastly carbon-black face watched them, then with total control and stealth it lowered the blanket and became motionless.

Keller rewound, zoomed the image onto the robot's face and hit freezeframe. "It's really alive," he muttered, suddenly aware that it was there, only a few feet from him and between himself and the doorway, which now suddenly seemed a long, long way away.

"Can you hear me?" he asked the darkness. An old terror gripped him. The same terror he first felt during the Nova-Insanity when patient after patient lay charred and dying in makeshift operating rooms. *Not enough resources. Too many. Too damaged...* He froze back then, overwhelmed, and motionless. All he could think of was running, hiding in the bathroom. Deserting his patients in their moment of critical need.

Breathe. Focus. With her I am safe and free. But she's not here! "Casi?" His voice croaked. "Casi... help me!" Still too quiet. He refocused on the real threat. "I know you can move. I saw you." He fought to inhale, to just expand his lungs. Fought the trembling in his hands; the urge to run and hide was so strong, but, as always, *just like back then,* he remained frozen to the spot. "Cas... help me." The world swam with shadows and watching eyes as the bench instruments ticked and hummed through the creepy silence.

A crash as the remote tumbled from his hand. The shock jolted him to his feet. *A survival rush!* He stared down the blanket, almost daring it to move, just a flutter of life. Maybe the video was fake, a joke, a hack from outside?

The bathroom. Yes, go hide in the bathroom. They'll never know. Never find me. I'll be safe there, recover, come back later when things calm down. I can move if it's towards the bathroom–

His legs came alive. In a single bound he crossed the room, shouldering past the hanging blanket, a lurking ghoul in the semi-darkness. He brushed by the cloth, expecting a ghastly robotic hand to lash out and grab him. He collided with the door frame, catching his elbow painfully on the way through, and then he was out and racing up the staircase. His voice wailing like the *Nevis*'s storm warning.

"Casi, Casi, that thing's alive. It's really alive."

CHAPTER 15

Qinghai Lake

Ogolai's salt map was now a spider web of lines and pictograms inside Steelos's mind. He didn't remember having a photographic memory when he was alive; just another perk of being a Burn, he assumed. Another perk was that he could run for days without stopping. His body was a machine, churning across the miles of salt and desert, just following the mental map.

Such energy. It reminded him of being a child.

"You're an evil child, Steelos." He heard his father's voice scolding him as he sat in the garden mud, pulling apart bugs and creatures he'd dug from the filth. Life had fascinated him back then, but only in the mechanical sense. How could something resembling a few twigs be alive and move? How could a tube of slime wriggle its way through the world, living, eating, and procreating? Did it think like he did? In truth, he searched for that soul other people told him existed in all living things. He never found it in his own mind, and certainly not in the worms and spiders in the garden. He saw components, linkages, objects attached by forces and fulcrums. They spun and rolled and jiggled through the universe, and sometimes... but only sometimes, they came together in his mind into a whole, into a thing like him. But it was still just an empty thing: an object.

Evil child. Evil youth. Evil man.

Lost in thought, miles of salt flats drifted by. Monasteries lined the distant shores, now far from the lake water which was at its lowest level in recorded history. Many were just ruins, but others remained vibrant communities servicing the stream of pilgrims and traders winding the ever-shifting pathways between Mongolia and the Tibetan plateau.

He wondered if Ogolai's map was real. Perhaps he'd sensed the danger in Steelos and sent him on a wild chase across China, making sure he was far away from his family caravan.

Steelos felt the twitch in his head. The berserk warrior, a passenger burning a throwaway body like rocket fuel. He'd get where he was going much faster, but would he be able to stop when he got there?

Evil.

Flies. Damned flies. His body was never his own, like a rental car with an insurance policy, a guarantee of having another if he screwed this one up. He shifted his perception away from the emotions of anger and frustration, and perceived the flies differently now, making them part of his extended self, almost like a sixth sense that ruffled his skin in response to changes in wind or course direction.

The meditation on extra senses passed more time. Afternoon dulled into evening and ahead Bird Island shimmered like a levitating castle above the salty mirages. The lake water had long receded, leaving the once magnificent island just a hump of dirt and rock above the pristine whiteness. Steelos circled its perimeter. A few elderly monks tended their ailing gardens, others clustered along what was once a road hoping to catch some passersby and sell them dried fish, salt carvings, or a stone jug of precious potable water.

A wooden path made of split logs and reeds led out over the salt to the distant water. Most of the able-bodied inhabitants had relocated their abodes closer to the water's edge. Steelos clopped along the walkway sounding like a horse on cobblestones. Distance was deceptive: miles of walkway but the harbor never seemed to get closer. Until suddenly, it shimmered into reality out of the colorful, unchanging mirage.

The harbor village was a grid of tents, wooden caravans, and brittle looking shacks that had been dragged a plank at a time from the mainland and set upon raised banks of salt that formed streets and neighborhoods.

Steelos headed straight for the water, passing under rows of colored flags knotted and strung across the road. As he neared the harbor, he saw the water had retreated more since the town last moved. The boats he thought were moored were actually grounded in the salt. People lived inside them now.

A new and thinner walkway extended out to another row of docking bollards. The salt flat between the village and the water was covered in resting birds, all pointing their beaks into the prevailing wind like thousands of black and white weathervanes.

"Where's Honneck?" he snapped at a dried-fish peddler sitting on a tricycle at a street corner. He didn't really expect an answer.

To his surprise the man pointed back up the street and bent his finger to the left. Steelos wandered up the road and asked more locals. It seemed everyone knew Honneck. Maybe because he was the only person in the town with a truck?

Honneck's cabin was a simple plank structure with shuttered doors and windows. A young girl sat on his doorstep playing a game with colored stones. "Honneck?" he demanded.

"Macau," she blurted.

"Shit! When?" She shrugged and stared him down with her huge, brown eyes. "Scram!" he yelled, sending her onto her feet and running. He waited until she rounded a corner, fearful of his own anger and what might happen to her if he didn't find what he was seeking.

Turning back to the cabin, Steelos ripped away the shutters, then leaned on the door until it popped open. Falling inside, he saw the room was empty except for a workbench and a photo of Honneck and his truck, pinned to the wall as if to denote the cabin's owner. The space smelled of oil and salted fish. Solder dotted the floor around the workbench. It seemed that Honneck had taken everything with him.

Steelos punched the bench angrily, shattering it neatly in two, and looked up at the ceiling, his gaze drilling through to the heavens above. Inhaling his dejection, he calmed his breathing and headed back out into the sun and the flies.

A status update chattered out of his Inner-I and onto Knoss's encrypted network: *We're looking for a man called Honneck. An elderly man living in a truck full of spare parts and robot fragments. Located somewhere between Bird Island and Macau.* He stared at Honneck's photo, allowing his Inner-I time to scan and send the image along with his words, and then cut the connection to avoid triangulation traces.

His body ached; his joints were starting to grind with wear. He walked down to the waterfront and sat, eyeing the birds on the flat. The birds eyed him back, but their eyes held no life, no hidden soul peering out. Just glassy beads adorning feathered heads, those boney crusts that protected an animal's survival algorithms that had evolved through trial and error over eons of births, deaths, and miniscule adaptions.

His Inner-I pinged to life and Knoss's chiseled metal helm appeared in his mind. "We'll find him. I'm sending a carrier for you now."

"Good," Steelos jumped to his feet. "I'll be out on the salt flats, running."

He leapt the harbor wall and landed amongst the birds, scattering them squawking and yelling into a monochromatic cloud of avian pixels. As he ran through them, they became birds again, whole and real, not beads and algorithms. He felt fairly sure they'd all live, and if he could get far enough away from the people of the village, then maybe they would all live as well.

CHAPTER 16

Leal

"Sir, have you heard the good news about the Future-Lord?"

"Madam, I have great news about–"

Jorben's blood boiled while his face grimaced out a smile, head bobbing in subservient politeness. *Six more days.* Looking wet and miserable should have been an asset for a recruiter in the Welkin business district, but, so far, Jorben had seen little benefit.

Rain poured, running down his neck and back, flowing like a river through the canyon of his butt-cheeks before cascading down his drainpipe legs and into his sodden shoes where it rushed forth into the world through holes in the toes and heels. He made squelching noises as he walked. His military surplus fatigues hung like sodden weights from his body. The damp chill sucked energy, sucked life. He felt his internal clock tick. *Six more days of penance!*

By day's end he had just one possible recruit. A charitable-faced young man had politely taken a brochure and promised to read... "at least some of it."

He wandered through the sunset and into darkness. The rain ceased, warm air followed the storm inland and his clothes began to steam themselves dry. His feet found the Gaia bar. Too early to be heaving with drunks and revelers. He wasn't going inside anyway, no money, no wish for that kind of company, and certainly no appetite to provoke more penance from Knoss.

Instead he found a lofty vantage point on the roof of a neighboring derelict. A housing project marked for demolition by the Broken. From there, he watched Krista coming down the street. His gaze followed her skinny backside as it wiggled through cones of light from the streetlamps, and around the corner toward the bar's front door. She seemed to sense him watching, paused, and turned, eyes scanning the dark. Her hand under her coat massaged the trigger of a concealed weapon.

He looked directly down onto the bar's shadowy, walled backyard filled with bins and chained bicycles. People milled behind a façade of frosted windows rimmed by pipes and vents that gushed steam, noise, and food odors out into the night.

Jorben settled into his aerie, his body dropping into meditation as he shut everything down except his eyes and ears, until he used less energy than the rats scampering around his hideout. A little healing after the rigors of the day. He felt old, worn, even though physically he was only a few months old. Mentally? He didn't even know how to go about computing that. His childhood memories seemed to come from about twenty-years back. Coriolis had been new and optimistic, and he'd been a deeply troubled teenager living with an estranged, bitter father. Could he really count those years since then? He'd been dead for a fair portion of them.

Hoots and shouts grew louder inside the bar. The rear doors opened to let air inside as a constant procession of cooks and bussers did sallies back and forth from the trash bins. Time went by faster in meditation and the moon had ridden the ecliptic up from the horizon to nearly overhead when he finally spotted Leal. Working the late shift, she scurried along the pavement, concealed inside a saggy, androgynous coat. He only realized it was her when she dropped the hood and sidled through the bar's rear door.

An hour later he saw her again, propping up an awning post and fumbling a light on a cigarette. She stood, eyes closed, dragging in the smoke, something nervous about her pose.

He eased upright, ironing the numbness from his legs with a firm massage, and opened his mouth to call to her. Maybe just a little talk, or even just a friendly wave. His words froze in his throat as he spotted another watcher in the bushes at the back of the yard.

Prickling with readiness, metabolism revving for a fight, Jorben dropped from the roof onto a balcony and eased down into the street. He heard voices now on the other side of the wall. Several people had entered the yard and were talking with Leal.

"You playing games with us?" An angry voice sounded like it came from a big man. "You see the size of that guy you tagged the other night? Fucking huge! I might think you're tryin' to get us killed or something."

"Sorry, Jay... really," Leal's voice, shrill with fear. "I didn't get any other marks that night. They kept me in the kitchen."

Jorben eased up onto the wall through bushes to keep hidden, thorns pricked and scratched his skin. Three men surrounded Leal. The one behind her had a hand gripping her shoulder making sure she didn't run.

He felt fully charged now. His metabolism raced; blood pumped through his body at a rate that would burst any normal human artery. Lubricants flooded his joints, cushioning them from shock and damage, senses sharpened. Time seemed to slow down.

"I did what you asked, Jay." Leal's voice trembled but was loud like she was calling for help. "I spiked his drink with that stuff, but it didn't do anything."

Jorben mentally labeled his foes: Three men, two of medium build; one with a hood and another with a balaclava. The third was a hulking human, quivering from an Amp shot. His face jittered between raging anger and lust as he tugged at the belt around his pants. Jorben noticed a cube of machinery slung off to the side, a reclamation pack for grinding bodies and extracting drugs, blood, and anything else of value. These were amateurs, a non-militia-sanctioned liching gang who picked on drugged and drunken targets leaving bars late at night.

"Maybe you need a little reminder?" Balaclava said.

"Please, no," Leal whispered, "I'll make good next time–"

The slap stung the air and made even Jorben jump. "Shut the fuck up," Balaclava hissed. Hood laughed while Amp tore off his pants, mouth foaming with anticipation.

Jorben landed right next to them, bent legs cushioning his landing and springing him into the action. *Elation...* near-orgasmic relief pounded through him as he slammed a fist into Hood's face. He kicked Balaclava in the crotch, lifting him clear off the ground, then spun on the spot clubbing Amp across the cheek with the back of his fist. What would normally be a killer blow to the average human just bounced off Amp's face, like slapping an elephant. Jorben heard, but didn't feel, the crunching sensation as he re-bunched his now shattered fist, and launched it again, straight punch, right at Amp's nasal bone.

But Amp was ready, riding his own high, senses jangling with internal energy and imaginary attackers. He caught Jorben's fist, spinning him into an arm lock. They rolled across the ground in a high-speed whirl scattering cans and bricks like a horizontal tornado. He heard Leal scream for help, but Amp roared in his ear, shattering an eardrum before biting the ear clean off.

Jorben roared, ripped his arm free and rolled Amp into a bear hug, pushing his head up under the man's chin. He felt Amp's neck dislocating, even as the man's fists pummeled his own head and shoulders.

The wrestlers crashed to the ground, Jorben spinning and twisting to land on top. But Amp's leg bent up around Jorben's neck, pulling him back into an escape roll. He landed on his feet, but Amp was there, barreling into combat like a prize-fighter. Toe-to-toe, they traded punches, slamming each other's faces, shoulders, and chests, oblivious to pain and damage. Neither even trying to avoid the other's strikes. Jorben sensed Amp's shot was running low and pressed his attack, smashing the man to the ground and stomping his neck, crushing the larynx.

As Amp gasped his last, frantic breath, Jorben felt a stabbing pain, a blast of agony as a knife tore upward into his ribs. In reactive rage, he snatched Amp's hair and swung him around like a grotesque fleshy battering ram. Balaclava collapsed under the crushing blow, but Jorben saw a new threat: Hood had a gun.

Balaclava rolled out from under Amp and rammed into Jorben's chest. His knife piercing Jorben's lung. The pain was the trigger. A switch flipped inside Jorben's mind. Sensation vanished and the world slowed further as humans became just targets, bags of flesh to puncture and rupture.

Like nitro injected into a drag-racer's engine, Jorben burned away the last of his body's resources in a single exquisite second. An elbow-uppercut shattered Balaclava's neck. He caught the collapsing body and heaved it at Hood as the shots rang out.

He followed the flying corpse, plunging face-first into a spray of guts and bullets. High kick, then the flat of his foot jammed Hood's head back into the wall, smashing his skull like an egg. The gun went silent. Bodies and weapons clattered to the ground.

The switch flipped off. Humans were human again. The shattered sacks of blood and offal were people. He stood, swaying, grief at what he'd done should have produced tears but there was no energy left for such things. He watched impassively as Leal crawled across the yard towards the bar door.

"What were you thinking, Leal? Selling me out to these creeps?" He still had anger, a soft, disappointed kind of anger.

A familiar feeling of being let down, deceived. The victim. "They give you a cut of the drugs they find?"

His knees gave way and he fell. *Dead soon.*

Other voices. He guessed people from the bar had heard the commotion. "It's that guy who was with Benz the other night," somebody said.

He heard Leal speak next. "Careful with him. He saved me."

Jorben felt a gentle snap as his mind broke free of the mortally wounded body. He drifted, just floating above it all, taking in every word until something inside tripped over an indeterminate threshold, and he simply switched off and died.

CHAPTER 17

Leaving Home

Rex called these types of mornings 'dynamic dawns.' The sun dwelled low on the horizon, with a damp, humid wind blowing straight out of its flickering face. Clouds scuttled over in layers, the low purplish-grey ones obscuring the slower-moving reds and oranges, which traversed the wispy backdrop of cauliflower white, high above. Birds leapt from ground to trees and back again, calling dibs on territories defined only inside their tiny brains, as leaves whipped past in mischievous vortices, rattling and chattering like mechanical bees.

He hadn't slept the previous night. Instead, he'd stalked the dark house, seeing Trabian's haunted face lurking behind curtains and in dark corners or peering through bushes and windows. When dawn came, he slipped out of the house and headed straight into the rising sun, trying not to think of Millie, peaceful and snoring in bed. As he passed through the rose arch, he took a glance back and saw John, sad-eyed, watching through the kitchen window.

"I knew you'd have to leave eventually," he'd said the previous night as their cards and drinks concluded. "There's always a place for you here when you're done saving the world."

Rex skipped over the grave and hopped the fence into the field. Bugs made tiny circular ripples on the lake surface as he passed. "I'm ready," he yelled into the wind.

He stooped over, swishing hands through the grass tops, watching seeds and pollen puff and swirl into the air. *Time to run!*

"Are you here?" he said, louder, grass whipping his legs, wind pinning his hair back and sapping the tears from his eyes. Faster through the wall of pain, blowing the dust and cobwebs from his soul.

His legs weakened and he slowed to a trot. The atrophy of easy family living taking its toll. "I'll go with you. But remember John and Millie, your promise to watch over them."

Cresting a hill, he staggered across a patch of grassland, nature's landing strip polished flat by wind and time. He saw movement, the grass here parted and bent in unnatural ways. He felt the eyes all around, the watchers inside stirring. Del was there too, but quiet, just a knowing smile. He'd won. He'd got his way in the end.

Why no fear? thought Rex. Does prey know when it's caught. When time is up?

Figures lurked on the edge of his vision, chameleon suits fighting nature's ever-shifting perspective. Machine sounds cut through the wind and the air crackled with energy. He felt a vast conspiracy taking place in the radio waves fluxing through his head. The atmosphere far above shimmered as if a great invisible bird pushed through the air currents.

"I want guards posted around John and Millie at all times." He stumbled to a halt. There was more that needed saying, but the figures emerging from thin air shut down his thoughts.

They were all around him, Sisters in chameleon cloaks, machines, furtive agents ducking through the long grass seeking a closer vantage. The air shimmered in front and suddenly a craft hovered just inches above the grassland. Its powerful down-jets pummeled the grass flat as it reversed to within meters of Rex.

"And another thing…" Rex had to spit the words out, but the sound never reached his own ears. "I want to deal with Sister-Zero at all times. No Reevas or Cycs or–"

The rear end of the craft dropped open and Sister-Zero stood in the entrance, a beckoning finger signaling him to come aboard. "Don't be afraid, Rex," she said, and for a few seconds his mind wanted nothing more than to turn him around, back to the safety of the house and the lake with the gun and the dead dog buried in the garden.

The Sister reached down and grasped his fingers, pulling him up and into the rear of the carrier with that tender grip that held such hidden power.

She steadied him as the craft lifted, tilting as the door closed behind. He got one last look across the plain, back to the distant village and the toy houses with their curls of rising smoke. He imagined two figures having morning tea out on the rear porch, surprised as they caught a glimpse of the strange flying craft, miles off over the hills. Perhaps John smiled and wished him well. Perhaps Millie watched as well. She remembered who he was in the mornings now, and that memory meant loss and sadness could once again enter her thoughts.

The craft rocked violently as if seized by a divine hand. A jolt of energy drained the power from the engines. "Inside," yelled the Sister, wrenching Rex into an interior compartment with soft, padded walls and restraining belts.

As the door cycled closed, he saw laser beams and smoke, heard gunfire. "The Alliance is trying to bring us down. They want you, Rex."

"But... John and Millie?"

"We have their house surrounded, but it was important that the Alliance saw you leave like this, Rex, fleeing into our protective custody. From now on, we are their targets. Not John and Millie."

CHAPTER 18

It Moves

"What do we do, Kell?" Casima sat in the bed, sheets pulled up tight around her neck as Keller sat on the end, rocking back and forth. They both stared at the frozen image on the bedroom screen. The charred, skeletal face leering down on them. Its fingers curled over the blanket that hid it from the world.

"We dump it in the sea. Just call it a bad purchase. I can smuggle it to the edge without anyone seeing, attach a chunk of metal so it sinks."

"Seems a bit cruel. What if it's sentient?"

His mouth dropped open as he stared her down. "You... you're siding with the robot?"

"Duh!" She waved her mechanical hands in front of his face, fingers rippling in a complex, inhuman pattern.

He stood and walked to the screen, thrusting an accusing finger at the frozen image. "It fell from orbit and survived. Not sure the ocean would do it much harm. Although it's a hell of a long one-handed crawl to any landmass from here under four miles of water."

"We should sell it."

"The *Nevis* is not exactly the pinnacle of human morality. I've heard all sorts of stories of people disappearing onboard here and deals-gone-wrong. They could just take it and dump us over the side. Or maybe we are in possession of something illegal, and they hand us over to... I don't know, someone even worse than them."

"Then we keep it, maybe talk to it?"

"Talk to it?" His laugh bordered on hysteria. "It's military. Who the hell knows what it thinks or what its orders are?" His voice rose in pitch and volume. "It could start blundering around here at any moment, tearing the place up." His eyes focused away from the screen and down to the floor. "It's only a few feet away, Casi. An arm's length of wood and insulation–"

"But it hasn't, Kell. It's only got one arm, no legs, and no muscle mass. But we'd best find out what it's about, now, before it grows more powerful."

Keller nodded. She was right, always a rational voice. "But you wanted that arm, that regenerative technology. This thing could be the key to saving you, Cas."

"We'll find something else. Besides, if it agrees to work with us then maybe we get the secret recipes and learn how to make our own parts."

"Okay... okay, that's a plan. A good plan." Keller huffed and choked as he tried to control his breathing. "How do we do that?"

She perked up and rolled out of bed to hold his sagging chin in her fingers and pull his face up to meet hers. "We ask it!"

They sent Grimace in first. He was given a simple set of orders to interrogate a possible intruder hiding underneath the blanket in the lab. Keller stood watch in the doorway, a high-voltage defense prod in one hand and Casima peering over his shoulder. Her magenta eyes wide and alert.

Grimace ambled over, metal legs hissing and clicking as he walked, and without hesitation, whipped the blanket off. "Please identify yourself." It stood awaiting a response, shifting from foot to foot as Keller had programmed him to do. It projected an impatient energy which was more intimidating to intruders.

"Please identify yourself," Grimace said again, and began frisking the dangling corpse. It lifted up the chest cavity and peered inside, then ran its hand up over the shoulder joints and behind the head. Cupping the skull, it turned it left and right, camera eyes scanning the macabre remnants. "The intruder is unarmed," it announced then flipped the entire body up and over, using the hook hand to probe the underneath.

After a few seconds of turning and scanning, Grimace dropped the bot back so it swung from the hoist chain and turned to Keller. "The intruder appears to be an inanimate object. Assessment: harmless, non-functional. This intruder is not a threat."

Keller gripped the prod with both hands and shuffled into the lab. "That's good, Grimace, now step back and remain alert. The intruder is pretending to be inactive but is capable of movement and possibly violence."

As Grimace moved around to the rear of the bot, Casima followed Keller into the room. "Maybe it ran out of power."

"Not buying it. Not buying it at all." Keller pushed the prod forward touching it on the bot's forehead. A small charge crackled from the end to ground through the hoist chain. The bot didn't move. "Not very conductive," he muttered.

"Maybe it can't hear us. It's got no ears."

Keller stood back, suddenly feeling stupid. "No ears! You could be right. We need to find another means of communication."

"We know it can see, so maybe it can read." Casima danced across the room and picked up a small whiteboard that Keller used for doodling designs on. She grabbed a marker pen and scrawled the words: "Hello. We are your friends. Nod if you understand." Then she held the board up in front of the robot's face.

They gasped as its eyes jiggled in their sockets as if straining to read the text. "It's moving," Keller hissed.

"True, but it's not nodding. I don't think it can focus on the words."

"It has no eye control musculature."

"Maybe closer." Casima pushed the board right in front of the face.

"Casi, no, you're too clo–"

The arm snatched out like a pit-viper flinging its forearm around her waist and hauling her bodily into contact with the broken chest cavity. Fingers encircled her back, growing longer and thinner, stretching up her neck, cupping her head and pressing it hard into the side of the grinning crystal skull.

"Casi!" Keller froze, his eyes on the electric prod, knowing that if he used it, he risked electrocuting her.

Grimace attacked from behind spinning the couple around the hoist chain and hooking the attacker's neck and grabbing its hand. It hauled the components apart trying to undo the deadly embrace. For a second, Grimace seemed to be winning and Casima almost wiggled free, but the bot ratcheted up its power and the arm pinned Casima back to its chest.

She screamed, a ghastly exhale as all the air was compressed from her lung. Grimace's arms crackled with short-circuited power, but the crushing force of the arm was too much. "No!" yelled Keller, a new level of terror snapping his frozen condition. He grabbed a hammer from his tool rack and rained double handed blows onto the bot's skull, feeling the impact shocking back up his arms, doing more damage to his body than to the robot.

The bot's fingers curled over the top of Casima's head, slowly turning her face so Keller couldn't avoid seeing the look of blank, uncomprehending terror in her eyes.

Keller's hammer dropped from his hands, and he fixated on some distant, imaginary place.

"Damn it, Keller, don't freeze on me now," she gurgled, fighting to keep her head straight and her eyes away from the crawling fingers. One of her hands was spasming, and her left foot began to spin on the joint as its control motors lost contact with the rest of her body.

Grimace whirled away as a hydraulic line ruptured in its arm, spraying black fluid across the lab. "Emergency shutdown," it rasped and dropped into a heap in the corner.

Casima thrust an arm under the crook of the bot's own limb and tried to lever it away, but all her strength did nothing. Keller could hear the bubbles in her electro-polymer muscles popping as they burst from the strain. He saw blood on her shoulder as the artificial arm started to detach from her body.

The bathroom. Run and hide in the bathroom!

She gasped with pain but kept pushing, eyes reddening with fear. The bot's hand spider-walked across her face, a finger probing her eye socket while a smaller digit explored her mouth, and another seemed to extrude longer and hook down around the nub of her chin.

"Kell... please–" He gaped as her mouth moved, animated by the bot's waggling fingers... open, closed... open. Through the forced motion Casima's own words struggled free. "Back off, Keller. It wants to talk."

He heard a buzzing sound like distant bees. For a moment he thought it was voices, the thousands of dying souls groaning and shouting for help from their gurneys and blankets on the hospital floor. *As I froze and did nothing!* But no, the noise came from the robot, from the small mushroom-shaped object projecting from its head.

Life came back to his limbs, and he staggered backwards away from the bot, hands raised in surrender.

The carbon-black fingers paused their motion. Casima's mouth stopped moving, and the pressure eased off her ribcage. She gasped in a desperate breath, choking on her own spittle.

The robot sound rose in pitch and had a clear sonic envelope that Keller could make no sense of. "Alphabet," Casima spluttered.

Sure enough, the sounds were of the alphabet "... M... N... O..." it enunciated in long, drawn-out buzz-sounds.

"It's calibrating its speech system. Hang in there, Casi, maybe it can understand us."

At the end of the alphabet the speaker whirred and clicked as if resetting and then attempted words. "I think weee are commune ick ate ting... now?"

"Yes, yes. I can hear you," Keller gabbled. "Can you hear me."

"I... hear... you..." The head tilted down so the eyes pointed roughly at Keller.

"Then let her go. Let her go now, you hear me? If you hurt her then I don't care what you are, how valuable or important, I will grind you down to atoms and rip out that shit in your head that acts like a brain and figure out its pain sensors and attach them to amplifiers for the rest of your miserable existence. You understand me?"

Keller forced himself back to a calmer state, focusing on the bot's eyes that jerked and segued between various targets in a confused, almost random, manner. Perhaps he was not dealing with a rational entity here? Did it have any idea *where* or even *what* it was? "So, what's your goal here? Your plan? Do you have orders?"

The grating voice came alive once more. "I need a fullerene bioreactor, FK87-minigun, and access to a high-orbital launch system."

Keller's jaw dropped, and he struggled to keep the sarcasm from his voice. "Oh sure, I'll see what I can knock together." His forced calm rose to a manic whine. "Have you looked around you? Do you know where you are?"

"Kell," Casima spluttered. "You're not breathing properly. Remember, box-breaths, in and hold, out and–"

"Then tell me," the bot said, with what sounded like a hint of resignation. "Who are you, and where am I?"

"I am Keller, you are holding Casima, and we are all onboard a barge somewhere in the middle of the Pacific Ocean."

After a long silence, the bot relaxed its grip on Casima, who inhaled her own deep, shuddering breath as it spoke. "You're not Alliance?"

"Not Alliance," Keller said. "Just... just a couple of traders trying to make money so we can buy Casima some replacement parts and better anti-rejection drugs."

The bot managed a crude but oddly human nod of its charred skull. "And I am your trade?"

"You were," Casima said. "We didn't know you were still active. Thought you were just spare parts, maybe something we could use or sell."

Keller slumped into a sitting position as his world began a sickening spin around his central axis. "Are you a combat bot of some sort?"

The bot's voice grew quiet. "No, but I fought the GFC."

"Then I guess you won. The GFC's gone, blown to hell. Other giant corporations like the Alliance run the world now." He closed his eyes, but the world kept revolving, curtains of bubbles and colored dots that shone at him through the darkness.

The bot became agitated. Its grip snaked tighter around Casima. "Then I am still in grave danger and must find my way back into Earth's orbital halo."

Casima twisted in the bot's grip. "Release me, damnit! I am never going into space with you, and to get there you're going to need our help. And in case you haven't noticed we're about to lose Keller."

"How can I trust any human to do what it says?"

"Then what?" Casima strained to turn her head and direct her angry stare right at the bot. "We stay here and stare at each other until we arrive in America?"

The bot's head seemed to scan the room again. "No, I need to be on equal footing. I need... I need legs."

Keller felt a tremor pass through him, an icy wave that paralyzed muscles and dissolved intentions. He heard Casima talking, probably calm words easing him down and back to reality. The bot spoke too, but all the words wafted over, leaving him unmoved. The fear of being confined, trapped, was itself a trap, and fear of that fear... another, deeper, more potent trap. A downward spiral of fear of fear of fear!

"Don't bug out now, Kell! Get curious. Think... curious!"

True, he thought, at this moment, she really needs me. She's trapped too, and supposing she has a full-on seizure, and I can't hit the transcranial stimulator or the hard system reboot? But *they* had all needed me too, and back *then*... I wasn't there.

Casima's words held an urgency, like the owner of a puppy tempting the animal out with a treat or a favorite toy. "We want to know how this thing works, right? Want access to some of the good parts, right? Think of the science, Kell, the engineering–"

Yes... the science. The engineering! The world came back, and it was clear, sharp, and relentlessly fascinating. "Legs?" The words emerged before he was consciously aware of them. "Yeah... right, I can do legs."

CHAPTER 19

Flies

"You have him?" Steelos asked, from inside the flattened windowless tube of the carrier as it zipped along just a meter above the ground to avoid radar detection.

"Maybe." Knoss's voice came through his Inner-I. "Our surveillance drone recorded a truck matching the image that you supplied moving away from Macau three days ago. We extrapolated a route back to Qinghai province and now have eyes on the vehicle from above."

The carrier cylinder rolled to a halt. The access panel slid open and Steelos dropped out onto a sandy patch beside a road made of compacted dirt and gravel. He gasped at the light and the air as the carrier's door hissed closed and it moved away, blinking invisible as its chameleon skin locked with its surroundings.

He stood motionless, soaking up the air, the insect sounds, and the merciful freedom from the vicious swarms of salt flies. A cloud of diesel fumes and dust puffed over the horizon. "Our carrier was detected," Knoss said. "The local militia is on its way. Alliance forces will be close behind. I estimate you have less than twenty minutes to achieve the mission objective." Knoss's voice vanished and Steelos cut his Inner-I to radio silence.

As the truck labored up the hill toward him, Steelos hid in

a bush awaiting its approach. This was the hard part, the part many of his fellow Burns failed. *Control*. He needed to fight to disable, not kill. Needed to interrogate, even act as if he was a real, feeling, empathic human. But all the time the switch was there, and each frustration or setback pushed it further into detent. The thought of what he could do made him sick, but as the switch moved, those acts became intriguing, beguiling… a raging need. *I want that. Why do I want that?*

The truck looked like something that had spent its life blundering across salt-flats and dirt roads. It took technical skill bordering on craftsmanship to keep an ancient wreck like that running for so long, over such treacherous terrain. The driver fitted his mental image of Honneck.

At the peak of the hill the truck barely managed walking pace. Steelos stepped confidently out of the bush in front of the vehicle and held out his hand in the universally understood gesture – stop!

Panic flickered across the driver's face as the truck made a series of gear-grinding noises. Then suddenly it revved and lurched forward with a surprising surge of speed. Steelos braced his shoulder against the vehicle and the pair collided with a crunch of metal and breaking headlights.

He locked his legs and dug his feet into the dirt, but the truck, with its steel-girder bumpers, had momentum, skidding Steelos backward until he abandoned the assault by rolling up over the truck's hood and making a grab for its side mirror. But Honneck was a wily driver, and a sharp, well-timed jolt of his steering wheel sent Steelos flying off into a clump of thorn bushes.

He rolled through the barbs and branches, down an embankment before finding his feet. "Come here you little shit!" He roared back up the slope as the truck accelerated down the hill. It topped forty miles-per-hour before Steelos managed to clamp a hand on the rear girder and haul himself up and over the wooden tailgate and into its yurt-like rear.

The damming evidence was all around: jangling rows of legs and arms, cables and staring robotic eyeballs. "Got you," he yelled, pawing through the bounty on his way to the truck's cab.

Honneck hit the brakes, slamming Steelos into the bulwark separating the truck's bed from its cab and burying him under a tumble of junk from the overhead storage shelves. Thrashing with anger, he kicked the side out of the truck and fell face-first onto the dirt. He lay still, letting the anger swim over and out of him. *Not now. Not here. But soon.*

He stared as the truck lost its holistic nature and became a collection of wheels, metal surfaces, and girders. *Detent.* That moment in between, of release and irresponsibility. *I can't be blamed for what I can't control. In madness, I am free.*

His head snapped up looking for the birds or even those damned flies, anything to distract, to bend that little switch in the other direction. Maybe a memory of his father. He felt the smack around his ear. "Get a grip or there'll be something much worse," he heard him say. No point fighting back, a weak, troubled boy against a full-grown man. "Oh, you wanna fight?" Another slap, it stung but that was not the thing that really hurt. No, this pain was mental, existential even, and it lanced right at the core of his being. "You keep going the way you're going, and I'll have to call them… you know, the men in the white coats. They'll come and take you away. Lock you up for good."

And suddenly Steelos was back.

Honneck had left the truck cab and was off and running, a long-barreled rifle in his hands. He watched him move, seeing joints and balance points, the flapping of clothing, wisps of his thinning hair blowing in the wind. All connected now into a living person. Somebody's father or grandparent. He laughed, letting the absurdity of the human form amuse him, the inefficiency, the sheer lumbering ineptness of the design.

"Never easy, is it." Steelos slapped his thigh, rose to his feet, and broke into a run feeling the grit in his joints fighting him all the way. There was nowhere for Honneck to go. The next village was miles ahead. The rest was open road.

The old man sensed his peril and turned, tilting the rifle up, steady hand, eagle-eyed. Steelos jolted sideways as he saw the muzzle flash, but somehow the annoying little man anticipated his move and the bullet thumped into the plate over his heart knocking the wind out of him and spinning him off the road into yet more thorn bushes.

"Fuck!" His metabolism roared higher. Time slowed. He saw the next bullet coming but was still too slow to evade it completely, catching it in his shoulder as Honneck tracked him through the bushes.

"Fucker! Fucker! Fucker!" He veered sideways, and the next bullet hissed past his head. Leaping from cover to cover, he spun up and over the road embankment and clean over Honneck's head. An instant later he snatched the rifle away and landed behind the bemused old man.

Steelos skidded to a halt, sliding on the dirt to fall flat on his backside. In that moment Honneck was off again, old legs pounding like a champion runner.

He sighed. This game was over. Shrugging off the frustration, he rolled to his feet, took a second to brush the dirt off his clothing, and sprang after Honneck, catching him and pinning him to the ground.

Honneck was all arms, legs, punches, and kicks. He spat and bit, aiming headbutts at Steelos's nose bridge while maneuvering the tiny dagger that had appeared in his left hand up toward his assailant's throat.

Steelos felt the calm of victory wash over him as he meticulously pinned each of Honneck's flailing limbs to the ground with his own hands and knees and twisted the tiny dagger from his fingers.

Just a few more seconds, he thought, I get the information then I can let go, rip his face off and make him eat it.

He tried Cantonese and Portuguese, but Honneck stared blankly. English seemed to catch his attention. "You sold a robot, one that fell from the sky. I need to know who you sold it to."

Honneck choked on his words until Steelos lightened his grip. "Don't hurt me." Honneck managed a terrified grin and rubbed his thumb over his fingers. "Information is cheap."

"Tell me!" Steelos yelled, staggering to his feet, and hauling Honneck up with him.

"Okay, okay... it's in my notebook. In my truck. I record all of my trades."

Steelos frog-marched Honneck back to the truck, keeping his hand around the man's neck. Simultaneously sickened and elated by thoughts of what he was going to do to the old man after he got the information.

Honneck rummaged around, taking way more time to find the notebook than should have been necessary. His eyes kept flickering behind him to Steelos as if gauging how much he could push his luck before Steelos snapped. Finally, he found the book and began flipping through pages of cryptic writing.

"Come on," Steelos slapped at his face and Honneck mumbled his way through the notes.

"Yes, yes. I remember him well, nice fellow, maybe American."

Steelos pulled him down from the truck cab and the two stood facing each other. In height and build they were similar, but Steelos had Burn metabolism, and a psycho-switch hovering in detent. "Name?"

Honneck shook his head and let his gaze drop to his feet. "If I tell you, you'll kill me, right?"

"I'm going to kill you very slowly if you don't."

Suddenly Honneck smiled. "Are you a gambling man... Mister–?"

"No, I am not. Now give me the name!"

"I saw you run, faster than should be possible," Honneck

pointed up the road to a gnarled looking tree. "I'll tell you everything you need if you give me that much of a head start."

Steelos glanced at the tree and the miles of empty road after it. "Sure, you can have a head start. I'll even give you a few seconds more. Now tell me."

"Let me go first."

Steelos screamed with rage, feeling the man in his grip losing his humanity and becoming meat and bones. The switch in his head jammed hard against the detent, ready to pop over to the dark side. The side he now wanted so very, very much.

He dropped Honneck, who backed away, hands raised in surrender. "The man you are after, the name of this man that you are seeking... his name, the one that is so important to you and that you absolutely, completely, and utterly must–"

"Fuck!" Steelos lunged forward but pulled up just short of punching Honneck.

"–Keller Morten. He lives on a barge in Macau harbor." Honneck turned and ran. It was the pathetic, stumbling run of a terrified old man. But Steelos saw no man, just a jangling collection of loosely animated objects, something to dismantle and maybe put back together again in a different, more interesting, order.

He heard a click behind and turned around.

A dozen trembling militia stood in the road, rifles, stun guns, entrapment nets, and grenade launchers all pointing in his direction. More were in the bushes on each side. Somehow they had crept up on him without a sound. He smiled, angry at his stupidity, delighted with the turn of events. "Oh... silly me. You win Honneck, nicely played." He glanced back at the old man who continued running, clearly having no real faith in the militia.

One of the militiamen yelled at him, motioning for him to lie on the ground. Steelos pinged his Inner-I back online. It crackled angrily with static. Somebody was blocking his transmission. He amped up the power, singeing the life from

the device's amplifier as if it were a Burn in the final throes
of combat.

"Steelos?" Knoss's voice crackled through.

"Keller Morten. American. Lives on a barge in Macau
harbor."

"Good work, Steelos."

"I'm about to be arrested."

Knoss paused. "I wouldn't let that happen."

"Will I remember this?"

"Comms bandwidth is too low for a mind dump."

"Oh well," Steelos said.

"Enjoy," Knoss's voice cut away to static.

Steelos roared at the truck. As the militiamen watched,
their faces evolving masks of confusion, he rampaged around
pounding metal panels and screaming at the sky. The guns
followed him as he tore the flesh from his knuckles with his
teeth and punched holes in the steel truck chassis. He tore
through detent, on into the white fury of unknowable territory,
ripping the steel girder off the truck's front and wielding it like
an oversized club.

He took one last look at Honneck's fleeing back and hurled
himself and the girder at the screaming militiamen.

A barrage of lead, wire, and energy came at him. But the
experience of that glorious moment never made it from the
immediacy of consciousness into any short-term memory
store, and an instant later, the moment was lost.

CHAPTER 20

The Can

Being dead didn't feel that different from being alive.

Jorben woke inside a debriefing tube. The voice of Knoss asked him to relay anything he recalled about his last mission. He remembered some: the hooded guy with the gun. Amp with the wild eyes and foaming mouth, and Leal.

He ached when he thought of Leal, a heavy, seeping pain that seemed to spread from his brainstem and down his neck.

The tube snapped away and he found himself in what the Burns called the Can. The afterlife. Really just a virtual waiting room for an untethered mind until a new body became available for him to inhabit back in the Real. He hoped he'd be used again, and that this wasn't the end. *I failed. I lost control. Killed people and deviated from my path of redemption.*

Being in the Can wasn't that bad though. No discomfort, no chores, just wander, learn, and contemplate The Logic. He thought of it as just another part of the Enclave, but one with no doors to the outside. He guessed it could be anywhere. Knoss called it convolution-space. Whatever that meant.

"You have a visitor, Jorben." The voice boomed from the ceiling.

"A visitor?" *In the Can?* "But I don't–"

"Your new body is ready for cognitive transfer."

He felt a shudder and the world went black. *Strange. I've never been rebodied this quickly before.*

His eyes opened on a hospital room. A male nurse unplugged his arms from various tubes and detached sticky pads from his chest. Jorben waved his hands in front of his eyes, checking out the fresh, unblemished skin. The fluid, oily feel of strong, new joints. *Same hulking body but brand, spanking new!*

"Okay, stand up," commanded the nurse, through teeth clenched so tightly he appeared as if his jaw were wired shut. "You might feel a bit dizzy at first but I'm here to catch you."

Jorben struggled to sit. The stiffness felt like cables pinning him in place, but blood started flowing and he came alive like an inflating balloon. Before he could put his feet down, the door to the room opened and a woman stepped in.

"Thank goodness you're alive," Leal said, rushing to his side. "Jeez, they kept me waiting. It was like they didn't want me to see you." Her face dulled with confusion as she eyed his glistening, new body. "But how–"

"What do you care?" Jorben's rage felt fresh and raw in a new body. "You tried to sell me to a liching gang."

"You don't understand–"

"Money talks, right? Shouts real loud and you can't help but listen."

"They know where I live. Know my family, my friends. I didn't have a choice." Leal's chin dropped to her chest. She stood in silence, sniffed, wiped her eyes on a sleeve, and looked around the room as the nurse left, quietly closing the door, leaving Jorben to find his own feet. "How come you're alive?" Real concern creased her brow. "You look good as new."

"I am new. New body. Old mind. One of the Convolvers' experiments in human-machine hybrids. I have an artificial brain, electronics and stuff." He tapped his skull. "Body's grown in a vat without a brain and they rebody me when the old one wears out or–" His voice rose. "Or gets killed when stupidly trying to help someone out of a shit situation."

"Wow... you're a robot?" She sounded disappointed.

"No! I'm a real person. I died and they copied my mind and let me live again. They call these bodies Burns because they wear out fast. But while alive, they're capable of superhuman feats. They literally *burn up* from exertion. We kind of go berserk, lose our minds. That seems to be a trait of all Burns, something the Convolvers want from experimental soldiers."

"So, you are a soldier?"

"I was never a soldier. I just have a bad temper. Putting me inside a Burn body... it's training, anger management. I don't get to go berserk. I get to sidle up to rich folks and sell them on the Future-Lord." He cracked a smile at the absurdity. Leal smiled through her tears and dropped into a waiting chair next to him.

"Well, I'm not on with that Future-Lord stuff, but since you wiped Jay and his guys out of my life, maybe I can be safe. Either way, I promise never to tag anyone again. I'll go down fighting rather than let them rule me like that."

Jorben snorted, face a mask of skepticism. "Anyone who reforms that quickly is not really reformed. Just making a new play."

He lumbered upright and made for the doorway, wondering if he'd actually be able to leave and find his room. *Real or Not real?*

Leal was suddenly by his side. She thrust a small card into his hand. "Come visit me. I'll make you some real food. Show you my life. I can help you with that temper, and maybe... you can help me."

Jorben pushed past her, out into the corridor. His body felt so very alive. He just wanted to run, to fight... to burn! "Another trap, Leal?" He dropped her card on the ground, slammed the door and jogged away, eager to get outside.

CHAPTER 21

Solent

Rex pressed his nose up against the small plastic window and watched the greenish-brown landscape below turn to the churning blue of the ocean. The Sisters' aircraft banked sharply dropping below the cliff rim to hug the pumice edifice and presumably vanish from any watching radar screens.

"Are you okay?" Sister-Zero asked.

"The coastline is different out here," he replied, absorbed by the passing view. "Kind of unfinished." He'd been numb through the chase, oblivious to the Alliance crafts and interceptors that pursued. This all felt so horribly familiar, trusting the Sisters, just waiting for the lies to begin all over again.

"We've evaded the Alliance for now."

The craft leaned left, pushing Rex hard onto the window. The shear, smooth grey cliffs dropped off over a thousand meters into the boiling ocean. "I've never seen a plane like this before." He dared to look around expecting to see fearsome militarized Sisters closing around him, but the cabin was small and only Sister-Zero stood in its center, apparently immune to the motions of the aircraft.

"It's an experimental close combat assault craft. It's air-worthy, amphibious, well-armed and camouflaged."

"Why the big guns, Sister?"

"Times have changed. Enemies are all around."

"Who are your enemies these days?" He dropped back from the window, sudden motion sickness churning his stomach. The plane skimmed the waves only meters from the cliffs, hugging their smooth profile in tight curves.

"Strange new minds control much of what happens in the world these days." The features on the Sister's face seemed to all angle towards Rex as she spoke. "Culture is a form of memory; it recovers, heals, and washes over the gaps that conflicts and atrophy create. The Internet is reforming, and with that comes the threat of more nova-bombs and much worse."

He nodded knowingly. "Those Star-River prophecies again, Sister?"

"No prophecies, just common sense."

"I've never seen a supernova bomb in my wanderings with Del, Sister. We see other things… wireframe things, outlines of machines and people that used to exist but are now monsters."

Something close to a smile crossed Sister-Zero's face. "Our Rex has come such a long way. The simple drug addict we found in an alley knows so much now."

Rex's mouth dropped open to speak, but he was lost for words for once. It was true that he often said things and even did things that he didn't think were his own ideas, but he no longer felt Del or Felix or anyone else taking control.

"I believe, Rex, that your many personas are bleeding together. They exist inside a stable shell, a structure so strong it holds them like a crucible, forging the parts into one powerful intellect." As Rex's mouth flapped silently, she continued. "We are interested in your ability to hold these Glow networks in a single stable persona. Why are you not craving more Glow? Why does it not attack you? Others with your levels of saturation are driven to madness and self-destruction."

He forced his poker face, no smile. *Don't you know? I am the plague. I am Glow!* He remembered the secret to surviving Sister-Zero's nightly interrogations, back from when he lived at the hostel: give her something close to the truth, but not the truth itself. He stumbled across the tilting floor and sat cross-legged in front of her. "We share memories when I am dreaming, and sometimes Del takes control when I sleep. But when awake, only one of us can be in control, and these days, it's me."

"Interesting." She leaned in close enough for Rex to see the pixels of her face. "When dreaming, your weakened hold on reality allows two personas to coexist, kind of a superposition. But when awake, a conscious mind must be grounded in some way, either through a real body or a body that it *thinks* is real. You only have one body, Rex, therefore one waking persona."

Rex had a sudden horrific vision of his body ripping into two separate pieces, each fragment ruled by a different mind. "What do you know about Felix?" he asked, feeling an ache of panic at saying the name out loud.

"Felix ablated his consciousness. It was a form of mental suicide, leaving behind his memories in an unconscious shell. A vessel for Del to occupy and use. But consciousness is an emergent property of complex, interconnected systems. Assuming that most of his memories are intact it is not inconceivable that given the right stimulus, he could reform."

"He did reform." He watched as the Sister's eye circles grew wider. "The nova-bomb that destroyed the cathedral building brought him back, but seeing my Master – I mean John – again, grounded me, gave me back control."

"Has Felix ever returned?"

Rex shook his head. "I can see a lot more of his memories now, but I try not to. It seems disrespectful, like going into a dead person's bedroom and touching their stuff. And I know he doesn't want to come back. I think he used to want to ride along and watch Del fix the world, but after being in damnation for so long, he just wanted to leave. To end."

In that moment the Sister seemed to grasp Rex's pain. "We will help you deal with those feelings, Rex."

"It's worse than dying, Sister. Being trapped inside someone else's mind. Falling through darkness and catching fleeting moments of reality through another's senses. If I am going to die, then it needs to be complete. No damnation. Felix didn't understand that when he volunteered."

The Sister gazed off out of the window as if consulting some distant oracle. Rex guessed she was silently passing on any new nuggets of information to her fellow Sisters. The moment shattered his view of her as an empathic being. Really, she was little more than a communications port for some colossal process hidden in a vault somewhere. He looked away and the doubts flooded back into his mind. "You will look after John and Millie, no matter what happens to me, right?"

"Of course, Rex."

He eased back to his feet, left the Sister and pushed his face back against the window. Foaming wave caps flashed by only meters below. Surf bucked up and over the front of the aircraft, which cut right through them like a sailing ship. Ahead, the sea assailed a gaunt, water-washed plateau of pumice, the tip of a peninsula that pushed out from the cliff base into the ocean. The aircraft rolled, pitched, and yawed all at once as it set down precisely in the middle of a raised, circular landing pad.

A bizarre structure grew up from the plateau, like a towering lighthouse, but much wider. The sea licked at its base but was too tame to assault the monolith. Above the base, the building branched like a cactus, sending arms out and up towards the sky. Tiny rectangular windows dotted the protrusions, destroying the illusion that the building was a gargantuan plant.

"Where are we?" Rex asked.

"This is Solent, one of our research facilities. We began construction after the Welkin nova-bomb destroyed our downtown base. It is a work in progress."

"It looks alive."

"An auto-structure, a building that grows organically

from seeds using only the available materials – in this case, pumice. We developed this technology to set up bases on other planets. We expect to be able to auto-create entire cities and infrastructures for human colonists to come and populate."

Rex walked down the rear entry ramp and into the brisk sea wind. Six landing platforms spread out from Solent's base, connected via walkways that curved like twigs bearing the weight of fat, round leaves. Several entities detached from the side of the craft and dropped down to guard the vehicle. Tall, bipedal machines with weapons instead of arms. Their heads were hexagonal stacks of sensor arrays pointing out in all directions.

"This way, Rex." The Sister glided off along the pumice curve toward Solent. Rex fell in behind her, aware of the troopers following. The bonded pumice surface looked glossy and slippery in the wet, but his shoes stuck to it as if it were well-trodden gum. By the time he arrived at the undistinguished-looking doorway in the base of the tower, he had perfected a method of walking by rolling his feet off the surface and breaking the suction hold gently.

The door opened into a storage warehouse. Robotic forklifts shuffled crates and pallets around piles and racks. Sister-Zero paused and looked back toward the cliff face. "There's a mark on the bottom of the cliff there, Rex." She pointed and he followed her finger to a small cross etched in the pumice. "There's a stairway inside the cliff, a long climb for a human, but it brings you out on the cliff top. From there you can just see the tallest spires of downtown Coriolis in the distance. It's probably two days walk from here to the edge of town, but you can leave us any time you wish, with or without permission or an escort."

He ignored the temptation to run straight for the stairway. Instead, he turned and stepped inside his latest prison. "Won't the Alliance find us here?"

"They will. We have many such facilities, and the cost in

troops and equipment will be high for them. But they will come."

His thoughts drifted back to Del guiding him through the Star-River. *Reality, thoughts, dreams, all the same thing, just running on different substrates.* Rex took comfort knowing that in some other dimension, somewhere in the Multiverse, everything might be working out just fine.

CHAPTER 22

Hostage

Keller didn't understand all the factors that contributed to Casima's seizures. He guessed that having her body pinned rigid and confined might be one. Others likely included stress, addition or excision of body parts, not taking her drugs on time, and injuries, such as the damage she'd sustained from her tussle with the charred, black robot.

She had suffered three such episodes in the last few hours as Keller struggled to keep himself busy working on new legs for the bot. "You're killing her!" he'd ranted at the impassive, carbon-black skull, while daring to move closer. When the bot didn't demand that he stop, Keller reached for Casima and caressed her various subdermal reset and calibration buttons, jolting her from a trembling wreck, back into a dazed but cohesive whole.

"It's the only way this works, Keller," the bot replied. "I get legs, then I release her."

"Each time she seizes there's damage, the connections in her brain fail and rewire making this more likely to happen again. The pressure on her body gets worse–"

"Stop it, Kell." Casima's voice was a sad moan. "Breathe, focus, and do what it says. If you space on us now, then we're screwed."

He took a few seconds to just hang in her arms, letting the

hoist take all three of their weights, feeling her strength ebbing, watching the tiny dots of blood drip from her damaged jaw onto the lab floor. "I'm so proud of you, Kell," she whispered. "You came back from the edge. Came back to me. So proud!"

He positioned Grimace under the hoist that held the dangling robot. Once powered down, Grimace's body plates were easily pried apart to expose the Kevlar mesh that protected its inner components. Inside the neck, Keller disconnected the cables that joined body to head. A pair of easy-release bolts dropped the head off and into Grimace's conveniently positioned arms. Keller lowered the hoist and the bizarre chimera came together: the mechanical two-armed lower body and torso, with the single-armed, charred remnants of a body mounted on its shoulders, all wrapped around the slumped body of Casima, whose eyes remained closed as her lips mouthed some silent prayer or affirmation.

He ran straps up and under Grimace's armpits and over the shoulders of the bot, securing the two parts together, then added cables through the bot's torso and through the carry-loops on Grimace's shoulders to ensure a sturdy join.

"You should be able to interface now," he said, standing back, shoulders slumping as he inspected his work.

"My fibers are seeking out control connections, infiltration software will do the rest."

Keller watched as tiny, silken fibers squirmed from the raggedy ends of the charred corpse down into Grimace's dormant mechanics. He didn't expect to survive the next few moments. The bot was powerful, with its own agenda that probably didn't include preserving human lives. But if it was good on its word and released Casima, maybe she was still strong enough to escape.

Keller removed the hoist, relying on Grimace's lower-body stability to hold everything upright. The bot was now free, free-standing, free of restraint.

He thought of running, hiding, of deserting his love. Sweat

poured from his underarms, and the shakes came in hard, rhythmic pulses. *Here I go,* he thought. *This is the moment.*

The connections were made, and Grimace's body lurched into action, placing his disconnected head gently off to the side. Grimace's machine arms embraced Casima, allowing the dark and powerful hand to release her head from its fearsome grip. Its fingers curled away from her jaw, posing Casima's head in an upright position, letting her neck take the weight.

The hybrid robot-human cluster shambled over to the lab door and secured it shut with its third hand. Turning back to the room, the Grimace part of the chimera released its grip on Casima, and she rolled off into Keller's waiting arms. The pair wept, holding each other tight. He fussed with her face, finding towels to wipe away the blood. "Look what you've done to her, you shit. Just look."

"Here is the plan," said the bot. "You can leave for medical supplies and food, but she stays here as hostage. You seem to be a knowledgeable man, so while we are working, you will tell me everything important that's been happening. What happened to the GFC? Who are the main players in the world, corporations, alliances, political situations, everything newsworthy, understand?"

Keller nodded, still shaking off the surprise that they were both still alive.

Casima found her feet, stood, straightened her back and ran her fingers through her blood-streaked hair as if prepping for an important interview. Her eyes met the charred face of the robot. "Do you have a name?" she said, eyes flashing with defiant flecks of silver.

The bot hesitated as if having trouble recalling who or what it was. When it seemed to remember, its carbon-black face turned, and the shiny beady eyes fixed her in its glare. "I do. You can call me Ursurper Gale."

CHAPTER 23

The Insider

Like a magically shifting maze, the inside of the Sisters' Solent research station boggled Rex's mind. He knew it was slowly growing, adding layers and branches, but the structure seemed to reconfigure internally on a daily basis. Could it all also be a part of the natural expansion process or a way of hiding things?

Rex insisted on seeing every cupboard, storage room, laboratory, and manufacturing block. At the end of these tours, he still felt he'd missed something, something important. By the end of his first week, he had to admit that there might actually be nothing to hide.

His assigned room was high inside one of the cactus-arm spires. Through one window rose the sheer basalt cliffs of Coriolis Island. Another showed the ocean, a uniform flat and blue from so high up. The room comprised the most space he'd ever been privy to in his life; lounge, bedroom, bathroom, and a study with books and a desk.

One evening he lay exhausted, reflecting on the things he'd seen that day: warehouses full of assault craft, armored vehicles, planes and helicopters. Behind vault doors he'd spied rows of robotic troopers, their hexagonal heads tracking him as he perused their ranks. Other rows contained the more traditional militarized Sisters, blank-faced and wide of shoulder, all just standing, gathering dust. One machine resembled a wireframe from his nightmares, thin bundles of metal framework held together by plastic ligament. He'd stood staring at it, willing it to move. Something about its stick-like nature made him want to chase after it.

"It's just a reconfigurable field antenna, Rex," said Sister-Zero, moving him along to the next room.

What had become of the so-called benevolent Sisters of Salvitor? Created to aid humanity in its moments of crisis, they seemed less fixated on guiding people towards the Future-Lord and more concerned with military power and politics. Perhaps the discovery of the Convolver sect hidden within them had changed their focus.

A soft beep jolted him from his daydream. A projection screen lit the wall across from his easy chair. "News bulletin." The urgent flash was accompanied by dramatic music as a serious-faced young woman appeared on the screen holding an overly large microphone. "This just in: the World Voting Rights Bureau has upheld the Breakout Alliance's claim to govern Coriolis Island. In last month's revote, the Alliance received more confirmed votes than any other contender. Winning forty-six percent of the total vote, the Alliance comfortably defeated the Xenith Military Equipment Corporation at twenty-two percent, and an unusual challenge from the Sisters of Salvitor, who garnered a mere eight.

"The Alliance states that it will be landing an embassy craft in Coriolis City in the coming days to seize control of city infrastructure and management back from the terrorist organizations and militias that currently run the island. A spokesperson for the Alliance stated that big and positive changes were coming to Coriolis, and that it would soon rise again as a hub of technological achievement and a beacon of freedom to the oppressed around the world."

Rex sat bolt upright. *The Sisters had tried to take control of Coriolis?* Suddenly the military bulk made some sense. The screen went blank, and his thoughts turned to John and Millie, back home, pinned to the news as they always were. "Sister-Zero?" he asked the wall.

"Yes, Rex." Her pale face appeared on the wall projection.

"What does the Alliance coming to Coriolis mean to us, I mean… to the Sisters?"

"Our intelligence suggests that the Alliance has been experimenting with weaponizing Glow-based plague networks and may be using them to spread its influence. I suggest avoiding the city for now. Such takeovers inevitably lead to outbreaks of violence."

"Thank you, Sister." He paused, waiting for her to say something, but she just stared back. He knew what she wanted but managed a few seconds of resistance before giving in. "Sister, I think I am ready to begin debriefing."

"Excellent. I will be waiting for you in the main lab."

The Sisters had painted the walls white along the route to the lab. All he had to do was follow the trail and ignore the gray, uncoated side turnings. He dawdled, delaying the inevitable, but as slowly as he walked, he still found himself standing in the medical lab's doorway.

He counted ten empty beds, each surrounded by machinery. Huge convex windows looked out over the ocean, magnifying and distorting the water's movements. Through an open door he saw a surgical theater with a robot perched like a colossal insect over the head of an operating table. A metallic mantis head with three sets of eyes stared down at the blank surface as if anticipating the arrival of its prey.

Surgery! Damnation! The terror gripped his throat.

"Ready to save the world, Rex?" Sister-Zero glided out of a side room. Her artificial smile lingering just a bit too long.

"I'm not going on that." Rex pointed a trembling finger at the surgical robot.

"We won't need anything like that, Rex."

He sat on a bed surrounded by buzzing scanners. A three-dimensional image of his body projected into the air close enough that he could wave his fingers through the laser light, making it scatter and reflect. It showed bones and blood vessels, organs and arteries, all color coded and frozen in time as the computer layered and combined images into a more detailed map. As the scan built in resolution, patterns of energy clustered inside his head and in nodes around his chest. "Is that me?" He dabbed a finger at the bright patch around his heart.

"These are the primary energy concentrations. We are seeing the density of electromagnetic energy emanating from the clusters. Billions of Glow nodes making trillions of connections, just like inside a real, biological brain but diffused throughout your whole body. Such complexity is impossible to analyze, but this kind of general overview helps create a picture of where you are mentally, and where other personas reside."

He watched, heart thumping as the projection reformed, shifted, colors changed and oozed like running oil. "What do you hope to accomplish here?" he asked, tearing his eyes away from his beating heart. *Felix Siger's beating heart!*

"Once we locate your centers of consciousness, we can figure out how to switch between them. From this initial scan I can see that your primary consciousness resides here." The image spun and zoomed in on the region around his heart.

I am Glow. I am the plague. Can they truly know me? "I hoped I was somewhere there," he smiled. "I could just feel it." He held his hand flat to his chest to check there was still a beat.

"To control and monitor a body, a network must pervade many biological systems. The dominant persona gains absolute control. While the smaller ones don't possess the informational density to cohere into full consciousness, they do contribute functionality to the network as a whole. They remain just fleeting memories to the ruling intellect."

Rex's eyes moved up from the image of his heart, and there... there it was, a small egg-shaped shadow lodged in the back of his brain. *The Star-River.* He felt Del quiver inside of him and saw sparkles of electrical energy pop around the dark shape. "Del?"

The Sister nodded. "We suspect Del's Glow nodes have migrated nearer to the Star-River. His center of consciousness is quite separate from your own and should be easy to detect."

"Do you think you really could separate me from Del... remove him from my body?" Rex winced at his own statement. Watching Felix's heart was a constant reminder that it was *not* truly his body.

"Technically yes, but we are not there yet. Personas overlap and their nodes share resources. Removing one could destroy or irretrievably damage the other or even both. With other–" she paused seeking the right word, "–volunteers, we have had some success using powerful, focused magnetic fields to knock node clusters offline, disrupting the local network without firing up Glow's fearsome self-defense systems. With one persona offline we can map the nodes of the one that becomes active. Once we've mapped all the persona centers, we can plan a removal strategy."

"How do you know you can bring me back once another persona takes charge?"

"We perform the same process, knock the usurper offline and then we assume you will regain coherence and control of your body."

"Assume?"

"We are exploring unknown territory, Rex."

Rex stared out the window. He felt like he was poised to sign his own death warrant, and what he really wanted to ask was: why would you bring me back? But instead, a different idea seemed more important. "Do I get to dream?"

Sister-Zero shrugged. "You can give us a full report on your experience when you return."

He looked up at her with watery eyes, wondering if he'd ever see John and Millie again. "Okay then," he said, slowly closing his eyes on the crisp, pristine reality of the Sisters' world.

"We have locked the magnetic pulses onto the most active cognitive regions and can put them to sleep whenever you are ready."

Put to sleep? The same term humans used when saying goodbye to their pets. "Okay, put me to sleep, Sister."

He saw virtual projections of field lines and beams lancing through his body. No sensation, just light, and a brief, high-pitch whistle as some machinery gathered its charge. A relay clunked and then he was a cube with six eyes, peering out into falling darkness with only the thinnest skein of space-time fabric separating him from the yammering madness of a thousand cloying souls.

CHAPTER 24

Run Free

Free!

Jorben's final day of additional penance had passed with no incidents, no violence, not even a snarky comment on his behalf. True, he'd recruited zero new Convolvers from the wealthy Welkin business district, but no one was killed or maimed in the process. It felt like a success.

"Take a day of rest and contemplation," Knoss offered, the confession tube snapping up and away, leaving Jorben with a sense of: *Great! What do I do now?*

He'd found Leal's card in his room, poised on the small shelf over his sink. He didn't remember putting it there, but it caught his eye. *Rest and contemplation?*

An hour later, he was looking down on the satellite town of Arlen from a neighboring hill. Coriolis City rose, grey and menacing, behind him. A scrappy mile of green bushes and scrubland separated the two. From high up, Arlen was a grid of concrete cube-homes that looked like they had all been excreted from the same square-shaped orifice of some gigantic machine and secured to the landscape by a web of creepers and washing lines.

As he jogged downhill towards the town's security barrier, he noticed subtle differences in the homes. Some cubes were piled into two-story units, others sported garage cubes, or sunroom cubes off to the sides. Other cubes were longer, with more windows. Technically not cubes anymore, thought Jorben, surprised by his architectural observations and relieved at how little anger such conformity raised inside his newly reembodied mind.

Burn bodies aged rapidly. The first few days of re-embodiment felt sensually crisp and sharp bringing on a carefree curiosity towards life. In days, the body blasted through a rudimentary teenage existence, with flashes of hormonal anger and skin outbreaks, followed by full adulthood, where things calmed down and made more sense. *I feel like me again*, he pondered as he approached a barrier restricting access to the community.

"Badge?" barked an angry looking security guard through the slot window of his post.

He felt a twinge of annoyance. A typical young-man's resistance to authority, to any adult telling him what to do. "I'm just visiting." Jorben kept walking while the guard yelled at his back. He heard the guardpost door open, and a gun click behind him. "Stop! Where's your badge?"

Jorben ducked under the barrier, paused to straighten his clothing, and then rotated his head in a slow, ominous turn to look back over his shoulder at the quaking guard. A seismic tremble shook the man's arm and the gun dropped away to his side. After a short pause, he turned, snorted, slunk back inside his cube and quietly closed its door.

Leal's house consisted of two cubes joined by a wooden walkway. Straggly plants clawed their way up the sides, smudging the relentless grey with hints of pastel color.

She greeted him at the door, oddly unsurprised by his appearance, wearing a long, flowery housedress with her hair lifted and bundled into a knot at the back. "I knew you'd come." She went to embrace him, thought better of it, and stood aside, inviting him in.

Jorben ducked his head and turned sideways to fit through

the doorway. He tingled with combat alertness. Even this felt like a trap.

"Thank you for inviting me," he said, following her into the dining room where a long table was clothed and set with oval bowls filled with food. Jorben smelled meat and rice, spiced and sauced, things he had forgotten existed. He counted four place settings.

"Give me a moment," Leal said, heading into the kitchen. "I'll fetch you a plate."

Two small girls came through the door from the adjoining cube. "You have kids?" Jorben shouted after her.

"Kimmy and Jess," Leal said, patting each one on the head as they bobbed politely before him. "They're on loan for a while." Her eyes watered slightly at the word *loan*. She ignored his questioning stare and went about creating another place setting around the table.

"Mommy and Daddy went away," Jess blurted, clearly excited by the new visitor. "They'll come back for us one day soon." Those words were someone else's words. Adult words replicated through the minds and vocal apparatus of children.

A skinny man with strange side-swept brown hair and a sour face followed the children into the room. His eyes grew wide at the sight of Jorben, and his mouth formed a silent "What the–?"

"This is Nathan," Leal said, heading off any questions. "And this–" she patted Jorben's shoulder, "–is the man who saved my life back at the Gaia bar." Her eyes dropped with guilt and an uneasy silence crashed over the room. "Right! Food," she chirped and headed back into the kitchen.

Jorben reached out a hand to Nathan. He ignored it and swept past to his chair. As he sat, his hair dropped down over his eyes. He swept it back into position with a well-practiced handwave.

"Husband?" Jorben asked, while trying not to sound disappointed.

"Friend and neighbor," said Nathan, refusing eye contact. "I'm helping Leal with the kids and stuff around the house."

They sat and ate. Cheap jug wine and food made from odds-and-ends, leftovers from the better cuts of meat paired with scant and well-trimmed vegetables. Jorben ate heartily even though his stomach was small and unused to large amounts of food.

"This is very good," he commented. "I've forgotten what real food tastes like."

"They don't feed you at the Enclave?" Nathan said, spitting crumbs across the table. A stern look from Leal sent his gaze back down into his bowl.

"Convolver nutrition rations, a few mouthfuls feed a man for a day." Jorben forced a smile and stared down Nathan, trying to see through the man's façade to his intentions. He wondered if there was a connection between Nathan and the gang that assaulted Leal. Had the Future-Lord brought Jorben here to eliminate that connection? To free Leal from some toxic relationship that still lingered even after the threads of its power had been severed. Surely not in front of the kids?

Leal kept the small talk going, favorite foods, drinks, pets, and styles of house decor, nothing controversial, nothing Jorben had any real opinion about. The meal finished and the children left the table, found some toys, and vanished into a tiny side room to play.

Nathan waited for the door to close before piping up in a loud voice. "Leal tells me that you're some kind of Convolver experiment?" Jorben nodded. "That you died and were reborn in this... new body?" He nodded again. "How very Jesus of you." Nathan carefully placed his fork down and leaned across the table as if trying to intimidate Jorben. "So, pray tell me... what did this original Jorben die of?"

Jorben swallowed, but he had no food in his mouth. "I was executed."

"Ah! Executed!" Nathan rocked back in his chair waving the

fork like a rallying banner. Leal's mouth dropped open and the sounds of children playing next door went silent.

"I... I have no memory of my crimes. But it is possible that I murdered my family."

"Possible? Possible?" Nathan was on his feet, oddly excited by this revelation. "If it was just *possible* then surely you'd still be alive, still be the 'original Jorben' and not some simulacrum? I'd say 'certainly' is more likely. You *certainly* murdered your family." He dropped back into his chair. "Wouldn't you agree?"

Jorben nodded. "I should probably leave now." He rose and turned to the door.

But Leal was on her feet too, blocking his path. "But they brought him back to life, didn't they? Surely that takes away that certainty?"

There was definitely fear in her eyes. Not of him, but of Nathan.

"Wonderful," barked Nathan. "A murderer's mind reembodied in a hulking-oaf's corpse appears on our doorstep to convert us all to Convolverism or whatever religious nuttery you claim to believe in."

"Not a religion," snapped Jorben, feeling oddly compelled to defend the Convolution. "It's an Intention. We *intend* to build a god. Intend to transform future humanity into a galactic species. There's no blind faith here!" Jorben pinned Nathan in his gaze. "What is it you *intend* to do here and with the rest of *your* life, I wonder?"

Nathan raged to his feet and stormed around the table wagging the sharp end of his fork at Jorben. "Well that's perfect, because I am just wondering... what the fuck are you really doing here in this household!"

Jorben felt the danger in the moment. His temperature rising. Nathan's homogenic humanity peeling away into fleshy blobs, bladders and orifices. He imagined the noises he'd hear as he popped those bladders, ruptured those blobs, and rammed an angry fist into that noisiest and most annoying of orifices.

Anger management! Pages from The Logic flashed into his mind: *Do not give others power over your own thoughts.* He's controlling my mind, making me angry, provoking a response. He has no idea how dangerous I am, and what I will do to him. Right here… in front of Leal and the kids.

Unacceptable.

He wrestled back his thoughts, seeing them from above and outside the temporary hunk of meat that was his body. Sounds returned. Images unfroze. The disparate collection of offal and objects became Nathan once again.

"I came by to check on Leal. I'm sorry to have bothered you," Jorben said, scooting around Leal, trying to read her face. *What's wrong here?* He felt pride that he'd not beaten Nathan to a pulp. He'd been civil, controlled. Surely if Knoss dug into his mind and saw this, he would see his progress.

"Stay away from us!" Nathan yelled.

"Nathan, please," Leal protested. "He's my guest. I just wanted to show him a real life and know who he helped."

"How can you not remember murdering someone?" Nathan continued, clearly emboldened by seeing Jorben's retreating back. "There must be records. Things to jolt your memory."

Jorben thanked Leal for the food and handed her a small, abbreviated copy of The Logic along with a children's version full of pictures of robots and spaceships.

"I hope I hear from you again," she said.

He stared at her. Willing her to tell him the truth. But she just stared back until Kimmy peeked her grinning face around the corner and whispered. "Are you a real murderer?"

I don't know anymore, he thought as he jogged back out of Arlen past the cowering security guard, and up into the hills. *But surely somebody knows?*

CHAPTER 25

Confinement

"At least we're still alive," Keller said, folding Casima into his arms as they huddled on the makeshift bed under the lab's workbench. He had been allowed outside the lab twice. Once to get medical supplies and food from the kitchen, then again as night fell to bring bedding and a mattress.

"Of course we are," she said. Her voice soft but bitter. "It needs us for history lessons and fetching things." She looked like someone had punched her squarely in the mouth. Her lips were swollen, and a wad of bandage covered her lower jaw. The unmarred perfection of her plastic face-parts stood out in stark contrast to the bloated, angry tissues of her damaged, living flesh.

"If you work with me then I won't hurt you," Gale said from the other side of the room. "I may be able to help you with your seizures. I have ways of infiltrating machinery and–"

"Don't touch me," she snapped, and Gale went silent.

Gale blundered and rattled around the lab all night. He clearly didn't want or need rest. Keller was alarmed at how fast he worked and how easily he found his way around the lab equipment, stripping out circuit boards, patching and welding, grafting together scraps and items from bins and buckets. Keller didn't ask what he was doing, but some of the patches were showing up on Grimace's body and disconnected head.

The curious part of his mind wanted to see, like a boy watching his father in the garage. The things he could learn. But that felt like a betrayal of Casima.

As he watched the clock tick around past four in the morning, Keller decided it was pointless trying to sleep. With all the noise Gale made in his hybrid body it was a wonder they ever slept at all. Instead, he went over to their portable mini-oven and made toasted sandwiches while Casima found a mirror and stared at her face.

He had managed to shore up the broken seams around her shoulder, and the electro-polymer muscles worked despite some rips. Adding more drugs to her regimen reduced spasm frequency, and relaxants prevented mechanical lockups. Keller wondered what effect this was all having on her floundering biology.

Casima turned the mirror around, so it reflected Gale instead. "We've spent hours telling you about the world. Answering your questions. How about a little reciprocation? Tell us about the battles you fought and what you plan to achieve here on Earth."

Gale didn't turn around. His grim features lit blue by a tiny welding arc from his latest project. "I rammed my ship into the GFC's Cloud9 orbital. I won the war for the Breakout Alliance with a single blow." His voice still issued from the mushroom on his forehead. The clarity had become better with practice, but still sounded muffled and imprecise.

"We should call the Alliance," she replied. "I expect they'd love to meet you, give you a nice fat reward and probably a new body."

"I destroyed a lot of what they were trying to capture. I doubt they'd see fit to reward me."

"Are the Alliance really so evil?" Keller asked.

Gale paused his tinkering. "Did you ever wonder what the Alliance is an alliance of?" They both shook their heads. "An alliance of machine minds and human military equipment corporations, cemented together by Hmech, one of the most dangerous and defective minds the world has seen. When my creator set me loose, he asked that I bring down the GFC, but warned me that Hmech's Alliance was a greater danger yet."

"What is your plan then?" Casima asked. "Attack the Alliance, or maybe find a nice robot wife, settle down, have some kids, maybe a dog?"

A snort that could have been a laugh came back from the mushroom speaker. "Humanity will have to learn to tame their destructive creations on their own, for the moment. I have other priorities."

Casima's turn to snort. "What could be a bigger priority than that?"

Gale stopped welding and came over to face her. He bent Grimace's knees, adopting a squatting pose before their makeshift bed. "I am a new type of biological entity, a Voidian, a being able to survive the rigors of space and thrive on alien worlds. I am a leftover, scrap from the GFC's galactic expansion research. Part of their EVE, Engineered Vacuum Ecology, project. A whole ecosystem designed to flourish in the void between the stars. My goal is to return to space, rekindle EVE and spread our species throughout the Galaxy. In doing so we take humanity along with us, like parasites, and save them from their own inevitable, self-induced destruction."

Casima just stared, unsure as to whether Gale was serious or demonstrating that he had a sense of humor.

"That's quite a goal," Keller said. "Not sure I can help you with that whole space-launch thing. Maybe the Convolvers can. They love bio-experiments and human-machine hybrids."

Casima glanced back at her mirror. "So why the hurt? Why the violence?"

"What would you do to save your species, Casima?" Gale leaned close to her face and touched some of the damaged spots gently with his finger.

"Don't touch her!" Keller leapt to his feet and for a second towered menacingly over Gale's squatting form before his hands started shaking and he collapsed back down onto the bed. "You're not a species, you're an experiment that went wrong."

Gale nodded. "True enough. I would very much like to meet my creator and discuss options with him."

"Who was your creator?"

"One of the GFC's founders, Del Krondeck. I think we would have much to discuss."

"Wasn't he blown to smithereens when you rammed into Cloud9?" Keller asked.

Gale remained statue-still and silent.

"The machine that wants to meet God," Casima said in her wistful, singsong voice.

"So how will you get back into space?" Keller asked. "Grimace's robot body won't hold up under vacuum conditions. It was designed for the sea and cracking a few drunken heads together and that's about all."

"On that subject–" Gale rose to his ponderous robotic feet and reached for something on Keller's shelf, "–I am open to suggestions." The tiny test tube in his fingers contained a black liquid. Gale eyed it carefully.

"Fullerenes," Keller said.

"I need more of this," Gale said. "Lots more."

CHAPTER 26

Reassigned

Reassigned?

"What is this?" Jorben had roared at Knoss as he punched the side of the confession tube. "Is this because I went and saw that woman? You tell me my mind is my own and then punish me when I use it?"

"Calm yourself, Jorben," Knoss said. "I've taken into account your need for some more challenging form of redemption."

"But fighting... killing?"

"You just confessed to me that you thought Nathan to be a danger to Leal, and that you were considering violence against him. I've removed the temptation, which would assuredly destroy your redemption path, and refocused you on a more worthy cause. A soldier's role is not just to fight but to build trust, shore up alliances, and put the security and safety of our beloved citizens first."

Jorben pondered his *reassignment* while sitting strapped in a jump seat of a military carrier alongside a squad of fellow Burns. He nursed a small scar on his temple from where, earlier, a surgeon had upgraded his simple Can data-link to a combat-grade Inner-I. He'd never had such a thing before. Sure, it gave him access to the Enclave's information network and all kinds of battle maps and statistics, but he couldn't help feeling that Knoss and the other Burn commanders were watching not just everything he saw and heard, but everything he thought as well.

The air turned rough as they approached Transit Mountain, bouncing and stalling, inducing whoops and hollers from his fellow warriors. Knoss had revealed that the Convolvers had sided with the local militia against the incoming Alliance forces. Which sounded like a tremendously bad decision to Jorben, but who was he to question the wisdom of Knoss. They went to defend Transit Mountain which, although defunct as a space-elevator or as a railgun mass-driver for many years now, was still considered a great prize and a key strategic position near the center of Coriolis Island.

Forty Burns sat in a double row, clutching weapons. His armor felt like a mobile cage, compressing and confining him in all the wrong places. "Damned cheap military surplus crap!" Commander Barc had complained as they filed onboard the carrier.

The lightweight multi-gun felt good and familiar from his basic training. Dangling from overhead straps was the fifty-kilo backpack-mounted rotary goshgun.

"Jorben gets the big gun," Barc joked as he lurched to his feet and moved to the carrier's front. "He's the only one freakin' big enough to carry it."

Jorben saw Transit Mountain off to the side as the carrier began a sideways maneuver lining-up with a landing pad that, compared to the colossal mountain, looked like a tree fungus growing halfway up a gnarled, old oak trunk.

"Listen up vac-heads," Barc bellowed. "The Alliance is coming to take Transit Mountain. They don't give a pig's turd about us or Coriolis. It's all about capturing the Mountain and its mass-driver space-launch system. Most of the enemy troops will be with the embassy ship that's going to land downtown, but there will be a considerable shock force sent to secure the mountain.

"Our mission, along with our militia brothers, is to protect the mountain long enough for our troops in town to repel the invasion. There are over a thousand militiamen dug in up here and we're going to support them and make those mofos pay dearly. Everyone good?"

The Burns grunted their unanimous approval.

They bumped to a halt on the landing platform, part of the flat ring that formed the boundary between Transit Mountain's plateau-five and the even taller, but considerably thinner, plateau-six. Jorben saw military emplacements spread around the ring along with the reinforced tops of bunkers with periscopic cameras pointing out over the landing area. From here, defenders could hole-up and rain hell down onto anyone and anything that came at them from all directions. Above, Transit Mountain was solid, no more landing areas or entrances. If they wanted in up there, they'd have to break through walls and risk damaging the very thing they had come to steal.

A militia captain emerged from a circular metal door that looked like it led to a bank vault. He spoke briefly with Barc and the two of them strolled around pointing out features on the terrain as they planned the joint defense.

The Burns disembarked and Jorben stood awaiting orders, soaking-up the cold, fresh air. His eyes wandered along his fellow soldiers; no one he knew well, but then he didn't know anyone really that well. Burns came and went, living and dying like bugs, sometimes returning in different bodies. Few seemed to get the privilege of being the exact same person on every iteration. He wondered if they were all executed criminals. Wondered why they always grew the same hulking, unwieldy body for him.

"Where's the bad guys at?" Gnurl grunted. He was even taller than Jorben, but thin and bent in the middle. "Feel myself flipping. If I don't get to kill something soon, I'm going to lose it."

A different Burn spoke from behind Jorben as Barc and the

militia commander moved out of earshot. "You dumb shits don't get it do you? What do you think happens if the militia can't repel the Alliance?"

Another, smug-sounding voice piped up from the rear of the group. "We blow the shit out of the mountain. I've got the explosives right here." Jorben recognized that man. His reputation was legendary. Geoff the Grenade, who blew himself to pieces on almost every mission. It was a standing joke that if Grenade was with you, then you were destined for a stay in the Can and a brand-new body.

This is a suicide mission. Jorben stroked his own arm: smooth, new flesh. He'd barely had a chance to run this body in; now he was going to die again. Hard combat made the connection to the Can notoriously unreliable, forcing reincarnations to rely on stored, outdated personality copies. He felt a heavy weight of sadness. Would the next Jorben remember Leal? Or would it come from a distant version, from a time before they met? *But I want to remember her.*

"Fuck yeah!" somebody roared. Laughter rolled along the Burn line, silenced as Barc returned giving them all the evil-eye. He yelled orders and the Burns surged into motion, but Jorben just stood staring over the edge at the cavernous plunge through the clouds. That would be quite a ride, he thought, me and a million tons of crumbling pumice in one gargantuan avalanche.

"Are you deaf, or just fucking stupid?" Barc yelled into Jorben's ear. His feet lurched into motion, and he followed his fellow troops through the blast door. He emerged on the level's defensive ring, a corridor that ran the entire circle of the plateau, connecting eight equally spaced bunkers that looked out over the island. Each bunker was equipped with arrays of screens and periscopes to gather and distribute data to the fire control of auto-guns that circled the plateau. A detachment of militia manned each bunker, lightly armed for close combat; they expected to take on enemy troops that made landing, either on the ground outside or inside the ring corridor.

Like the spokes of a wheel, other corridors led from each bunker to the center of the mountain. Here the thick metal tube of the mass-driver railgun thrust up from below on its way to the tip of the mountain. When operational, it was really a giant vacuum tube with field-coils wound along its entire length. In the days before the space-elevator, it had powered capsules along the tube from the ground station until they exited the mountain top at speeds fast enough to achieve geostationary orbit. It was a revolution in space access, cheap and safe; more than a billion tons of freight had been sent into orbit on the mass-driver before the elevator took over the heavy lifting work.

Geoff the Grenade began setting up an explosive ring around the mass-driver tube while Barc lined up the troops for a briefing. "The militia was going to setup the blow, but Geoff here is more experienced in such things. We let the militia do all the first-contact work. We're here as last resort, to hold the fort long enough for any surviving militia to escape down one of the elevators if our defense goes balls-up. Happy shooting, vac-heads. See you all back in the Can."

Jorben, Gnurl and two other Burns were sent to oversee bunker-six. It had a stunning view out over town. Through the high-grade crystal he could see the distant Enclave and the jagged teeth of the Fringe surrounding the glistening flats of the Welkin nova-lake.

Around fifty militiamen were positioned in bunker-six. Some were wired into machines and monitors; most were cleaning guns and playfully targeting each other, psyching themselves up for the impending battle. They looked at the Burns, suspicious of the strangers but glad for any help they could get.

The central access tunnel branched four ways. Two went to the ring tunnel, one left and one right, one to the bunker, and another back to the mountain's center and the mass-drive tube. A Burn took up position at each branch. An attack could come from either direction on the ring-tunnel or from a breach in a viewing window.

Jorben sat on the edge of the access tunnel and began assembling his main weapon. The massive goshgun was a two-handed affair even for him, one of the more advanced, recoilless versions that mounted under his forearm. Its fluted barrel opened out under his hand allowing him to grip the barrel-stabilizer straps. He joined on the crossbar that connected the gun across his chest to his other hand, where the firing trigger rested comfortably under his thumb. The bar acted as steering for the barrel giving a precision aim. A tube connected to the pack on his back that contained the metallic-hydrogen pellets. He holstered his multi-gun next to his firing hand for quick access and checked that the goshgun's exhaust recoil port pointed behind, making sure nobody was inside its destructive zone. Unlike the more precision guns, the goshgun didn't have any computerized aiming mechanism. Used for close range destruction, it generated a wall of supersonic gas and shrapnel and couldn't really miss. Jorben clamped the metal crampons to the soles of his shoes to grip the pumice surface and anchor him in place.

He opened his Inner-I combat window showing a tactical map with the locations of his fellow troops. A quick nutrition bar stoked his muscles with calories as he sat upright and let his body sink into relaxation.

Somewhere down there, between here and Coriolis City, but too small to see, he knew Leal, Kimmy and Jess were probably having breakfast. Maybe Nathan was there too? He was, after all, a 'good friend.' But how good? Leal's invite had felt more like a cry for help. Something else was wrong, but something he just didn't see or didn't get.

His world sank into calmness. *Real or not real?*

The mountain was real. He was real. He stroked the barrel of the gun. *This was real.*

Did that really matter?

It mattered to those on the other side of the gun. It meant everything to them.

Red alerts and shifting shapes lit up his Inner-I.

"Listen up, vac-heads." Barc's voice filled his head. "Enemy's here. Let's welcome them through the gates of hell!"

CHAPTER 27

Del

"Del? Are you in there?"

Del? He definitely knew that name. Del Krondeck, GFC cofounder, prison escapee, invader of plague networks, and man imprisoned in someone else's body?

"Come on, Del. Come towards the light."

The light! But the dog was always guarding the light. Rex… always circling, always watching. Rex was the plague. Rex was Glow… or was Rex what came after?

It had been easy with that other body, what was his name, Xell Vollarer? A weak man, who just wanted the simple things: drugs, sex, maybe some food now and then. Dull and suspicious, it was simple enough to worm his way into Xell's thoughts. Flash some gruesome prophecies into his dreams, some paranoid fantasies across his senses when awake. Xell had killed himself, but not before trapping Del in a different body. It was the body he'd intended to inhabit, that of Felix Siger, "the volunteer." But the transfer happened too late, after a parasite had moved in. One grown from the cognitive seeds of a dog's mind. Grow it had, like a snowball racing downhill, grubbing up the stems and roots of all the other, weaker personas the Glow had picked up along the way and globing them together into… into Rex.

How is he so cohesive? So strong? So resilient?

Stupid! Of course, he *is* the plague. No wonder he doesn't attack himself, he assimilates, absorbs, corrals it all neatly under one roof, a great castle... and through those dazzling halls slinks a mouse – a mouse named Del. A parasite within the parasite, whose memories bleed-over into ideas that Rex thinks are his own.

"Del, you have to listen. Hear my voice. Come. Towards. My. Voice."

I can't; the dog will see me.

But the dog was gone, punched out of existence like a singularity in the fabric of spacetime.

Del blinked. *But I have no eyes.* And suddenly he was sitting upright, muscles locked rigid in fear of... something? A dog?

He caught himself slumping forward off the bed, eyes swimming through the barrage of incoming stimuli. There was so much to do, being in-charge of a body again: breathing, balancing, holding a head upright, coordinating eye movements, itches to scratch, distractions to attend, so much, too much!

"Steady. Just breathe, stay calm." A robotic female voice was a gentle hum in his ear. He felt a girder-strong grip propping him up.

Del breathed slowly, seating himself gently in control before attempting to see and hear and think again. Everything was so clear, so perfect now it was uncontaminated by... *by him!*

"He's gone?" he said. Surprised how his words sounded through this voice box. So different from the one inside his thoughts. "And you must be Sister-Zero?" He nodded at his supporting companion, recognizing her from the flashes of imagery he'd gleaned through Rex's eyes.

"Del?" the Sister asked. "Is this really you?"

He nodded, taking in the mass of machinery, tracing the linkages to paddles and sensors on his chest and arms. "Is it safe for me to move around?"

"It would aid us if you remained near the scanner. We are mapping the active Glow nodes inside Felix's body."

"Well, I didn't exactly feel like running anyway." Del swung his feet over the bed and stared out of the window. The sun skittered off the wave crests heading toward their inevitable collision with the coast. He still thought of Earth as a large ball across cold, distant space. His few sojourns into the realm of Earthly reality had been brief and traumatic, no time to soak in the details, just run and survive.

"When you have a mapping will you be able to remove Rex from *my* body?"

"The multiple personas are too intertwined."

"It seems to me you could knock out the nodes as you've done here but permanently; damage them in some way so they can't come back online."

"Dangerous, Del. There are overlaps. For example, the network that models *Felix's* body is spread across both persona maps. It will take time to assess what areas can be removed without permanent loss of function or memory."

"But he's a parasite, an entity that's not supposed to be in this... *my* body–"

"In *Felix's* body," she corrected. "Besides, this is an opportunity to study a very small but persistent form of the plague, one that has remained in a stable and cohesive persona for a considerable time now."

Del's hopes of a quick and permanent fix for his condition vanished. His newly acquired body seemed to deflate under the Sister's withering stare. "Why am I here? What exactly do you want from me?"

"Technology. The GFC's knowledge predates the Nova-Insanity. Help us take back this knowledge. In our hands alone will the future be safe. After all, Del, were we not created to be the benevolent machines, the helpers of humanity, saviors of the lost cause?"

Del remembered his fellow GFC cofounder, Jocelyn Salvitor. How she'd quit the GFC just months before the Nova-Insanity and returned to Earth to create her robotic sisterhood. They'd both seen the Nova-Insanity inside the Star-River. Del had convinced the GFC directors that military might and precision strikes were the only way to stop it. Jocelyn disagreed and had her own ideas about what was needed.

"Tell me what you've learned about the plague while I've been dormant."

"Glow is unconstrained Simmorta with its communication encryption and network limitations removed. We don't know how the Convolvers cracked the constraints."

"They didn't."

The Sister nodded as if Del had just confirmed her own deeply held belief. "True, they never admitted to doing that, just distributing the drug as part of one of Knoss's insanely dangerous experiments in human-machine hybridization. I assume you, Del, you cracked the code?"

He laughed, a feeling that felt oddly painful and good all at once. "The best theory I can come up with is that it cracked itself, probably with some help from an interested party. A party that wanted a backdoor into the GFC, a way to destroy it without wrecking all that priceless technology."

"The Alliance?"

"The GFC let Simmorta degrade; they abused it, didn't use their maintenance patches. Some even switched the thing to dormant and let their bodies rot *au naturel*. Leaky Simmorta in a confined group like that became its own network, a nascent but powerful computational intelligence. The Alliance figured a way to control these rogue networks and utilize its vast reservoir of computing power hiding unseen inside its unwitting enemies."

The Sister became strangely animated. "This could very well be the same mechanism driving the plague, here on Earth."

Del nodded. "Glow is Simmorta, so it understands the protocols. Every person who ever took that or any other somanetic longevity drug is vulnerable to the plague, which I imagine manifests itself largely as voices inside the victims' heads."

"Glowworms."

Del smirked. "Here I am, a real-life glowworm!"

"You know so much for someone locked away in a prison for years."

"I've had my external sources and access to one of the best future-simulators that humanity has ever made." He gave the sister a disarming grin. "Maybe I am your prophet after all."

Sister-Zero's pixelated gaze seemed to turn inwards. "And what does this prophet have to say about the re-emergence of the Internet, of nova-devices, and even bigger, more dangerous versions: Supernova devices?"

Del shrugged. "They happen, kind of dead branches in the tree-chart of existence with nothing ahead, no observers to make prophecies or predictions. No Future-Lords to reach back through time and influence the past."

"Is that not a more immediate threat than plague?"

"The GFC stopped it once before–"

"The GFC no longer exists."

Del stopped short. Suddenly many things made sense at once. "And you want, no, you *need* to become the new GFC."

The Sister nodded. "We are here to protect and preserve." Something like a smile flicked across her face screen. "Shall we get started?" She handed Del a headset. "Sister-Six will become your remote telepresence unit. You can rest here, and she will guide you around the Solent and our technology. Feel free to suggest improvements as we go. Afterwards, we'd like to talk about picoforms and how we can start a fullerene production facility."

Del glanced at the scanner and the faintly pulsing network nodes around his chest. "And then we'll bust into a somanetic network and see how it works under controlled circumstances?"

"We have one waiting for you, Del."

"And Rex?"

"Rex can sleep a while. A rest from reality will do him good."

CHAPTER 28

Back Stab

Jorben watched with slack-jawed horror as the Alliance's gargantuan embassy-class invasion ship assaulted the militia defenses of distant Coriolis City.

The ship didn't fly into Coriolis. It didn't hover or descend or even freefall. It powered down from the heavens like god's hammer, parting the clouds, distorting the air into a bulging lens ahead of the pyramid-shaped menace.

It braked hard above Welkin Lake, heatshield blazing red from friction and deflected munitions. The massive vehicle's sides split away forming shields as hundreds of robotic landing craft spilled out from internal hangers and strafed targets across the city.

Jorben and every other Burn and militiaman gasped at the ferocity of the attack. He expected the attackers to engulf the Convolver Enclave, but they appeared to avoid it entirely, perhaps saving the biggest morsel for last.

The ship slowed just meters above the lake and settled down to a graceful standstill on the crystal like some aging statesman, right next to the Convolver Enclave. Seconds later, the side-shields crash-landed, embedding into the ground forming a stout outer wall defense around the main craft.

A murmur of fear swept across the militia. "Sweet Salvitor, we don't stand a chance." Jorben saw their commander desperately tapping at his earpiece as if it had suddenly gone dead.

Barc's voice jolted Jorben from his stare. "Here they come vac-heads. Stand ready!" He saw a dark cloud ascend from the city, swirl, and gather, and then head towards the mountain, arrow straight. All the city's defenders were neutralized, dead, obliterated. *Just us left now.*

The notion of mutiny spread through the militia as a visual ripple. Their eyes seeking out the Burns, the corners, the escape routes, easing back from their positions. Even their commander appeared lost and was sidling away, fingers fumbling over his holstered gun.

"Eyes forward," yelled Barc. "All of you." He pointed his gun past the Burns at the militia. Jorben followed, swinging the massive goshgun in an arc across their allies and their bunker.

"Five-thousand meters and closing fast." The militia commander's voice came across Jorben's Inner-I. "Prepare missile shield, prep goal-keeper guns for firing. Defenses to auto."

"Ready to fry some ass?" He heard Gnurl's snide voice over his Inner-I.

"It's a slaughter," Jorben muttered back. "All we have is this close-ranged shit. They'll just pick us off from a distance."

Gnurl laughed that bitter, demeaning hack that Jorben hated so much. "You really are a dumb fuck, Jorben. You still don't get it, do you?"

In that moment he did get it, just a single second before the words flashed up in red on his Inner-I. "Change of orders." The message came directly from Barc. "Light them up!"

All eyes were suddenly on him, a frozen moment of sheer disbelief. "Light... *them*... up?"

"Do it man, clear out the whole section. Eliminate the militia. Light them up!"

He heard the jet-plane whine of rotary goshguns coming from other parts of the mountain. The screams of militiamen instantly silenced as the avalanche of devastation swept them and their defenses out through the viewing blisters and into thin air.

In his mind, he squashed that trigger, feeling the catastrophic expansion of the hyper-compressed gases pounding through his body and thighs and down into the ground where the metal spikes anchored him in place. He swept the landing, killing without thought or remorse. But these weren't Burns, these weren't robots. These were one-shot, all-or-nothing humans, and for them: *This was real!*

What happened next was a reaction, not unlike him flipping into berserk state, but in a sense, the complete opposite – a catastrophic stand down, utter resignation, the belief that he'd throw away all his future lives and everything he'd worked for, in order not to obliterate these people.

He hit the mount release and the goshgun dropped to the ground. In the same instant, he turned and ran, a single demented idea filled his mind. That he could somehow reach Leal, do one last deed before he was gone: maybe take out Nathan or whoever was troubling her and then it would be over. His redemption would be complete.

He fled down the inner corridor to the core of Transit Mountain. Gunshots smattered and churned behind as his fellow Burns diligently went about their business of murdering the remaining militiamen. The betrayal was complete. The Convolvers and the Alliance were now partners.

Barc's words seemed to follow him down the corridor as he fled. "And somebody pop that treasonous son-of-a-bitch before he escapes." Now the bullets came for him, slapping his armor, spinning him around, gyrating him through a wild, stochastic dance along the corridor. He fell around a corner, multi-gun blazing at a closed, metal doorway ahead.

The door buckled, shredded, but it was tough and refused to give. A hard impact smacked into his back, thrusting him forwards. He felt his armor hold, but something shattered in his spine. Another burst from his multi-gun ripped a line down the center of the door. Jorben leapt at it, angling sideways taking the impact on his shoulder. He smashed into the damaged door, bursting through – into thin air.

As he plunged into the mass-driver tube he realized the horrible mistake he'd made. Far too late to stop or grab a handhold, he saluted the darkness and fell, laughing, into the void.

CHAPTER 29

Dead Man's Hangover

Rex groaned awake to a diesel-powered hangover. A single erratically gyrating cylinder thumped and ground through his skull while his exhaust emissions were positively toxic. "Mother of–" He heaved over the side of the bed and crashed onto his knees. "Sister... What the–?"

The room spun for a while as his eyes tried to lock onto stationary items and pin his awareness to a single spot. *My room? Not the lab?* "Are you there, Sister?"

The door opened and Sister-Zero glided silently inside. "How are you feeling, Rex?"

"What happened?" He pumped a fist at his aching head.

"Del wanted to... enjoy... being in a body before he gave it back."

"He left me with a hangover? Thanks, Del."

"You are resilient, Rex. Your Glow network will–"

"I know. I know... just let me sit for a while." He punched a button on the bedside remote and a wall lit with a projection of the local news: scenes from downtown Coriolis, angry crowds, gunfire and smoke canisters. The excited drone of a news anchor narrated the whole thing. Something was going on, but Rex didn't care. His mind was out of sync with reality, an awkward, hollow feeling, as if life were a fever-induced delusion. "I feel weird. Why am I here and not in the lab?"

"We carried you back here after the suppression experiments. The Rex persona returned after we removed the magnetic field but remained only semi-conscious due to the high degree of systemic intoxication."

"And how is Del, in the flesh? In *my* flesh?"

"We had productive talks."

Rex pondered the bizarre moment, the madness of being trapped in a body-sharing scheme. "I'm alive. That suggests I'm to be involved in his plans in some way."

"You are the most important part, Rex."

He pottered over to the window, morning sun sparkled off a calm, friendly sea. "Will you tell me what you found out?"

She explained Del's ideas about the plague's origin and its emergent intelligence. "Del regards plague as humanity's most dire exigency. We, however, consider the reformation of the Internet and a potential supernova device to be a more immediate danger."

"I've been inside Del's prophecies. It's all wireframe plague-monsters and bombs, tilting us into the endless unconscious void from which nothing ever returns."

"Consider, Rex, that Del shapes these prophecies from his own obsessions, the results of which may well bleed over to you."

"Oddly cynical, Sister?"

The Sister changed the subject. "The Alliance embassy ship has landed on the Welkin nova-lake. Hmech's forces have subdued the militia and taken over the running of the city."

Rex's feeling of temporal disconnection returned. "Exactly how long have I been out?"

"More time has passed than you think." The Sister paused as if deciding how much of a lie she could get away with. "Seven days in total."

"You let Del run me for seven days?"

"He needs time mentally anchored in the real world."

Was that their plan? To let him live but take his life away a piece at a time, gradually forcing him into the background until he didn't or couldn't emerge into conscious existence again.

An uncomfortable chill settled over him. "Why did you really bring me back, Sister?"

She moved nearer to Rex and he found himself stepping backward, the cold glass of the ocean window pressing into his back. "We need Del's insights. As you connect more and more with him we believe your personalities will increasingly overlap and eventually merge. You will gain access to his memories as he gains access to yours."

"You want me to spy on Del?" Rex laughed at the irony of *having to spy upon himself.* "You understand now, don't you Sister. I am the plague. There never was a Rex before all this…" he waved his hand across his head and body, "got mixed-up and thrown out into the world."

"A plague confined to a single body," she said, turning away and sliding silently through the door. "I will leave you to rest. I suggest you meditate on Del, try forging new connections to his memories. When you are ready to let Del return then please let me know."

Rex watched her leave. *So, I am still useful. Not just an annoying parasite.* The Sisters' plan involved him becoming Del, merging, spying – the ultimate game of cat and mouse, spy versus spy… and all inside his own head.

CHAPTER 30

Capgras

"Is it Capgras? You know… Capgras Syndrome. I've read about Capgras." Steelos's dad, Ray, leaned into the physician as she thumbed notes across a tablet's screen. Steelos watched her face. Creased with concern, it reminded him of the runoff patterns he saw in the garden after flood waters had swept over the vegetable patches and on down into the stream.

"No, but similar," she said. "Capgras patients see imposters instead of the actual people. Steelos seems to have a problem perceiving holistic objects rather than just their component parts." Her eyes sought the ceiling as if her textbooks were somehow scrawled across the white polystyrene tiles. "Some form of associative agnosia possibly linked to a deficiency in the lateral occipital complex."

Ray blinked slowly, not taking in any of the technical jargon. "He takes after his mum," he said. "She saw horrors in every corner. Drove her to suicide in the end. Can't say that I blamed her for that. But doing it in front of young Steelos… that was unforgivable."

The physician appeared to reach a decision and flicked the screen off. "It's a small genetic defect that affects the way the brain develops. It manifests differently in each person since the brain is such a fickle organ. A few errant twists here, some extra neural growth there, can completely alter a person's behavior."

"Is he a psycho then?"

Steelos looked away. He knew he should feel embarrassed by such a statement but didn't really know what embarrassment felt like.

"We don't use that term anymore, Mister Arkland, and no, this doesn't mean young Steelos will become a killer or be anything abnormal. In fact, it might work in his favor, giving him a singular focus that you can channel into an excellent career or pastime. Such detail-oriented people often become engineers or accountants."

An accountant? Steelos felt the life ebb from him like a deflating bladder. He gazed around the room as the doctor droned on. So many interesting distractions, but for some reason his father's ear captured his attention. Fractal in shape, it curled in upon itself to swallow sound into a pit of hairs and wax. What happened next was a mystery to him, a strange interfacing as the compression waves, or noises, plucked the strings, banged the drums, and wrangled the chimes of the inner ear, converting pressure changes into nerve impulses that burrowed through dense layers of brain cells triggering and creating simulations and recollections, down, and onwards, into the soul... the consciousness.

Father's ear was almost the same level as Steelos's eyes. He was growing fast. Catching his parent up. They often fought, sometimes for real. Dad won, of course. Even though they were similar in size now, he possessed that adult strength and knew some sneaky tricks that allowed him to pin Steelos helpless to the ground.

That was usually when he lost his mind, screaming and crying, while being talked back down by his father's now calming voice. He knew he'd win one day. And he wondered if he'd need to talk his father down. Wondered if he'd be able to stop himself from doing permanent or even terminal damage.

The doctor's voice changed, going from dull drone of explanation to a more sparkly, interactive, salesperson tone.

"We do have treatments available, Mister Arkland. Treatments that have only just become mainstream thanks to the prevalence of nanotech drugs like Simmorta."

Ray looked concerned. "Oh... we can't afford Simmorta. I already work extra shifts just to feed the boy. He grows bigger every day, you know. It's like having a locust swarm as a pet is having a teenage boy."

"No, no, these treatments are much cheaper. Single-shot drugs that target very specific brain areas and bridge gaps and deficiencies in neural networks. We use them all the time on stroke victims. The effects can be slightly... unpredictable. In many patients, recovery is incomplete, but does give the recipient more control. Kind of like having a switch inside your head to turn off unpleasant thoughts or emotions."

"More drugs!" said Steelos out loud, channeling memories of his mother as she protested injections and spat drug cocktails back at the doctors. His heart raced and the doctor's desk seemed to join with his father's arm, making him part of the furniture. The doctor became an overstuffed couch with flowery arms and a large, round pillow as a head. He shielded his eyes. What he could not see, he couldn't hurt.

He heard his dad speak, voice sad and resigned. "See... he's losing it again. Losing it, just like his mum did–"

"Steelos!" A different voice commanded. "Calm down."

"Steelos?" Someone gently slapped his cheek and he popped awake.

He lay on a soft bed. A warm breeze flowed through an open window and birds sang their springtime love songs outside. It all felt warm and familiar, like being mildly stoned.

He looked to his side and saw a nurse. "Bad dreams?" she asked.

"The Can?"

She nodded. "Welcome back."

He thought for a moment, couldn't recall anything of importance happening recently. "My last mission?"

"Big success, but the low bandwidth connection to the Enclave prohibited a mind dump protocol. Knoss can brief you on the details if you're interested?"

"Not really." He eased out of bed enjoying the painless, liquid-like flow of fresh, new joints and muscles. The past was just a dream, something he cared nothing about.

The nurse turned back to him as she left the room. For a second she reminded him of his mother. Perhaps Knoss had dredged her image from his childhood memories to recreate her in VR. "You'd best get down to the gym, work that new body image in," she said. "Make sure you're ready for upload. Rumor has it you're being recalled for a follow-up mission very soon."

He looked at his hands, much bigger, powerful fingers, muscles rippled up his arms and he twitched his thighs and pecks feeling the pent-up power. *A combat body!*

He didn't bother with clothes as there never seemed to be anybody else in the Can but him. He ran to the gym, eager to work out, even if it wasn't a *real* physical workout. The bags and buffers in the boxing arena now appeared remarkably similar to the form and features that made up his father in the dream, and this time he was big and strong enough to win.

CHAPTER 31

Conflation of the Unlikely

"Here!" Rex shouted at the blank wall halfway along the corridor on one of the far eastern wings of Solent. He kicked the wall a few times for emphasis. The wall felt solid, felt real, but an intuition told him otherwise. "I know there's something here."

Behind him a silent panel slid open, and Sister-Zero stepped out. "Please stop attacking the walls, Rex."

"You told me you wouldn't hide anything... bullshit!"

"Rex, please." Her hand on his shoulder silenced him.

"That's what you wanted right, Sister, for me to infiltrate Del's memories?" Suddenly Rex felt stupid, the victim of an obvious game. It was all deliberate, a way for the Sisters to judge the degree of memory seepage, a cruel version of hide-and-seek. Whenever he found one of their hidden troves, that was a marker on some graph somewhere, a waypoint on their progress map for him infiltrating Del.

"Rex, it's good that you are accessing his memories, but we don't need to show you everything. A better test would be for you to tell us what you think is behind–"

"No! Show me it. Now!" Rex couldn't explain his anger toward whatever lay hidden behind the wall.

A puff of air and a crackling sound made him step backwards. A thin rectangular line appeared on the wall. A panel slid sideways unveiling an opening into a metal vault with walls thicker than his waist. It smelled like a cleanroom, stark and sterile. Lines of racks covered walls that towered over his head. Each rack had rails etched into its surface and each rail was notched like a row of eggcups and each cup held a single, spherical egg that looked like a silvery golf ball.

"Rex!" she startled as he reached out and took one.

"What is this?" Hard and very heavy like gold or lead, it had a thin red band around its equator and a small red circular infrared port at one of the poles.

"Weapons, Rex. Nothing you need be concerned with."

The truth welled up from somewhere inside him. "Nova-bombs. Are you insane?" Rex gripped the sphere as if to crush it.

"We don't yet have the ultra-fine silicon fabrication plants from before the Nova-Insanity, so these devices are low yield, but still a considerable deterrent to anyone wishing to strike down the Sisterhood."

Rex shook his head as Felix's memories of the Nova-Insanity stirred. "The next Nova-Insanity is almost upon us, Sister."

"We agree. But back then, Rex, such technology was in the hands of everybody – governments, factions, dictators, criminals, and zealots. Now only military superpowers possess them, but that is changing. The Internet is coming alive again, people are connecting, old technologies like opensource engineering and print-on-demand manufacturing are reappearing."

He shook his head in disgust. "But we'll all be safe as long as the good-ol' Sisterhood has the weapons of mass annihilation." Rex eyed the rows of bombs again. "You have one of your supernova devices stashed away here somewhere?"

"We're not insane, Rex. But others create them just like before, when it took a collaboration of governments and the GFC to decimate Earth's infrastructure and stop–"

"I know, Sister. I've seen inside Del's mind. I know what the

GFC did." He almost slapped a silencing hand over his mouth, but it was too late, he'd given them another point on their graph. He turned a sad eye upon her. "Were you there, Sister? Were you a part of that coalition of destruction?"

"No," she said. "But I have access to memories from some who were. Events happened so fast leading up to the Insanity, but the supernova bomb happened even more rapidly. Many cognizant parties realized that the nova-devices could be ringed into spherical structures that would create massive explosions and simultaneous implosions. World-busters!

"Governments turned to the only people who could help... The GFC. It was as if they had seen this coming and were prepared. A series of devastating, simultaneous strikes on Internet infrastructure across the world, hundreds of thousands of precision attacks on nations and individuals likely to be working on such devices. Electromagnetic pulses erased history, bank accounts, databases, websites, and even the memory chips inside of our robots and machinery. To the general population this was all just the Nova-Insanity escalating, but in truth it was an eradication of civilization unparalleled in human history."

Rex put the nova-bomb back on its rack and stood staring at it. "And you are planning on unleashing all of these and many more to smash civilization back to the pre-information age... again."

"We do what we must to save humanity from itself."

Rex shook in disbelief. *Who am I to criticize them?* A deep sadness trembled his jaw. *Inside me reside Felix Siger and Del Krondeck. I'm a vessel containing all of humanity's sins.*

He stood in silence, hearing the noises of the Solent; buzzing machinery, the hissing and clicking of doors, heating and cooling systems. *All for me*, he suddenly realized. There were no other living things here except him. The Sisters didn't need heat or air conditioning, food, drink or even lights. It was a profound thought: Humanity so powerful and corrupt it was inevitably going to destroy itself. Yet it was too short-sighted to let something smarter or more morally responsible take over. Instead, the very devices humanity created took it into their own hands and became the guardians.

"How will you know?" he asked. "Who makes that decision?"

"The devices are out there, Rex. Somebody could use one at any moment, and the world ends. There is no science behind this decision anymore, no intelligence gathering, no warning system. Instead, we wait for a sign, a prophecy."

Rex staggered backwards, choking and laughing hysterically. "You... you still think I'm some kind of prophet?"

"Those that hid amongst us, those calling themselves the Convolvers, once believed this, Rex. That within you hid humanity's greatest creators and destroyers, along with a device that could be used to test prophecies.

"You were their crucible, holding that creative fusion together. And their version of the Future-Lord would come from the convolution of man and machine. Through this conflation of the unlikely, miracles would occur." Her guiding hand pushed Rex gently out of the weapons vault and the door slid closed behind. "We, at the Sisterhood, do not believe such things." She turned lightly towards him and looked up at the ceiling. Her eyes seemed to range far, far beyond the smooth, pumice façade, and deep into the heavens above. "The sign we seek has to come from Him."

CHAPTER 32

Terminal Velocity

Jorben probably hit terminal velocity before his mind fully registered what a stupid mistake he'd just made.

Ha! Running straight into the mass-driver shaft! The boys back in the Can would rib the heck out of him over that, forevermore. Of course, there wouldn't be a 'forever more.' He was a traitor. Knoss would revoke his redemption, and he'd either never wake up again or find himself in *real* Hell.

But then why is there light?

No white light at the end of the tunnel. No doctor's lamp shining in his eyes. *This isn't the Can.* He saw a large, industrial light cluster hanging high overhead. He stared for a while and then tried to turn his head.

How am I still alive? Impossible.

His world lurched through ninety-degrees. He was in a vast chamber, body crunched up against what looked like a set of railway buffers, big old mechanical pistons laying horizontally along metal tracks. His mind wandered back to childhood memories, of seeing the mass-driver on the news. A parabolic track that used massive magnetic fields to launch capsules into orbit. Perhaps the shape of the track had a braking effect? *But a five-kilometer fall?* True, he was in a new Burn body, tough as heck, and wearing armor. He touched his brow, felt the dents in his skull. Swathes of skin shredded away unveiling bare bone.

But the wounds were already scabbing over. *I am healing.* Old Burn bodies healed slowly, but a sparkling new Burn had an accelerated healing rate. *I really am alive!*

Something's wrong though.

He turned his head again, facing up at the lights. He could *feel* his head turning, but his view of the world stayed the same: a sideways look across a loading bay. Then, seconds later, his vision caught up and he was looking straight up. "Shit! Visual interface." Those bits of electronics between his real, biological eyes, and his artificial brain were malfunctioning.

He eased upright. Eyes firmly closed to suppress the nausea caused by the visual disconnection. He felt the grind and pain from multiple bone fractures, light-headedness from blood loss.

I've aged a lot the last few hours. I'm almost spent.

Something tickled his cheek. A breath of warm air. *A way out?* He cracked and groaned to his feet, dropping off the rail to crash to the ground. He risked a look around, head segueing through a one-eighty, then pausing to let his brain gather and process the scene. *Nobody here.*

Move. Pause. Stare.

Wait for my mind to catch up.

Move… pause… stare… perceived existence now consisted of still-frame images.

In excruciating slow-motion, Jorben worked his way through the empty building, past an abandoned security post and into the foothills of Transit Mountain. "You there Knoss?" he asked his Inner-I, but it remained blank. He was cut off from the Convolver world.

A wonderous thought arose. *I am free!* The Burns assumed he was dead. With no comms and a broken Inner-I maybe even Knoss assumed he was dead. Perhaps Knoss was reviving a snapshot of his mind back from the Can into a new body at this very moment.

Just maybe… maybe I am free!

He knew he didn't have long left, possibly just days. Perhaps with some coddling and careful living he could extend his lifespan into weeks, maybe even months. A few, worthy, real months.

"Leal!" he gasped. "Got to find my way to Leal."

Hours went by in a blur. He pinned distant buildings in his vision, familiar Coriolis landmarks like the Enclave or the Parallax Tower, cross-referenced them in his mind, and set a new course blundering across wasteland and through small farming communities towards the edge of town and Arlen.

He had almost nothing left in the tank, a broken engine with no oil, and only fumes for gas. He rested in doorways, amazed that he had survived and that he still continued to survive despite his injuries. He guessed his intimidating size and bloody looks gave any would-be attackers second thoughts.

He got into one fight. Someone trying to rob him. It wasn't really a fight, just him screaming in frustration and swinging wildly at thin air. Trying to estimate where his opponent would be around four-seconds after he last saw him. Awaiting a knife thrust or punch that would take him down. He had a few flash images of his assailant: youthful, but with a filthy, pockmarked face. He'd snap him like a twig normally, rip his spine from his still-twitching corpse.

A different voice yelled. Another scuffle broke out and things went quiet. He saw the frozen image of an elderly man before him. Walking stick in hand. "Where you heading, soldier?" he asked.

"Arlen."

"I'll walk you in the right direction. Name's Woijeck."

"Jorben."

Woijeck spoke of the war he'd just missed. Of the Alliance taking over the city and the mass-driver. "Things are going to be great from now on," he proclaimed. "Hmech'll see us alright. No more thugs in the streets, and there'll be food and jobs for everyone."

Woijeck left Jorben staring at the frozen image of the security post that guarded Leal's housing estate. He had nothing to offer the old man except his thanks. Which seemed enough.

He staggered up to the tiny hut. He'd perfected the art of guessing a vector based on direction and number of paces. Then he could simply walk that section from memory and blindly arrive where he needed.

He stopped, waited, and sure enough the surprised and very alarmed face of the security guard appeared only inches from him. "Please, I need to see Leal."

He waited, saw the guard nod, and faced forward. Maybe he'd be shot in the back as he walked. Maybe the guard saw a seriously damaged piece of military equipment and decided to let him pass.

Leal's doorstep cut a stark image that filled his vision. From the angle of the step, he guessed he was laying down, chin propped on the concrete where he had fallen. He heard his knuckles rapping on the door and then somebody grabbed his shoulder and turned him over.

"Jorben! What happened to you?" Leal's face swam into vision, frozen in mid-sentence, hair billowing in the evening breeze.

"I fell off Transit Mountain."

"And you landed here?" she said, amusement lighting her damp eyes.

"Yeah," Jorben said, feeling himself falling into those eyes. "I've been falling a long time."

And then came the beautiful silence.

CHAPTER 33

Plague

"There... it happened right then."

Del leapt to his feet, pressing his face against the thick one-way glass of the observation room. The room spun slightly, and his stomach lurched. He'd woken this morning with an inexplicable hangover, clutching a note that simply read: "F.U."

He guessed it was some childish vengeance from Rex protesting Del's earlier hedonistic transgression. Taking a swig of the herbal tonic the Sisters had prepared for him, he peered through the glass into a holding cell which was set up as a typical suburban living area, complete with table, couch, and chairs. A family consisting of a middle-aged father, slightly younger mother and two children, a boy, and a girl, both in their early teens, lounged around the chairs, apparently watching TV. A viewing screen next to Del showed Sister-Zero watching the same scene. "Rewind the recording."

Earlier experiments proved the father to be the dominant node in this small, family-sized plague network, but even he was not totally under network control. Momentary breaks in the network's hold allowed him to awaken, look around, and act confused until the network distracted him with some sensory quip and pulled him back under its control.

"There," Del poked a finger at the recording. "A flash of terror. That 'where the fuck am I' moment, and then his face goes blank."

Sister-Zero's voice came over Del's earplugs. "At that exact moment, the rest of the family breaks control as well, but for an even briefer period. Body scans show similar amounts of network energy in each individual. The mother seems the most..." The Sister searched for an apt descriptive "...loaded of them all. In our estimation she was the initial user in the family. The father also used Simmorta, but the children were sequestered later, possibly by force-feeding them Glow, or maybe there was some natural seepage from the parents into those in very close proximity?"

Del nodded. "Wonder why he's the boss. Maybe a more cohesive artificial persona? Maybe he thinks he's a dog like... you-know-who." He took another swig of tonic and tried to breathe the room back to a stationary state.

Sister-Zero kept talking. "We should also ask what motivates this network. Does it have an objective, a function, or is it just existing?"

"It appears purposeless," Del pondered. "Just biding time. It doesn't study its environment. It certainly doesn't seem aware of us, even though you captured it and brought it here as a family unit. I think we are dealing with a nascent intelligence, something not that well-formed. Unless it is much smarter than we think, and it's really studying us."

"Do you wish to proceed with the infiltration program, Del?"

Del agreed and a burly militarized Sister escorted him from the observation room. His magnetic field generator trailed behind on an auto-dolly making sure Rex stayed asleep and Del very much awake.

A group of Sister-orderlies gathered the family members onto individual gurneys and strapped them in place with their own suppression coils and scanners encasing them like giant, metal sarcophagi.

Del settled into his upright gurney, gently testing his leg and arm straps. He didn't like confinement, especially as embodiment was still a new and precious feeling, but it could prove necessary if the plague sequestered him. An odd sense of fear crept over, like pre-flight nerves.

"How are you feeling, Del?" The Sister's voice remained soft and reassuring over the room speaker. The robotic orderlies left the room and secured the door leaving Del alone with the family. Many observers clustered around observation windows and screens, watching the experiment with great interest.

"Uncomfortable," said Del. "Feels like someone's poking my brain with a cold, metal pole."

"All monitors and field coils are on standby. Awaiting your command."

Del arched his back as painful prickles scooted across his skin, paused, and then appeared to dive in through the center of his chest. "Something's digging! Like a worm burrowing in my body."

"I'm switching on the holographic visual overlay so you can track the field lines and the intensity of network traffic," Sister-Zero said.

Del's view of the scene became augmented with colored lines, flowing and warping like some crazy weather map. Contours formed a perfect envelope around the family, concentrations bulged from nodes in their chests and heads. A large, ominous bulge loomed from the father across the gap and into Del's middle."

"Woah! How's it doing that?" Del gasped, feeling violated and supremely vulnerable. He had no concept of how to defend from this attack. If it was even an attack.

"This is a new behavior," the Sister said. "Something that has emerged from these larger, more complex plague networks. It's using phased-array techniques to direct an energy bulge, kind of like a focused radar beam."

Del fought the discomfort. He felt fragile, like he might suddenly wink out of existence. *Decoherence!* Who would take over then with Rex suppressed and him gone? "Okay, ease me closer." His gurney began moving, closing the gap between himself and the family. The field bulge grew wider, engulfing him like a hungry amoeba.

"I see inside it now. It's letting me in. No... sucking me in. It sees the world differently, no physical boundaries, everything is open. I'm just another part of it, a store of curious information. It's messing with my head... I'm seeing things. Hearing things. There's music in here, looping over and over. All of it is a VR simulation running on the underlying drug network. A mixture of memories and reality. The victims' senses can be fed by either reality or simulated reality... or even some combination of both." He felt himself slipping further into the scene, losing his mind, but focused on the hangover to bring him back to physical reality. "That's how it controls people, by manipulating their reality." The dominant network bulge seemed to surge at him as if somehow angry that he'd plundered its secrets. "I'm feeling faint, losing grip, slipping down a slope into something, but I can't see what – okay, do it, take it down."

The field coil behind the father node thumped, its magnetic field jolting the gurneys and monitor blocks on their racks. The field-line distribution changed wildly as the father-node was bludgeoned offline. Del saw the large field bubble pop, and the smaller bubbles coalesce around the mother and children as their eyes flicked open and their heads rolled sideways, their eyes suddenly pleading for help.

"Anesthetizing sub-hosts," Sister-Zero said.

Life and energy drained from their eyes. With the powerful probe gone from his body, Del could breathe again, and explore. "I'm kind of free and unconstrained in here. I can step out and into each individual persona. They're wide open. Like... like splayed books."

His consciousness flicked from one perspective to another and then back to his own. Momentarily becoming each individual, seeing through their memories like a vast perceptual filter. Del heard his own voice babbling to the sisters. "Memories are like balls of string. You can see the whole thing. Know it exists but don't really understand until you pick an end and pull the thread."

"Stay calm, Del." Sister-Zero's cool, pragmatic voice refocused him.

"They are trapped, but their sense of self is still here, compressed into a tight ball. I'm looking through glass, miles and miles of glass, and able to read all the little scratches and stains like holograms."

"Del, you need to take control, don't let it take you over."

"I'm seeing the father's memories, everything flatlined. It's like the Star-River: a mind with no point-of-view, no observer."

And suddenly he was fully immersed. No longer seeing field lines or gurneys, but just another node inside the virtual world, as alive and real as anything external.

"I could navigate this forever." He felt elation, like flying through canyons of memories. But different from the Star-River which worked within the parameters of its preprogrammed simulation. This network didn't have such constraints. Its limit was the total life experience of this group of people. Everything they'd ever seen and done, merged into a singular, interactive landscape. An infinite toolbox from which a user could forge new realities, new delusions.

"How did they get like this?" he marveled. "How did entire human memory-scapes get converted into... into just data?"

"We need you to speak to us, Del."

"Who is Del?"

"Del? If you don't speak in the next two seconds. I'm activating your suppression field."

"I'm here, don't touch me," he said, unsure of which mouth the words now came from.

Cohesion! Everything snapped into focus, becoming not five bodies but just one. "I've done it," he cried. "I've become an embodied network." He didn't see people anymore, just sensors, fingers, hands and noses, eyeballs pulling in light and ears filtering sounds. He didn't see personas, individuals, just troves of memories, stores of experience and heuristics. It was all *his* body now.

He felt a smile spread across his five faces. "I'm in control." They all said at the exact same time, but the next voice came out of Del's mouth alone. "Okay, lower the suppression fields. I want to see if I can maintain control when they are fully functional."

The droning, electric thrum of the coils dropped, and around Del the other minds began to reform. For a second his giant awareness reached outside the small, local bubble… *was there such thing as an outside?* And out of nothing, another presence appeared. Much bigger than the others, one in possession of a pristine clarity as if it had no thoughts, just pure, distilled existence.

For a moment, Del was suspended in water. He felt the warm pressure pushing into his ears, eyes, mouth… down into his lungs, and then it slowly turned to gel, choking, freezing… growing ever colder until motion stopped altogether.

He had a flashback to childhood, of spilling an entire tube of monster-glue over his hands. That panic, everything he touched, clothes, fingers, his own legs and face.

He tried to talk, to cry out, but as the temperature of his virtual surroundings plunged towards nothing, his world solidified to an absolute halt. *It's got me… help!*

Thump!

"We lost him. Suppress the networks. Bring Del back." He felt orderlies fussing over him, breathing tubes, needles… something messing with his eyelids.

"I'm back," he choked alive, pulse pounding in his ears. The elation of new discovery and wisdom filling his heart. "I need to go back inside, figure out how it shuts me down like that."

"Rest awhile, Del," Sister-Zero said. "Then, if you are up for it, you can go in again."

CHAPTER 34

Shuttered

Silence. Peace. Nothing.

Jorben remembered hearing about a condition that afflicted Burns known as being *shuttered*. Like a derelict house, windows boarded, planks of wood nailed across the doorways. The more medically minded called it locked-in syndrome. When a Burn's body failed but the machine mind ticked on. No inputs. No outputs. No way of contacting the outside world.

To a shuttered Burn, time didn't pass at all. It just felt infinite, and the utter silence and darkness could tinker with a person's sanity.

Real or not real? Neither. Just darkness.

Shuttered minds often descended into mental worlds of their own creation, believing them to be real to the point that they lived and flourished, even died again, all inside the confines of their own imaginations. Their own personal convolution-space.

There was no orientation, no up nor down. No gravity, heartbeat, or breath, not even the ringing of silence inside the inner ear or the gurgles and bubbles as the enteric nervous system massaged food and liquid through the miles of intestinal tubing. Just silence.

Like white noise mixed with silk and oil, Jorben's darkness stirred. He felt a sound, saw a texture. And then tasted... a voice? "What the hell is he? I've never seen anything like this before." An odd vibrato male voice as if Jorben had awoken during an operatic aria.

"He's a Burn, one of the Convolvers' experimental soldiers." A female voice.

"I don't know whether you need a doctor or an electrician. I suggest you take him back to the Enclave. They might be able to fix him there."

No, don't send me back there. I'm a traitor. A deserter!

"He might not live that long," she protested.

Leal? Is that you?

"He should be dead ten times over. Every bone in his body has some fracture or trauma."

I'm here. Don't throw me away.

"Look… connectors. It's like the guts of a TV inside his head. This one's loose. I can wiggle it–"

A feeling like an airhorn blast hit all his senses at once. An image jumped into Jorben's mind, Leal and a middle-aged man wearing a white cap and shirt.

Blackness returned as Leal spoke. "His eyes moved. Jiggle it again."

"Probably just a reaction, dead nerves firing or–"

More airhorn noises, followed by a pink haze, an out-of-focus hand across his face… then blackness.

"Maybe you're right. Let me see if I can't make a more permanent connection–"

Jorben stared up into the doctor's eyes through thick-rimmed spectacles framed by oily, grey hair. The next image was of the ceiling with Leal bending over him, examining one of his eyeballs. "Definitely moving." He heard her say, but her mouth didn't move.

He felt himself rolling sideways.

"This sponge-thing inside the base of his neck may be a motor cortex interface. Bunch of damaged connectors at the top here."

He heard grunts and gasps as Leal and the doctor pried apart bits of his head and jabbed around inside.

"His flesh is already healing," the doctor said. "Look at this scarring around these wounds, and his heartbeat is more stable than it was half an hour ago."

"Try that there... good god! So much blood."

"I'm here!" Jorben's voice burst free of its cage. His arms and legs twitched striking the people on each side of the bed sending them flying back against the walls.

"He's alive!"

Jorben rolled upright. The room was still frozen but voices babbled around him. He saw Nathan in the doorway, cowering back behind the doorframe. The shock-faced doctor sprawled against the wall, and Leal was halfway back to her feet. He jumped as her hands touched his shoulders even though in his mind, she was still several feet away.

"Jorben, we're here. We're your friends. This is Doctor Nasent from down the road, I'm Leal, remember? And this is Nathan."

"I thought you were going to send me back there." His words tumbled out and flowed back into his mind through the normal feedback loops, but the world remained stationary.

"What's happening to you, Jorben?"

"I see still-frame photographs instead of video."

"Probably damaged his visual pre-processing," Nasent said. "That's all in the electronic part of you. Nothing I can do there except jiggle connectors and hope."

"We need to get you back to the Enclave. We can't help you here."

"No, Leal. I betrayed them. Ran away from a fight. Knoss won't forgive me for that."

Her voice rose in angst. "You need a new body. This one's shot to bits."

"Patch me up. I'll stay here. Help you as best I can. I don't have much time but what I have... it's yours." He sensed her shaking her head.

"I'll get you some food. The doc here will fix what he can."

The doctor grunted his reluctant approval. "We'll get some splints on these limbs and stitch your head back together. We can't have your circuit-board-brains dropping out all over the place, can we?"

Jorben flopped back down on the bed. Leal leaned over his face, and he caught a good image of her, of her deeply concerned smile. He closed his eyes, hoping to block any further images from entering his mind. He focused on the one he had, and wondered if he could hold onto it forever and build his own internal world around it, and never see any of the horrors of the real world, ever again.

CHAPTER 35

The Imaginary Imagining the Unimaginable

Rex often tried to rationalize away his need for sleep. Why would a network of bio-mechanical nodes need rest? Either Felix's biology still ruled at the most fundamental level and his Glow network adhered to those ancient, biological regimens, or the network was indeed a perfect simulation of the human condition, warts and all.

He felt sleep coming, that sagging weariness dragging down the body and mind, but the fears of falling and darkness remained strong. So instead of heading for his bed, he walked.

Out past the hidden weapons vaults and the movable walls, down the stony steps and into the night air, away from Solent and along the grey beach under the shadows of the massive cliffs. The beach extended out under the water, sloping gently down, forming a shallow shelf around the island, a small concession to ocean ecology; the creation of a whole new ecosystem that hadn't existed out here in the middle of the deep ocean before Coriolis was constructed. Seeded with corals, the shallow water shelf became a giant reef swarming with fish. Nubs of coral protruded from the ocean like the petrified corpses of sunken mariners wading ashore. Rex swore that sometimes, when he wasn't quite looking, they moved.

He'd seen the Sisters' maps and knew that further out to sea the slope dropped off much faster, down to another underwater cliff leading to a deep-water haven where sharks and squid patrolled. Another cliff lay beyond that, the very edge of the artificial continental shelf that was Coriolis Island, down through the miles of darkness that made up most of the great ocean's volume. There resided things with no eyes, hunted by slow moving sharks that lived hundreds of years without ever meeting another of their kind. Worms as old as forest giants and creatures still unknown to science lurked. For a moment it all existed inside Rex's head, the whole system of living things, oblivious under a shroud of human-created perils like *plagues and supernova bombs!*

The half-moon cast a doubtful shadow across the beach, just enough light to see things with many legs creeping out from the water to scuttle across the grey pumice sand. The sky was lit with stars and the orbiting vehicles of mankind. They grew in number every night, a billion unblinking eyes forming new bands of stars swaddling Earth's girdle. Most were Alliance orbitals and satellites, but the Convolvers were out there too. Rats fleeing the sinking ship, arks containing DNA and the memories of that broken culture Sister-Zero had spoken of. The culture that never forgot and would take its own destruction with it, wherever it went in the Universe.

He lay down, drifting, numbing to the hard rock beneath his back as voices came into his head. "Why am I here? My legs walked me here, but my mind just wanted bed."

I need to work. The voice seemed to drift down from the sky like stardust.

"I saw what you did to that family. Experimenting on them like… like cockroaches. I was there, in the background, watching you. Like a bad dream, a really bad dream."

Come on, Rex, plague victims are already lost. Their sacrifice gives us the knowledge we need to save billions.

He felt calm, unusual for him beneath all those watching eyes. But the stars seemed more alive, more real than the ever-present cameras and white faceplates of the Sisters. Everything watching everything else, back ad-infinitum. Observers all the way down. Unpicking that knot created reality, light, music, some great self-referencing tangle of the imaginary imagining the unimaginable.

He fell into the darkness, tried to come awake, but it was no use. *You got me, Del!* But falling was different now, lucid falling, unlike in those days past when he just barreled on down through hell. *The yammering void.* He could watch for a while, shrug, and look away to somewhere else, dream, think, even go find the Star-River. But no, he was not Del, not going to get lost for years in that warren of possibilities.

He popped awake, back but feeling oddly uncomfortable as if he'd only just lay down on the rock.

A full moon crept up from below the horizon. "You can't fool me, Del. How long was I out?" He looked out into the stillness and for a second touched all the life around him, every single mote of awareness, joined in some global network that had existed for billions of years. "Take the body, Del, save the world. I'm busy sleeping." He turned over, rolling off the rock and onto the grey sand. Crabs skittered across the beach like tiny robots as he faded into another dream. A dream where he was many different people walking across the sands, kicking a ball to himself as he went, practicing coordination, experimenting with how far from the others he could go and still maintain control.

He reached for the surface like a hand grabbing waves out of the shallow waters. "Are you finished with that family now?"

I've learned everything I can from them, Del said. *The Sisterhood will grant me more experiments but in return they want picoforms. They're crazy, you know.*

"I know," Rex said, running handfuls of grey sand through his fingers. "How did I get back out here, Del?"

I asked the Sisters to carry you out here, same spot each night, and then take away the magnetic suppression units. All my idea.

"Did you think I wouldn't notice?"

Not really. I just wanted to fool the Sisters. Make them think we weren't talking yet. Takes the pressure off you to spy on me.

"Can I ever learn to trust you, Del?"

How do people ever trust each other? They see inside each other's thoughts and intentions, resonate with their ideas, and take a leap of faith. That should be easier for us; we're overlapping minds sharing the same existential substrate.

Rex chuckled. "What should we do, Del?"

Leave. Put our destinies back in our own hands.

"Will they let us go?"

There's only one way to find out.

"I can't endanger John and Millie."

Let's try leaving. Maybe stop by and visit some old friends, and then we come back here and see how that sits with our robotic overlords.

Rex felt the prickle of sadness. He wanted nothing more than to see Mrs O. again and the dogs, maybe walk in true freedom one last time before Del immersed them inside the plague. "You'd really let me go there again?"

He felt Del's virtual smile. *I want you to go there. A quick stop and then... then maybe we go to work.*

CHAPTER 36

Cyborg-Sickness

"She needs to leave. Needs proper medical attention." Keller paced angrily before ducking back down next to Casima and planting a palm on her forehead. She was burning hot, and the real flesh and blood parts of her body were turning an awful, jaundiced yellow.

Gale paused his tinkering. "Casima is cunning, and I don't trust her." After quickly absorbing Keller's small phial of liquid fullerenes, he'd spent a full day and night combing their possessions for any useable forms of carbon such as Keller's stash of electro-polymer limbs, carbon fiber patches and clothing. Even rods of graphite and the fake diamonds from Casima's jewelry collection were taken. Having no way to directly absorb or repurpose such objects, he simply strapped them over his grotesque body like bejeweled bandages and let his auto-repair systems chisel what they could from the materials.

"It's her liver," Keller stammered, feeling his old panic return at the very thought of a surgical procedure. "She's on her third one and it's under a lot of pressure now her cybernetics are all out of tune."

"I've offered to help," Gale said. "I can infiltrate her cybernetics, rebalance things, add new software."

"You... don't touch me," she slurred, her eyes opening and swimming into focus on Gale.

The Gale-Grimace hybrid clumped over and adopted the now familiar squat position in front of her. "Keller will never betray me. He's terrified of what I'll do. You, however, have a rebellious streak. I think you like danger. That's why you provoke me."

"Come on, Casi," Keller pleaded, "let him try and help."

"No, never! I don't know what he'll do to me. What software viruses he loads me up with. You've seen how he infiltrated Grimace with those freaky tendrils. I just need a doctor, some suppression shots, and a liver-booster, and then I'll be fine."

"Fine," said Gale, much to Keller's surprise. He stood and plucked a handful of small boxes linked together by straps and chains from the workbench. "I made something for you." The device looked like a safety harness. "You can leave here if you wear this. It has cameras and microphones and if you try to remove it or say something inadvisable to anybody then I will know, and Keller will pay the ultimate price."

"I'm not wearing your stinking wire," she protested, but after an hour of Keller pleading with her, she agreed.

Gale spot-welded the belt around her middle. Straps looped up over her shoulders and another under her crotch and welded to the back of the belt. The whole contraption was concealed under her coat with the main forward camera poking out the front like a large, unstylish button. "Keep the camera out at all times. If it goes dark–" Gale let the threat hang in the air.

She said nothing, just a sad backwards glance at Keller as she left.

He trembled as the door closed. Gale was probably right; she was going to do something reckless. Gale's words rang inside his head. "What would you do to save your own species?" It took a particular kind of bravery to think like that, something Keller lacked, but Casima didn't.

Keller lay watching the screens as Casima hopped from barge to barge heading for the main *Nevis* mall. The sounds of her deck shoes on the metal clacked loudly. A smaller screen held a view down the front of her coat, showing the coat buttons and the main camera. It looked down past her waist to her legs and feet.

Gale stared, as fixated to the screens as Keller, as she walked the shops, found a doctor, booked an appointment, and went back to the shops assumedly awaiting her allotted time. Keller sank into a fitful slumber before awakening with a start as Gale resumed his destruction of anything plastic that could contribute to his repairs.

Gale's eyes left the monitoring screens, but Keller's were now fixated again. Casima had been gone a long time and this was the second time she had visited in the same shop. He wondered if Gale noticed. Willing his hands to become steady, he rolled carefully out from under the bench. If this was to be the end, then he should go down fighting. Whatever Casima was doing he had to back her up, or at least create a distraction. A real fighter would make the sacrifice, cause a commotion so *Nevis*'s security came and disposed of Gale before Casima became aware of what he'd done. His hand curled around a wrench; voice choked in his throat. *I can't. Just can't.*

A different, more sane idea came to mind. "How did you survive crashing into the GFC ship and freefalling back to Earth?" He shuffled closer trying to make Gale turn away from the screens.

Gale ignored him and carried on with his work.

"I would love to know. I'm sure it will make a great story."

Gale looked carefully at the screens. Keller cursed himself for trying such an obvious ruse.

"Fascinating!" Keller said, mustering as much sarcasm as his petrified voice box could convey. "Please… tell me more." His eyes widened as he realized Casima had hovered in front of a row of cosmetics for an absurdly long time. Her feet remaining stationary.

To his surprise and relief, Gale suddenly started talking. "I escaped destruction by climbing out of my ship moments before impact with Cloud9. My plan was to let momentum carry me into a higher orbit and then use a small drive unit to maneuver to a safer location amongst the abandoned GFC orbitals. A distraction delayed my exit and I clipped the Cloud9 debris field. That changed my trajectory and destroyed the maneuver drive I was carrying.

"After many spins around the Earth, I skimmed the atmosphere and headed for a crash-reentry. I feathered my reentry vector as best I could by adjusting my aerodynamic profile, aiming myself at a remote region of Asia. I used my burning limbs to create turbulent airflow and steer myself towards the snow-covered downslopes of a mountain. My last memory is a frozen image just inches above the snow."

"Headfirst! I knew it," Keller snapped his fingers, pleased with his earlier deduction.

Gale stared down at Keller. His shiny, bead eyes jittering in their sockets. He caught Keller's furtive glances at the screens and went over to examine them more closely.

The images still hadn't changed, but as Gale moved closer the view turned and moved along to the next stand of goods. The motion was awkward, a single staggering step at a time, not the flowing natural motion of real walking.

"Something's wrong," Gale muttered. "Is she trying something?" He turned up the sound level and the lab filled with the buzz of people shopping, their footfalls became explosions.

"It's okay," Keller stammered. "She's got her fancy legs on. They don't work that well on the ship, so she's probably in pain... you know... limping along." Keller eyed the door. Gale kept it barred with heavy crossbeams locked together with chains and padlocks. Even with tools it would take minutes to break through, something he had spent hours rehearsing in his mind.

Gale turned knobs and pushed buttons on his camera control pad. The main screen panned fully left and right and then back to center. The cosmetics were moving along at a steady pace as if Casima were shuffling sideways along the row, but her hands never came into view, they never reached out and touched anything. "Fancy legs?" Gale sounded confused.

"Yes, the ones I made for her."

Gale turned to him. "She can change out her legs?"

"Of course–" Keller clamped his hand to his mouth as his words betrayed them both, and suddenly the scenes on the screen made a lot more sense.

Gale lunged, careening through the benches and equipment racks, grabbing at Keller as he fled. Keller leapt for the door, hurling everything that came to hand behind him. He snatched at the cluster of locks, heaving with both hands in a futile attempt to snap them free.

He felt Gale's fullerene claw snag his shirt and jerk him backwards. A moment later, Grimace's mechanical arms folded him into a deathly embrace. He pondered with sadness how fast he'd moved, purposeful, no, *decisive*! How fluid, how unobstructed by thoughts and hang-ups from *back then*. Casi would be proud. He hung limp waiting for his neck to snap.

"What has she done?" Gale bellowed from the small speaker now right next to his ear.

Keller shook his head and felt it slip down into the body of his shirt. Maybe he could wriggle free and leave his clothes hanging in Gale's grasp. "I don't know. She has her own plan," he said, playing for time.

Grimace's arms tightened around his waist and hauled him off the ground. "We're leaving. Now! How do we detach the barge from *Nevis*?"

"You can't. We're locked and loaded. Not going anywhere." His head slipped farther down the shirt, and he heaved his shoulders, shrugging the fabric free.

"So be it," Gale said, his voice oddly soft and resigned.

And suddenly Keller was free, sprawling across the lab floor while trying to find an exit hole in his shirt big enough for his head. As his face tugged free, he saw Gale gazing down at the floor, clearly sizing up the best place to bore a hole down to the ocean beneath.

"You're... not... going to kill me?"

Gale's voice blared at him, and he toppled backwards. "Why on this confounded Earth would I kill you?" Gale reached down to the floor just as an intense thump jolted the barge.

"Casi!" Keller yelled, as the ceiling exploded above them. Debris crashed down as a massive metal claw reached through and grabbed Gale, swallowing his entire upper body and head, and hauling him upwards through the hole in the ceiling.

Keller lay there in shock watching Grimace's sturdy, metal legs treading air above him. Other faces peered down through the shattered deck. One was Casima. She had no legs and was perched on the rim of the hole using just her arms to hold herself upright. "Kell?" she asked, eyes frantically searching the wreckage below.

"I'm okay," his words came out in a hysterical laugh.

"Thank god, I'm so sorry Keller. Forgive me."

She looked up at Gale dangling in the grip of the vast longshore-bot. His head bent hard around, crushed inside the claw as his single arm grappled futilely with the hunk of engulfing hardened steel.

"Not so clever now, are you?" she spat at him as he lifted up past her and out into the gusting pacific air.

The boat was a sleek wedge of colored stripes endowed with overly large outboard engines. A blond hunk of a man in a Hawaiian shirt, sporting sunglasses and a grin that only the son of a billionaire could maintain, manned the helm. He gunned the massive engines and spun the boat through a series of donuts, delighting the bathing beauties that clung to the boat's rail and dousing *Nevis*'s starboard pleasure dock with water. Those sunbathing along the dock shook off the drenching.

Some waved, some clapped hands, others cheered or waved derogatory finger gestures from many different cultures at the boat's retreating rear end.

The engines gunned again, and the boat roared away, performed the nautical equivalent of a handbrake turn and sat, bobbing in the waves facing the *Nevis*, revving and prepping for its next pass.

Hidden below the party boat's deck, away from any hope of fun, was a very different scene. Sixteen Burns crunched shoulder to shoulder inside the tiny hull. They all stared down at their boots, deep in meditation, preserving their pristine new combat bodies for the coming mission.

Every few hours, Steelos stirred and looked around, raising his pulse a few beats to push some extra blood through his sleeping limbs. He sat at the rear of the boat. As the group leader, he got a handspan of extra shoulder room. Glancing along the row of slack faces, he saw soulless, empty eyes. Just the tools of some larger algorithm to be bent and ruined for a cause he could never understand.

A viewing screen opposite Steelos came alive, emitting a gentle alarm tone that stirred the rest of the Burns to life. He watched their eyes refocus, remember their last missions, and register where they were and what they were doing. Dour, slack faces lit with grins as they looked across at their opposite numbers, then along the line to Steelos, nodding recognition as they rolled shoulders and massaged knees back to life.

The screen changed, showing the view outside, blurred and grainy from the camera's extreme zoom. A huge docking machine strode across the *Nevis*. Something black dangled in the grip of its immense claw, something that still struggled despite the colossal pressure the claw exerted. A timer ran down in the upper left of the screen, and right on cue came the bang as one of the party boat's engines developed a sudden and catastrophic fault and exploded sending parts hurtling across the open water and a puff of dense and very noticeable smoke up and across the watchers on board the *Nevis*.

A cheer arose from the *Nevis*. Rich boy had blown an engine out here in the middle of nowhere. He'd be forced to pay the exorbitant open-ocean retrieval and docking fees and the even more exorbitant repair costs.

Steelos stood and rubbed his hands together. The row of soldiers before him flashed between being people and a singular mass of limbs, eyeballs, and weapons, then back to humans again. "Listen up vac-heads," Steelos said, finding his voice for the first time in days. "Let's go bag ourselves a space-robot."

CHAPTER 37

Leaving Home… Again

Rex came alive as the sun's warmth touched his face. A discordant song of seagull and tern calls rode a crashing backbeat of waves and surf. *Hungry,* he thought, *No hangover, but definitely hungry.* He looked back along the beach to the distant spires of Solent and decided that didn't matter.

Is it time? came Del's voice. Although he didn't really think of it as Del anymore, more just a different point of view, kind of like a change of mind.

"Yes, it is time." He worked his way along the beach, legs aching from treading the deep sand. "Do you think they'll let us leave?"

I believe they will.

"They got what they needed? Picoforms? Bombs?"

Few nuggets, some false leads, and a lot of promises.

The entrance to the cliff stairwell lay unguarded. He paused and looked back at Solent. He'd miss the beach, but not that tower of deceit.

Different muscles burned as he ascended the spiraling stone steps, leaning into the climb, hands bracing his knees against the strain. Pitch darkness came immediately as he rounded the third turn. A few tentative steps into the blackness and he saw light from a slot window above. He paused next to the sliver of brightness, nose thrust through the crack, sucking in the heady sea air, then on and up into more darkness. A hint of light from above urged him onward.

Birds' nests lined the window ledges; cracks in the pumice led back into hidden caves. He smelled bats, dead gulls, and years of accumulated guano. The sound of the sea mellowed, and a warmer breeze washed down from sun-drenched Coriolis Island above.

He spilled out onto the cliff top and stood gasping in the sunlight, staring at the figure just standing, waiting for him to exit. "Are you going somewhere, Rex?" Sister-Zero asked.

"You said I could leave anytime I wanted."

"Where will you go?"

"Friends."

"John and Millie are perfectly safe–"

"Different friends."

He kept walking, skirting around her as if she were just an annoying bush or fence post. "I should come with you," she said, falling in step behind him.

"Why?"

"Coriolis is dangerous. Even more so with the unrest caused by Hmech's takeover. I would make a good bodyguard."

He shrugged. "Sure, why not. I'm sure you are watching from hidden cameras and satellites and drones and all the other things you have, so why not be here in person too?"

"How long will you be gone?"

"I'm not sure. I just need to see some friendly faces for a while."

"I can break all my connections to the Sisterhood if you wish, Rex, become an independent agent."

Rex stopped in his tracks and turned back to face her. "Is that even possible?"

"I wish to stay with you and regain your trust, and yes, I have permission."

"Not sure I can bring myself to believe you, Sister."

Something close to a smile graced her features. "One of my beliefs, Rex, is that I have beliefs."

Rex shook his head and kept walking. "I can't stop you following me."

Transit Mountain loomed in the distance. Sister-Zero zipped past him and stood still on the cliff edge, pointed feet jutting fearlessly out over the precipice, like a lost soul contemplating a final jump. He could easily push her over. She was off balance. One nudge and he'd be alone.

He walked behind her, contemplating the surprising observation that the Sister had feet. He'd always assumed they hovered or slid along the ground like hockey pucks. Maybe Sister-Zero wore a special outside body. He loitered, eyeing her silky, black habit, then moved to stand by her other side, his own toes creeping dangerously close to the edge. She never moved or even flinched, never even looked over her shoulder. He realized it was all an act of trust, like falling backwards into the arms of a companion. He let out a gentle sigh, knowing that despite how the Sisters had mistreated him in the past, he could never push one of them over a cliff. He wondered if Del thought differently.

"Let's see if we can hit the city's edge before lunch. I'm as hungry as a seagull with no beak. And about those clothes, Sister, bit conspicuous. Maybe we can find you something more… real." He nearly said *like Mira*, but those words stuck hard in his throat.

CHAPTER 38

The Pointy End

"We're so dead," Casima muttered to Keller. The pair formed part of a bizarre procession with Casima up front in a wheelchair, her detached, spare legs slung across her shoulder. Keller walked behind pushing the chair, eyes scanning the surrounding halo of *Nevis* security personnel armed with an array of epoch-spanning weaponry from swords and hatchets to goshguns and laser carbines. A cluster of soldiers in full armor held a long metal pole from which dangled the detached torso of Ursurper Gale swinging like a rib roast on a rotisserie. They had cautiously rolled him in reams of duct tape assumedly to prevent his arm from grabbing anyone. Keller doubted that tape would hold, but where would Gale go with no legs?

"We can just leave this with you," Keller pointed at Gale, "and head for the doctor. Casi needs urgent treatment." A soldier with a gas-masked face prodded him on with his gun barrel and said nothing. "Are we under arrest?" Keller tried.

"Quit it," Casima snapped. "These guys aren't talking."

He leaned over the chair back and spoke right into her ear as they rolled on through the seemingly endless corridors. "How did you escape?"

Casima's fingers flickered in what Keller assumed to be some form of sign-language. "Hidden talents. I finger-signed a Macanese shop assistant and convinced her to help me. We redirected the cameras with face-mirrors and detached my legs so I could slip out of Gale's harness. We contacted the *Nevis*'s security. They thought I was nuts, but I gave them the codes to the barge's security network and they tapped into the lab cameras. Once they clapped eyes on Gale things happened really fast."

Keller shook his head in disbelief. "Risky, Casi, real risky."

They funneled into *Nevis*'s forward tanker, passing through extensive networks of barracks and residences. "This where the *Nevis* family live?" Casima whispered.

Keller nodded as they entered a massive wedge-shaped space at the prow of the ship, a single multi-level apartment with huge windows looking out across the open sea. The metallic interior décor resembled the insides of an ancient but pristine combustion engine.

"Nice place," Casima said, easing out of her wheelchair and into the couch next to Keller.

The soldiers hung Gale like a prize fish from a hook that dropped down from the distant ceiling. A rectangular woman with clipped, black hair and a fearsome boxy face emerged from a side room and stood staring at Gale.

A man in a wheelchair followed the square-lady. Small, old, and frail, his head propped up by a support, he worked a joystick with both hands to maneuver the chair into position behind Keller and Casima.

Square-lady shook her head in disbelief. "I should be very upset with you for bringing such a dangerous article aboard my ship."

Keller stood and presented his hand. "I'm sorry, we haven't met. Keller Morten and this is my partner Casima Salean."

She glanced at the hand but didn't take it. "I'm Reet and this is Ben." She pointed at the wheelchair man. "Our family owns the *Nevis*. These are my sons and daughters and a few friends who I won't bore you with." She pointed to a crowd of others who crept silently into the room to examine Gale.

"A robot from space, eh?" Reet moved closer to the dangling and motionless Gale.

"That's what it told us," Casima said.

Keller walked to her side. "Don't get too close. He's very strong and quite clever."

"Not that clever," Casima said under her breath.

"He doesn't look that dangerous either." Reet moved closer as if daring Gale to try something.

Keller winced as she put her face right up against the crystal black skull. Gale's eyes were now fully formed and staring straight ahead. "He's playing dead, you've seen the video. You know what he can do."

"What's it worth?" Reet asked.

"A lot."

"Why is it worth anything?"

Keller sat back down. "New technology, more biological than mechanical. It's made of fullerenes, and it regenerates. Something like this could change robotics forever."

Reet suddenly looked interested. "None of us have the knowledge to pull this thing apart and use it. Any suggestions?" She looked around at Ben and the crowd of silent watchers.

A striking young man stepped forward. His red hair looked like flames around his head and a long, forked tongue flicked from his overly red lips. "It's easy," he hissed, pointing at Keller. "Dump him overboard, sell the robot to the Alliance, and I'll find a use for her." He leaned over Casima, tongue flicking like a snake sensing a dead rat.

Keller now understood the horror they had stumbled into, what kind of people he'd been travelling with all these years. "Here we go," Casima said, shaking her head and looking away from the snake-man.

"A fine suggestion, Glin," Reet said, cracking a toothy smile. "Any objections?"

"Yes!" Casima and Keller both yelled, and Keller made it to his feet before Reet pulled a pistol and jammed the muzzle into his face. Keller fought the urge to shut his mouth, as if that would stop the bullet, and kept talking. "This thing is worth good money, but if it were whole, it would be worth a fortune. You could become the next GFC. And we–" he clutched at Casima's shoulder, "know how to make it as good as new."

Reet lowered the pistol. "Now you're talking my language. What do we need to fix it?"

Keller waved a hand over Gale's body. "Fullerenes."

Reet shrugged. "I don't know what that shit is, let alone where to get it."

"I do," Glin said, stepping up to Gale, suddenly more interested in the money than what he was going to do to Casima. "We wring a bunch of it out of the reprocessing plant every day. Glow, Simmorta, there's also bits of it around in antiques, you know... stuff that fell off the space-elevator cable when it crashed and burned. People keep things like that as trophies, also the cables that fasten artificial islands to the seabed... all fullerenes."

Reet chuckled. "So we sail to Coriolis and hack the mooring cables out from under the Alliance. Nice plan, Glin, very nice."

Rage flickered across Glin's face. The boy clearly had anger issues and didn't like being insulted by his own mother.

"Alright people, here's our plan." Reet put her hands on her hips and, even though shorter than everyone present, she suddenly appeared much taller. "Put the robot in our holding cell, make sure it's tied down good – don't want no one-armed freaky robot crawling through this place in the night. Keller and Casima are our guests for a few days while we figure things out. Give them a nice room and treat them right." She punched a finger at the ceiling. "Do it!" she yelled, and everyone, even the old man in the wheelchair, snapped into action.

CHAPTER 39

Breakfast in the Head

"Where are the kids?" Jorben asked Leal as she served him a steaming plate of eggs and toast for his breakfast.

"With Nathan. I figure it's best if they don't see you in this state."

It had been a horrible three days. There was nothing Jorben could do, no exercise, no movement, just lay there staring at the ceiling. *Heal... that's what I'm doing.* He healed, but not enough. His joints remained arthritic, muscles weakened, their tissues scared and strained. Telltale blemishes spread across his body portending organ malfunction and failure.

"How is my big soldier feeling today?" Leal asked.

"Fine soldier I would make. I can't even feed myself without pulling a tendon." He ate in silence, each motion a measured performance. Leal watched from the doorway as if unsure about coming too close. As he finished the last morsel, his curiosity got the better. "What's the deal with Nathan?"

Her voice went quiet. "He lives down the street, helps out when he can. He has... problems." She touched a finger to her temple, a gesture that Jorben caught in one of his freezeframe moments of clarity. "Paranoia or something, thinks the world's not real. It's hard for him to keep a steady job or find a girl or... anything really. Everything is one great big conspiracy... work, militias, governments, you... even me. We're all out to screw him over and pull the wool over his eyes. He thinks the kids are real... the only things that are real. I guess he loves them in his own, special way, and that makes them real."

"So you let him stick around."

She shrugged. "He's good to me... mostly." She shrugged again, and Jorben thought he caught a tear forming in her eye.

"They're not even your kids," he pressed.

"My sister's." She flushed with anger. "Not everyone gets to come back with a shiny new body when life screws them over, you know."

"Sorry. I feel like a right shit." In that moment, he gained a new appreciation of the gift Knoss and the Convolvers had given him.

She turned back into the kitchen and emerged with more eggs and toast.

He spooned the eggs into his mouth, feeling their slimy texture, but his sense of taste had been lost along with his sense of smell and pain perception. But hunger remained, more as an empty, hollow feeling than anything unpleasant. It told him functionally: *eat, and eat more,* but didn't let him enjoy the process.

He navigated feeding the same way he navigated the house, using memory of layout and distances in hand-widths and strides. Collisions were frequent, spoons of egg were rammed up nostrils; most slopped onto the table to be re-scooped when it made it into his attention. But there was no feeling of frustration anymore. Perhaps the switch that connected that particular emotion was broken. He liked to think it was a product of his new freedom. *My mind is my own.*

He decided to change the subject. Back to himself. "My vision works like my memory now. Individual moments that I have to join together, like one of those kids' puzzles where you draw lines between the dots until you see a face or a cat."

She finally stopped moving, dropping down in the chair opposite. "I can't understand how you went from being a living person to a computer program. That just shouldn't be possible."

Jorben waited for his vision to settle into a perfect picture in his mind. "Not that hard, really. Especially if the... subject... was a complete Glow-head. I was loaded with that shit, so much so that I kind of became it, or rather it became me. When they passed the death sentence on me, Knoss bought the reclamation rights to my body and just plucked that Glow right out. The hard bit was extracting the program, which is me. Apparently, that's never been done before. Anyway, it worked; I think I'm that guy, the one who did bad things and died. There's a lot missing though. Glow doesn't remember everything about me and more got lost in the extraction and processing."

"Have you been... dead, you know, re-embodied before?"

"Sure, lots of times. You die a lot when you're a Convolver recruiter working the Fringe all day. You die a lot more when you don't give a shit about dying."

"But is it really you that comes back or just a copy?"

It was Jorben's turn to shrug now. "Feels like me. The original version lives on a computer server, Knoss calls it convolution-space or something. Burns just call it the Can. When we get killed, our mind-states that live on computer chips in our skulls find their way back to the Can and merge with a stored, dormant original. So I remember everything this version of me did. Unless I get blown apart completely or the connection to the Can never makes. Then I don't remember the mission I was on, but I do recall all the stuff before that."

She leaned in, suddenly more concerned. "But... you're not connected to this... Can, now, are you?"

He shook his head, feeling a small crush of anxiety in his chest. "The Canned version of me thinks this version is dead and gone."

"Wild," she said, rolling back to her feet as if to put a little distance between them. "You really don't remember what you did to get executed?"

"That bit got lost. I'd like to know though. As bad as that sounds, I'd like to understand my past and make peace with it. If that's even possible."

"Sounds like you need a session with my friend at work. Calls herself Madam Seer and claims to be a psychic. Really, she's just a Glow-head like you were, but she uses that stuff to get inside people's heads. She claims to read any mind, man or machine, and can dig up old memories, and even give you new ones. She can implant memories about being screwed by this super-hot guy and you really believe that you actually–"

"She can dig up old memories?"

"Sure, ones you didn't even know you had."

"How can I meet her?"

"Easy, she hangs at the Gaia bar couple of nights a week. The punters love her. We just need to get you out there one evening."

Jorben's hands dropped to his side in a gesture of futility. "I can barely move."

"I told you Nathan was useful." Leal's eyes shifted, suggesting something behind her. "He has a car."

CHAPTER 40

Reconnection

They stumbled upon their first guard station as they crossed an open expanse of ground on the edge of the Cosmos district. "You need an ID to enter the city now," said the guard.

Sister-Zero stepped forward. "This man has been in rehab. I am transferring him to the Welkin district to look for work there." She flashed an ID card from inside the cape she had acquired from a market stand. Despite covering her from head to toe it did nothing to hide who and what she really was.

"That's all very well... madam, but he still needs ID." Another guard appeared with a pocket-sized camera, and a fingerprint and DNA scanner.

Rex stood obediently staring into the camera lens as the other guard searched him, prodded him, and syphoned off skin cells with a tiny vacuum unit. He eyed the man as he worked, small and nervous, bearing a passing resemblance to himself a few years back. His flesh showed addiction scars and his eyes were haunted by something only he could see. "How long have you worked for the Alliance?" Rex asked, suddenly feeling superior.

The guard raised an eyebrow, unsure whether he should answer the civilian's questions. "About a week."

"Are there jobs available?" Rex lightened up the mood.

"Thousands. Jobs everywhere, and they pay good, too. The

Alliance is recruiting guards all over town, laborers on Transit Mountain, recruiters, trash collectors, police... everything. It's like they're just building a whole city from scratch taking all the unused population and putting them to use. Must be costing a fortune. Future-Lord only knows where they get the money from."

The guard waved them on, and Rex examined his shiny new ID card with its embedded chip full of personal information. He went to throw it away, but Sister-Zero stopped him. "That may well prove useful, Rex."

They travelled across East Firmament, Rex marveling at the changes in this part of town. Just days after the Alliance's arrival there were shiny new buses, open shops, and rows of robo-trucks bringing food and provisions to stock the once-empty shelves. Heavy machines ploughed away the old ruins and laid foundations for new buildings. They passed a patrol, a group of two-dozen young men in ill-fitting uniforms marching up the road with wooden guns over their shoulders as if performing an historical reenactment.

An hour later Rex and Sister-Zero arrived at the familiar ragged wire fence. He gazed across the dusty yard ringed with kennels and dotted with dog toys. They watched a woman scuttling around the yard with a broom. She looked young, maybe forty or fifty at the most, but her clothing style and energy were unmistakable. "Mrs O!" Rex said, unable to keep the excitement from his voice. "She must have taken longevity meds."

He opened the creaking gate. Memories of the lich and the fight brought on tears and palpitations. He thought of poor, heroic Goliath who had saved them all, and Mira leaving... just leaving him after all they'd been through together.

Mrs O. stared in disbelief as he approached, smiling and crying at the same time. Sister-Zero hung back a half-step.

Dogs poured from the kennels, swamping him as he dropped to his knees and fell into the sea of muzzles and fur. Many new and curious souls mingled with familiar faces. Mrs O.'s hands cupped his face and lifted him from the melee. She kissed his forehead and embraced him. "I thought you were dead and gone, Rex."

"Just surfing your wave, Mrs O."

"And you have a friend." She hugged Sister-Zero, seeming not to notice her pale plastic face.

"She's more of a..." Rex struggled for the right word, *companion, suppressor, bodyguard?* "...kindred soul," he said, hating the words as they came out.

"Well, that's an important start, Rex. You make a lovely couple." She winked at the Sister, initiating that knowing connection between two females that, in truth, probably went right over Sister-Zero's head. He imagined her mentally flicking through her vast database of human gestures and emotional cues trying to make sense of that.

"You can call me Zee," Sister-Zero winked back at Mrs O.

"Well Rex, Zee, come and meet the new gang. You have a lot of catching up to do. We have lots of volunteers these days, no shortage of help and money. I've already been approached by the new Alliance chaps. They want to train dogs as sniffer dogs for security duties. I think that's a wonderful idea, give them a purpose in life. Dogs like to work you know, like to feel part of the pack just like the rest of us. Well, come on through. You have to stay, simply have to. I have a guest room or would you prefer separate rooms for the moment." She winked again as she led them across the yard and into the house. "I won't tell. I was young once, just me and dear Harold... Oh the things we got up to in those fast, carefree days, you just wouldn't believe it..."

CHAPTER 41

Regen

Keller stood in an echoingly large, windowless, metal prison cell facing Ursurper Gale, the robot that fell from the sky. Gale hung from colossal loops of the ship's anchor chain, wrapped in an elaborate weave of restraints that terminated in a welded collar around Gale's neck with additional metal bars crisscrossing his skull like a miniature cage.

Keller wanted to gloat, but there was something implicitly sad about anything confined in such a way. Gale's left arm was almost full size now even if most of it consisted of a transparent web of ultrathin fibers. Clearly he'd been shuffling material away from his other arm as it was now just a stub. He still had no legs, although his lower torso had rounded off as if the ragged edges of his wounds were healing over.

Another of Reet's sons called Bov had dragged Keller from their holding cell early that morning, leaving Casima alone. They'd only just managed to reattach Casima's legs, an all-night ordeal with no tools other than a few bent pieces of wire he'd scavenged from the cell's corners.

Bov was a strong, quiet youth. Keller assumed it was some unspoken *Nevis*-family policy that none should possess a name consisting of more than one syllable.

"Fix it," Bov grunted, prodding Keller with a chubby finger and then pointing upwards at Gale.

Keller examined the available tools laid out on a table next to Gale, various non-lethal wrenches, pliers and short-bladed cutters, and a syringe that Keller assumed contained a cocktail of Glow, Simmorta and whatever other fullerenes they had rustled up for use. "You realize I need pounds of this stuff to fully repair its body?" Keller complained. But Bov's face registered nothing.

Keller sighed. Gale's eyes jiggled in their sockets and focused on Keller. The first time Gale had shown any sign of life since the incident. "You should have worked with me, Keller." His voice was quiet, like a distant aircraft leaving.

"You can't honestly tell me you were going to let me and Casi go?"

Gale's eyes dropped focus and he was once again just a charred corpse. Bov inched closer, suddenly interested as the robot spoke. There were cameras all around, nothing that happened here went unnoticed or unrecorded.

Keller held the syringe in front of Gale's sagging eyes. "Fullerenes. Is it of any use?"

"Some, although raw hyper-fullerenes are better, stronger, and far less costly in human terms."

Keller placed the syringe back on the table, suddenly sickened by the implications of what he was holding. How many people had died and been recycled to reclaim this tiny amount?

Gale's head tilted and a small clump of fibers around his neck writhed and unfurled. "I've created a port for you here."

Keller looked closer and saw a single strand breaking free from the others, like a wisp of black silk.

"I need some specialist tools," Keller said, turning to Bov. "Nanoneedles and a very small pump." He saw the frustration and incomprehension flicker across Bov's face. "I'll make you a list." He turned away as Bov grabbed his shoulder.

"Just do it," Bov roared, sweat beading on his forehead, fist pushed hard against Keller's cheekbone.

"I'll do it when you get me the right tools." Keller braced for the blow, watched the fist shake, the emotions flicker across the boyish face. He offered Bov the syringe. "Perhaps you'd like to handle this yourself?"

Bov's fist dropped and he stalked away. *Not so stupid after all.* Keller turned back to Gale and glanced down at his own hands. To his complete surprise, they were not shaking.

CHAPTER 42

Seer

Leal eased Jorben into a chair in the far corner of the downstairs lounge of the Gaia bar. Even the short drive across town, hunched inside Nathan's plastic pod-car, had exhausted him.

She eyed him up and down as he sat gasping for breath. "I gotta go to work now. You amuse yourself until she gets here."

He had no money, but Leal petitioned the barman using a "wounded soldier" argument to get him a free drink. She lied and told him that Jorben had fought for the militia, that he was a hero of the people. The barman inspected his wounds and announced that, "This man can drink for free the entire night."

Madam Seer sped into the bar around an hour before closing. In a theatrical entrance, she whirled across the floor in a spray of green and purple silks. Jorben had a perfect freeze-frame of her poised in the middle of the room, an expression of mild disappointment forming on her face as she realized how empty the bar was.

He tried to follow her progress around the scarce clientele, but just as he got a good fix on her, she moved on. Her gravelly voice and cackling laughs now emanating from a different corner of the room.

He zoned out for a while, wishing he could actually taste his beer or that it would make him drunk and forgetful. He wondered where all the militia had gone, and what had happened to Benz and his gang. A voice off to his right made him jump. "Nice lady back in the kitchen tipped me to come see you, son."

Son? He felt her breath on his face, but still couldn't see her. He stretched out his hands and felt her take his fingers in her palms. "You blind, son?"

"I don't see too well."

"You got demons need evicting?"

"I think I did something bad, and I want to know if I really did."

"We all got those demons. Met them all before. They don't scare me." Suddenly she was there in the chair, pale, wrinkled face made-up to look even more ancient. Like a classic fairytale witch, she had a hooked nose and piercing green eyes and was wrapped in a silk shawl and headdress. Her hands were on the backs of his, but he felt them moving up to his elbows.

"Got to get a little closer here, son, see what you have in there. Real demons or glowworms or something different."

"How does this work?"

She chuckled, the perfect cackle.

"I'm a sea of tiny radios, so popping with Glow I travel with bodyguards to keep the lichs away from my old bones." Her hands were on his shoulders, and he felt something touch his forehead, something boney. He guessed it was her own head pressing to his. "Gotta get the interfacing right. Don't want to be triggering any nasty self-destructions."

He felt a tingle in his head as if cold water flowed into his skull and sloshed around the edges of his brain. "Ah… you're one of them artificial types. Easy to read, standard interfacing, although… this one's not so standard. Convolver, I'm guessing." His next image was of her face only inches from his own. Taut with concentration, hands gripping the back of his neck as if hauling him into a lover's embrace, she groaned and grunted as if fighting some inner demon of her own.

"I see Leal in here. She's on your mind a lot. You kind of like her, eh?"

Jorben nodded. The grip and caress of her fingers felt good on his neck.

"Lucky girl." She exhaled making a deep, rumbling noise from somewhere in her throat. "Now, you relax. Try and think around the particular event that's troubling you."

Jorben thought hard, bringing up his few fleeting images from before his execution. A woman's shocked face. Screaming child. Flashes of red... blood.

"Ahh... yes. A man, a woman, and two little girls."

"Two?" Jorben's body shook. "But I only remember one."

"Nothing here, son. No connections, just still-frames like they were planted. Someone's done an edit job on you. All dead ends, leading nowhere... wait... tiny thread leading to here."

Jorben saw a dusty town, probably out on the far side of Transit Mountain in the rain shadow where the island was most desert-like. He stood, looking down the middle of an arrow-straight street. A wooden sign hung over the road read: *Welcome to Elford City.*

"Ever seen that town before, son?"

The memory itched, but he couldn't scratch it. "No."

"Looks like a memory plant to me. Somebody wanted you to find it. Although might be a leftover from a long chain of things that all got chipped away. It's hard to edit from the outside. You don't see the mind the same way, don't see those connections that you can only find when you grub around inside."

She pulled her fingers away and the images vanished. For a few seconds Jorben was in darkness until a fresh picture of the witch formed, showing her sitting back looking around the room for her next client.

"That's it? That's all you can find?"

"Well, there's threads going off and on here and there, but

too fine for me to follow. Maybe if you go to Elford City, take a look around. It might traumatize your mind into freshening some of those connections. Come back and see me after. Maybe something'll stick."

"But why would somebody edit my memories?" He waited for an answer, but the sense of her presence was gone even as he saw her still frozen in the chair. He fumbled around, found his beer. Madam Seer appeared on the other side of the bar, tempted away by a newly arrived group of youngsters, their eyes blazing with drugs, alcohol, and zeal.

He could faintly remember being just like that once, easily fooled, easily lured. Easily drunk or stoned. He missed that Jorben. Damned artificial minds! The needs and limitations of the human body were often what made it so great to be alive.

He imagined a series of buttons down his neck each embossed with a label for easy location. The button called *horny* was obvious enough. Another labeled *hungry* so he could enjoy food again, one called *shutter* for when he just wanted to exist in a quiet space, and another called *scramble* for when he wanted to feel drunk and carefree.

Before he could conjure other buttons into existence, a hand gripped his arm. "Coming home, soldier?" Leal said. "You find out what you need?"

"Elford City," he grumbled, easing to his feet. "Gotta go there. Try and remember."

"I'm off work tomorrow," she said. "And I know where Elford is. Let's go take a drive."

CHAPTER 43

The Legend of Rex

The evening Rex arrived at the Forever Friends Rescue Sanctuary, Mrs O. declared a party.

Kennel doors remained open, and dogs came and went as they pleased. Some hung around the kitchen, draped across couches and chairs, while others scrambled around Rex's knees vying for attention. All the sanctuary's helpers were welcome, and as the evening went on and the wine worked its way into the biological part of Rex's brain, he started to lose track of who was who and who did what. It turned out he was kind of a legend in the field of dog-walkers. Stories of his exploits were told and retold. Growing larger and less recognizable with each telling. But they all ended in sadness as the great champion of canine-kind had been tracked down by a heartless monster from space and finally killed in a massive explosion. And now, somehow, he was back. The risen prophet, a legend rekindled, and everybody wanted to know exactly how.

As the cool night breeze blew through the house, rustling curtains and blinds, calm returned. Dogs slept or went back to their kennels, and Mrs O. brought out her special cognac. "I see you didn't eat or drink anything," she said to Sister-Zero, who had spent the whole evening hovering aimlessly in the background. "Try a little cognac at least, it really is very fine."

"She's a robot," Rex whispered to her for the third time that evening.

Mrs O. laughed and slapped his shoulder. "I know, Rex. I'm not senile. Doesn't mean she can't partake in our little celebrations, does it?"

The wonderful liquid burned a smooth trail into Rex's stomach. It seemed to stir Del from his dreams and Rex felt the "Where the hell are we?" moment seeping through as Del glimpsed a secondhand view of the world around.

"Your being alive, Rex, has certainly renewed my faith in the Future-Lord and in my own personal future." Mrs O.'s voice took on a mellow slur.

Rex nodded. "I never had you down as somebody that could lose faith, Mrs O?"

"I lost it all after you left and the cathedral exploded. It seemed the world was coming to an end, and that I would never find my Harold. But I soldiered on, just hoping that one day there would be a sign. And here you are as if sent back from the very future itself." Her smile seemed to split her face in two. "I feel so sure of things, that I just know Harold is there, in Haven at the end of time waiting for me."

Rex nodded again. He hadn't quite figured out how Mrs O. looked younger. He still recalled the terrible things that had happened to her, being attacked by the lich, and by militia, and yet, somehow, she always seemed to survive.

He watched Sister-Zero creeping closer at the mention of the Future-Lord. He explained to the Sister how Mrs O. had lost her husband, Harold, in the Nova-Insanity and how she was determined to remain immortal and meet him in Haven.

"Everyone sees the Future-Lord in a different context," said the Sister.

Mrs O. reached out her arms to encompass all the dogs. "More good fortune. Hmech and the Alliance coming to fix Coriolis, and with new money coming in from them and other donors, things just keep getting better and better." She banged the glass on the table and tipped the liquid down her throat. "Cheers to you all. May you all be with me forevermore." She looked thoughtful, and drunk. "Where are you two lovebirds off to next?"

"We're not sure," said Rex as his thoughts wandered briefly back to the Sisters and their stockpiles of nova-bombs, just waiting to bathe the planet with destruction. All they needed was *a sign*. He glanced at Sister-Zero and took a big gulp of cognac. "I just wanted to see you and the dogs one last time."

They took the separate rooms, even though Rex was curious what the Sister did during the night. She certainly didn't sleep and probably just stood there in the darkness computing something. The thought creeped him out, and he knew he would sleep better without her looming over him.

That's one whacky old lady. Del's thoughts percolated through the informational membrane.

"She believes that the Future-Lord is reaching back through time and helping her to keep on living so she can be reunited with her dead husband, Harold, in Haven at the end of time."

That's quite the long-term plan she has, but I like her vision!

"Where are we going next, Del?" He didn't detect an answer and decided it didn't matter. He was going to sleep, and if Del took them off somewhere then maybe that was okay. He assumed Sister-Zero would follow along and make sure nothing happened to his body.

CHAPTER 44

A Smile is Still a Smile

It was a simple enough idea, or so Keller thought at the time. Slip a few small tools into his pockets while the dull but ever-watchful eyes of his overseer, Bov, were looking the other way, and build a hidden toolkit back inside their cell, so that at some future moment he and Casima could engineer their escape.

The plan went awry when Keller pressed his luck and pocketed a more sizable multi-wrench. "Hey!" He heard someone yell, and Bov's fist came at his face like a fleshy meteor.

He floated through darkness before the velvet void coalesced into curves and contours that the pattern recognition circuits inside of his brain resolved into a human face.

It was interesting to Keller how a smile was still a smile even if the face wearing it was beaten, swollen, and bruised almost to the point of not being a face anymore. He stared into Casima's magenta eyes, noting that the eyes were where the smile hid. He went to move but the ache in his head and the bruises down his back reminded him that he was damaged goods as well.

"What happened?" He struggled into a sitting position while massaging what felt like a fracture in his jaw.

"Bov knocked you clean out and they dumped you back here. You must have pissed him off."

214

"Oh…" He remembered the wrench incident and suddenly felt stupid. "No… I mean what happened to you?" He touched her damaged cheek noticing that her jaw was slightly out of alignment.

"After the doc came and gave me some of the shots I needed, Glin popped in to try out his new toy."

"Bastard, I'll kill–"

"Hush… it's okay, Kell. Glin looks worse than you now. I figured they wouldn't kill me as they needed your cooperation." Her smile grew sad as she smoothed away Keller's tears. "The guards heard him scream, I think they waited a moment longer than they should, maybe enjoyed seeing Glin get what he deserved."

"Things are not going so well for us at the moment, are they?" he said. "And they'll probably get worse tomorrow, when he comes back to try again."

She wrapped her arms around him, and he sank into her familiar warmth, their mouths touching each other's ears to shield their whispers from any hidden microphones. "I'll get us out, Kell."

"No, too dangerous. These people are psychos. Worse… gangster-psychos."

"What then? We obey and hope they let us go when the Gale-robot-thing is fully repaired?" She pushed her face in closer to his ear. "Befriend it."

"Gale?"

"Sure. You've seen how powerful it could be. At some point we release it, cause chaos, and break free during the distraction."

"After our betrayal, I doubt Gale is open to our friendship."

"Come on," she smiled again, and through the pain and damage Keller's world lit up. "Who could resist a cutey like you?"

"Sure," Keller stroked his bruised face. "I'm such a charmer."

CHAPTER 45

Ghost in the Wrong Machine

Rex had the strangest dream. As a massless, silent, invisible mote, he left Mrs O.'s guest room and floated the sanctuary halls like a ghost. He paused in front of her easy chair, sniffed the empty cognac glass on the side-table before drifting closer to her eyes. She wasn't sleeping, just staring. Her face a mask of doubt, eyes searching the darkness as if she knew he was there. "Hello?" she said quietly. Her watery eyes held the hidden horror that someone or something might actually answer.

"I'm right here," Rex said, as close to her face as he dared get. But she looked straight through him.

Moving backwards, he passed through the solid walls into the yard, out to the dog kennels. Dismayed that they couldn't see him either, he looked down and saw he was no longer a disembodied spirit: he had legs. Though wispy and transparent, they were legs, good legs none the less. He decided to walk – or rather someone else decided to walk for him.

"Where are you taking me, Del?"

To work. The Sisters weren't cooperating, not unless I gave them dangerous technology. The air was suddenly cold, and the dark of night felt very real. *I'm sorry, Rex.*

"Sorry... for what?" Like a drowning man, Rex panicked and began swimming to the surface, clawing through layers of torpid dreams even as a weight dragged him back down.

"What have you done, Del?" He peered through the darkness and saw people shambling around him in a tightening circle, their eyes fixated on infinity just like Mrs O. and the dogs.

A voice startled Rex, a voice that came from Sister-Zero but through some trick of focusing sounded right inside his ear. "These people are controlled by plague. This is a fringe cluster on the edge of a massive plague network that we believe originated inside the Alliance's embassy craft." The Sister stood off to the side as more and more people rushed from the shadows to surround them.

"You betrayed me... again." Rex's voice struggled through the numbness of his drugged body.

"This is for the good of everyone, Rex. Del must be released into the plague, and, once inside, we believe he can find a way to control it."

The crowd jostled inwards, compressing their remaining space down to a small circle. Hundreds of them wandering out from the darkness just outside the rescue sanctuary as if they'd been waiting in the bushes all night for Rex to emerge. Of course, Del and his Convolver friends had set the whole thing up. Even Sister-Zero was a Convolver plant.

You have to free me, Rex, so I can take control of this cluster like I practiced at the Solent lab.

"Why would I help you?" he spluttered. "All you do is lie to me, filling my head with false horrors and hopes." But he knew it was futile. He'd agreed to help. Even Felix had volunteered, and in some convoluted way, Del and the Sister were also unwilling participants in the Convolver plan.

Rex felt a great pressure on his mind, like a huge distraction pulling his senses in a single, inexorable direction. The figures around him jumped and changed and he realized he was losing track of time. Objects and spaces appeared blocky as if made from tiny bricks.

He looked for Cyc's destruction meme, that mental thread etched into his psych that had killed his mind and let Del take command as he fled from Jett. That thread was gone, but he saw something else, something that he hated but understood only too well. A hole, a gaping, black pit from which bitter, angry voices raged. *The yammering void!*

The Sister's voice grew louder, more urgent. "Do it, Rex. Before it's too late."

"For John and Millie," he shouted as he toppled forward, nose first, like a good dog.

The voices grew louder as familiar concentric rings of darkness flashed past and he fell through somebody else's memory of tumbling down Transit Mountain. To his surprise, he could still see and hear the real world, like being at the back of an amphitheater watching reality on a fuzzy, black-and-white movie screen.

In that glimpse of reality, he saw his own hands rise above his head in surrender. Around him, the mindless bodies of the attackers wavered, some staggered backwards, others turned away as if seeking a different calling. "Thank you," Del yelled through Rex's vocal cords. "I have them. I contain them. I am them, and they are me."

Rex felt it too, as if all these people were just extensions of his body, more eyes and mouths, more lungs sucking in more air. Their hands touching his face and body felt like his own hands.

"So unstable," gasped Del as he wrestled to keep control. "This is a much larger network than I practiced on at the lab."

Something hung on the edge of Rex's awareness, like a sheen around reality, a strange blurring of edges and lines. As he focused harder, he saw what appeared to be a parallel reality, a superposition of objects and people but somehow inside a great house. A mansion of many rooms, each room its own small world.

"What is this place?" Rex mentally flicked through the rooms like a deck of poker cards, seeking a familiar pattern. *There…* Sister-Zero in her own room. She existed as fragments, pinned in a line like washing across the room. Her mind still existed but as a small, confused cog sandwiched inside an unyielding machine.

Something akin to an earthquake rattled the seams of the network. He heard Del's voice cry out from elsewhere in the mansion. "It's too much. Too strong."

"That's it?" Rex cried. "Your great plan." But Del was unable to comment. All the free-floating, disparate minds occupying the network suddenly aligned like particles of iron in a magnetic field. Inside the mansion, the virtual doors connecting the virtual rooms slammed hard shut.

An echo of Del's last thoughts came through to Rex. *It's up to you now, do what you always do, Rex, exist, survive. Hold the crucible together while I work this out from the inside.*

Like a mote of impurity inside a crystal lattice, Rex was suddenly locked in place. His inner watchdog hauled against its new, virtual leash. That same predatory instinct that had kept him sane, kept him Rex, even as Glow memories from myriad different personas had tried to overwhelm him. It knew no other way. No odds, no plans, doubts, or regrets; just reactions.

Another mind entered the network. He felt its presence like a storm hanging over the mansion, seeping in through the gaps and rafters, examining and sampling as it came. No... not *entered*, not even controlled, or encompassed... *it dominated*! An overseer. The overseer. *Hmech.*

"At last," Hmech said. His words just a whisper of seething power inside of Rex's mind. "I've been waiting for you." Rex had another, single glimpse of the real world. He was laying down, people standing over him, crushed tight together, shoulder to shoulder, palms stretched out just barely touching him. "You are everything I hoped you would be."

As one, the people reached down and lifted Rex off the ground. They swept along the dark, deserted streets like a swollen river with Rex raised high above their heads like a trophy.

CHAPTER 46

Find a Way

"No more work unless she comes with me." Keller screamed his demand into Reet's face while doing his best to tower over her and maintain eye contact. "Good luck figuring out how to do the infusions yourself." In truth, he knew it wasn't that hard, but he'd made a big deal out of setting up precision pumps and monitors and having them break down at regular intervals in the most self-destructive of ways, thus making sure only he could put the whole thing back together again.

Reet's hand twitched for the gun on her belt holster, but instead she shrugged and walked away, and both Keller and Casima were led from the cell to Gale's prison. Keller winked at her. The plan was working so far. Casima felt that the *Nevis* family were working on a deadline, something or somebody had laid out a timeline and they were falling behind. Knocking Keller out or arguing with him would only delay things further.

After days of accumulated fullerene shots, Gale was developing nubs for legs and wisp-like structures enmeshed his lower torso. Keller studied him up close, fascinated as always. The amount of material added to Gale's mass only made up a few ounces, but his repair system wove the fullerenes into webs that were stronger than steel and as light as a breeze. It was like looking through a human made of spiderweb.

Even Gale's bones and muscles were little more than outlines bridged by a fog of fine threads.

Reet examined the experiment and seemed happy to let it continue. Keller felt he needed to appease her to some degree, so he rigged up a secondary pump system, and Gale obligingly extruded another port near what could loosely be described as his pelvis. The additional material infusions allowed Gale's legs to sprout to full length, splaying at the ends into long, hooked toes. Keller caught him testing them, shifting position as new muscle fibers came online. He moved slowly as if a rush of air would blow him away, but Keller had seen the strength of the material. He eyed the steel chains and caging and wondered if it would be enough.

"Better get a move on," Reet said. "I've got a delegation from the Alliance flying in tomorrow to see the goods and make an offer."

"What happens to us when the bot has gone?" Keller asked.

She shrugged. "Maybe they'll buy you off us as well. You're the expert, after all. If not..." She shrugged again. "We'll find a use for the pair of you."

Casima lay curled on a bench in the far corner of the room. Her role in their escape plan was to mentally map the way to Gale's holding prison and all possible escape routes. So far, nothing viable appeared. Too many cameras and guards, but at least she had the lie of the land, and, as an ex-professional guide, she committed the whole setup to memory.

Keller struggled with depression. He felt he was in his final days, unfair days. The surgeon who lost his will and ability to work on his first day on the job, who retrained as a robot expert and was now going to die either at the hands of one of his robots or as the result of some deal-gone-wrong, and all just as he'd acknowledged a true love of Casima, his first... and his last.

"I'm going to be killed," he muttered softly to himself, feeling sanity slipping, "but I think she has it worse." He'd wondered several times if they should try to kill themselves, an act that would spare her the vile fate that assuredly awaited her. When he'd suggested suicide, she shook her head and whispered. "Patience, Kell, something will come up."

Patience! He thrust his face close to Gale's translucent skull. "What should I do?" he whispered. "If you were freed, would you let us live?"

Sound issued from several different parts of Gale's body forming a focused, directional beam into Keller's ear. "Free me and I'll make sure *she* lives." That was an angle Keller wasn't expecting, *a sacrifice*. His life for Gale's freedom. A noble exit from a life of terrible decisions.

"Deal," he said, and felt a wash of cold, calculated calm ease away the years of fear and pain.

CHAPTER 47

The Wild, Wild West

"Where are we, the freaking wild west?" Jorben looked up from the puddle of vomit around his knees, over a landscape of grey pumice dunes and brown dirt basins.

"Rain shadow, kind of a small desert," Leal said, gazing off to the south toward Transit Mountain. "You should have told me you didn't like cars."

Jorben spat bile and eased upwards. "I used to be fine until I fell off a damn mountain." The car's front seat was too small for him, so he folded into the rear looking like some mad-science project with his face and limbs pressed up against the windows. "It doesn't help that it smells so bad, either."

Leal dropped back into the driver's seat and fired up the electric motor. "Yeah, it's a bit of a stinker. Nathan plugs it into the sewage system overnight. It's a free battery charge."

They'd driven most of the day to reach the north-eastern tip of Coriolis Island, scouting around the Sidereal Sea, watching the terrain change from hills and farms to hills of sand. The car was old. Something in the drivetrain kept slipping and spinning, emitting a fearsome howl, and jolting them to a near halt before catching and lurching back into motion with a vomit-inducing jerk.

An old labor camp for Transit Mountain, Elford City was a sprawling grid of dilapidated houses, storefronts, and bars. It showed no sign of human life, only birds, jackrabbits, and the relentlessly whining cicadas that haunted every tree and post like the ghosts of ancient air raid sirens.

"Stop!" yelled Jorben. They pulled over again and he tumbled out and into a nearby bush.

"Christ, Jorben," Leal watched him in the mirror. "What's with all the puke. I didn't feed you that much."

"Guts are failing... like the rest of me."

"You're going to get a new body after all this, right?"

He groaned to his feet and crashed back across the rear seat. A pair of eyes glinting in the sun caught his attention. He shielded his gaze and saw a fox standing on its back legs watching him over the dirt. As he swept his gaze full circle, he saw other animals, rabbits, rats, reptiles, and birds, all looking his way.

"We should leave," he said quietly, trying not to be alarmed.

Leal laughed. "We're new out here, critters are gonna stare."

They lurched into town passing under the *Welcome to Elford City* sign that Madam Seer had pulled from his memory. "Definitely been here before," Jorben said. "I recognize these buildings, that bar, the strip-mall."

Leal looked skeptical. "They look pretty much like the ones in my neighborhood, without the people and with extra sand and grit."

"Turn here." Jorben pointed left and they stalled into a sharp corner, waited for the engine to catch, and lurched into a side street. "I grew up here, caught the school bus on this corner every day. I hated school until we started biology, animals, bodies, I loved all that stuff."

"That's great, Jorben. Now, tell me where you used to live."

"Live... live?" They trundled around town, but nothing sparked a memory. "There's a black-hole in my head where those memories should be." His aging eyes fought the failing light.

"Looks like we're spending the night," Leal said, pulling

alongside a ramshackle guesthouse. A vacancy sign still hung from a board out front. "And we're in luck, they have rooms."

The building was a gutted shell, but they made it homely with car mats, seat cushions and a picnic blanket. Jorben crashed into meditation, conserving what little life energy he had remaining and hoping for some overnight healing.

He came out of his trance sometime early morning. The grasshopper creaks and buzzes sounded eerily close, and the moon shone through gaps in the boarded-up window as if trying to squint a look inside.

He rolled upright and stepped outside, feeling fresher after rest and for not being jammed inside a car. A sickening hunger radiated from his empty gut, triggering some of his old Burn compulsions: the need to move, to run… *to fight!* He broke into a stumbling jog. The glass still ground through his joints, but motion added a little oil to the system and they loosened up. He just let his body go, legs finding their own way right down the center of the moonlit street.

He sensed the animals around him. A million tiny eyes connected to tiny brains and their minute sparks of consciousness.

Real or not real? Surreal! How can I be here? With her? After all I've been through?

He saw a bus-stop. A bent orange disk, somebody had spray painted over the "Bu" of *bus* and replaced it with an "As." *Not me. I didn't do childish things like that. I got into more adult trouble, like fights.*

Jorben felt the weighty lunchbox and book bag dangling from his shoulder strap. He stood, shuffling his feet, just waiting, waiting for that distant engine sound. Even then, he'd had a mechanical leaning, visualizing the pumping pistons and spinning cams. The sounds triggered images of the moving parts. *Everything was just parts back then.* "An engineer or an accountant", he remembered somebody telling him. *But I became neither.*

Time warped around him, hours, days, and months of just standing right here… waiting for buses. His body grew larger and stronger each day. Even as his mind became jaded, losing any childish glee for life. Boredom replaced curiosity, etched into him through dull repetition.

"Your mind is your own, Jorben." Which teacher told him that? His mind *was* his own, so he took off walking. *Screw the school bus, and classes, and teachers.* Side alleys hid him from prying eyes, weaving across the town grid, a hundred different ways to get to the same place, and he'd tried them all.

The weight of teenage angst lifted from his shoulders. He was a man now, confident of stride. A man who caught the exact, same bus, but earlier before the sun rose. No sweaty, farting kids on this bus, just smoky workers, angrily silent, with moody, far-off stares. Off to the Mountain they went, to work their butts off to pay their way only to come home unfulfilled, exhausted, and worst of all, *suspicious*.

Today he came home very early, deliberately early, passing the neighbors' windows, aware of all the eyes following him through cracks in the curtains. Their smothered whispers followed him like a constant breeze.

"He's home."

"There'll be trouble this evening."

"Not right in the head is that one."

Old Edwards was always in his front garden, kneeling over his plants like he was praying. The Boyan kids sat smug in their garage, giggling at his failings. They all knew. Everyone here knew.

A car sat in his driveway. *Not my car. I can't afford a car. That's why I get on the fucking bus every day.* His step quickened, past rows of cube homes where deadbeat drug-addicts lived off the charity of the town, past Jeff's place with his giant TV that could be seen from three streets over. Always on, burning money, just to show everyone how well-off he was.

Into the driveway, wanting to key the car, spike some tires, smash the windshield, but why waste time? The house's front door was locked, catching on the deadbolt as he turned his key.

Alarmed voices sounded from the upstairs window. He felt his control slipping away, punched the door and broke his knuckles, kicked the door and hurt his foot, "fuck!" Kicked it again, harder, the rage piling up as the door fought back. The screams and yells from inside only fueled the fury, bending some invisible switch inside his mind from the sanity setting over to the insane.

The door yielded to his boot, crashing open with a soft, sickening thud as it silenced the short scream from little Arian who was on the inside trying to peer out through a crack around the lower door hinge.

He scooped her up feeling the softness of her skull, the way the bits moved under his fingers, trying to hold them in place as blood seeped from her slack mouth.

Somebody screamed. "What have you done?" *Leal?* No, this was somebody else, from his old life. Her name removed or traumatized from his memory. She came at him, fingernails tearing the flesh from his face. Not the first time, but this was going to be the last.

"You did this. It's all on you," he yelled, shoving her backwards onto the floor. He saw him then, hopping away towards the backdoor, pulling his pants up around his waist as he went.

And suddenly Jorben was awake.

Not walking at all, but hunched on the guesthouse floor, mind still lost in the story as Leal stroked the back of his neck. "Keep going, Jorben. You're doing great," she whispered.

"I lost my mind when I saw him leaving our house. I chased him through the streets, stalked him, slow, almost methodical, so he knew I was coming, that his end was near. I did him in the middle of the road, people watching, witnesses. Strange that nobody came to help him. I rang his neck until the life was gone from his eyes, and then I just stood up and went back home.

"She was there waiting for me with a kitchen knife. Think I broke her arm getting that knife away, but she managed to run up the stairs. Don't know why she did that, the front door was wide open. Yes, I do, I remember, she was going for Angel in her crib. I really didn't mean to kill Angel, but she kind of got in the way.

"A neighbor shot me in the back as I straddled her. I must have stabbed her a hundred times, but still she cried out. It was the crying that did it, shunting that switch in my head, crashing it against the end stop. Every time she shouted, I stabbed, and she shouted... and I... I stabbed more. She pleaded with me to stop, even though I couldn't. Couldn't figure out how to, and how was she making all that fucking noise? "No Steelos. Please Steelos!"

"Steelos?" Jorben was suddenly fully awake, moonlit dust particles swirling around him like nanoscopic ghosts. *A ghost for each stab of that knife.* "Steelos?"

Jorben walked out into the street and Leal ran after.

He paused, noting how utterly numb and broken he felt. He ground to a halt as if striking some invisible wall, then slowly turned to face Leal who stopped in her tracks, face a mask of fear and confusion. He took a single step towards her and crashed face first into the dirt. "Who the fuck was Steelos?"

CHAPTER 48

The Delegation

Keller called their prison cell, hidden deep in the prow of the *Nevis*, the ringing void.

Everything around was metal. Even the luxury apartments that housed the *Nevis* family were decorated, appointed, and constructed from metal girders, sheets, mesh, and foils, and it all existed inside what was basically a giant bell. The tanker body amplified and propagated every sound. The white noise from the ocean was filtered and resonated into odd rising tones, that, to Keller, sounded like ancient recordings of whale song. Voices and footsteps travelled vast distances. Looping back on themselves, they transformed, morphed, taking on demented, alien qualities that seeped and crawled through the waveguides of the ship into Keller's ears. And all in the pristine, utter darkness of the cell.

Am I going mad? he pondered, as the sounds fermented his thoughts. *A sacrifice? The man who froze at the first sign of conflict was going to throw his life away in an attempt to free a robotic monster, trusting it to keep its promise and keep the love of his life alive.*

He stirred in their cramped bed, feeling the weight of Casima's head pressing into his shoulder. Something in the soundscape had shifted. The distorted, organic noises of the ocean had taken on more human sounds, crashes, voices, aircraft banking and landing. "They're here," he said, easing Casima off him.

"Who?" she muttered through the darkness.

"The Alliance." *A sacrifice*! In the complete darkness of the cell and the utter depth of his depression, it made total sense. *I can do it for her.*

Moments later their cell flew open and Glin and four companions came inside. "Out, now," he demanded, grabbing Keller's elbow, and hauling him to his feet, while strategically avoiding any contact with Casima. Two sidekicks took her, an arm each, and marched her out after him.

"Kell?" she grumbled, rubbing the sleep from her eyes and smoothing her prison-issue nightgown to cover any exposed flesh or plastic parts of her body. "Where are the morons taking us now?"

Gale's vast holding cell now buzzed with people. Reet's entire family and dozens of guards jammed the space, but from the point of sheer intimidation the three beings from the Alliance had them all dwarfed.

The central figure caught Keller's eye. He had an uncanny plastic face, or maybe flesh surgically repaired from burns. The intense disfigurement marred what could have been boyish good looks. A snakeskin cape spiraled around his tall, lean body, reaching all the way to the floor and hiding feet and hands, making it hard to tell if the figure was human or not.

His two guards were fully a meter taller than any normal person and appeared to be made of translucent glass filled with blue water. The glass flexed as they moved, more like a gel than any solid. Inside them, Keller saw what looked like bones, mechanical actuators and electrical boxes strung together by plastic muscle strands and colored cables. The bulbous heads of the guards were transparent; multiple eyeballs swam freely inside, rising and falling like bored fish as they peered out through the transparent gel-skull in all directions. The guards held stubby firearms cradled close to their chests by massive, oversized hands.

"What the f–" mumbled Casima, clutching Keller's arm so hard he thought it would snap.

"It's okay," he whispered as Glin tugged him towards the daunting leader. "These people might be our ticket out of here."

"This must be Keller Morten," the snakeskin-caped man said, his voice ringing with friendship and optimism. "I am Trabian Folley." He reached out an enormous hand and Keller shook it. The hand felt like cold steel and had the weight of a dumbbell.

"An honor to meet you, sir." Keller bowed his head and wondered if he would ever get his hand back.

"Casima." Trabian offered Casima his hand and she took it reluctantly. "I am here in the role of negotiator and trouble-shooter for the esteemed Breakout Alliance."

"It will be my pleasure to answer any questions you have about *my* robot," Keller said, aware that his gamble caused sharp intakes of breath from Reet and her whole family.

"Excellent!" Trabian threw up his hands. "I hear *your* robot is regenerating. What do you need to complete this process, Keller?"

"Fullerenes are working well. Hyper-fullerenes would be better."

"Excellent! I will have more shipped out here by the morning. You understand, Reet, that we will be staying here until we can assess how safe it is to move this machine."

Reet nodded, suddenly meek and small in Trabian's presence.

"And what price will you be asking?" Trabian addressed the question straight at Reet.

Reet licked her lips as if trying to pluck a number out of thin air, but not wanting to get it wrong. "We want payment in eight different currencies, totaling one-billion Euro-credits. Half in advance now and half at the time of taking charge of the machine."

"That's an absurd amount of money," Trabian said, seeming to grow even taller.

Silence settled on the room. Keller noticed trigger fingers twitching. The gel-troopers remained totally motionless. Their discombobulated eyeballs seemed to pick faces from the crowd and fixate on them until they wilted under the unflinching stare and turned away.

"It's a valuable property," Reet said, crossing her arms over her chest. Even on tiptoe, she came only halfway up Trabian's body and had to crane her neck to meet his gaze. "It's worth ten times that and you know it. I'll even throw in Keller and Machine-Girl here as a bonus."

Keller bit his lip. He wanted to scream out that they were not property, and that the robot was actually *his*. He squeezed Casima's hand, and she squeezed back. The Alliance was a powerful, global organization. Surely they'd be safer with them than with the *Nevis* family.

"Excellent!" Trabian said softly. "I will arrange payment." The tension popped and everyone's shoulders slumped forward in relief. "Now, I wish to spend some time alone with my purchase. Keller and Casima can stay with me as they are part of the deal. Everyone else can leave."

"We're not leaving," Reet said. "It's not yours until you've paid for it." And suddenly the tension was back.

Trabian's chest expanded, a mighty inhalation that seemed to suck all the air from the room leaving everyone else struggling to breathe. "Let's be very clear. I will stay, and I will perform my investigations, and, at the end of it all, I will leave here with this robot. If you wish me to show you the courtesy of paying you and leaving your heaving mass of nautical relics afloat, then you will not challenge me again."

"Reet!" Ben coughed her name from his wheelchair in the corner. She glanced around at the old man and made a good decision.

"Okay, everyone out," she said.

"We'll take your guest wing for our operations center," Trabian called after her.

Reet and her clan shuffled out the door, slamming it behind them with an added touch of impudent momentum.

"Secure the room," Trabian ordered, rubbing his hands together.

The gel-troopers animated, their eyes swimming and pointing in all directions. Holographic virtual displays and instruments sprang out of thin air around their heads. A tiny spinning mirror inside each guard's head directed laser beams to multiple points around the room. Reet's security cameras smoldered and popped, sending debris hissing to the floor. Sharper beams bored holes into the walls routing out hidden microphones, fiber optics and other nefarious devices.

"Isn't technology wonderful?" Trabian addressed Keller while unwinding his long snakeskin cape, and letting it drop carelessly to the floor.

Keller stared in stunned silence as he realized Trabian was also some kind of gel-trooper, a transparent body with carbon-black bones. He wondered if this was an Alliance attempt at recreating Gale's fullerene biology. Trabian's head was either a perfect replica of a real head or, even more terrifyingly, it might have been a real head that ended right at the neck where it seemed to merge with the gel while sending thick, octopus tentacles down into the gel body.

Trabian noted Keller's admiring gaze. "The brains of captured GFC personnel yielded a bounty of new technology. Free of their suppression we now advance with great speed. Would you like to be part of this advancement, Keller Morten?"

He nodded. Beside him, Casima nodded too.

The troopers finished their scans and adopted frozen poses with their backs to the walls. Keller felt his ears pop as a noise cancellation field silenced the external world and smothered them in artificial silence.

Trabian stepped up to Gale, his gel-feet extruding longer toes that lifted him up until his face was directly in front of Gale's. They stood eye to eye for a few seconds before Trabian spoke. "Ursurper Gale, I presume?"

"Trabian," Gale said in what sounded like a sad or even shocked tone. "Which of us has changed the most?"

"First let me convey the Alliance's gratitude to you for your role in defeating the GFC."

"A shuttle ride into high orbit with a hold full of equipment would be thanks enough."

Trabian chuckled, his face pressing up to Gale's. Keller shuffled closer to hear the exchange. "Ursurper, our world cringes on the edge of utter destruction. At any moment, a supernova device might obliterate everything. The Universe will become a dark and empty place once again. We have no time for games, no time for niceties or conventions. I don't expect you to understand the picoforms that created your artificial biology, but my minds will pull you apart atom by atom, and we will understand your biology, and we will harvest whatever scraps of Del and his priceless memories that remain inside that mind."

Gale just stared. Keller wondered if the robot would ever get the chance to regenerate his face. And he tried to imagine what expression such a face would be making right now. Silence rang in his ears as he glanced at Casima, whose eyes were so wide he could see one of the gel-troopers in full reflection in her pupil.

"Excellent!" Trabian clapped hands and pinned Keller with his very human gaze, a gaze that held both youthful curiosity and crushing sadness. "You will both stay in my suite. I have questions for you Keller, and Casima looks like she could use proper medical attention."

"We just want our freedom back," Casima said, shrinking into Keller's side to avoid Trabian's direct gaze. She winced as Trabian's hand reached out and clasped her shoulder in what was supposed to be a reassuring gesture.

"On behalf of Hmech and the Alliance, I can offer you a

unique type of freedom inside our organization. I think you will find it far better than the alternatives," Trabian said. "Your brains are in possession of too much sensitive data for any better way out."

The noise cancellation switched off and the ringing void returned. Trabian led the way out of the cell, Keller and Casima following close behind. "We have some hope, right, Kell?" she asked in a small, coy voice.

He managed a smile and nodded, eyes scanning Gale's elaborate restraints, and Trabian with his gel-troop bodyguards. There was hope, but he wondered what Trabian's 'unique type of freedom' meant, and whether it included either of them remaining alive.

CHAPTER 49

The Way Home

They rode in silence, back through the darkness into a blood-smeared dawn sky. Leal kept nodding asleep at the wheel, jolting awake as the car sidled off and back on to the road. Jorben propped himself in the back, broodily watching the unfinished wasteland of Coriolis Island pass by the side window. He refused to look at Leal, had nothing to say. Didn't even really know what to think. *Steelos?*

Without warning he opened the door, rolled out of the car, and plunged down a sandy embankment, crashing to a halt near the bottom.

He heard screaming brakes, a door opened and slammed shut. "What the fuck, Jorben?" The sound of Leal's soft house shoes scything through the dirt as she descended the slope after him.

"Go! Leave me," he yelled, struggling to his feet and stumbling away. "I'm a monster. You can't be near me." His words slurred like a drunk's. It was truly the closest thing to inebriation he could remember. His body was shot. Eating itself alive trying to drain enough sustenance to feed his metabolism's stress reaction.

"Get a grip. You're not this... this Steelos guy. You didn't do those things."

"I remember it! I am him or he is me. Somebody changed my name. Deleted some memories–"

"Or added some," she screamed back. "Think, Jorben, did your mother ever call you Steelos? School teachers? Lovers? Anybody? You've never mentioned that name. Even with the best edit job or the most complete amnesia in the world, if you'd ever been Steelos there would be more left to remember."

Jorben curled into a hunched heap and grabbed at his temples. "Then what is this game? Why give me these memories? Is this a punishment of some kind? A test? Anger management?" He laughed, remembering Knoss lecturing him on controlling his temper. *How can I control something that I literally have no control over?*

Leal cradled his head. The sweat from her armpit tingled his nose. "You said it yourself: Burns die and go into the Can. Maybe you get mixed up and spat back out. Shit, Jorben, maybe you really did do this back when you were Steelos, but you're a different person now, one who paid with his life and is now working through redemption." She clutched him tighter. "I see a good man inside here. You told me how you ran away rather than murder those militia guys in cold blood. They gave you free rein to maim and murder at will and you… you risked your life and fled. And where did you come? You came to help me."

"I told you about that?" Jorben scratched at his head. He wasn't even sure that had happened and that it wasn't a Can-sim or a bad dream. *Real or not real?* "What do I do now, Leal?" His huge arms circled her, feeling the bones and structures of her delicate body slipping and popping beneath his monstrous fingers. "I'm so lost, finished."

"I remember being a kid, watching this movie, a ton of people died. It was horrible. I went to sleep that night and woke up convinced it was real. I'd been there, seen those things." Leal gave a sad chuckle. "Parents stopped me watching films after that." She eased out of his grip, stood, and offered him a helping hand to stand up. "That's you, Jorben, a kid-brain in a soldier's body, watching movies, and you think it's all real."

"Now you're making me sound like Nathan." Jorben eased to his feet, swayed a little and began the haul back up the slope towards Nathan's car. "Take me to the Enclave, Leal. Let's get this over with."

She nodded. "I'll take you, and I'll wait and demand that you get a new body. I'm not leaving until I get Jorben back."

He laughed. "You'll get something back. Maybe it'll even say it's me. Maybe it'll *be* me... some version–"

"I'll know the difference. After, you can stay with me and the kids. I'll help you get a real job away from all that Convolver crap. They owe you that much, an attempt at a real life."

"And Nathan?"

"I kicked him out a few days back. His conspiracy shit was starting to affect the children. I worried what he might do to them or to me if he flipped and lost it completely." A sudden thought seemed to strike her. "He's going to be really pissed that I borrowed his car for so long."

He looked into her face and saw hope. "If you can get me back from the Enclave, then I promise to keep you safe from Nathan and anybody else that wants to harm you."

CHAPTER 50

Fullerene Dreams

The *Nevis* guest suite should have been a wonderful treat after days in the cramped, metal cell, but captivity was still captivity even if it had a double-king bed, a swimming pool bath, and an enormous glass viewing window that looked back along the *Nevis*.

Keller and Casima sat in the loveseat gazing back at the monstrous ships. "We should at least see if there's a way out of here," Keller sighed, struggling to his feet. The emotional exhaustion from the previous days' events felt like a weight far heavier than his physical wounds.

"Already checked." Casima dismissed his idea with a hand wave. "There's only one door, and it's locked, and there's one of those freaky gel-troopers standing outside. You can see it through the peep-hole."

"Maybe there's another way." Keller dabbed at the thick glass with a plastic chopstick he'd found in an odds-and-ends basket in the bathroom. Even if he broke through, the drop down to the ocean would be fatal.

Earlier, they had been hustled out to a dining area by a gel-trooper. They sat at an outlandishly long table as a group of men in chef's outfits delivered plates of food and drinks. As they sat staring at the banquet, Trabian entered and sat oddly close to them, considering the scale of setting. He didn't eat or drink, which enhanced Keller's already high level of suspicion regarding the food.

"Eat!" boomed Trabian. "My troops personally supervised the food production."

Keller wasn't reassured, but they ate anyway, satiating the hunger gnawing at his innards.

Trabian asked disappointingly few questions as Keller outlined how he came into possession of Gale. He expected to be quizzed on all the details of his experiments, the levels of regeneration, and his notes on biomechanics and behavior. But Trabian just watched him as if reading his mind and bypassing his words. Keller assumed either his views were worthless or that the real Trabian was not actually there. He wondered what the real Trabian looked like.

A gel-trooper returned them to their room, passing more identical looking troops coming down from the landing deck above. A charming doctor visited Casima, took some scans and issued some different drugs. After she left, Keller shook his head in disbelief. "Amazing. I think she was a robot too."

Casima nodded, a gleam of envy in her eye. "Although there was still a touch of human in there, somewhere."

Despite the huge bed, they slept in the very middle, unwilling to break free from each other. They slept in fits; startling awake as destructive dreams haunted their thoughts. Around them the ship rang with life as neither Trabian nor his troops seemed to require rest. Keller felt they were organizing defenses, but against who? Perhaps the *Nevis* family and its loyal retainers. He doubted they would stand a chance against even one of the Alliance's inhuman troopers. That idea played out inside Keller's dreams as few things would give him more pleasure than seeing Reet and her abhorrent sons squished under a robotic boot.

It was barely light when a trooper roused them. "Report for duty," it said with a voice like an electric shock.

Keller dressed but Casima just rolled over in bed. The

consultation with the doctor the previous day had yielded only minor hope. New drugs propped up her ailing organs, but for how long? Her flesh and blood just weren't playing well with her numerous prosthetics. She needed transplants or a powerful somanetic drug like Simmorta to coerce her body back into a whole.

Keller carefully re-tucked her bed covers and tiptoed out the room after the trooper.

Back inside Gale's cavernous prison cell, he noticed a large, silver cylinder nearly the size of his leg. "Hyper-fullerenes," the escort trooper intoned. A collection of sleek, modern surgical instruments, pumps and monitors were stacked nearby. Things that would make Keller's job much easier. He doubted he'd get to do much more than setup the fullerene drip and adjust the dosing. Once Trabian witnessed the process, he was redundant.

"That's a shitload of fullerenes!" he exclaimed to no one in particular as he rigged up a drip, made some adjustments, and pulled up a chair in front of Gale to observe.

Like watching paint dry, nothing happened. He zoned out, just wandering through his thoughts and regrets. Moments ticked by into hours, and only then, over such an extended time frame, he noticed changes in Gale's physiology.

The flimsy legs filled out, growing thicker, as ever-smaller fibers sprouted from the trunk-fibers and meshed over the gaps. The ultrathin structural fibers became wrapped in sheaves of fine cables like muscles which sprouted branches, shoring up the body and adding degrees of freedom to Gale's motion. Gale's skull grew a face, or at least the basic structure of a face. That seemed like an extravagant waste of material, but it began to make sense: Gale's repair system was stockpiling excess fullerenes wherever it could, almost like humans deposited fat. Gale was gorging on raw material, absorbing it so fast he couldn't use it all... yet.

Day dulled into night; Keller watched in morbid fascination as Gale's lower jaw curved out of the knotted mass of his pseudo-face. His neck puffed with cords of muscle making him look more like a charred bodybuilder.

The room was suspiciously empty, no troopers, no Trabian. As Keller sat in silence, he realized this was Trabian's plan. Let him be alone with Gale and talk, maybe reveal something Trabian was unable to interrogate out of Gale. And Gale must know it too. They both just stared at each other, equally trapped, equally lost. Eventually, Keller rolled into a corner and for the first time in days he fell into a deep sleep.

The babbling noise woke him hours later. A disturbing sound like dozens of people speaking languages he'd never heard before.

The noise came from Gale.

As he listened, the sounds cohered and started making sense. He guessed Gale was calibrating his newly formed vocal plate, which Keller examined with a flashlight. He figured it must work like a speaker membrane as it needed no air from any lungs to create sounds.

Gale talked of the war with the GFC, how he evaded capture and plunged his small craft into the heart of their capital ship while swinging free at the last moment. He spoke of assassins and heated debates among GFC council members over his existence, of imprisonment, escape, allies and betrayals, years of living and evading, building secret labs, squirreling away resources, and watching as they were discovered and confiscated.

He recalled the sudden realization that reality was not as he remembered. That, although he'd thought of himself as Del Krondeck, that was so, so long ago; and that since then he'd lived his own life and become Ursurper Gale, effectively growing a new mind stacked on top of that original persona. He understood that most of his life was a complete fraud; implanted memories manipulated his beliefs and the very framework upon which his whole personality was based. Despite the doubts about who and what he was, Gale had carried on anyway, becoming his own being while always just managing to stay ahead of his enemies – until now.

Keller listened, head down as if in prayer. He got the message, understood what Gale was saying with this stream of low-importance babble. He was saying, "I'm ready. I am as powerful as I can get. It's time for your sacrifice."

"How?" he said, standing, craning his neck up at the mass of chains, clamps and tethers. "What can I possibly do?"

He jumped as the cell door slammed open and Trabian stormed in at the head of a group of six troopers and the doctor.

"Making deals with the Devil are we Keller?" Trabian said, shoving him aside. "I've seen enough. Take him down."

As Keller stumbled off to the side. He saw Gale twist and writhe in his restraints. His body took on a sheen, flowing like fibrous oil through and around the chains. His flesh seemed to dissolve into whips and tentacles that flowed upward through the welded neck restraint to reform around his head which remained locked, rigid in the clamp.

"Disable him, now!" roared Trabian.

As Keller stumbled away from the insanity, many things happened all at once. A gel-trooper stepped forward, carrying what looked like a huge gun with plastic coils along its barrel. Gale's amorphous body seemed to boil around his own head before exploding outwards in a mass of hooked tentacles that ripped and tore into the metal head-clamp, which disintegrated in a flare of sparks and shrapnel. Trabian sprang sideways, alarmingly fast for such a large man, as Gale toppled free. One of his whip-like appendages scythed a nearby gel-trooper clean in two as he dropped to the ground.

Another trooper powered up the coil weapon, which made a sound like a cracked bell followed by a subsonic thump. Gale jerked rigid and held for a full second before resuming movement in slow motion. Fighting the induced pain, he became a vortex, sucking his drooping tentacles back into his body and spinning them into a snake-like torso. His head lashed forward at the gel-trooper, but the energy field coming from the trooper's gun slowed his motion, stalling it just inches from the trooper's multi-eyed head. A second trooper wearing an identical rig stepped in and clamped the gun barrel to Gale's skull. Together they pushed, forcing Gale to the ground inside what Keller assumed was some kind of containment field.

For seconds Gale crackled with energy. His face turned to Keller imploring him to help. But Keller remained frozen, his own eyes now far away in a distant surgery, his hands covered in blood, surrounded by bodies he could never fix.

"He's out," one of the troopers said. "One-hundred percent loss of functionality."

"Excellent!" Trabian said. "Load him onto a containment gurney, then move him to my shuttle. We're leaving." He pointed to Keller. "He may be useful, bring him along."

Keller choked back to the present moment, finding his own voice hidden amongst the knots of angst. "But Casima?" He made a stumbling move for the door but a trooper's solid grip stopped him.

Something shifted in the air. A subtle tilt in the vast ship's poise; a distant but violent compression wave rippled through the ringing void like a thunderclap. A moment later, the floor lurched upwards as if the *Nevis* had experienced an earthquake.

"Report?" Trabian spoke into the air above his head.

"Someone just torpedoed the rear end of the *Nevis*." The voice came from somewhere above. "We're under attack, sir."

CHAPTER 51

A Ship in a Storm

Steelos and his squad of Burns blasted through a wall from the *Nevis* repair dock where their party boat was moored awaiting its very expensive repairs. Convolver spies had long ago mapped the vast ship complex, and Steelos saw the battle plan clearly in his mind's eye.

They burst into the crowded *Nevis* shopping mall, parting the dense mass of people like arrows through foliage while using the panicked masses as cover from cameras and sniper fire. They attacked in a wedge, the tip aimed squarely at the security cordon at the far end of the mall.

Wearing the insignias from various global corporations, the Burns carried carefully planted scraps of forensic evidence: fibers charged with Chinese air molecules, materials from European Amtech corporations, and memory chips and components carefully sourced from illicit central African foundries and other autonomous manufacturing plants. Anything to hide the fact they were Convolvers. Anything to divert Hmech's accusing eye onto somebody else.

Steelos hung back on the left flank, eyes on his fellow Burns. They all had their own switches, their own thresholds, that moment when it all became too much and they lost control. Some held on to their humanity for just seconds; others, like Steelos, kept their sanity for much longer. The randomness of their violence and berserk nature made them impossible to predict, even for their commanders, and a nightmare for any defensive forces seeking logic, a plan, or just a limit to how destructive or vicious an enemy combatant could be.

People ran for cover, packing into the rows of boutique shops and eateries. In seconds, the mall emptied, just two-hundred meters of open tile to the security cordon. From outside, Steelos's combat helmet was an eyeless wedge of metal-alloy, but from within it was all transparent glass and holographic combat glyphs. His sensors tracked guards and gun emplacements, marked targets and potential hostiles with color-coded icons. His helmet AI picked off targets that Steelos didn't acknowledge, using the tiny missile launchers mounted on his shoulders. The Burn squad embodied pure concentrated chaos, a distributed organism that moved and shifted shape while emitting barrages of small munitions, guided anti-personnel missiles, energy beams, slow moving wall-busters, and stun grenades.

Other attack boats swept in from the sides, conspicuously visible, obvious decoys to create panic and spread the *Nevis*'s defenses across as wide a front as possible. The timing was perfect to within a second. Steelos's tactical display showed one of their suicide boats striking the rear of *Nevis*. The explosive-laden craft detonated on impact sending a massive concussion wave rippling along the ship and under their feet.

The Burns leapt into the air as the deck bucked, and their split-second-timed barrage of wall-busters found their targets. Everything ahead changed, walls vanished, soldiers fell in shreds, grenades blew minds and eardrums. His combat maps updated and he kept running. *Detent*. Its absolution of responsibility crept into the red. Everything and everyone became just shapes in motion, pegs to fit into holes. Linkages and fulcrums to be exploited, disabled, destroyed.

Heavier firepower emanated from the main barracks nestled strategically within *Nevis*'s outer residential zone, isolating the more affluent residents and the *Nevis* family apartments from the rest of the ship. The Burns strafed the doorways and side rooms as they passed, seeding tiny explosive mines behind them. They were never going back. It was always a one-way, single direction mission.

Fire sprayed from a guard post. Steelos veered nimbly, bullets ricocheting off his armor. Some pierced but he felt nothing. Combat bodies had minimal nerve endings. Mortal wounds tickled rather than hurt. A Burn's role was to soak up damage, not shy away. The more broken and shredded a body, the more one could boast and revel back in the Can.

They leaned into the hail of munitions like runners through a blizzard that shifted and angled, concentrating fire into corridors of death that tore bodies to fragments. In the heightened combat awareness of Steelos's hyper-accelerated mind, they seemed to keep running as blood-red shadows before fading and vanishing completely.

His counter showed *thirteen* Burns remaining.

Now *twelve*–

Their own fire struck the end guard post, vanquishing walls and routing defenders as their morale failed, and they made that instinctive decision that this was not the moment they wished to die.

Eleven Burns remained.

Over more wreckage and into the inner apartments. Here, the decor was lush: ornate vases, pictures of fruit, alabaster statues in alcoves, and fine tapestries adorned the walls. The density of soldiers and targets was smaller, just loyal family retainers. The Burns split into pairs to best utilize available cover.

Ten Burns left.

He paused for a second to admire a painting. A deer caught in the open, eyes wide as its brain vacillated between standing still and running. *Reset the switch, calm the insanity. I might need to be human again soon.*

A nearby Burn lost control, ripping off his helmet, spinning, spraying bullets like a rogue sprinkler system. His companions ducked and dodged, giving him the space to berserk freely. As the crazed Burn took on fire from every defender, Steelos and the remaining troops used that free second to retarget, reassess cover, reset their own sanity, and blast every defensive bastion to dust.

On cue, two more explosions ripped through the ship. New lights appeared on Steelos's command screen as thirty-two fresh Burns entered the *Nevis* through hull breaches. Immediately four of them vanished under heavy fire. They assaulted locations where the Alliance forces were believed to be barracked. Real troops, far more deadly than the *Nevis* militia, they favored autonomous mechs with fullerene skeletons and algorithmic brains, monitored by remote human operators.

Steelos felt the ground tilting backwards. The *Nevis* had begun to sink. Another timer appeared in his peripheral vision, an estimate of how long it would take the massive vessel to upend and slide beneath the waves – eight minutes.

Overhead, the sky battle was heating up as Alliance support aircraft engaged a swarm of drones launched from a Convolver-submarine. The sub pummeled *Nevis* with EMPs which would hinder the communications between the Alliance troops and their remote controllers. Once the gel-troopers were running on local intelligence only, they became reactionary algorithms that were easier to outsmart.

Nine Burns left... *Eight*... *Seven*. A powerful hidden auto-gun tore two to shreds before succumbing to fire.

Three gel-troopers appeared to the front, sending out a blaze of munitions that tore away the Burns' cover while fragmenting entire rooms. Steelos's combat suit launched a series of countermeasures taking down a cluster of anti-personnel missiles that winged his way.

Six...

Five Burns…

The enemy troops didn't die easily. Their gel-suits channeled energy around internal components and soaked up momentum, heat, and shockwaves.

Steelos shoulder-barged another trooper emerging from the hiding place. They tumbled across the floor, its powerful arms locking around his waist. He fired his multi-gun up into the chest cavity. Bullets ricocheted, some hit targets, most missed. He pulled out the barrel and rammed it at the gel-head, but the trooper was too strong and deflected his gun, hyper-velocity bullets ripping through ceiling panels and up into the decks above.

He felt the thump of an EMP torpedo detonating under the ship, followed by an instant of dizzying silence as every electronic system glitched and reset. His own radiation-hardened mind recovered fastest and, while the gel-trooper's eyes still swam lazily in its transparent head, he pushed the gun where the face should have been and fired. The gel blew apart and the body went limp. Steelos rolled to his feet, running and ducking under more incoming fire.

Four Burns left.

CHAPTER 52

Sinking

"We have to go back for Casima," Keller raged as the gel-trooper dragged him along by a cord connected to his wrist. They seemed to be moving upwards but he didn't remember there being any inclined corridors inside the *Nevis*. Gale's containment gurney headed the procession, closely followed by Trabian and his gel-troopers. "You won't get any cooperation from me without her," he yelled, but Trabian seemed not to hear. In the end, Keller just sat down, and the trooper dragged him bodily across the floor. *An inclined floor? Are we sinking?*

In his mind he saw Glin and Bov and the rest of the obscene *Nevis* clan descending on Casima and hauling her off like a prize. But surely, if the ship were sinking, escape and preserving their own miserable lives would be their priority. But how would Casima escape the locked apartment? *I am never going to see her again.*

The bizarre train of humans and mechanoids moved up through the lavish family quarters then out into an interior courtyard with steps spiraling up onto what was once the conning tower of the great ship. Keller clung to iron railings, but the trooper snapped his fingers free like a baby's and, with a rather human-like loss of temper, threw him over its shoulder and continued climbing.

Two more explosions rocked the *Nevis*, right underneath

them. The ship lifted slightly and dropped back into the ocean, the million-ton hull heaving like a harpooned leviathan. He imagined the chaotic movement spreading back along the chain of ships and connecting structures to the harbor and its neighboring twin-tanker catamarans. The ripples of force spreading across the barges challenging the latching mechanisms that held them all together.

Somewhere in the mess lay the *CyberSea*, and somewhere below in the bowels of the ringing void Casima must realize what was happening. Perhaps she slept, never to awaken, just gently slip beneath the ocean and into the darkness. Spared whatever nightmares this vicious world had planned for her next.

"Shit!" Casima felt the torpedo hit the ship and sat bolt upright, suddenly aware of how very, very long, and how deathly deep she'd been asleep. "Kell?"

She pounded on the apartment door, eyed the peephole and saw no trooper outside. Using a curtain rod as a lever, she pried the solid wooden bedpost free of the bedframe and assaulted the door with her makeshift battering ram. The hinges gave slowly, and she'd almost broken through when the door flew open and in stepped Glin with a pistol pointed at her.

"Die, creep!" She flung the ram at him and dived in for the rugby tackle, not noticing the stun wand in his other hand that sent her sizzling and jolting back to the floor.

He pushed the gun barrel hard into her numbed face, screwing it in a circular motion as if drilling a hole into her head. "You're coming with me," he said. "Bring her to my plane," he yelled over his shoulder. "We're getting the fuck out of here, now."

Casima felt her cybernetics twitch and begin their reboot and self-test sequence. She mentally powered them down making sure she remained limp and helpless, just staring dead-eyed at the ceiling above.

Bov and two of the food delivery chefs swept around Glin and grappled Casima to her feet. They dragged her out and along a row of circular cross-section hallways that looked like submarine launch tubes. The rooms became more lavish, and she noticed expansive side-chambers with huge viewing windows looking out over the sea. These were clearly the family residences. She wondered where they were all hiding. Doubtless they had panic-rooms and escape capsules lined up.

The floor was definitely tilting as they struggled into what appeared to be a ballroom with side doors leading to kitchens and TV rooms. She wondered if Keller was with Gale. Surely the Alliance forces were evacuating but had they taken Keller as well? The tears welled into her eyes, and she sobbed. "Kell... I'm sorry."

Bov's simian face thrust into hers, a mask of mockery and spite. "Aw... she's all sad about something."

The glyph in Casima's mind turned green as all her mechanical systems came fully back online. She eased her power back on, feeling sensation returning to her cybernetic parts while her real flesh remained numb. Her electro-polymer muscles bunched, and her left leg snapped upward, planting a sumptuous blow right into Bov's crotch. There was a satisfying crunch as his testicles ruptured against his pelvic bone and he dropped to the floor projectile vomiting out across the splendid, art-deco tiles.

She whirled around, side-smacking the head of one of the chef-thugs and sending him sprawling. Something hard struck the back of her head and she stumbled, arms wrapping behind her skull in a protective reflex as the world flashed from light to dark and then to grey. Somebody grabbed at her. She fought as she always fought, with everything she had, torquing awkward circles and bending into impossible shapes, anything to confuse, damage, or gain an advantage.

A stronger arm snaked around her throat, dragging her backwards while somebody else had her legs. All the while,

Casima's ears rang with a wailing sound like a siren that might have been the ship sinking or Bov lamenting the obliteration of his manhood.

"You'll pay for that," rasped Glin. His grip on her throat was much stronger than any normal human's. "You have no idea how much you're going to pay."

CHAPTER 53

Pink Cadillac

Gale's massive securing chain still swung from the ceiling as Steelos and his three remaining Burns crashed through into the holding cell. "The target's been moved." He eyed the hunk of metal that now resembled a twist of foil. "Split up," he barked, sending Burns off in separate directions.

He took off down the corridor toward the family quarters. The top deck and landing pad were the ultimate destination for all his Burns, but there were many routes to cover.

Steelos found a man curled on the floor, clutching his crotch. He appeared to be mumbling some sort of incantation or chant into a puddle of vomit. The man looked up, his dull gaze regarding Steelos with a resigned sadness. "Please..." He begged as Steelos's impassive wedge-helm thrust into his face. "They went that way." He pointed off through a wide doorway and up to the ceiling. Steelos didn't even need to threaten him.

"Who?" Steelos demanded. "Who went up there?"

"Glin and the cyborg bitch."

Cyborg bitch? He snatched the screaming man from the floor and used his scrawny body as a missile, flinging it at the door and following through to use it as cover. Stepping over the twisted corpse, Steelos moved on past decadent rooms and hallways, around a corner, along a corridor with a door at the end. He saw a woman being hauled backwards through the doorway, her feet held up by a terrified woman with a bloody face who looked frantically back at him.

He shot the woman just as the other two figures tumbled backwards into the room and slammed the door shut.

Steelos shoulder-rammed the door, striking it so hard the entire hallway shook. He felt some bones fracture, but the door held, and he heard laughter on the other side.

His map showed other rooms adjacent to the target room so he ran around the periphery, his helm sonar scanning the walls, feeding back estimates of wall strength and composition.

On the opposite side to where he had entered, he detected a thin wall, just aluminum plate. Steelos scanned it with a broad laser fan that cut a pattern of tiny grooves into the panel, then he struck it with his other, unbroken, shoulder. A neat, square wall section collapsed inwards, and he rolled into the room and back to his feet.

Straight ahead was a grotesque pink bed with the woman secured to the bedpost by a chain. A man knelt on the bed, clicking the chain in place, a snub-nosed shotgun cradled under his arm. He whirled around and discharged the gun. The cone of pellets struck Steelos in the chest, parting around his armor and pausing his forward motion for just a half-second.

Steelos batted the gun aside and hauled the man against the wall by his throat. "Where's the robot that fell from space?"

"I know where it is," the woman yelled. "I'll take you there right now."

"No... she doesn't know shit–" the man squawked from Steelos's grip.

Steelos looked across at the source of the voice. He saw components: machinery, plastics, threads, and fibers, but also flesh parts like limbs, joints, eyes, and an open mouth. All of that suddenly coalesced into... into a truly striking woman. He stared as her blazing magenta eyes filled with hate for the man in his grasp. Without a thought, he clenched his fist crushing the man's windpipe and silenced his screams.

"Take me there." He grabbed the chain securing her to the
bed and ripped it from the post.

She ran to the huge plate glass windows that opened
out onto a balcony. "They're probably outside, evacuating
from the roof. We have to hurry." She stepped outside and
Steelos followed, feeling mildly disturbed at how easily he'd
surrendered command to this person.

Occupying most of the small balcony was a ridiculous looking
aircraft: a pink Cadillac with a gimbaled turbofan mounted on
each corner. The cockpit had the stark, white canopy of an old
convertible car and the interior was pink leather with white
piping and trim. There were two sets of steering wheels and
foot controls, one for each front seat. She leapt in on the left
side and fumbled with the starter button.

"You can fly that?" Steelos felt a distant tug of fear. The
tilting deck had lifted the prow of the *Nevis* clean out of the
water and they were probably a hundred meters above the
ocean's surface by now.

"I drove old-fashioned cars all the time in Macau."

Steelos stepped in, and the turbofans roared to life. The
pleasure-plane lifted unsteadily off the deck and tilted over the
edge of the balcony. A dizzying drop opened before them, a
staggering dive into the foaming sea.

"Name's Casima," she said, gripping the wheel and pushing
it forward.

"Steelos." He fixed his eyes on the drop and felt his stomach
lurch as they plunged over the edge. The fans caught air, and
she revved the motors. The aircraft sailed out from the ship's
side and angled upwards. For a second, they looked back along
the *Nevis*, now separated from the twin catamaran-tankers
that veered off in opposite directions spilling the thousands of
barges out from the broken harbor across the ocean.

Steelos checked his Inner-I. Fierce battles still raged; reports
of the target being sighted on the upper deck glowed red and
urgent. The plane sailed up and over the rim of the ship's

towering superstructure, where he saw the Alliance carrier plane planted firmly in the middle of a helipad, its turbofans blowing down along the tilting deck to prevent it from sliding off.

A gel-trooper maneuvered a gurney up the carrier ramp. Steelos saw his target, carbon-black – the robot he'd been chasing all these weeks, strapped to the gurney and held in some kind of stasis by a wedge of attached machinery.

"Keller!" Casima gasped, pointing down at a terrified looking man entering the carrier's hull. The air below filled with munitions as the remaining Burns closed in around the helipad. "It's leaving. We're too late," she cried as the carrier rose from the deck. An escort of a half-dozen combat craft formed a ring around the carrier, all pointing outwards to engage the Burn forces emerging from the *Nevis*.

Steelos grabbed his own steering wheel and accessed a basic knowledge base about how the craft might fly. "Are you ready to die for that man down there?"

She looked at him, shrugged, let go of the wheel, and raised her hands above her head. "Heck no, but let's go kill those bastards anyway."

Steelos pushed the steering column fully forwards and the craft plunged into a spiraling nosedive.

The gel-trooper released Keller's arm restraint and flung him, bodily, up through a hatch and outside onto the deck of the *Nevis*. "Stay down," warned the trooper as combat craft whirled overhead, high-speed guns buzzing bullet traces across the sky.

Trabian and a group of troopers moved ahead, cowering behind mooring bollards and chain piles. A carrier plane hovered inches above the *Nevis*'s deck, its four turbo-fan engines straining to hold it steady as its loading ramp dropped down to receive Trabian and his fleeing soldiers.

The carrier's ramp was a straight run, but fire came from

all directions. Keller's own guard trooper came under attack, lurching and twisting under the barrage of hits. He was amazed he was still breathing, guessing that the attackers wanted him alive or that somebody's god was watching out for him after all.

A spray of tiny missiles arched up from a hidden deck position before plummeting back down, each one targeting a gel-trooper. Countermeasures and tiny drones hissed outward in defense, but a missile still made it through, smacking into the trooper's chest only inches from Keller. He saw the tiny pencil-sized weapon lodge inside the gel and rolled trying to put distance between himself and the doomed soldier. The explosion was small and contained inside its body. The trooper slumped to the ground, dissolving into a puddle of lumpy ooze.

More gel-troopers closed around him facing outwards forming a last circle of defense. Trabian appeared by his side, thrusting Keller toward the carrier. With one hand he swung Keller up and onto the ramp and the other pushed Ursurrper Gale's gurney into the carrier hold and over to a corner. He saw the gel-troopers falling as enemy troops closed-in.

"Go!" yelled Trabian to the pilot.

Keller grabbed hold of a metal floor loop as the craft angled upwards. Trabian stumbled into the corner and fastened Gale's gurney to a wall mount.

Gazing down the length of the ramp, Keller felt his last hopes of ever seeing Casima again topple away. The hulk of the *Nevis* receded beneath him. He thought of jumping, thought of ending it right now, but his legs were no longer his own, just mush and gel attached to a spineless torso.

He turned back to Gale, laying prone on the containment gurney, pinned rigid by forces emanating from the giant coils and battery pack that comprised the bulk of the gurney. Mounted lower down, behind Gale's head, was a control console; a screen showed status, energy levels, and field strengths. Beneath the screen Keller saw a chunky, military-grade keypad. Recessed into the bottom corner was an off-button, smaller than the other buttons with a raised bezzle and red warning sticker. Keller stumbled closer, finger reaching out to the button. *Sacrifice or suicide?*

His finger trembled and curled away. What was the point if she wasn't here? Would Gale return to the *Nevis* to save her?

Something pink flashed past his vision, plummeting down from above only to pull up at the last instant into a tight parabolic curve and slam through the still open entrance of the carrier's cargo door. A pink aircraft, really a flying car – in its seats he saw a wedge-headed robot or maybe an armored soldier, and there... like some miracle materialized out of his very thoughts, "Casima!" Her face a frozen mask of horror, mouth and eyes wide open.

The carrier lurched under the impact and the sudden dump of extra weight. Keller and Trabian sprawled backwards onto the waist-high bulwark that separated the carrier's hold from its cockpit. With a woosh of engine noise, the pink aircraft jammed into the carrier's entrance, wedging firmly in place as its motors ground metal and came to a smoking halt.

Casima remained lodged upside down hanging from her seat belts, but the metallic soldier had no such restraints; momentum catapulted him out of his seat and into the hold. He rebounded off the ceiling and landed feet-first like a cat ready for combat. A swift up-kick sent Trabian's gun sailing off to the side, but before the soldier could get his own shot off, Trabian barreled into him, and they spun around in a crazy vortex of armored limbs.

Trabian's combat style was thoughtful, precise, stylized blows and kicks that seemed slightly delayed. In comparison, the soldier was a high-speed animation, a whirlwind of violence and berserk zeal. He seemed to have no plan, little coordination, and no regard for his own life. A strategy that the more powerful Trabian appeared stymied and confused by.

The carrier stabilized, absorbing the rogue impact, and Keller crawled across the floor toward Trabian's gun, but the carrier suddenly shifted, angling upwards to accelerate away from the rising prow of the sinking *Nevis*. The gun skittered away back down past the pink airplane and out into open air. Keller's stomach reeled at the sight of the *Nevis* below, nearing vertical as if saluting the world before its long slide down into the ocean depths. Debris and troops flailed along its decks before tumbling off into the sea. *But she's here, and we are nearly safe.*

The soldier straddled Trabian, pounding blows into his face like a jackhammer. Trabian's plastic head ruptured and underneath the topical, plastic facade Keller saw whirling eyeballs inside a gel ball. He nearly gagged as he realized that they were real eyeballs and were attached to what looked like small clumps of living brain matter. Trabian clamped a powerful hand onto the soldier's eyeless faceplate and ripped the helmet free. What Keller saw stunned him. This was no robot, but the face was not that of a human either – flesh and blood for sure, but the eyes held nothing Keller interpreted as life. Icy and detached, this being saw the world in a way Keller never could.

As Trabian's hand groped for a hold on the enemy, the soldier drew a pistol from a back holster and jammed it deep into the gel head. He fired a half-dozen rapid shots, angling each differently into the head and down into the body cavity. Trabian flopped limp, gel and fluid spread across the decking. One of his still twitching eyeballs rode along on the stream.

A bang rang from the cockpit as the pilot turned and fired his pistol. A piece of the soldier's skull fragmented away in a puff of red, but the creature didn't blink, didn't react, just returned fire blowing the pilot's brains over the cockpit window.

"Keller!" He heard Casima scream as she struggled to free herself from the wreckage of the pink flying machine.

The soldier turned the gun on her and fired. Bullets ricocheted off the metalwork as the carrier bucked under heavy turbulence as the autopilot system seized control of the now pilotless aircraft and tried to stabilize.

The soldier stumbled forward, foot lashing out at the pink flyer. It jolted almost tearing free.

"No, please!" Keller found his feet, but the carrier was spiraling madly, throwing filth and body parts into a whirling mix of confusion. The soldier's foot struck again, and the pink flyer ripped free. Casima leapt up and grabbed an overhead securing loop. "Thanks a freakin' bunch, you bastard," she yelled, as the twisted, pink contraption tumbled clear, spinning like a toy toward the disappearing prow of the *Nevis*.

Keller staggered upright again. In the back of his mind he was aware that he felt oddly calm, strangely alive, as if all the fears and freezes of his past years had been just his imagination, just bad dreams. Now he'd awoken to find he was normal again, that same, calm, surgical Keller that he remembered from his youth.

The word *sacrifice* suddenly felt so true, so right as he launched himself bodily at Gale's containment gurney, finger out for the off-button. "For you, my love!"

"No!" he heard Casima yell as he saw the bullet punch out the front of his chest. A fraction later another shattered his shoulder joint. As he fell, the world exited in slow-motion, his severed arm whirling free in a perfect arc, blood spray marking its passage through the air. As his thoughts seeped away to some different realm, he wondered if maybe his finger would still find that off-button. But sadly, he thought, things like that only happened in cartoons and fairytales.

"Please, no!" Casima careened into Steelos as his gun flicked toward her face. They spun to the ground, Casima landing on top, legs curling around his torso as her arms whipped around his neck in a double-fisted headlock.

She screamed. She raged.

She twisted.

She stared past the coldest, deadest eyes she'd ever seen, up into the missing fragment of Steelos's skull. Metal mesh gleamed and glinted through the gap. "What are you?" she cried, realizing that she was fighting some kind of cyborg, a militarized version of herself. But none of that mattered. The two cyborgs fought while the only real human left was sprawled across the deck, shot, maybe dead. She had to get to him.

Steelos's neck bent and cracked but wouldn't break. For a moment it seemed as if he'd lost the ability to fight, perhaps terminally damaged, perhaps the will to keep on killing had deserted him. The lifeless eyes seemed to search her face, scanning, eye, eye, nose, mouth – as if fascinated by the order or the symmetry of the features.

And then they seemed to find her, swimming into focus at a point somewhere inside her skull. The spark of recognition surged the body back to life. Like a mechanical ratchet, he meticulously unclamped Casima's hands and legs from his body and rolled out from beneath her.

She aimed a finger-punch at the hole in his head, but he caught her hand midflight and bent the finger back until it snapped, forcing her down as he rolled his bulk up and over, pinning her to the ground.

"Keller, I need you!" she cried, but she'd seen the hole appear in his back, seen his arm whirl away. There was no Keller anymore. The thought of never again feeling his warmth, his breath, his love, crushed the fight from her. "What's wrong with you, you sick fuck. I helped you... I ... What do you want?" But the creature that called itself Steelos didn't see her and heard nothing of her voice. It seemed fascinated by her bent and broken finger, fascinated enough to grab it with both hands, pulling it up to its face. It began tearing the hand apart, plucking wires, popping out joints, breaking it down into ever smaller components as if seeking the smallest fragment, the very soul of the part of Casima that she thought of as her hand.

And then it was done with the hand and reaching for her face.

"Fucker!" she screamed, suddenly finding her rage. Their arms clashed in midair. Casima landed a clever, arching hit that ruptured Steelos's mouth, sending teeth clattering to the carrier's floor. Her next punch tried to ram his nose back through his skull. But Steelos's bones were thick with reinforcements and his head snapped back, bloody and smiling, now even closer to hers.

In that instant, he was suddenly human again, as if some hidden switch jolted a lost soul back from the dead. "Come on!" he roared. "Fight me! Finish me! Put me out of my fucking misery for good!" He snapped an open-handed chop to her head. Casima shielded her face with the stump of her ruined hand while clawing at his eyes with the other, seeking that rent in his skull. *If I can get a finger in there, then maybe–*

"You've got more than that." Steelos punched a hole in the flooring beside her head as she scampered sideways. She knew it was over, her body felt cold, weak, a trembling gel. Nerve pain ripped through her as components and systems failed to talk and lost their interfaces. *I'm failing, Kell. Forgive me.*

As Steelos's inhuman grip grasped the back of her neck and pushed her once more to the floor, she screamed out loud, "Keller!" Determined that his name should be the last thing that she heard.

Just meters away, Keller was blissfully unaware of anything. What was left of his consciousness had wandered toward the light, wondering what came next. *Old school Heaven, Hell, or maybe there really was a Future-Lord and he'd get to see Casima again in Haven at the end of time.*

"You have another arm you know." The voice pulled him back from the final step.

"Who... what?"

"Another arm. You know, humans... they have two arms and you've lost one of them."

"Are you the Future-Lord?"

The voice remained silent.

"I guess just one part of me talking to another part."

Somebody called his name. Somebody he once loved calling him back, back from a new and more peaceful existence. Back to finish something he'd left behind.

His eyes flicked open, and he tried to raise a hand but nothing happened. *Frozen as usual.* The other hand *did* work though. He marveled as it raised up, almost as if under its own will and power, and waggled in front of his face. "Well look at that! Not shaking!" Blood poured out his mouth, warm and wet down both cheeks. He turned his head, a reflex really, something to try and shake all that annoying blood off his face.

The world was black-and-white, a distant phenomenon far off down a tunnel. He felt the light of the afterlife on his shoulder, urging him to turn, walk. *Walk into the light!*

Down that tunnel, he saw Casima pinned under a dead-faced solider. Her head flopping side to side under a relentless stream of blows. *Poor Casima, she didn't deserve this. All she ever wanted was a good and peaceful life… with him, and maybe a body that wasn't always trying to kill her… in a world that wasn't always trying to maim her or knock her down.*

His longing for her reached out across the space, and to his surprise her magenta eyes found him, and she smiled.

"Fight me, come on, fight me!" screamed the vile humanoid that straddled her. "Come on… kill me, fuck you, kill me. Send me back to the Can."

Keller's dead hand reached across the pool of his own blood toward the machine under the gurney, fingers spider-walking blindly over buttons and cables. The trembling digit found the one he needed, the one recessed to avoid any chance of an accidental press. His fingertip traced around the raised bezel, for a moment it was her lips, and she was leaning in for a kiss. *So easy to sink into that kiss and be gone, forever.*

He heard the hiss of his dying breath leaving his body and formed his numb lips into one last smile. He focused back on those fading, magenta eyes, and then, with one last effort, he jabbed down on the button.

* * *

Steelos didn't hear the soft beeps as the machine counted down the seconds until it powered off, a little warning to those around that whatever it was suppressing was about to be imminently unsuppressed. Even the final, loudest beep never registered on his mind.

Fist poised above Casima, he wanted to deal the death blow, but something was shifting in his mind: *detent*. The bruised, damaged mess quivering just beyond his fist was becoming a woman again, and with that came a mixture of feelings: hatred, confusion, relief. A rush to get as much consequence-free violence in as possible before the constraints of conscience and empathy clicked in. The grim awareness that he would puke his guts out if he ever got to reflect upon what he had done.

His fist paused. The woman's face turned back to him, and he felt the prickle of her gaze, of her soul, trying fruitlessly to connect with his. She looked up through the blood and gore and saw him for what he really was: *A monster!*

He couldn't have that. Couldn't have somebody else knowing. When a memory was just his memory, then it could be forgotten, justified... reconfigured, but if somebody else knew–

A monster that could only be created by... by who? Another monster!

He clicked his knuckles again, ready to punch... but no. Something felt different this time. Had he pushed so far past detent that he'd busted through the berserk, the insanity, and out into something new? But what? Was he fixed? Cured? Normal? Enlightened?

Fascinating eyes. The color, the way they glinted in the light, reflecting the blood smeared inside of the carrier, reflecting him... *the monster.* In the center of that eye was a tiny hole, a tunnel, which led back into a mind, a memory structure haunted by a past, and terrified by something that just hadn't happened, yet.

My future is unlimited, infinite, but why don't I have a past? Not a real past like a real person, just dads and doctors, bugs in mud holes.

Why? Because that's how monsters are created! Edit the memories, shape reality, nourish with lies, and then... then give them a gift: the illusion of control, a switch or a choice, and send them out into the world wearing their choices like shields against whatever morality still existed within.

He reached down to pluck the eyeball free and examine it closer, only vaguely aware of the shadow rising off the gurney behind him. He did see something loom in his peripheral vision as Casima's eyes widened. Her gaze looking past him into some imagined future, one even sadder and more terrifying than this present.

He rolled off her and upright in one fluid motion, eyes taking in his new opponent as it flowed and heaved before him, weaving from a heap of oil-black tendrils up into a bipedal body with a grinning, carbon-black skull perched on a neck made of serpents and coils.

"A monster to slay a monster," Steelos said. He searched his mind, seeking *detent*, the switch that had ruled his life since even before a corrupt doctor and her flaky drug concoctions had messed things up even more.

It's still there!

With joy in his heart, Steelos roared, shrugging off any semblance of humanity, and slamming the switch in his mind from detent to blind, raging berserk.

Eight-hundredths of a second later, that version of Steelos ceased to exist, and never felt, heard, saw, or perceived anything ever again.

CHAPTER 54

Flight and Fight

Ursurper Gale leapt over the bulwark and into the cockpit of the carrier leaving Casima pumping Keller's chest and blowing air into his mouth. Gale knew it was futile. The man's torso had been ripped apart. And weak, fragile human biology didn't survive damage like that, although he gave Keller immense credit for somehow staying alive just long enough to hit the crucial off-switch that freed him.

He launched infiltration routines from his Inner-I into the flight control. A small electronic battle ensued as the less-sophisticated, post-insanity Alliance technology attempted to repulse his attack. A second later his vision lit up with flight parameters, tactical screens, and weapons, as he took over the onboard systems.

Gale's head swam with voices. *Poison!* Somehow Trabian had infected his thoughts. He guessed the hyper-fullerenes he'd been fed were more than just raw chemical compounds. Tiny biomech infiltrators, and, maybe by sheer numbers alone, some had evaded his auto-repair systems and lodged inside of him.

At first the drug had plunged Gale into a black void. A strange convolution of outer-space mixed with the experience of city living, of being surrounded and pressed against a million different people. But, as he fell, Gale felt his repair routines working, seeking and destroying, tracking down anything that attempted to control or communicate with his body that was outside of his machine mind. Gradually his thoughts cleared as if a bunch of separate mental fragments coalesced into one big idea. One that now chose to remain quiet.

Gale set the carrier to a stationary hover two kilometers above the vertical hulk of the *Nevis,* now poised to drop beneath the waves. The air below filled with fumes as the other tankers, platforms, and ships that made up the bulk of the *Nevis* nation ship powered away from the sinking hulk along with a flotilla of thousands of barges and auxiliary craft.

Fleeing was pointless at the moment as the carrier was surrounded by six sleek fighter craft that hung in the air in a ring. Gale's only advantage was uncertainty: The fighters didn't know what had happened. They assumed Trabian was on board but probably had standing orders to annihilate him and the ship if the operation was compromised.

Frantic coms pings came from each direction as they tried to ascertain his status. It would be only seconds before they decided something was wrong and that someone else was in control of the carrier. Gale pondered his options: attack or bail out, drop into the ocean and sink to the bottom. It would be a long swim back to land, but Jett had managed it on his original mission to Coriolis Island.

One of the fighters nudged closer, slowly circling around to the carrier's cockpit for a view of who or what was in control. Something that would be difficult to ascertain through the blood and brain smeared glass.

Gale glanced back at Casima, still crying and pounding on Keller's chest. *I made a promise.*

He pulled up the weapon systems data: dual mini-guns, various missiles and drones. And a bomb. Not just any bomb, a nova-bomb! That made sense. If the mission failed, then everything, including Trabian, was expendable and could be vaporized. His fingers flicked across the door control panel, and he heard the cargo bay doors hiss shut and seal.

The sleek fighter craft hovering in front began backing

away. The pilot had made his assessment. Gale stared into a wall of missile tubes and mini-gun barrels. Someone behind that shiny black flight helmet had their finger on the triggers and was about to blow them out of the sky.

Gale flipped the autopilot off and opened fire with both mini-guns. They made a soft buzzing noise and the enemy fighter vanished in a cloud of debris. At the same instant, Gale cut power to all four turbofans and the carrier plummeted out of the sky straight down toward the sea.

He heard Casima shriek as she, Keller's corpse and whatever remained of the strange and berserk soldier crashed to the ceiling. Nose down, Gale saw the whirling water vortex left behind by the *Nevis* shrouded in smoke and fumes.

His Inner-I lit with warnings: incoming missiles, radar locks, bullet fields. He re-fired the engines as the carrier dropped below the water line and into the vortex. He powered toward the vortex's edge, an imploding, circular waterfall of froth and debris. The carrier's engines cut and folded inside their protective casings as it transformed into its aquatic mode and plunged into the foaming whirlpool, following the massive backend of the *Nevis* into the depths. The carrier's hydro-jet engines whined in protest as Gale tried steering it sideways out from the direct pull of the *Nevis*.

His tactical screens showed the positions of the other enemy fighter planes. Several had followed him down into the vortex while others spiraled the rim waiting for him to resurface. Forward radar showed the receding hulk of the *Nevis* speeding toward its final resting place on the seabed. He eased his descent, riding the curving water, then powered out and away, darkness swamped his front view as they were hauled down farther, one-hundred meters, then two. The damaged seals on the rear cargo door began leaking and the hull of the craft groaned and popped under the mounting pressure.

Gale ran a quick mental simulation, set the detonation program on the nova-bomb, and jettisoned the device out the

rear weapons port. He pulled the steering rudder fully upwards
and revved the hydro-jets into their red-zone. The craft climbed
the impossible gradient, slowly breaking the hold of the vortex.
Behind, he saw four other craft attempting the same breakout
maneuver, along with a small flotilla of torpedoes and guided
munitions. He watched the clock on the bomb tick down as
daylight leeched through the churning waters.

He launched all the carrier's torpedoes sending the enemy
scrambling into their evasive maneuvers. His Inner-I tracked
a dozen drones and sub-munitions in the water around him,
closing fast. More filled the air above.

Gale sent out a small prayer that the sinking nova device
would hold up from the pressure long enough to explode.

It did.

The sea turned white. His screen showed the supersonic
compression waves thundering outwards as a billion tons of
seawater boiled into superheated steam. The four craft behind him
were crushed by the wave, vaporized by the heat. Gale's carrier
nosed up to the surface, only meters ahead of the compression
wave. He broke the surface, and the sea followed him upwards in
a vast, curving dome. He engaged the turbofans and lifted clear of
the surge and the deadly pressure-wave that passed beneath him.

He cut power again, fired all forward missiles at the waiting
enemies, and dropped back through the oncoming shock wave
into the receding mountain of ocean. The red dots in his mind
that marked the enemy craft winked out as they succumbed to
either the shockwave or Gale's missile barrage.

He dropped through roiling steam and foam, finally finding
a cushion in the cold, dense waters far beyond the sunlight.
Gale reengaged the engines and calmly set the autopilot to
take them away from the swirling vortex and the mayhem
surrounding whatever was left of the *Nevis*.

He flopped down in pilot's seat and for the first time looked
at himself reflected in the cockpit glass. At last, he was whole
again, and, more importantly, he was free.

CHAPTER 55

Incarceration

Rex felt he had spent an awful lot of his life incarcerated. In Felix's memory, he was the child, a prisoner of a brutal and unstable mother. After that, detained in a government home for unloved, unwanted boys. As a young adult, he became a captive of his own obsessions, walled behind books and papers, a desk cell in a library, or fixated on computer screens. Later, it was the prison of guilt which led to suicidal depression, drugs, and addiction. The loneliest prison of all, the inside of one's own head, an outcast from society. Since then, he'd become Rex and been held by the Convolvers, by the Sisters of Salvitor, by Reeva and Cyc, by a carbon-black monster from space, and now… he had to admit, he was held by one of his own kind: a plague entity, and this was a very different type of incarceration altogether.

His current prison was a gurney in the middle of a transparent, glass cube. The cube itself sat in a huge, windowless space, possibly an underground bunker. From Rex's limited perspective, it reminded him of a school playground. Except that milling around this playground were not children but plague-sequestered adults, thousands of them. Their ghoulish faces pressed against the glass, leering inside without really seeing, noses and lips squashing, smearing the glass until they fell away and were replaced by those behind.

Rex heard their voices inside his head. *Glowworms!* Each one a spike in a huge communications network that resided on a single substrate that spread across many individual bodies. Day and night they battered his mind, plucking at neural connections like relentless fingers on overtight knots. They deceived his senses, sending impressions of smell and touch, creeping sensations and stenches, prickling fingers, and distant voices. But he was Rex, the plague, the Crucible, and he was not going to crumble, not going to be breached.

Just existing and observing, as he now did, Rex realized there were two basic types of memory experience that interested Hmech. The first was all those subjective experiences that made him Rex, the emotions, loves and likes, the stories he told, and the stuff he believed.

The second flavor was everything outside of that. The things he'd seen and heard, the tunes, smells, and tastes, that all felt pretty similar no matter what mind they were hijacked from. One person's image of Transit Mountain was very much like another's, a kind of Platonic form that defined the real object in a limited but sensory kind of way.

Once separated from their host's minds, these forms became part of the great wash of experiences that comprised the network itself, each contributing and reinforcing an existing view. These memes created Del's convolution-space. Effectively, Hmech had crowdsourced virtual reality by blowing-up minds and rebuilding the useful bits back into a different whole. A clever way to construct a perfect, imaginary copy of the world without having to actually build anything at all.

Rex felt pleased with his observations and hoped that Del could see them too, and maybe put them to good use.

The continuous mental probing was bad enough, but harder to take were the full-on assaults that occurred numerous times each day. The door to the glass cell buzzed open and figures tumbled inside, cramming into the tiny space as if their only purpose was to steal all his oxygen. Their hands pushed into his body and face, stifling him, their fingers entering places fingers should never enter.

The mental attacks became harder then, closer, no glass or distance to dampen the effects. The real world took on fuzzy edges, and Rex glimpsed the portals to those 'other' worlds, the ones constructed by Hmech and designed to entrap and disassemble a weakened mind.

As he peeked at those tempting worlds, Rex realized that they were just like reality – some so close it would be hard to tell that they were false and made up by Hmech. Maybe when inside it would be alright, kind of like Haven, a utopia; one could even forget that this was not real. And besides, reality was overrated. His experience of reality had been largely terrible. Maybe he deserved this escape. This final and eternal resting place.

This… this… *damnation!*

No! I am Rex. I am Glow. He steeled his resolve for the thousandth time and focused his attention away from portals and fuzzy edges, back to the truth of the here and now. "They are getting to me, Del. Eventually they'll win."

He sensed nothing from Del. Maybe he'd retreated from existence, either roaming the halls of his sacred Star-River or lost in Hmech's convolution-space. Perhaps he'd decohered, broken apart, under the assault of his own glowworms.

"Come back, Del. I don't know how to defeat this on my own."

He wondered why they didn't just knock him offline, like the Sisters had, using an electromagnetic pulse. Perhaps Hmech needed him conscious, that whole, intact structure that he could capture as a single entity, and not as useless fragments? Conscious, he was more than the sum of his parts, an ongoing narrative with intent and meaning. But broken apart, he was random words from a page, no narrative at all.

He tried jousting back at the network, probing Hmech to see and feel what he truly was. He sensed that he was something other than a dog mind, not even an ape like Cyc, something different, and that they didn't yet comprehend each other.

Act crazy. Act dead! Run like Hell. Fight! He laughed at the naïve simplicity of his old mantra. Nothing worked here – even fight was only temporary resistance. *Defend, hide, cohere… better, but still no. Believe?*

Believe in Rex!

He felt the old dog not in his soul but *as* his soul. The loyal pack member surging from under the table to attack the lich. Spinning circles in the Forever Friends Rescue Sanctuary yard, shovel in hand, defending Mira and Mrs O. and the rest of the pack. Loyal Rex. Good boy Rex. The crucible Rex!

He took a deep breath, forced a grin to his face, and let the dog run loose, not as a shepherd, corralling lost souls into a pen, but as a defender, a sentinel, a force on the network that pushed back the invaders or laced their attention with distractions. He felt the shift, the easing of pressure as the hands left his body and the dull lights of sequestered minds refocused elsewhere. Through waning willpower, he pushed the people back out of the glass cell. As the final one exited, the door slammed, and the mental attacks dropped from a hollering crowd to an insidious whisper.

He imagined Hmech watching from the background, slow clapping, nodding approval. *Well played, Rex. Lesson learned. Next, I'll try something new.*

The faces pressed back to the glass, the mental probes began again, building to the next moment the door burst open and Hmech's wave came blundering in.

CHAPTER 56

Born Again

Jorben stood at the bus stop just outside Arlen, hands in pockets, waiting for the familiar sound of the approaching engine. It all felt so normal. As if he'd done this his whole life. But in reality it was just a few days, although it seemed so much longer.

Still fresh and sweet in his mind was the memory of him collapsing outside the Convolver Enclave, of his promise to be there for Leal if he made it back in a new body, and, of course, if he remembered who he and she were.

As promised, she'd been there when he awoke. He'd slithered out from the hospital room like an oiled fish, convinced that Knoss would stop him. Guards would arrest him for his betrayal on Transit Mountain. But nothing. Nobody even acknowledged his continued existence. As he left the Enclave, arm-in-arm with Leal, a message had appeared in his Inner-I from Knoss. "Your mind is your own, Jorben."

Was that really just days ago? No, weeks, maybe months. Prosaic, working life, normal life, was like that. Each day the same. Days rolled into years. A Burn could easily lose track of his allotted time.

And so, here he was, living with Leal and the children. *Crazy!* Who in their right mind would take on an unstable, murderous mind housed in a military-grade body? But then he'd largely made peace with the idea that maybe Steelos was the criminal. Steelos was executed. Steelos was a horrible violent person. And he, Jorben, was a copy-and-trimmed version of Steelos. An entity not responsible for those actions. He wondered if the Future Lord would see it that way. His path to redemption was now clear, released from his service to Knoss and the Enclave, he just had to lead a normal life.

The bus turned the corner at the end of the street and bumbled slowly toward him through a haze of morning mirages and desert dust. He shuffled his feet in anticipation. Leal had found the job opening at Transit Mountain only days after he moved in. He didn't mind the work. Wanted to work, to be physically active and contribute to their new life together. The job was easy, mainly standing around guarding supplies, guarding doorways or corridors. The monotony was broken by spells of intense loading, unloading, carrying, storing, and hauling boxes and crates up and down ladders. His memories of recruiting in the Fringe, of fighting on Transit Mountain, of the journey to Elford City and all its revelations, had largely smoothed over in his thoughts. Like a barely remembered dream that he'd spoken about and embellished, so that in his mind it was really just a tall tale, a fun yarn to spin at parties... if he ever went to such things.

The bus drew close, and he glanced back up the street, imagining the sequence of turns that would take him back to Leal's house. Wondering what he'd find back there if he ignored the bus and went on home. The last few days he'd come back from work and sensed someone else had been there. When he confronted Leal, she admitted Nathan had popped by to check on her. Nathan was worried about her. He'd shaken that off, told himself he was being stupid, paranoid even. After all, how could a friend not be worried based on the strange life choices Leal had made?

And then–

Last night, Nathan's car had passed him as he walked from

the bus stop, coming the other way, possibly from his home. The slimy man had hunched down in his seat, thinking Jorben couldn't see, but he saw. He felt a prickle of rage but breathed it back down. He shouldn't be upset; Nathan had helped Leal, and in the end, there seemed to be nothing terrible about the man other than some weird beliefs and an overly controlling nature.

The bus squealed to a halt next to him and the door hissed open. No driver, automatic, it waited for him to step inside and wave his Alliance pass at the scanner. His feet shuffled again, pointing back home, then onto the bus... back home or–

"Sir?" A mechanical voice enquired. "Do you wish to take this bus?"

"Not really," Jorben said stepping onboard. The door hissed shut and another day of guarding and laboring loomed ahead. *Normal life.*

CHAPTER 57

Hidden Bliss

Rex's days of captivity blurred into one single long session of pain. A constant vigil. Like being on watch and not being allowed to fall asleep. His head nodded. His window on the world faded. And gently he spiraled down, down to where the edges of the world grew fuzzy, reality faded into a new, identical reality, right there underneath!

"Wake up, Rex! No sleeping on the job."

"So you're back, then," Rex jolted alert, his mind turning away from the edge of the underworld he'd so nearly fallen into once again. "Have you learned anything?"

"He has a tool," Del said. "An algorithm, something I don't yet understand. Once inside convolution-space you are vulnerable. Somehow it reads you, pulls you to pieces making you part of the network. I can't know how it works until I am inside. And I'm scared, Rex, scared to go in, to not be ready, to never see the real world ever again."

"It's called *Damnation*, Del. Get over it."

Suddenly Goliath was beside him and a grassy plane stretched out before his gaze. "No!" Rex tried to open his eyes, but the grass was still there.

"It's okay," Del said. "I got you, buddy. This is my world. The Star-River. We can hide here for a while."

But who's guarding the house?

Rex let go and ran, feeling the wind and grass, seeds tickling his ears and eyes. The restraints of real life fell away, and, achingly slowly, he eased upright, hands exploring his ribs and bones and jutting... *what... what is this?* Nubs of material growing out from his shoulders and elbows, hard under his skin, stakes and spikes growing from his bones. "What's happening?"

"Another of Hmech's new algorithms, loaded into your body network by the plague. Your Glow nodes can now take carbon leached from your body or your diet or from spent Glow or Simmorta and repurpose it into structural elements inside your body, like a secondary skeleton."

"I'm becoming one of those wireframe things." Rex's mind filled with the horrific visions of the shimmering energy creatures stalking the land, tatters of their host's flesh still dangling from their sleek, metallic frames.

"Now you see exactly how the plague takes us over and replaces us, Rex. Now you see what I fight to prevent and how we must win."

He snapped awake as the cell door crashed open, but instead of a horde of people, he saw Sister-Zero, her face plate a blank of static. She freed his arms and legs. He lunged at her, just wanting to kill the traitor, and for a surprising second he almost overpowered her until she recovered her poise, and locked him in a painful shoulder hold. She marched him out of the cell, across the creepy, but now deserted playground, and through a door into a roughhewn basalt tunnel. Her grip on him never slipped, never yielded; in fact, it ratcheted tighter as if she were determined to squeeze all the blood from his body.

In such close proximity he was easily able to reach across Hmech's network to her mind. He saw her now through one of the fuzzy-edged portals, a single room in some great castle that held everything she once was. Something insidious lived in that room, something that was still in the process of devouring Sister-Zero's thoughts and turning them into Hmech's reusable memes.

As the thing inside her stirred, Rex recoiled in horror, back into his own reality. But before he left he caught a glimpse of something tiny, something private. Her own miniature Rex, a mouse-like personality routine, complete and pristine, something the Sisters were clearly working on perfecting. A way of sealing off a miniscule part of the machine mind behind a firewall, and at the same time making it so small, so uninteresting, that Hmech's algorithms rolled right over it, ignored it, and went on their busy way.

For an instant they connected, and the compact persona opened to him, a flash glimpse of something designed to show him hope, to keep him fighting.

What was that?

A bomb? A nova-bomb?

Would the Sisters really dare to plant such an infiltrator into the heart of Hmech's empire? He felt a malign joy, the hope of a brief flash of white incineration, and then peace. No yammering void... nothing. "Yes," he mouthed silently, "please, Sister, please."

Back in reality, he pushed him into a room and the door slammed shut. He stood facing a small man in grand attire who swept toward him like a king in stately robes. His hair was short and brown and sawn-off in a straight line around his head. Fearless bright brown eyes regarded Rex from his pudgy, greyish-pink face. Tiny black lines radiated like spokes from his pupils. "Rex and Del," he nodded a greeting. "I am Hmech."

A power exuded from the man. Not a physical presence but something that held a great weight of information, of confidence, a power to control that only the network overseer could possess. Rex felt any fight vanish from his body and sank into a heap on the ground.

"You are fascinating," Hmech whispered. "A disparate mass of thought processes, inside a hardened shell, protecting Del and his GFC secrets. A man who clings to his Star-River as if it were a prophetical miracle."

"How do you know so much about us?" Rex's mouth moved although he felt Del was actually speaking.

Hmech stepped closer. Rex felt the network field overlap. This was a different kind of attack, strong, but focused, pinning him bodily while leaving his mind free and clear.

"We are not so different, you and I, Rex. Instead of a guard dog, I have a child, a curious and insatiable child, who just wants to fill its mind with life's new experiences."

"What do you want from me then?"

"Our destiny grows within you now, Rex. You can feel it." He reached out and massaged Rex's shoulder. The nub of material growing from his bones ground against the flesh, making him wince. "These creatures possess copies of their host's minds, their knowledge and experience, organized and categorized with none of the messy emotions of consciousness.

"These new bodies are experimental, made from carbon fibers and simple fullerenes, a dozen times the strength of steel. Hyper-fullerenes are an order of magnitude stronger still, but we can only get those in useful quantities using GFC picoforms, that elusive manufacturing technology that may only exist now inside of Del's mind. Imagine the power of these creatures, unstoppable forces with minds controlled by their world view, that are, in turn, controlled entirely by me.

"As much of a curiosity as you are, Rex, you are of little worth compared with Del. If he won't work with me then I need his mind dismantled and sequestered into my algorithms. Give me him and I'll surgically remove the Star-River and let you go. Free to eat and run and shit and whatever it is you dogs do."

Rex nodded. Of course it was all about the picoforms, that was all anyone really wanted; the ultimate combat machine coupled to the ultimate subservient mind.

"What do you think, Del?" he asked out loud.

I think he kills you and tears my mind into fragments to get everything he wants.

Rex looked around the room, noticing for the first time the mass of humans surrounding them. All had bumps on their joints, many much larger than his, stretching the fabric of their clothes. Some had even pierced through as translucent black needles. The ones with the largest protrusions had the deadest faces. Their eyes held no shine. "Del seems to think it's a bad idea and I kind of agree," he said.

Hmech twitched and Rex flinched expecting to be struck or attacked by another psychic wave, but instead he leaned in and whispered in his ear. "I could even load your mind into a dog, Rex. Just imagine, having one of those sleek, immortal bodies. What do they call them? Ah yes, forever friends. Maybe we could drop you off with that delightful Mrs O. and you could live out eternity surrounded by your own kind."

Rex could do nothing but sob as he visualized the old lady and her dogs being dragged away by Hmech, and all because of him.

"It doesn't have to be that way, Rex." Hmech's voice became gentle and distant. "My standard infiltration methods have failed, but I have many others. I can simply knock you out using an EMP, or I can isolate each node that comprises you and surgically remove it – an option that might take months and truly try my patience. And such brute-force options risk damaging Del's valuable memory. Imagine how one crucial fact going missing could cost me years in research." Hmech turned away and Rex felt his grip relax. Other arms grasped him from behind, stopping him collapsing to the ground. "I'll leave you to consider my offer, Rex, talk it over with your friends." Hmech laughed, "I hope you do the right thing, and soon. I am not a patient person."

CHAPTER 58

Lament

Casima perceived little of the battle raging around her. Keller was gone and nothing she could do was bringing him back. She'd found a medi-pack and hooked it into a vein but with no pulse the nanomeds were slow to diffuse, and she knew in her heart that even they couldn't fix this amount of damage.

She cradled his head, rocking him in her arms, but the grief was beyond mere crying and tears. His eyes still held something, an evanescent sparkle that faded like a distant sunset. A smile that suggested he knew she was safe. Even though in her mind she accepted that she wouldn't make it far in this crazy world with no meds and Gale at the helm of her existence.

As the glow in his eyes withered, the ship dropped into a nosedive, and they were hurled around the carrier's cargo bay. She clutched him tighter with her single, functional hand as loose parts, machinery and fragments of Steelos's still warm corpse clattered and splashed around her. She made sure the medical package stayed attached to Keller's arm, and together they simply rolled through the filth, crashing from roof, to floor, wall to wall like brazen lovers. Her mind drifted back to those precious moments in the lab, becoming so lost in them that she almost believed them to be real. But when she opened her eyes, Keller was still dead.

The lights faltered, darkness engulfed them, and then came

the light of a nuclear fire. *I'm coming Kell. I'm coming!* The blazing white seemed to pierce the skin of the carrier, on through her eyelids like fire cleansing her soul.

She rushed towards the light, but, like hope itself, the light faded, and after the insane ride ended and near darkness returned, she was left gazing into Keller's glassy eyes. He really was gone, and she was truly alone in the world.

She stroked his eyelids closed with a pair of gentle fingers, and the tears finally came, dripping down onto his face.

A shadow came over her and she looked up to see Gale standing over them. He looked different. The crazy limbs and tentacles had all folded back into a neat, compact bipedal body, and his crystal skull was now covered in knots of fiber that formed a simple face.

"Can we get this over with?" she asked, her voice devoid of any tone. "Just finish it."

"I promised him I'd keep you safe."

"Do robots keep promises?"

"Maybe, but I am not a robot."

She worked her way along a row of storage lockers until she found a blanket and wrapped it around Keller, his face poking out of the end. She laid him on the gurney which was still miraculously attached to the carrier wall.

"What do you need, Casima?" Gale asked.

"I need him back."

"I don't know how to do that."

"All my life, nobody wanted me. The unwanted girl in a family of boys. And then even they were gone, and I was just a freak, a nobody, a… a piece of meat to be slapped around, used up, and thrown away. But I made something of myself, met Keller, and we helped each other. Together, we were something special."

Gale nodded. "I believe he valued your life over his own."

"Then I want what you have – power. I want never to have anyone pin me down helpless again. Or drag away my beloved in front of my eyes. I never want to be held in some asshole's prison or hostage by some... some–" She waved a dismissive hand at Gale.

Gale backed away and climbed over into the cockpit. "I'm going to Coriolis Island. You can come with me, or I can leave you somewhere on the way."

"Why there?"

Gale shrugged, something Casima assumed a robot just wouldn't do. "Many reasons. Transit Mountain's mass-driver, unfinished business. The last known whereabouts of my creator."

"Can you swing past Macau on the way?" Gale stared at her as if trying to figure out if she was serious. She shook her head and let out a bitter laugh. "Great! A pilgrimage to Coriolis Island then." Gale adjusted the controls on the carrier, and she felt it turn and accelerate.

"I've been examining news feeds," said Gale. "The Alliance has taken control of the Coriolis mass-driver. It's an opportunity for me to get back into orbit."

"The Alliance hates us, and they want to dismantle you. Plus, I doubt they're giving away free rides."

"Continued existence has never been an easy prospect for me either, Casima."

She sighed. "Okay then, just go." She looked across at Keller. "But first we need to find somewhere suitable for a burial." She nearly said 'to bury him' but knew that was not really true. As she folded herself around Keller, she felt the ice in her veins, and the jangling nerve pain. Her cybernetics hummed with disfunction. A strange living rigor mortis of organ and mechanical failure tightened her around Keller like a cocoon. *Not bury him*, she thought, now feeling warmly resigned and content. *Bury us.*

CHAPTER 59

Mass Driver

A docile Rex followed Hmech down into the bowels of Transit Mountain. They boarded a magnetic train that whisked them around sharp banking curves. Rex's ears popped and his neck strained against the acceleration as the metal walls blurred past. His mind was silent. No sign of Del stirring trouble inside. *Do you know that I'm going to betray you soon? To mentally fold and hand the keys to the castle over to Hmech.*

Sister-Zero's revelation about the concealed bomb had played on his mind the last few days, even as he'd tried to suppress any such thoughts. At first, he'd seen it as a sign, a glimmer of hope that there was an end, something beyond damnation, but as he considered it more, then what was the point of holding out? Maybe the bomb only went off when he collapsed. A form of dead-man's switch. Why wait? Why prolong the agony, unless there was some reason, something else he was supposed to do first?

They emerged into a staggeringly large cavern filled with what looked like the end of a railway line: The mass driver, an electromagnetic railgun that swept upwards on a parabolic curve from the flat rest where he stood to vertical as it reached the gun barrel exit at the top of Transit Mountain.

The whole contraption started here, at a spring-loaded buffer. Rex stood gazing down the line, a full kilometer long before tilting upwards and vanishing through the cavern ceiling. Field coils hummed with energy along the rails and a stack of sleek, steely capsules hung from gantries, awaiting their turn to launch.

Here, dull-eyed people moved slowly but with purpose under Hmech's relentless sequestration. Viewing windows looked down on the whole scene. The people there had clearer eyes. Perhaps they still had minds.

"Welcome to my investment in Earth's future." Hmech opened his arms encompassing the whole cavern. "I'm sure Del remembers back to the pre-Nova-Insanity, pre-space-elevator days and this piece of innovative machinery. Maybe Del even worked on it back when he was a young, fired-up engineer, devoted to mankind's galactic expansion."

Rex stood waiting for Del's retort, but nothing came. He noticed that Hmech had interesting onion-like layers of security surrounding him at all times, even on the train. The closest guards were a thick cluster of lightly armed humans and robots, including Sister-Zero. He assumed these were the easiest minds to dominate, the utterly loyal troops that he could control perfectly. Then there was a gap and a ring of what appeared to be cyborgs, their bodies and faces hidden under wraps and cloaks. Their movements betrayed their nature; jerky, fast actions followed by statue stillness. Maybe they were the wireframe creatures from his nightmares, hiding from view so as not to alarm visitors or spark rebellious notions in those that still had their own thoughts.

The outer layer hung back on the periphery, the tough skin of the onion, a motley bunch of heavyset humans in military uniforms. They lounged around cleaning and checking their guns. An elite outer guard not as trusted as the inner circle. The shell of the nut, the firewall between Hmech and outside reality.

"Our first test runs have gone very well," Hmech said. "Not quite the power we need to reach geostationary orbit. I'm sure Del will appreciate the difficulties of tuning the system harmonics to resonate correctly. The pulse timing of the coils is critical, and the materials balance inside the launch capsules is something we are still experimenting with.

"And then there's the nose heatshield which burns up as the capsule leaves the vacuum tube and plunges through the atmosphere. Too much shielding is inefficient, too little and the capsule fries. The rate of burn is key. A perfect launch will have close to zero shield-mass as it leaves the atmosphere." He pointed to a huge screen showing a graph covered in colored dots. "Each node is a test launch. A point of education from which we learn and improve our performance."

They sauntered over to the end zone buffer and Hmech looked up at a capsule dangling from the overhead gantry. "This one is our next… volunteer. In fact, it leaves imminently."

He waved a hand at the watching crane-crew, who jumped to attention and began lowering the capsule. It slipped slowly down and onto the rail and decoupled from the crane. A hum of power filled the cavern and the capsule rose an inch above the lines. Hmech reached down and popped open a rectangular door flap on the top. Rex saw a coffin-sized space, enough for a payload the size of a small person.

"Why don't you hop down into there, try it out for size." Hmech pointed down into the tiny space.

Rex backed away. Just looking into that cramped coffin made his skin crawl.

"I really do insist," said Hmech as hands grabbed Rex from each side lifting him off the ground and dumping him into the opening. All four of Rex's limbs clung to the edge like a cat resisting its travel box. "If you won't give me the informational access I need, then you are of no use to me. I might as well get some experimental value out of you instead."

Rex felt the capsule bob up and down on the magnetic field as he yelled and clawed at the surrounding faces, but the hands worked against him as a coordinated group. More joined the fight, two for each limb, prying his body free and cramming him into the tiny space. The lid slammed shut, its curved metal surface squashing his nose against his face, hands pinned hard to his sides. He couldn't even turn his head.

"Commence firing countdown," Hmech said.

Words tumbled out of Rex's mouth, a senseless blur of phonemes and pleadings. "Quiet down," he heard Del suddenly back in his head. "He's not going to fire. He wants picoforms, remember?"

But supposing Hmech had picoforms? Maybe he'd found some amongst the GFC wreckage, or they'd made one of their own design. Perhaps they didn't need Del anymore—

He thrashed, voice rising hysterically. Del was yelling too. Hmech spoke loud and clear from outside. "You ever wonder how tough you are as a somanetic being, Rex? How long those Glow nodes will keep you alive in space, rotting, confined, unable to even move or scratch or breathe. Just rotting, Rex, eternally rotting in your own putrid little atmosphere..."

He felt himself coming apart. The darkness filled with fuzzy-edged portals to safer places: John and Millie's house, the rescue sanctuary, a wonderful castle full of memories and waiting friends. *All fake. All Hmech!*

A mechanical voice talked over Hmech's calm words. "Five... Four..."

He shrieked and twisted, feeling his neck cramping, body dissolving, falling, on through the yammering void to whatever virtual world Hmech had waiting.

"Three..."

"Two..."

Foaming mouth... the dog was running now, heading off across the grass toward the sun as he lost his mind, floating free.

No, Rex. No! Del implored. *Hold on just a bit longer.*

"One..."

And then he was free, tumbling out of the capsule, gasping

in air as Hmech's guards laughed and slapped each other's backs. "All just a bit of fun!" Hmech chuckled as Rex staggered to his feet, surprised to find that he was laughing as well. Somehow everybody was friends now and he felt lighter, more alive, colors brighter, and so much more real–

It's a lie, Rex. Del said. *A Convolution-space creation. Deny it. Refuse it. See only what's real.*

And suddenly he was back inside the coffin, grinding elbows into the walls, straining at the impossible bonds. *I am Rex. I am the crucible.*

"Zero!"

The attack ceased. The door popped open, and Rex spilled out, eyes fighting the lights, vomit clung to his chin and matted his hair. He felt so sick, so defeated, that this had to be real.

Nearby Hmech stood laughing. "Rex, you know how this farce ends, and yet you still resist me."

Rex rolled on to his back. "Fire!" yelled Hmech. The power fields ramped like a hysterical jet engine and the capsule roared off down the rail. Two seconds later a muffled bang hit his ears as it cracked the sound barrier, followed by a pop as it breached the field separating the air-filled tube from the vacuum pipe. The capsule tilted upwards and began its climb up the ten-thousand-meter mountain. Images on screens around the cavern showed it roaring past cameras and sensor points, numbers rose higher as the whole mountain hummed in mechanical resonance.

"Remarkable isn't it," Hmech said as the capsule burst from the mountain's peak into the thinning air, its nose a glow of orange-red fire.

As they watched the screens, it made it up to the edge of space, then carried on, slow and silent as it slipped through the blackness, no energy required, possessing all the momentum it needed to reach orbit.

Cheers went up around the cavern as announcers proclaimed a successful launch. Rex watched as the first green dot appeared on Hmech's graph. "Congratulations on witnessing history," Hmech said, patting Rex's shoulder as he sat mopping the vomit off his face. "Maybe on the next launch you will play an even bigger role."

CHAPTER 6

Funeral

Two trails of footprints wound across the fine grey pumice sand of the beach. One set meandered, taking the longer route with small, irregular steps, almost deliberately hanging back from the other set whose strides were even, perfectly measured, twice as long, straight and direct. The sand's color matched the clouds, and the churning sea, and Casima's grim mood.

"What did you do to me?" Casima stumbled as she focused on her feet while waving the stump of her shattered hand around in front of her face. She carried the blanket-wrapped body of her love over her shoulder. Keller's corpse felt oddly light and her body uncannily strong.

"I took the medi-pack off Keller and put it on you," Gale said. "He didn't need it anymore. Then I infiltrated your cybernetic systems, tuned them, added some military-spec upgrade patches. Everything should work together for a while."

"You infiltrated me." She expected a rise of anger, but nothing seemed to matter. She was disappointed when she awoke, alive, when the carrier landed, but surprisingly relieved she wasn't inside some sealed coffin with Keller.

They'd flown for hours, skimming the ocean surface until Gale found the western edge of Coriolis Island, a long way from the city or any population centers. He guided the carrier into one of the many small coves. The cliffs towered over the beach, their slow erosion and sudden catastrophic collapses forming the sands that had begun the millennia-long process of piling into dunes.

"They will be coming for us," Gale announced. "We must move inland and blend with the crowds."

Blend? she thought. A magenta-eyed cyborg and a close approximation of the Grim Reaper. Oh yes, they would blend right in.

They left the carrier under a rocky overhang and scouted along the beach, seeking a suitable burial site. A few hundred meters in, they climbed up onto a cliff ledge that led to a quiet inland valley looking back out over the sea. "Don't you dare touch him," she snapped when Gale offered to carry Keller.

Grey rock and dirt in all directions. Land set aside for future development, never farmed or terraformed, like lunar regolith. Keller always wanted to go into space, but never showed any desire to go to the moon or to be buried there. There was life, though: bird droppings and dust gathered in cracks and rills, and, over the years, seeds had taken root. Tiny green shoots wormed their way out of every crevasse like little fingers of denial, demanding a hold on the world, a silent display that announced life's arrival even into this harshest of realms.

"This will do," she said, and laid Keller on the ground. "I think he'd kind of like it here. Peaceful. No people or hospitals or–" The words turned to ash in her throat. A raised bump of rock resembled an altar. Around its base, gnarled leaves and tiny flowers bowed in supplication. "Yes. This is the spot."

She stepped back as Gale tore into the rock with his hands, clawing basalt aside like wet sand. In seconds he burrowed out a rectangle as long and wide as a man and deep enough for Casima to stand in and not see out. She placed Keller carefully next to the grave and dropped down into the pit, reaching up and easing him in after her as Gale shuffled backwards, his own head bowed in what looked like respect. She arranged Keller in a comfortable sideways pose, as if he was curled in their bed, sleeping, then carefully rolled herself up and out of the pit.

Her hand found the hidden fold at her waist, and she pulled out the wad of creased, torn photos and thumbed through to the end where she stood grinning and besotted next to Keller, her new friend. "There's nobody left in here," she said. "All gone." She twitched as if to throw the photos into the grave. Instead, she folded them back into her clothes.

They stood side-by-side gazing down, hands automatically taking the form of a prayer. "I want to say something, but I just don't know what," she said.

"Which god do you worship? I have a database of human wisdom and traditions."

She shrugged. "Not sure I ever believed in one, let alone worshipped one." She looked up as the sun tried to peek through the clouds, sending columns of gods-light down over the sea. She focused on the light rays, the wind, and the song of distant birds, letting nature convey the words that she could not find. "Goodbye my love." She dropped a handful of dust into the grave and stepped away leaving Gale to fill the hole.

Seconds later, he loomed silently behind her. "It is done."

"Do you believe in gods and afterlives?" she asked.

"I despise the idea of non-existence as much as any creature."

"You've been up there." She nodded at the sky. "Up in space. Didn't you see something... anything?"

"No ghosts, no spirits, no aliens. As far as I can tell, the Universe is empty. All that lives, breathes, and thinks is here."

"That's pretty poetic for a killer robot." She managed a somber smile. "I think that would have been a good prayer. One that Keller would have liked." She walked slowly back to the beach kicking at the sand as if each grain were the object of her bitterness. "If you make it back into space, will you remember him for me?"

"Yes, I will remember him for you."

She nodded her approval. "Where are we going next?"

"I think we are about to find out."

She stopped as she noticed a man sitting on the beach. Cloaked in a multi-colored checkered blanket, he sat hunched against the wind, looking up at them as they approached.

Gale moved out in front of Casima and confronted the man, who's features remained calm and virtuous, with lips set in a somber greeting.

"My condolences on your loss." He nodded politely. "I am Braer, and I have come from the Convolver Enclave on the wishes of Knoss to tell you about the wonders that await you in your coming life in Haven at the end of all time."

"What do you know about this?" she demanded, pointing back at the grave. "Who did this to my Keller?"

Braer looked confused. "I have no information about this, but Knoss may be able to help." He glanced at his watch. His sympathy seemed to wash away replaced by a mechanical, pragmatic calm. "The Alliance will be here soon. I suggest coming with me to the Enclave." He turned and addressed Gale, oddly unfazed by his first encounter with the voidian. "Our enlightened leader, Knoss, has a proposition for you, Ursurper. A deal to get you back into space." He turned back to Casima, clearly more nervous of her than of the carbon-black monstrosity. "You should come too. I believe you will find the Convolvers are most sympathetic to your cause."

"What do you know of my cause?"

Braer reached up to his forehead and to Casima's shock it dropped away into his hand like an access panel. Beneath, she saw the mechanisms that bunched his facial muscles and moved his eyeballs. Behind it all lay circuit modules and tiny, winking lights. "I was fully human at birth, but injury and disease made my flesh-and-blood body unsustainable. The Convolvers helped me to migrate my essence into an artificial substrate. We can do this for you too, Casima."

Her mouth dropped open as she struggled for words before turning back and pointing at Keller's grave. "What about him?"

Braer shook his head. "We can't raise the dead. Your faith needs to be with the Future-Lord."

She turned away, pondering the long, dangerous walk across Coriolis Island to the city. And then what? A life on the streets? Become a guide?

Gale flowed into action and moved toward the carrier back on the beach. "I'll come with you," he said.

Casima sighed and looked over to where Keller was buried. *What should I do, my love?* The wind said nothing, neither did the birds or the breakers crashing up the beach. *You, me, and the Future-Lord makes three?*

She turned and followed Gale. "You still protecting me?" she asked him, when Braer was out of earshot.

"I am."

She kicked the sand, hard. "Fine, then I'll come."

CHAPTER 61

The Enclave

A sudden change of direction lurched Casima awake. Her mind felt hollow, all emotion gouged out by some razor-edged spoon and dumped back on that grey beach where Keller lay under six feet of pumice sand.

The carrier dropped from the edge of the atmosphere after its short, arching flight across Coriolis Island. Transit Mountain looked like a wasp's nest, its airspace abuzz with patrol craft, fighters and material haulers, angry dots circling their newly acquired nest.

She stared as a plume of smoke erupted from the top of the mountain and a flaming capsule headed for the heavens leaving a contrail of dissolving heatshield in its wake.

She heard the boom. Shook her head. "You want to ride on that?" she asked Gale who seemed intent on watching the autopilot controls as Braer remotely operated their craft down to the Convolver Enclave.

They came in about halfway up the massive spiraling structure. Casima's eyes were drawn to the levels above that tapered to a frighteningly thin point devoid of any windows. The craft jolted as the Enclave's air traffic control took over the landing, guiding them onto a pad just below the spire. Dozens of planes and carriers were lined up across landing strips or hanging from transport cranes.

The spire was covered in transparent observation blisters and tiny turrets with needle-like gun barrels that tracked their motion as they arrived. A network of pylons sprouted outwards at odd angles. They crackled with energy that played games with the air, lensing and warping the world into shimmering mirages.

"We're never leaving this place alive," she muttered. Gale turned and looked at her, and for a single second she thought he was going to say something reassuring. *Of course not*, she thought, looking into Gale's beady, black eyes. *Is he even alive?*

The carrier touched down. Its door opened and a burst of frigid air caught Casima by surprise. She could adjust the senses on her cyborg limbs to not feel the chill, but the real parts of her flesh erupted in goosebumps as the cold seeped in. She stepped out onto the shiny, grey landing pad, clutching her shattered hand like a comfort toy. A set of white lines flickered on and off, guiding them to a gaping hole in the side of the spire.

"Good luck," Gale said, as he stood on the carrier's ramp, eyeing his surroundings. In that moment, Casima thought he looked vulnerable, almost human in his hunched, bipedal form with makeshift clothes spun from his surface fibers.

Braer stepped out of his own aircraft and joined them, nodding a curt acknowledgement at their safe arrival. He led the way forward into a steely corridor. Blowers hummed and groaned as they pumped warm air through the tunnels which escaped into the cold outside like the steamy breath of some dreaming monster.

The tunnel led straight to a great hall crisscrossed with thick tubes that sprouted from the floor then rose up through tangled knots to a distant vanishing point way up in the roof. The pipes pulsed gently as if sucking nutrients from a store residing in the levels below their feet.

At the head of the room towered a throne with a huge robotic figure sitting like a king, solid and motionless, hands on the chair arms. Its head was a mediaeval knight's helm that peaked in a vertical ridge down the front of its face. Casima saw no holes for eyes, no ears or mouth, and no neck.

"Oh shit, shit... shit, shit..." she repeated looking back to the entrance door, but it had gone. "More fucking robots. Giant robots." The hall held a sense of awe, a subliminal rumbling that influenced her on an emotional level. It sapped the strength from her knees increasing her uncanny urge to fall in supplication before this gigantic figurehead.

Gale strode purposefully toward the figure, seemingly unintimidated by its size and presence. He stood within striking range, the top of his head almost level with the giant machine's kneecaps. Casima struggled to his side and stood shoulder to shoulder with Gale. *He promised to protect me. But then, I promised to protect Keller.*

A rumbling voice came from the seated figure. "Ursurper Gale, Casima Salean. I am Knoss. I grieve for your loss, Casima. You may log the life of Keller Morten in our archives if you wish to do so. His life story will endure to the time of our Future-Lord."

Casima's mouth dropped open to retort, but Gale spoke first. "I am not one of your gullible humans. Let me see the real Knoss. At least show me that respect."

Casima's mouth snapped shut. To her surprise, a set of double doors appeared between the robot's feet, sliding silently aside to reveal a hidden room. Gale stepped forward and she tagged along behind. The room was small but appeared infinite as its walls swam with holograms showing endless landscapes with wheeling arcs of stars overhead. A figure stood in the middle of the room. A woman. Casima gasped at her appearance. Long black hair framed a face covered in striking, angular makeup. Her head appeared to have been sliced in two, diagonally from her left temple through her nose to her right cheek, and then sewn back together, but with a small but very disconcerting offset. Her eyes were huge, and they twinkled like cerulean diamonds.

"Don't be afraid, Casima." Her voice floated through the air to catch right inside Casima's head. "We have much in common." The woman flexed her hands and tilted her wrists. Casima observed the odd range of motion, the purr of high-end cybernetics. Her head twitched sideways, and those radiant eyes focused on Gale. "You know me, Ursurper, or does this copy of Del Krondeck not remember its origins?"

Gale bowed his head. "Jocelyn Salvitor," he said, and for a second Casima thought he was going to drop to his knees.

"Jocelyn Salv–" The name struck a chord with Casima as she struggled to recall basic history. She remembered the GFC and its four founding members, and that one of them had returned to Earth just before the Nova-Insanity, but nothing beyond that. "You are a Convolver?" was all she could think to say.

"*The* Convolver," Jocelyn corrected. "I joined the GFC to change the world, the very direction of the human race. Del promised he'd make us a galactic species. When I realized that was no longer their edict, I left. The Convolvers are my research and development arm, my push and thrust against normalcy. I started the Sisters of Salvitor as a gift, to aid humanity through hard times, but also as a tool that I could call upon when needed."

The moment of wonder seemed to fade and Casima's anger returned. "I don't believe in your fairy tales. I just want my Keller back."

"That's too bad. Belief is the first stage of any cognition-driven creation, Casima. Believe that you can–"

"I must return to space, to my people," Gale interrupted, clearly unwilling to debate philosophy.

"You have people, Ursurper?"

"The seeds are sown, and they are as real as your Future-Lord."

The woman calling herself Knoss nodded. "The plague that ravages the world originated with the Alliance. It has taken control of Coriolis Island, and Hmech himself is in charge of test-firing the mass-driver. The Earth halo will soon fill with their creations. Perhaps, Ursurper, you could be amongst them?"

"Why would you help me?" Gale asked.

"The voidian may be one of humanity's better ideas, Ursurper. If we can't manage our own affairs, be good custodians of the Earth, and colonize space, then perhaps the voidian can."

Gale eased closer. "I am to capture the mass-driver?"

"I have assets in place for this mission. You, Ursurper, are the missing and essential part."

Gale seemed to heave, almost boil a little. The fake clothing shrouding his body turned to wisps of fibers and he appeared to dissolve downwards becoming a mass of limbs and reinforcing cables. Casima staggered backwards, shocked by his sudden transformation. Even his face unwound, dropping down to his neck, becoming cords of muscle and mesh. In a second, the humanoid Gale had changed into some kind of fighting machine, a body designed to run, to batter walls, to leap and bludgeon. To destroy. "What will you take from me in return?" he asked.

Jocelyn seemed unmoved by Gale's transformation. "I'll take your power and fighting prowess, nothing more. Setting one of the few viable alternatives to humanity back on its course is reward enough." She smiled at Gale, but her eyes remained stony cold.

"No," Gale said, his now bare skull shaking in doubt. "There's more going on here. It's a distraction. You want me to distract Hmech from something else you have planned."

Jocelyn nodded. "I have time constraints on this mission and poor military resources compared to the Alliance. Having a voidian lead my assets will improve the odds of success."

"Show me these assets," Gale demanded.

A door opened back into the main chamber behind, and a dozen powerfully built soldiers emerged, bare shouldered and muscled they stood in a line for inspection.

"Don't worry, they can't see you," Jocelyn said. "They see nothing outside of the world I project into their minds, and that can be the real world or one which is completely false, or some combination of both. This VR runs on the very hardware controlling their bodies and minds. I got the idea from studying plague networks where such convolution-spaces have emerged as the dominant control mechanisms that have allowed the plague to propagate through humanity with terrifying efficiency."

She walked past Gale, closer to the soldiers. "I call them Burns. They are expendable bodies, in this case highly augmented cyborgs, with simulated human minds – a similar concept to your own, Ursurper. I think you will find in them the degree of proficiency and fanatical loyalty that you will need to fulfill this mission."

Casima watched in horror as the Burns performed a series of ultra-high-speed combat maneuvers fighting with bare hands and knives. After just seconds only a single Burn remained, beaten and bloody. He turned, saluted, dropped his knife, and gripped the sides of his head, palms cupped under each side of his jawbone. With a mighty jolt, he thrust upwards tearing his own head free from his neck. For a moment, he hung there holding his head, eyes rolling upwards in apparent ecstasy, then collapsed to the ground.

"Jesus–!" Casima gagged, turning away and shoving her knuckles into her mouth.

"Exceptional, inhuman loyalty," Jocelyn said, turning slowly back to Gale.

"I want to leave," Casima managed to say. "There's nothing here for me."

"I'm afraid you must stay. The Enclave exists through a tenuous agreement with the Alliance, and any hint of our misdealing will result in the destruction of all my Coriolis assets. I'm sure you understand."

Casima turned on Gale. "You promised Keller you'd protect me."

"You mustn't harm her," Gale said to Jocelyn. "That's part of the deal."

"Casima, you are my guest, and free to explore all the things the Convolution has to offer. Knowledge of the Future-Lord will help you cope with your loss. My engineers will fix your broken hand and upgrade your cybernetics. You should check out the Migrators or the Burns, perhaps there's a path for you there."

Casima found herself sobbing and staring down at the dead Burns. For the first time she could remember, she doubted herself, that fanatical need to become a machine, a part of this disturbing, immoral future that lay before the entire human race.

Maybe I don't want any of this. Maybe I just want to be a human, after all.

CHAPTER 62

The Secret Life of a Gurney

Rex felt the gurney on which he lay had become part of his extended body. After all, with the strange carbon-based struts emerging from his shoulders and elbows, he was becoming a frame, a place to arrange and perch the useless flesh of his biological body. Not much different to a gurney, really.

Unable to move, his mind broke free of its body and wandered, down, deep into Del's Star-River. Today he found himself inside a house – more of a castle really, but more cosy, almost homely.

"Where am I, Del?"

"Oh, this old place? Just a little somewhere I knocked-up to keep me sane. Kind of a repository for my memories, a safehouse. Somewhere I can go and remember who I am and what I was."

Del led him through corridors lined with pictures of friends, family, fellow GFC founders and coworkers. Rex zoned out through most of Del's tour; nothing of interest here. The side rooms were episodes from Del's life: schoolrooms, holiday places, great open spaces, and boardrooms filled with excited investors. More interesting, but–

It reminded him of the house at the rescue sanctuary, and Mrs O. Her life and history partitioned into easily assimilated chunks and arranged in chronological order.

Del led him down some creaky, wooden stairs into the mansion's basement and a dusty, derelict theatre, where he plopped down into a heavy cushioned seat, middle row, center position. Rex thought he looked old, tired, defeated. Long silver hair hung lank down the sides of his face. Rex saw no eyes, just shadowed hollows. His head faced forward, now engrossed by the movie screen.

The movie showed wireframe creatures tearing across the world, crushing and blasting towns and cities. Militaries combined and launched assaults, but the wireframes were impervious, they dropped into the ground re-emerging anywhere they liked, folding themselves into tiny spheres that vanished under the sea or sprung up like fleas into space where they spun around and returned, attacking someplace else.

"I can't let it be," Del said. "This is all I think about. All I see. Is it real Rex? Or did I make this whole thing up?"

Rex stroked the bulges on his joints. They seemed bigger today. He wondered how big they were back in the real world. Maybe he was already gone, a sentient gurney, with just tatters of Rex's – no, Felix's – ruined flesh hanging on that frame.

The destruction he saw on the screen had the inevitability of the Nova-Insanity. Maybe there was only one way out and that was the one humanity had taken back then: *controlled destruction. Would the Sisters dare take that shot? What sign from the Future-Lord were they hoping for?*

"The wireframes save us," Rex muttered as disparate thoughts coalesced into sense. "Last time the GFC bombed the world's infrastructure; but this time there's no GFC, and the Sisterhood, well–" He performed a screwy-motion with his finger near his temple.

"How?" Del asked. "How could these... machines, save us?"

"They become us, the entire human race, and stop us doing stupid things. One lesser-apocalypse to prevent another, bigger one." Rex felt vaguely dazzled by his own wisdom, but realized the thoughts were probably coming from Del.

"The problem is... there's no path back," Del said. "No path to repossess humanity from these machines. We're just lost, gone, replaced by something else that comes next. That's why all that I see beyond this is darkness. If there is nothing conscious in the future, then there's nothing to resonate with us, here and now."

Rex thought that sounded like something Mrs O. would say. Just a crazy string of ideas and words, *but it felt so true.* "But they are us." Rex patted Del's shoulder, suddenly feeling sorry for the troubled man. "I'm conscious even though I'm kind of a machine. They will be too. And maybe not as destructive as we think? Maybe that's just us projecting our own violent, repressed past into our predictions of the future."

"One lesser-apocalypse to prevent another, bigger one!" Del laughed and shook his head. "I like your ideas, Rex."

"Your ideas, Del. You just want me to think they're mine." Rex remembered Sister-Zero talking about human nature, how violence was human culture, and how it would go with us, and grow, reform, spread, wherever we went in the Universe, and in whatever form.

Del looked thoughtful. "Let's just call it *our* idea. A mixture of us both."

Rex hopped over the seat and sat next to Del, determined to see into his eyes, but Del turned his head away. "Either way, you still have to take over Hmech's network. All that rehearsing with the Sisters must have given you some insights."

"Hmech is too strong. It's like fighting an algorithmic version of yourself, something optimized for speed that knows everything that you know. You're always going to be outgunned and outclassed."

A boyhood memory surfaced. Young Rex, or really young Felix. An obsession with chess and other games of strategy. "Speed isn't everything. Look at that chess prodigy, Moy or whatever her name was. She thrashed every chess machine in the world long after chess algorithms were deemed unbeatable."

"Yeah… she was something, alright," Del said fondly, hands reaching behind his head as he seemed to relax. His face angled back toward Rex but not enough to be seen clearly. "She invented a totally new approach to the game. Of course, it only worked for a few days until the AIs adapted. She never won another game against a machine. I don't think anybody did."

"That's all we need though, right? One victory, smash the network, take control?"

Del sighed. "I think Hmech is a subset of something bigger that even he doesn't understand. The plague consists of disparate collections of networks all just obeying orders from some higher power. Hmech figured out a better control system. For the moment he's the big dog, at least in this part of the world."

"You changed the world before, Del. You can change it again."

Del laughed. "The illusion of free will. The idea that anything we do changes anything. When all we do, really, is circle around a predefined series of attractor states – inevitabilities – the Nova-Insanity, supernovas, steam engines, spears and arrows. Freewill only works in the gaps between. In the end, all of our choices are gravitationally bound to an inexorable set of end states: immoveable blackholes that cannot be changed."

"Yeah, I was pretty sure you and the Sisters would betray me again, lead me into a trap, but I went anyway."

"I had to get in here before Hmech became too big or the Sisters received their 'sign' from above and blew us all to crap."

"But surely you had a better plan than this… just drop in and hope. Hope for what? That I can hold Hmech's attacks off indefinitely? That you'd come up with something in the end?"

Del finally turned to face Rex. He did have eyes, wispy blue in seas of grey-white cloud. Each looked like peering down into the atmosphere of some vast and alien planet. "There is a plan, Rex. Help is coming. Don't lose hope."

A rattling noise jolted Rex out of the Star-River and back to his gurney inside the glass prison. The cell door was open, but no sequestered humans lumbered inside. Instead, Rex saw a hulking human with remnants of Convolver tattoos on each cheek. His eyes held the blank half-stare of the subjugated. "Time to go see the boss," he said in a gruff, lethargic voice.

"Tell the boss to go fuck himself." Rex smiled and tried to roll over away from the man.

When he regained consciousness, he was moving, draped over the shoulder of the hulking guard. Others plodded along behind as he stared down at the metallic floor, watching as drops of blood from his nose formed a pattern that receded into the distance like guide marks through a maze: waypoints in time forming a path from the past, through the sad, incomprehensible present, and on to the future.

CHAPTER 63

Basic Training

Jorben was initially surprised at the sheer number of Burns that worked inside Transit Mountain. He supposed it made sense. Hmech and Knoss had formed an alliance, and now Hmech rented troops from the Convolvers to prop up his already ample defenses and do the dirty work that maybe his other soldiers didn't want to, or simply couldn't do.

Jorben's strength and diligence paid off quickly as he was promoted from construction work to Transit Mountain's military guard. He'd done his week of basic training, really just relentless labor, marching, digging holes and filling them back in again. A process designed to foster obedience and quell any sense of individuality a soldier might still possess.

After basic, they moved him into one of the defense regiments. That meant barracking for five days at a time at the Mountain. Now he only got to see Leal at weekends, and the house stank of Nathan when he returned even though the oily little man was never anywhere to be seen.

He didn't recognize his fellow Burns. Not that they ever spoke with each other. Each was a square-jawed, dead-eyed, slack-faced uniform hunk of robotic-humanity, a product of Knoss's cloning chambers and Hmech's training.

He felt poisoned. It grew stronger the longer he was inside Transit Mountain, fuzzing his mind, making it hard to think.

Days drifted past in that fog, interrupted by moments of combat clarity as they performed live-fire training and defensive drills.

They moved barracks, edging deeper into the mountain. Here, they mingled with stranger beings: real robots, but made of transparent fibers and rods. They clattered around the building at triple-speed, faceless and menacing. Some had guns built into their bodies. Others appeared to have remnants of human beings attached to them. He would normally have stared agog at such things, but inside the mountain nothing tweaked his interest. Everything just *was*... and that was somehow okay.

His head cleared a little on the bus ride home. He paused to scare Reggie the security guard as he always did. Sneaking up on him and rising from below his eyeline to yell and pull faces through his booth window. Now that he knew Reggie had no bullets in his gun, there was no danger anymore. The gag lost its appeal.

As he walked up the street, Nathan's car flashed past. *Always such precise timing!* He nearly leapt out in front, shoulder-barging it to a halt. He reckoned his odds were pretty good, and if he lost, they'd just rebody him anyway. The look on Nathan's face would be priceless. Instead, he stepped aside and watched it pass, catching a glimpse of Kimmy waving out of the back window.

He stormed into Leal's house. "Where's Nathan taking the kids?"

"They're spending the weekend with him," she said, fussing in the kitchen and trying not to meet Jorben's eye.

"What? Why?"

She dropped her cutting knife and faced him. "They don't feel safe, Jorben. You've been acting weird since working at the Mountain. I just feel they are better off with him until you get your head straight again."

Jorben dropped onto the couch, the shock of rejection eating him up. "Are you like... seeing him, again?"

"I can see who I want to. We're not married. Not even dating. You're here as a favor, and in return you're supposed to help me out with money and tasks around the house. Remember that agreement?"

That didn't help. In his very few conversations with other Burns at the Mountain, he'd told them he was married, described Leal in intimate detail, and painted a picture of a loving, normal relationship. It was something he had over them all, a life few other Burns seemed to achieve or even want.

"But you said that Nathan was unstable, the crazy one–" Jorben felt the argument draining from him. After a week at the Mountain, he just didn't have the energy.

"Nathan's not crazy, just a bit... odd. He's always good with the kids though. He's never hit them."

Something in her tone aroused his suspicion. "He hit you?"

"Once... maybe twice–" Jorben boiled to his feet, heading for the door but she blocked his way, wooden spoon held menacingly in front of her face. "It was an accident. He was on something that made his crazy ideas seem all too real." She took an awkward look at the spoon and dropped it back to her side. "Look, I can take care of myself. He didn't get away lightly." She smacked the spoon gently on Jorben's forehead and cracked a small smile.

"I'm sorry, just really tired."

"Come, I'll get us some food and you can tell me all about Transit Mountain defense duty, and then go sleep it off. Tomorrow is another day, and you look like shit, by the way. They are wearing you out real fast. Gonna have to take you back to the Enclave for a refund. Maybe trade you in for a younger model."

CHAPTER 64

Nosebleed Seats

"Stop his nose bleeding." The woman's voice was loud next to Rex's head as he was carried face down under a medical blanket through the warren of tunnels beneath Transit Mountain. "He's leaking valuable Glow all over the place." Someone jammed cotton swabs into his nostrils. He tried to sneeze them out but inhaled instead, sucking them deeper inside and choking.

I think this is it, Del. They're either firing me into space or cutting me to pieces.

He felt the muscles of the unstoppable soldier who was carrying him bunch and bulge, then dump him bodily onto a firm mattress or bed. Familiar restraints clamped him in place: wrists to metal sidebars, feet, legs, and knees secured with straps, and a wide band across his abdomen pinned him down. Clamps latched onto his skull and jaw, locking his head so it couldn't move.

Ah! The claustrophobia attack.

No, maybe the surgical attack?

Perhaps the 'hang me over a pit of fire and slowly lower me inside' attack?

The blanket whipped away, and his eyes roamed the huge room, soaking up its pure, sterile whiteness and the waiting machines and staring people.

Definitely the surgical attack.

A figure in white robes stood over him. A mask covered the lower part of his face, but his brown eyes glared out over the top. Rex saw the black spokes on his pupils rotating hypnotically. "Hello, Rex," said Hmech.

It was his nightmare, exactly as he remembered it! The machines, the tubes, tearing the dog from him and making him human.

"Oh," Rex said, sadly. "That old attack, again."

Hands reached over Rex's head and secured a mask over his mouth and nose. He held his breath until his lungs burned, then with a gasp he took the gas in great gulps. "Not too much, nurse," Hmech said. "We don't want Rex to miss anything."

The mask came off and Rex could still see. The world was clear, sharp, and loud, everything hyper-real except for his body that was numb like dead flesh. He tested his jaw, it still moved, words slurred out, and he felt the dribble run down his chin. "This all ya got, asshole?" Saliva mixed with his tears and pooled on the table, warm and clammy, around the back of his head.

Straight up, a mirror gave a full-length body shot. The absurd idea occurred to him that those memories of past surgeries were never real, but prophecies sent back by the Future-Lord. *But why? Why give a warning if the fate is inevitable?*

He froze from his struggle as a cluster of robotic machinery clattered alive and clawed its way up the surgical bed to hover menacingly over his head. He caught flashes of scalpels and clamps, and a small, circular saw in his peripheral vision. The machinery closed around his skull, and a shaving implement screamed a delicate, mechanical cry as his hair fell away into a vacuum tube, unveiling a mottled, bumpy scalp.

"Relax," Hmech said. Rex stared at the mirror as his head support dropped away leaving him held in the grasp of the robot. Hmech traced a line across Rex's forehead reaching down the sides and around the back of his freshly shaved head. A red line marked the trace, a perfect circle around the cap of his skull.

You got anything for me here, Del? Anything? When's the help arriving?

Sorry, Rex.

Hmech stepped back and the robotic surgeon powered up.

A laugh punched through Rex's anesthesia. *More convolution-space delusions. That's it. Wake up, Rex. Wake up!*

Nurses grafted tubes to his arms and legs. Blood raced off down coiled lengths to machinery that huffed and hummed before returning it back into his body. Another masked surgeon wheeled in a chair with a figure sitting in it. They placed the chair carefully to the side, just in Rex's cone of vision.

In the chair sat an androgynous figure, small and fragile like a person aged to the very end of life. But this person was made of glass. Its slim body had no head, and the spine extended up and rounded into a nodule on top of the shoulders with a pair of small spidery eyes looking out to the front. It sat motionless, hunched forward as if staring at the floor. Through the transparent skin Rex could see internal structures like bones and muscle fibers. "What is that?" he asked, realizing it was Del speaking.

"Your new body, Del," said Hmech. "I call it fullerite. It's similar to the framework growing inside of Rex at this very moment, but fully developed. We stripped away its mental nodes. Now it's just a bare body-frame awaiting a shiny new mind."

"How?" was all Del could say. Rex felt him fade and swell as if the pair of them almost occupied the same space and time.

"Timing here is crucial," said Hmech. "Most of the Rex-based nodes are clustered around his growing fullerite substrate as he's been the dominant personality longest and is most grounded in this body. But yours, Del... yours are attracted to the Star-River, your little haven, an obsession that will hand you over to me."

Something toyed with Rex's mind, exploratory fingers reaching from the surrounding nurses and networks, testing his resolve, seeking new weakness. The robotic surgeon clattered to life, and a ghastly sawing sound filled Rex's ears along with the smell of singed flesh and hacked bone. "No!" he screamed, but no sound made it to his lips.

"Still no surrender, Rex?" Hmech's quiet, calm voice was filled with scorn. "Well, that's just fine." Hmech stepped away and another figure entered his line of sight. A woman, head bowed, lank hair spilling over her face, drowned but somehow still alive as if shambling out of the mire.

Rex should have felt more horror, more gut-wrenching pain and grief, but there was simply nothing left inside of him to feel. "Mira," he croaked.

"It's okay, Rex... no pain anymore... no more pain," she said, reaching over and touching his cheek. "Your pain will end too." She bent over and kissed him gently on the lips. His mind snapped under the surge of hatred. He raged outwards mentally seeking her thoughts. They were all there... laid bare, organized, categorized, just as Hmech wanted. Her battle to survive Jett, the lich, the dens of depravation, and the death of her family. Once raw and bleeding emotion but now at peace. A repository, a database of what Mira once was.

Mira, Mira... his mind sang the words like a lament as he saw Jett squeezing her head, saw his tendrils of infiltration piercing her soul, raping her thoughts. *Where was I?* Rex wondered. *I, who let her walk away that day after the battle with the lich. I, who left her to this fate. I am the lowest scum, the worst filth. I am nothing... nothing.*

He felt a new presence in his head. Something physical, something cold and precise routing through the layers of glial cells and neurons, gently parting delicate blood vessels as it dug through brain matter seeking its prize.

He surrendered.

The dog fled, pausing briefly to look back, expecting its master to follow. But he remained pinned under Mira's dead stare. Even the green from her eyes had leeched away to grey.

No smile or twitch of facial features, no cuss words, no squirrel-like distractions sending her mind fleeing in new directions. *No more Mira.*

The edges of his world became fuzzy and imprecise. This time he tumbled toward those fake realities, almost willing them to come faster. Before his gaze, Mira came suddenly alive, the green in her eyes was back, and a smile seemed to welcome him inside this new realm.

"Fucking Christ, Rex," she said. "You can't be in here. Hmech's kid-monster will eat you alive."

"How are you talking to me? You're gone."

She shrugged. "Jett took a lot of me, and I took some of him. I think we both learned things from that experience. Hmech broke me apart but there were so many versions of me, so many facets that all think they are Mira, memories of memories of memories. Like little mini-Miras kind of rolled up and stuffed in the corners. Hmech hasn't managed to unravel them all yet."

Rex felt Hmech's child now, dipping a toe into the fresh waters of his mind. It froze for an instant, like a fox in the chicken pen, not knowing where to go first. *So much stuff to touch and see... and take!*

"No, Rex! No!" cried Del. "Snap out of it." But even as he spoke, Del tumbled away in pursuit of something, something he needed more than friendship, life, or even the hope of humankind. Something precious had been snatched away, and he had no choice but to follow.

"Go! Get the fuck out of here, Rex." Mira's gaze turned fierce, that look he knew so well and just couldn't refuse. "Do it for me."

The bubble seemed to pop, and Rex was back in the operating room, staring into Mira's dead face.

"Still here?" Hmech sounded surprised. "You should die now." Rex felt the jolt of electricity that stopped his heart. He imagined the Glow nodes comprising Del's mind-state racing for the exits of his body, seeking a new host as they fled the sinking ship, while the nodes comprising Rex still clung to the wreckage, the fullerite skeleton of his dying corpse.

A smile eased across Rex's lips. "Am I dead now?"

"Just for a moment, Rex, long enough to fulfill my need. But Rex, dear Rex. You are Glow. You are the plague. You can never die. Besides, I'm curious about your dogged resilience, and there's so much good science locked away inside Felix's brain."

The assaults came back, hard, relentless, but Rex knew what to do this time. His world narrowed to a dark tube with Hmech at the far end. He tumbled gently out the bottom into the yammering void. He knew this place so well, had even been born here, a product of the void itself as the fragments of damaged Glow personalities tumbled freely and came together as Rex, as Glow, as the crucible. It was his void, and even Hmech couldn't find him in here.

CHAPTER 65

Shoal Awareness

New motes of consciousness stirred inside Hmech's convolution-space network realm. Like a shoal of tiny minnows, they swam through a hostile ocean filled with predatory data, shifting and changing direction, clustering back together and slowly becoming something more than just the individual fish.

Del emerged from that darkness, disembodied, ungrounded, just floating but aware that he was still Del. The shoal of Glow comprising his mind coalesced around a reef, an anchor of sanctuary inside that void of confusion. He knew that reef by a different name: The Star-River. Just the idea of its presence sent a wave of relief through his imaginary body, a feeling of physical bliss inside a purely informational realm.

"Rex?" he asked, but no response came. "Are you still with me?" He should have felt elation at being free of his jailer, but instead he just felt cold and alone. Rex had been his shield, his protector. Now, he was a naked and vulnerable mind, a simple electric circuit, and a monster had its hands on all the control switches.

The myriad nodes comprising Del's proprioception and monitoring algorithms began the task of seeking out the new body's actuators, sensors, feedback loops and power sources. They attached to the fullerite structures and formed a thin shell of linked nodes ringing the entire body perimeter, mapping the physical limits of this new realm into their collective memory.

Quickly they built a body model, but no maps in their communal databases matched this one. There were no lungs, digestive tracts, glands, not even a brain. Power was everywhere in the form of tiny reactors, and the muscles and tendons were all strands of smart fiber that had small minds of their own. With no biological mind to override or monitor, they settled into the task of control, and Del's artificial body jolted and convulsed in its harness as they experimented with their new physical processes and brought the whole contraption online.

With this embodiment, Del's senses snapped to life. A voice like rolling thunder seemed to bring the entire network to attention. "Behold," shouted Hmech. "The perfect being. An artificial human mind inside a perfect, artificial body. And all under my control!"

Del fought using his deep understanding of mindscapes and networks, but he was just a mouse dangling from a cat's jaws, a tiny reaction against an immovable force.

He saw the room through his sharp, new, multi-spectrum eyes: Mira, a crumpled mess in the middle of the floor. Just a node on Hmech's vast network. An open book whose pages he could peruse at will.

Rex looked so different, small and pale, eyes open and staring up to Haven or wherever he believed he was going. A robot at the end of the bed held the top of his head in its claw. As he watched, it spun the bloody cap over and planted it back in place. A smaller set of claws began crimping and gluing Rex's flesh and bone back together.

Time jumped and wavered as Del lost focus, trying to reattach to the Star-River, seeking a bastion from which to mount a counterassault. He watched surgeons jolt the life back into Rex's corpse. His eyes remained wide open as if still dead, but Del felt him on Hmech's network, a feeble presence, either near death or deeply sleeping.

Del felt Hmech close off Rex's portals to the outside world.

The robot finished its work and Rex's head flopped back onto the bed and his eyes slowly closed. His mouth still moved, mumbling something. Del triggered what amounted to a newly discovered zoom function on his hearing and suddenly Rex came through loud and clear. "I'm not Rex. I am not Glow, and I am not the crucible," he said. "I am the creator. I am the void."

CHAPTER 66

Migration

Casima was surprised by the amount of freedom Knoss granted her inside the Convolver Enclave. She wandered the vast structure, testing the limits to her travel, which ended anywhere there was access to the outside world.

She visited the confessional hall with its bizarre tangle of tubes that engulfed its supplicants like giant feeding leeches. She passed through libraries and laboratories, open courtyards with fake skies and suns where acolytes trained and worshiped. She saw machines that looked like humans and humans that looked like machines, and some things that looked like nothing she had ever seen before. There were humans resembling grotesque biological experiments, ones with multiple heads and extra limbs, even examples of apparent cross-species morphing. The Enclave was a giant laboratory, a single multi-armed experiment into the nature of being.

Most bizarre of all were the shuffle-rooms, as she called them. They were dotted throughout the Enclave, tiny, square spaces behind large automatic doors. She'd wandered into one out of curiosity, unprepared for what lay inside: hundreds of people, jammed shoulder-to-shoulder, heads down, eyes closed, just shuffling around in a big circle. As she stared, one of the men broke free and left. As soon as he passed through the door back into the main Enclave his face lit, eyes sparked alive, and he was normal again.

"Sir?" she shouted, running after the next person to leave the room. "What were you doing in there?"

The man smiled and said, "I went for a walk outside."

Casima added it to her list of questions for Knoss.

Her quarters were opulent; fine couches, a giant viewing screen and a living bed that cuddled and warmed her like a gentle, considerate lover. Sleep came easy. Time passed quickly. But the ache of Keller's death remained a constant. She knew time would heal, but here, time had its own agenda.

The next day, a doctor appeared at her door. He inserted her damaged arm into a surgery tube which gently detached her smashed limb and replaced it with a new one that looked and felt just like a real forearm and hand. For the rest of the day, she sat admiring its perfection, the amazing fluidness of its motion, and the smooth, efficient strength. *Keller would love this*, she thought as she sank into a troubled sleep.

On her third day she noticed her shadow as she dawdled aimless and lost around the Enclave. The handsome young man wore a metallic grey turban and loose-fitting robes of scintillating colors. His smile was intoxicating.

She waited for him around a corner then triggered her ambush. Stepping out in front and stalling him to an awkward halt. "Name's Casima." She held out her new hand. "Is it me you are stalking?"

"Rarlis," he said, shaking her hand with youthful enthusiasm. "I was sent by Knoss. If you desire, I can give you a tour of the Enclave."

He took her to the tops of pinnacles with views out over the city and down into galleries of art and science where Convolvers flocked to seek inspiration and knowledge. He explained what it was to be a Migrator. How it started off as a simple neural interface to an external array of toys and games: little calculators and drawing programs that allowed the user to doodle remotely using their mind alone. Gradually the user learned more complex tasks such as storing and retrieving data and images from external memories that were not part of their brains. As the mental prosthetics became more useful, they took over from the biological substrate and gradually the user 'Migrated' their mind away from their biology and into a machine.

"That sounds dangerous," Casima said, even though it sounded intriguing.

"The goal is to achieve substrate-independence, a state of cognitive immortality where my entire conscious mind is migrated out of my brain. Then my brain can be shut down and removed. Something that sounds terrifying at the moment, but I'm assured will be perfectly reasonable when the time comes."

"Are there Migrators that have achieved this independence?" Casima asked.

He said he didn't know and that the upper echelons of Migrator culture were shielded in secrecy. "I asked Knoss about that and he told me that, like so many of his great experiments, this was a work in progress. I hear there was research into copying mind-states from dying people, but it only ever worked once out of hundreds of trials. Nothing's a given."

"Why so many failures?"

Rarlis shrugged. "It's hard. Minds don't hold together when transferred or copied. It takes a particularly cohesive type of individual to survive something so traumatic. I spend hours every day on focus exercises and meditations. It's a no-lose proposition, Casima. Even if I don't achieve immortality, I get to lead a more relaxed and creative life."

She had to admit it was a fascinating idea, the culmination of everything she had ever wanted – freedom from her treacherous biology.

The next day she ate alone in a small courtyard cafeteria frequented by silent, devout looking people who hid inside deep cowls. She tried to glance at their faces, but they didn't seem to have any.

Rarlis arrived as she finished eating and asked permission to join her. She accepted and he sat and drank tea and asked about her life and journey.

"If you're trying to seduce me then it won't work," she warned. "I'm not interested."

He gave her a coy grin, then proudly announced, "I'm a eunuch. The Enclave determines how the species propagates, not us individuals. We've evolved on from meat-age reproduction."

"What a revolting idea," she said. "If I wanted to Migrate my mind would I need to worship the Future-Lord?"

"You're never required to worship the Future-Lord. Why worship something that doesn't exist yet? By attending the teachings, you learn of the waypoints, the steps that must exist for the Future-Lord to come into being. The more of us who have this intention, the more likely the Future-Lord is to one day exist."

"Waypoints?"

"It's hard to think in terms of millions of years. We are products of the meat-age, and we think in years, maybe decades, not millennia. Bigger, better minds than ours work on those scales, but for us, we need personal waypoints, things we aspire to achieve, nexus points where we change who and what we are in fundamental ways."

"Tell me some of your waypoints." She looked into his brown eyes and saw a sense of wonder there that she had seen in Keller, that dreamer who saw the limitations of the Universe as challenges, not as walls.

"Well, many are private. Obviously near-term, I want to evolve into a full Migrator. Once my conscious mind exists on a new substrate, I'd like to join one of the Convolver's cosmic seed voyages."

"Seeds?"

"A plan to seed the cosmos with life. When minds exist as data on computer substrates, they can be loaded onto tiny seed ships that construct bodies for the minds when they reach distant stars. All human culture can be contained within a representative sample of human minds, copied and sent out to the stars in the billions."

"How do you know we're not already in some kind of seed capsule virtual reality show?"

Rarlis laughed. "There are people here that believe just that. This world is a simulation, and we are riding across the galaxy in a seed-ship. They believe their purpose is to live, grow, and exist inside this virtual reality, and to gain the skills they will need to bring a new planet into flourishing existence in the distant future. I can introduce you to one of them if you like?"

"That would certainly explain why I am locked inside of this place and not allowed to leave." She left her sarcasm hanging in the air, while Rarlis slowly and awkwardly finished his tea.

CHAPTER 67

Soul Transcription

"Why give me a body if you won't grant it freedom?" Del struggled against his restraints, but his new corporeal form felt deliberately frail and weak and was no match for Hmech's straps. He realized that there wasn't just physical restraint at work here. He'd been dropped into a living container, a sequestration snake that coiled around the outer perimeter of his physical existence, filtering and censoring his every move and sensation. Deciding precisely what he was and wasn't allowed to feel and do.

Hmech spoke directly into his mind. "An embodied cognition is a more complete cognition, Del. I need you grounded and complete, a whole mind with memories intact." Hmech pressed in closer, invisible, dominant, like a pressure jacket. "You can always work with me, now you're free of Rex. Perhaps some equations. I know the picoforms use fractal geometry to construct machines that are theoretically too small to be etched with masks or other physical tools. How is the math implemented? A hyperdimensional folding algorithm?"

Del felt those memories bubbling to the surface, as if Hmech were the fire beneath the pot containing his mind. Cranking up that heat made the memories roil and tumble, some started leaking through: the secrets to miniaturization, mathematics, techniques, blueprints, plans, and experiments. The whole history documenting the construction of the giant picoform machines on Earth to their miniaturization and proliferation in orbital arrays, free from gravitational distortion. Del didn't know it all, but he knew enough.

Claustrophobia grew stronger. The need to escape became intense. He saw Hmech's parallel world, convolution-space. An exact copy of reality snapshotted from his own captive senses, but somehow a nicer, neater, more desirable place to dwell.

It would be so easy to slip inside, believe it was all real, down... down... inside–

Down to Hmech's child or whatever horror awaits me.

Del saw glimpses of Hmech's process, and it was beautiful. Algorithms built from the ordered and catalogued experiences of the sequestered. Laid out like some fantasy toolkit, stocked and ready to build new and convincing realities. Drop in a vulnerable persona. Deconstruct it. Make new tools for the kit.

Del barely noticed the switch as his reality was cunningly and subtly replaced. He acknowledged the cleverness with a small, virtual smile, and the pressure on his being began to ease. The world was the same, except he knew it wasn't. On some subliminal level he'd accepted it, resigned, done what Rex had never done, and thrown himself, his beliefs, and his future away.

"You are weak, Del," he heard Hmech say. "You are not Rex. You cannot resist looking where you shouldn't look."

Okay, so I'm inside. Now what? How exactly are you going to dismantle my mind?

A gentle presence brushed past him accompanied by childish giggling. He could move now; this virtual version of himself had no restraints. He wandered straight to the door, but outside wasn't Transit Mountain, or the blank warren of corridors that riddled its insides. He was inside his house, the Star-River mansion he'd constructed to contain his memories.

Fine. Let's go explore.

The childish ghost flickered past like a breath of sweetness, tiny fingers brushing objects, almost touching but afraid of breaking.

He felt compelled to follow, sensing rather than seeing the child ahead as he turned and swept through another doorway. He saw a flash of multicolored light and suddenly he was a teenager. *Math class*, eyes fixated on the whiteboard as Mr Wallace enriched his thoughts with new, exciting knowledge that would change his life forever. "Chaos theory, Del, my boy. This is where mathematics will take us. From the solid certainty of algebraic equations and into the realms of fractal-uncertainty. Unknowable in some sense, but quantifiable through its limits. Taming this frontier will lead us to understand things we can't even imagine today."

That giggle again, so sweet, so innocent, just exploring, playing; it passed by invisibly and left the room – and so that room was gone, erased, and Del found himself back in the corridor, staring at a different door.

What was behind that door? He looked back trying to locate the place he'd just come from. *What door?* It didn't matter. There were others.

Physics class. Mrs Benson and her crooked-smile monologue on Rutherford models and baryons, even more fascinating, but no… that room was gone now and so was its door.

Del remembered his training with the Sisters. *I'm inside the plague. Not real!* "I don't have to be here," he cried, fighting back to reality, reconnecting with his senses and that frail, ridiculous body. "This is not real, Hmech. You can't fool me!"

But he'd seen the whole process now. Hmech's child. *Was it a real child or just a clever algorithm?* It sought out every part of his memory, touching, exploring, experiencing every moment for itself with the infinite patience of a being that had no time constraints, no goals and destinations. In doing so, it processed his memories through its own pristine senses, experiencing them for itself, and reencoding them as data. *Help me, Rex. I'm being dismantled by a living memory parser. It's transcribing my soul.*

For a moment he was back in the real world with its fuzzy edges, a human with arms and legs and eyes, sweeping the room desperately seeking help. He reached out across Hmech's network and suddenly Rex was there, running through the grass by his side, but this grass was wrong, odorless, with mute, uninteresting colors. The grassland vanished, the memory of it vanished, along with its door.

Not real! Del stumbled on down the corridor. "Wait," he cried. "Wait for me." But the child was way ahead of him and moving faster now. Deep in his heart he knew he'd never see reality again.

CHAPTER 68

Meltdown

Something roused Rex as he tumbled through the silent void, an itch of annoyance, an uncertainty, something he needed to attend to before the end of everything came.

"Can't you just leave me alone to die?" he yelled, struggling to the surface of consciousness to find himself still tethered to the surgical gurney. He watched through sad, empty eyes as nurses cleaned up his body, dressed the wounds left behind by the surgical robot, and fastened him to a new set of monitoring equipment.

Hmech stood over Del's transparent new body, fingers stroking the smooth surface as if it were a precious metal. But none of those things mattered enough to stir him back from death. Something else–

Sister-Zero stood by the doorway. He remembered Mira, or rather the image of Mira, *rolled up and stuffed in a corner*. Momentarily free of the constraints imposed by Hmech's fake realities, Rex reached across the network into the room containing Sister-Zero's dismantled mind.

There! In plain sight, or at least it was if you knew what to look for. A curled meme, tiny, like a crumpled piece of discarded newspaper. And inside was a switch – the trigger for the bomb! "You really want me to do this? Is this my purpose? The reason you sent me here, to blow everything to pieces?"

He moved closer. The meme contained words, thoughts, even a small part of the Sister. Not enough to have agency on its own – that would make it large and easily noticed by Hmech or his inquisitive child. He ruffled the meme and it spoke to him. "Not a bomb, Rex, but hope!"

Without a thought, he tugged on the switch and watched as tiny feelers reached out through the Sister's body, plucking invisibly small motes of machinery from disparate corners and clumping them back together as something new.

"What are you building?" Rex lurched back to the real world, yearning for the blinding light, that cleansing, incinerating heat.

The Sister twitched and jolted as if in the throes of some internal convulsion. "Yes," he gasped as smoke oozed from her plastic face plate. "Yes!" his yell escaped as the Sister's head crumpled, melting slowly from the inside. But there was no blast, no cleansing inferno, she simply fizzled, slowly curling in on herself like a plastic toy under a child's magnifying glass. *A self-destruct? How does that help me? It doesn't even give me hope.*

"Security breach," Hmech said, snapping away from Del and thrusting his palm at the melting Sister. The network of connections pervading Hmech's entire virtual creation jolted. Not really an explosion, more of an energy pulse that Rex felt as a ripple in the underlying reality.

Hmech waved at the door and it slammed shut as the Sister's flaming head toppled off her body. "What happened?" he demanded.

Virtual screens sprung up around Hmech. One showing a startled man sat at a desk surrounded by monitors and flashing lights. "EMP? Not enough to do any real harm. Might be a signal though."

A sign! Rex nearly choked. *Did I just signal the Sisters to destroy the world?*

"How did that get through our scans?" Hmech raged around

the room, his holographic viewing screens swirling around him as he moved.

The figure behind the monitors shifted, eyes filled with the fear of failure. "The device must have been tiny or maybe divided into many, small pieces."

"Lock the place down. Full security alert."

Sirens blared. Red lamps flashed overhead. A dull thud reverberated through the pumice walls, ringing the metal tunnel-linings like tubular gongs. Rex tried to sit but bonds secured him to the stretcher. His body remained numb, but he felt himself healing as his Glow network rushed to aid its ailing host.

More thuds rolled in like distant earthquakes, Rex counted seventeen in rapid succession. "Report!" Hmech demanded, as concerned faces appeared in separate boxes on his screens.

"We're under attack, sir. All directions."

"Who? Who's attacking us?" Anger darkened Hmech's face. "Maybe the Sisterhood wants you back." He waved a nurse over to Rex. "Prep my bunker and activate all our military reserves. All of them. It's time to show the world our true nature."

"We have the signal. Mission is a go!" Knoss's booming voice cut through the darkness of concealment. Gale's Inner-I lit with tactical information fed from their accompanying swarm of nano-drones and filtered through Knoss's convolution-space battle simulation environment.

"Hoo-Arrr!" Gale's fifteen Burn comrades let out a simultaneous grunt as the assault capsule launched from the back of the fake air-conditioning repair truck, acceleration pinning them hard against the support webbing.

Gale's Inner-I displayed a god's-eye view of the battle arena as it unfurled around him. The air-conditioning truck receded behind and Transit Mountain loomed straight ahead. The Burn infiltrator who had driven them through Hmech's checkpoints to position the truck less than a kilometer from their target ignited the incendiary device that would dissolve his truck, his body, and any forensic evidence of Convolver involvement into ashes.

As the assault capsule leveled off and began its short plunge toward Transit Mountain's base and the mass-driver complex, the Burns began their battle chant. Gale had been impressed with their performance during the three days of combat training. Not voidian performance, but exceptional for human-based combatants. Each Burn was a fusion of amped human flesh and state-of-the-art cybernetics, controlled by a computer simulation of a human mind and encased in the convolution-space fantasy that Knoss used to guide their actions.

"Impact in... four... three..." Knoss roared. The Burn's hunched forward in their restraints, eager to leave, and fight... and die. Their battle roles were defined by their armor, weapons, innate abilities, and the particular framing of reality fed to them through convolution-space. Suicide troops that needed a berserk rating saw a world of hostiles and chaos, where terrifying things came at them from all directions. For them, the only way to salvation was through a quick and glorious death. Burns that needed to remain rational and in control saw a calmer, more pragmatic reality. A clever spectrum of experiential shifts ranged between those two extremes, and Knoss's battle-AI decided how each Burn's false-reality morphed and changed.

All wore reactive armor, which would shred away under fire. The five shock troops, including Gale, wore modified back plates that allowed them to dive into forward rolls and become giant, armored wheels. The Burns had fully rotational shoulder sockets enabling them to poke guns out the sides of the wheel and fire as they rolled. Gale's body didn't work that way, one of the few limitations of his fiber construction. Instead, he wore a much thicker armor plating, and relied on weight and momentum for devastating effect.

"Two... one, and..."

Gale saw the gleam in his companions' eyes, fanatic, fearless. He was the only one who could die here. The only one with something real to lose.

"Zero!"

The capsule smashed into the outer pumice layer of Transit Mountain. A shockwave of small explosions emanated from the nosecone, rupturing and softening the pumice ahead, whilst slowing the capsule from supersonic speed to a relative crawl.

Around the mountain sixteen identical penetrator-craft hit their targets, each launched from a different concealment vehicle and timed to the second.

Gale felt the capsule stop as it completed its penetration of Transit Mountain's outer wall. A second of silent weightlessness as it dropped through some interior space and crashed to the ground, rolling on its deflating airbags to a halt. A bang detonated the rear door latch and light flooded inside. Gale saw none of that, his own vision was coupled to the Burns' augmented reality, giving him a wild three-sixty view of everything around them.

"And combat is live," said Knoss as they piled out through the capsule door, weapons blazing, death roars in their throats.

CHAPTER 69

Mind Game

"What do you want?" Del cried, as he chased feverishly along the corridors of his mind, pursuing the fleeting ghost of Hmech's child. "It's all just one big game to you, right? Not to me! Please stop." He felt its glee, its endless wonder – how could he hate such unfettered curiosity? It was like chastising himself as a child for being young. And like any child it had no sense of consequences; its unwitting destruction of whatever it touched. Turning vibrant, real memories from an essence of a life experience into cold, dry data.

"No... no! Not there, please–" Del rushed through a door and into his Gran's eightieth birthday party. A wonderful family gathering at their cabin in the Big Horn Mountains. But before he even reached the entrance, he felt the memory fading, and was back in the corridor again. "There must be something that will stop you?"

He thought back to his own childhood, curious Del, sticky fingers into everything. But those memories were all of him as a four or five-year old. He spoke, communicated, had interactions with parents and friends. Threw tantrums and made unreasonable demands. Had this child ever experienced such things?

More rooms opened. More windows on his past that flickered to life and vanished, leaving him with only the hollow understanding that something was once there. At some point nothing would be left, just memories of having had memories, and then maybe even those would be gone. Dementia. Artificial, accelerated dementia!

"That's the answer, force the memory. Use it or lose it. Gran, she existed, right? A cabin in the hills. I... no *we*, had a party... wedding anniversary?" His virtual head dropped in despair as the child raced past again, too fast to keep up with. This kid devoured his life whether he was there to see it or not.

"Toys. Warmth. Mother. A puppy? What the fuck are you seeking?"

Distraction! Show the kid things it wanted, no talking, no words, it didn't understand those. He conjured up mental pictures of everything a three-year old might want, focusing on smells and flavors, sweetness and fur, chewy, crunchy, sticky fun. But still this uninvited guest swept onwards as if Del's conscious efforts made no impression on its world.

No, not working. Must be some way–

More memories vanished. *I'm still Del. Still me.*

"Invented memories don't work." *They must be mine. Must be real, at least in my view.* In the Star-River memory system, his consciousness collapsed possible futures into scenarios partially of his making but guided by everything else that had previously happened inside that simulated universe. Human memory worked differently, by reconstruction, building impressions of an experience from stored cues and gist. When a person thought they knew something, they had a feeling, a feeling-of-knowing. That mental itch that told them that if they just kept looking, then they *would* remember. *It feeds on that, the feeling-of-knowing, uses it to home in on a memory. Once that feeling-of-knowing is satisfied, the itch is scratched and it moves on to somewhere else.*

Del threw out a familiar face, a kid he went to school with. Ron... that was his name. Ron Evans. They hung out together, played action roleplaying games with figures and maps drawn on graph paper. The image formed and Del felt the child coming along with him, whistling through rooms filled with memories of Ron Evans, vanishing them as it passed.

It's working. Now I can guide it away from important things by sacrificing the mundane... until I run out, of course. Damnit, Rex, how do I stop it?

His world lurched, kind of a reset, and suddenly he was back in his glass body, inside Hmech's bunker. The word "EMP" made it through his fogged senses and into his awareness before the world took on its fuzzy, fake edges once again.

Good. The attack has begun.

"What do you want, child? What are you seeking? Punishment? Reward? How can I make you stop this... this rampage through my mind?"

Del felt his mind slowly dissolving. The faster he thought the more memories he brought online. Just food for the insatiable predator.

Meditation?

Too hard to focus. How long could I really keep that up?

Instead, he halted in a long corridor that he just knew was full of funerals, obituaries, and dead relatives. *Go ahead, take those. I don't need them.*

The child moved quicker, seeming to gorge on the images of death and sadness. "Is that it? Are you curious about death?" Del conjured images of things dying, but these were too distant. Things, bugs, birds, friends, and soldiers – they lacked immediacy, that personal touch. *I have never actually died. My memories were extracted long before my original body gave out.* He tried to visualize his own death, which sparked a momentary change in the child's torrent of curiosity. "Your own death. That's what you want to understand. Non-existence. But that's the one thing a human mind can never show you. The one thing there is no memory of, and so you keep searching, never satisfied." *Clever, Hmech, clever. An invasive program that can never be stopped because the end it seeks can never be reached.*

Or can it? Del filled his mind with darkness and, when he sensed the child's attention, he sadly unfolded one of his favorite memories.

Years in the past, better times inside his lab on Cloud9. "This was my home," he narrated, unsure any of his words made it through to the child, but it helped him guide his thoughts, and perhaps radiating such strong emotions would catch its attention.

He stood before a carbon-black biped. "This will one day become a voidian called Ursurper Gale. It's a new biology designed for exploring and colonizing space. At the moment he has no brains. It's just an experimental body guided by remote control. He's got senses, even eyes. See those tiny camera bumps on his shoulders?"

I did this. I was really here. For a second, he dangled that familiarity, that feeling-of-knowing out there like bait. And then... he let the memory unfurl.

Bored, needing to go play with something fun, he eased into a GFC VR-couch and let his Inner-I take control, shutting down his body, feeding his mind with data from Gale's senses.

"This was me at my most content, just weeks before the Nova-Insanity ruined everything." He pinged Ellayna on his Inner-I comms. "I'm taking the new voidian exploration body out for a spin." Her face popped into his view. Her eyes still held the twinkle from their recent amorous encounter inside one of the centrifugal workout chambers.

"Knock yourself out, Del." She looked away, clearly distracted by other, more important tasks.

Del trooped Gale's body over to the airlock and executed the safety protocols. The hiss of vanishing air flowed over Gale's ultra-sensitive skin, tingling, alive as if the velocity and momentum vectors of every molecule meant something profound and delightful.

Alarms sounded, seals hissed and popped. Lights flashed. *The child is watching! Just watching. I have its attention.*

The airlock's outer door opened and Del thrust out into space, feeling the prickle of raw vacuum on his fullerene skin, untethered, unrestrained. He activated a small rocket pack on his back. Within seconds Cloud9 vanished to a speck behind him and the Earth was a glorious blue-grey ball hanging in front. He felt the child push past him, interested, no... *fascinated*. It reached out, tiny hands trying to grasp the Earthly globe as any child would, confused that it couldn't touch but enthralled by the colors and soft motion.

"Welcome to infinity," said Del, quietly. "Except for a few probes and colonists, this is, as far as we know, everything meaningful to ever exist. Our entire culture. This is an encapsulation of what it is to be alive."

The child kept reaching, wanting to touch, but then pulled back, perhaps frustration, perhaps the realization that this was something very large, very, very far away.

Del kept the narrative flowing. "This... this is the very definition of life." He turned gently away, skimming his vision over the dense core of the Milky Way and then up, out of the galactic plane to the darkest regions of space. "And this... this is everything else." He let the image settle, felt the quiet in the child's mind. "If all of life is behind us then this is the nearest to death I've ever experienced. An immense, endless, meaningless void." He activated the rocket and felt the ache of acceleration, but the Universe didn't change, nothing grew closer or larger. "And yet, gazing upon this dark infinity gives me hope. Hope that one day we'll go out there and sprinkle life throughout those stars."

He felt the child drifting ahead of him as if compelled to test the size and texture of everything in front of it. Del eased back gently, quietly, into reality.

CHAPTER 70

Waypoint

Ursurper Gale crashed out of the assault capsule, rolling into his combat wheel form, and passing the advanced Burns who took up defensive positions around the ruined penetrator vehicle. He flashed past the remnants of humans, their bones and brains shattered by the concussion wave from their assault craft. The Burns had already dispatched any survivors, and the ground was now clear for Gale and the other shock troops to roll forward on their designated vectors and begin the destruction of Hmech's defensive formations.

As Gale moved, he channeled memories from deep storage, that flash of information he'd received from Jett just before he exploded. He felt Jett's passion for combat, something he'd never really felt from his baseline existence as Del Krondeck, but something he needed right now.

His direction arrow jolted right, and he turned, almost a reflex, through a block wall and into an adjacent room. Incoming fire raked his armored plates as he unfurled out of his wheel and opened fire with his hyper-rifle. A single fire-controlled sweep dispatched the remaining foes, shattering their bodies into a red fog.

He ran now, instead of rolling, giving his Inner-I a few seconds of clarity to snapshot his surroundings before folding back into an assault wheel. Lasers burned pinholes through his frontal armor; one of his side plates absorbed a rocket propelled grenade hit. The plate crumbled and blew away. The explosion from his reactive armor sent him reeling sideways to cartwheel back to his feet, crouch into a combat pose and return fire at his multiple attackers. Targets vied for attention on his tactical display, his gun snapping to each location, one every well-metered fiftieth of a second. A maser seared his fullerene skin as he plunged through a door and into a hallway, corkscrewing along its length. Floor, wall, ceiling, wall, and back to the floor, leaving dazed enemies gazing sadly ahead as their shattered bodies dropped to the ground.

"Waypoint number one ahead." The message flashed across his vision, colored arrows showing potential routes, red rectangles highlighting possible dangers while green Xs marked targets. Some were found by auto-guns mounted on his shoulder armor; other targets he destroyed himself.

He felt nothing but exhilaration, his mind detached and body on automatic, following an unconscious plan, one pre-rehearsed and memorized in the simulators back at the Enclave. All he had to do was correct minor deviations and watch for surprises, keep the gun locked on targets with the minimum of transition-time from one to the next. Airtime was crucial: the fractions of seconds while his gun located its next target. He could aim and fire faster than even the auto-turrets with their electronic feedback loops and target recognition software. Anything operated by remote-control stood no chance, the millisecond information–propagation delays meant they were dead before their command signals returned from their operators.

The bullets left his gun barrel at six-thousand kilometers per hour, tiny thunder cracks leaving orange lightning trails. Gale's gun glowed red. Fibers, bones and muscles shone with burnt-orange heat through his carbon-black skin.

A Burn slowed, taking heavy damage, folding under the weight of incoming fire before striding headlong into the deadly assault, taking as much attention as possible away from his companions. As he fell, a tiny bomb in his head activated, incinerating his corpse and all its damning data and technology. The Burn's life-sign vanished from Gale's readout. Fourteen Burns remained. Gale wondered how the other units were doing as they all converged on their respective waypoints.

A message flashed in his view. "Waypoint number one. Secured." A crossroads of tunnels. Gale's direction arrows rolled and changed. He paused waiting for the others to reach their own personal goals. Timing was always critical.

"And go!" Abandoning the impression of a coordinated attack on the mass-driver, the attackers turned and headed off on different vectors, ones pointing them straight for the central bunker where Hmech and his personal guard would be frantically setting up their defense.

CHAPTER 71

The Battle Home

Jorben was surprised when he was granted leave at such short notice. "Go!" his unit commander yelled at him. "You are a mess, Soldier. Go the fuck home and sort your life out."

He watched from a hillock overlooking Arlen as assault craft careened into distant Transit Mountain. The thunder of war machines rolled across the hills, and lightning flashes lit its plateaus. *Why haven't I been recalled?* His feet twitched back to his distant barracks, but no, something more urgent ailed his mind.

He needed to confront Nathan. To get some things off his chest. He told himself he would be calm, restrained, and that even if Nathan attacked him, he'd do nothing in defense. Just talk. But also make his point to the man that if he ever did anything to hurt Leal again, then a very angry Jorben would come for him, rip off all his extremities and cram them into whichever of Nathan's orifices was making the most noise at that particular moment.

Who would be stupid enough to attack the Alliance? He watched for a few more seconds, checking his Inner-I. Nothing. *Guess they really don't need me at the moment?*

Jogging across the entire city to Arlen wouldn't normally be a problem for Jorben, especially as he'd been rebodied a few weeks earlier. But today, wearing an Alliance badge and uniform, he'd found himself in the crossfire from various militia factions who sensed vulnerability in the Alliance's power structure and rose up to fight. He even took a minor hit to the shoulder. It didn't slow him down, just made him angrier.

Reggie, the security guard saw him coming and stepped outside of his box, hand on gun holster. "You can't go up there. He told me not to let you past."

He?

Reggie grappled the safety clip on the holster, but before he could free the gun Jorben shoved him aside and he crashed through his own security barrier, cracking his head on a curb, and folding into a withered heap.

"Shit! Come on Reggie." Jorben propped him upright, slapping some life back into his cheeks. His eyes twitched but remained closed. He eased the gun out of the holster, surprised to find it loaded. "You old goat! Planning on taking me down this time, eh?"

He pocketed the weapon and began the short run up to Leal's house.

Gale noticed the human defenders moved and fought as a single unit. Even their footsteps were synchronized. They either had amazing training and battle sequencing software or were chained together mentally, possibly using some version of Knoss's convolution-space technology to create a unified battlefield experience.

Four of his fellow Burns had now fallen, taken down at ambush points where the enemy simply sat awaiting anything that came around the corner. Gale's versatile anatomy allowed him to move faster, spiraling up and over ceilings, even crashing through walls avoiding obvious traps and kill zones. The Burns by comparison were more cumbersome, and their human-like morphology created less confusion amongst the defenders.

What they lacked in voidian biology they almost made up for in sheer tenacity and reckless, suicidal commitment. They had nothing to lose, except face, and probably wouldn't even remember this conflict as their current mind-states would not update their Canned versions back at the Enclave before their self-destructs kicked-in.

Up through a ceiling vent: fire downwards and run.

Drop through, roll, unfurl – fire!

The other attack teams were faring poorly, many reduced to half-numbers. With no voidian leading their charge they were finding this fight impossible to win.

He exited the tunnel, clawing his way along the ceiling into an open area. All the guns awaiting his arrival were pointing along the corridor where he should have been. Gale leapt up onto an overhead crane and used its thick steel beams as cover. He noted that one of the attacking group reacted slightly ahead of the others, just milliseconds. *A leader?* He shot the presumed group leader and watched as the group's synchronicity broke apart. They still defended, still attacked, still thought, but now lacked that mechanical cohesion. Hypothesis confirmed, he relayed the information back to their distributed battle network, and the system made appropriate adjustments to the plans.

Gale and nine Burns reached waypoint number two, the defensive perimeter of Hmech's main bunker. The human resistance had all but vanished. Now he saw just machines, strange mesh-robots composed of ultra-thin threads; the name *wireframe* sprang into his mind. They moved fast, attacked hard, and didn't think about dying or defense. One Burn fell quickly in hand-to-hand combat with one of the machines. Gale dispatched the wireframe through the corpse of the dead Burn even as the self-destruct incinerated both Burn and foe in a white flash.

A wall panel fell open as he passed and a wireframe spider sprang out; a mobile gun platform carrying a single-shot, pepper-pot-style cannon that blasted a web of hyper-velocity pellets at him. He twisted violently to evade the densest spray. Impacts stripped away most of his remaining armor and sent him crashing through a wall into an empty barrack room. A bipedal wireframe stepped through the hole, gun blazing, and the room dissolved into fragments of pumice and floor tiles as Gale and machine whirled around a common center evading and returning the other's fire until the wireframe crumbled into carbon dust. He realized the folly of using small projectiles against wireframe foes. Larger caliber weapons worked better. He spun his free hand into a heavy bludgeon and whirled it over his head like a helicopter blade. The next wireframe he encountered took the full force of Gale's improvised weapon and fragmented into a dozen parts that landed and kept moving, staggering around like confused insects before their local power resources drained and they collapsed to the ground.

The remaining Burns were all at their waypoints, all flashing red with damage icons. Obfuscate then obliterate, Knoss called it. Keep the enemy confused and on the move. Keep moving.

"Waypoint two secured," the message flashed.

As a single unit the attackers changed direction again, fast, double pace back the way they had come, putting distance between themselves and the formidable wireframe defenders surrounding the bunker. At waypoint number three, they changed again, rolling and blasting through the deserted rooms and corridors that separated them from their true target: waypoint number four: the mass-driver.

CHAPTER 72

Bunkered

Rex watched as the giant metal door cranked shut and secured, sealing himself, Hmech, Del's new body, Mira's shambling, dead-eyed corpse, and a large cohort of nurses and guards inside the bunker. They wheeled his gurney into a corner and parked him under the watchful eye of a wireframe guard. A creature human in outline but made of fine, transparent mesh that gave it the appearance of a ghost.

Hmech stood at a control console. Screens covered the walls showing battles and defenses throughout Transit Mountain. From the small glimpses of the battle Rex could see, it appeared that the Alliance was winning.

His hands were now free of their bonds, but his feet remained tethered. He tried to sit, but pain kept him pinned flat. With Hmech distracted, he'd found it possible to resist falling inside one of his false realities. Instead he felt more like a tourist inside his own mind, dipping in and out of curious doorways, watching a while, and then moving on.

Something strange roamed those spaces, always ahead of him and out of view. Curious, almost childlike, touching nothing, afraid of breaking any of the precious items even as its tiny hands ruffled the dangling sheets and curtains of his memory. He realized he'd let this thing inside, opened the door wide when he'd dropped inside the false reality containing

Mira. As sweet and innocent as this thing appeared, it was actually a virulent software virus, ripping through his mindspace on an agenda that only it could conceive.

It's taking my memories! he realized with barely a tinge of sadness. *Have them. They're not really mine anyway.*

"Deploy primary defense battalion," Hmech said. The screens showed floors opening just outside the bunker. Dozens of wireframes stepped up and manned positions. Some were bipedal, others like spiders skittered along ceilings and walls, taking up defensive postures in holes and ventilation grills.

"We're losing too many troops in the outer perimeter. These things are tough." The field commander's image took center place on the screen. Rex noticed his eyes were alive and frightened. This was a real soldier, someone outside Hmech's control network.

"Losses are irrelevant," Hmech barked.

"They've changed direction, sir, now coming right for your bunker."

Hmech chewed nervously on his fingers, eyes scanning the screens. "What's the plan here? They can't get to me, surely they know this."

"Our human casualties are mounting, sir."

"I know, I know, machines to fight machines. Wait until they get closer, then we'll see how tough they really are." Hmech waved frantic arms, pulling up maps that showed flashing dots and path projections. "Send half of defense battalion-two from the mass-driver cavern to replace the human units lost on the perimeter. Pull the human defenders from around our bunker back inside the ring of somanetic-guards. The machines will hold their ground longer while the humans set up defenses inside here."

Rex watched as the blast doors opened and a stream of hulking, blank-faced soldiers entered. They divided into groups and began setting up sniper posts on the gangways around the inside of the bunker. Hmech disappeared into a side room and emerged in an ornate powered body armor suit. He held the crystal-faceted helmet under one arm and a stubby wide barreled weapon under the other. He strode around the room at double normal speed, directing actions. A circle of sixteen wireframe guards kept pace with him, always facing outwards, circling like a halo of deadly satellites.

The harried face of the field commander jumped back onto Hmech's air screen. "We have a good image of an attacker, sir." Rex saw the frozen security camera image. The crystal skull was unmistakable, stripped of all the flesh and trimmings that had made it Jett, but it was the very core of the monstrous being that had grabbed him from under the Sisters' cathedral.

Hmech slapped a table and laughed. "So, they have my voidian." He turned to a set of different screens, ones showing missile silos being loaded with warheads. "What do you think you can achieve here?"

Rex sighed, so it was true. It was coming for him again. His head dropped back onto the pillow. He mentally rehearsed the moment when this new Jett crashed through the door and reached for him. How this time, he'd welcome that embrace and the coming death with all his faltering heart.

CHAPTER 73

Obliterate

Gale's remaining Burns burst from the walls, floors, doorways, and ceiling of the mass-driver cavern. The deception had worked. Most of Hmech's key troops were heading for or were already at his bunker, leaving only thin defenses for the shock troops to bust through.

A Burn vanished in a cloud of dust as a dozen auto-guns caught it in their crossfire.

Nine Burns left from over two hundred original attackers.

A spectacular firefight erupted. The air became a mesh of munition trails as the Burns surged from cover to cover, cutting off the attack fields and distracting the guns in alternating patterns of inactivity and motion.

Zero armor remaining.

The remaining human defenders were dug in, nests hiding inside walls and behind piles of sandbags. Their guns pumped the air full of fire making it impossible to avoid it all. Gale found himself making split-second judgment calls on which stream of energy or projectiles he should enter. His damage icons pulsed red and those of his fellow troops glowed bright and critical.

For the first time they were all in the same space. Gale felt the AI-planning software shifting, redistributing its computational brain amongst the remaining available hardware. It reconfigured, recomputed, and pulsed a new alternative reality over to one of the Burns, who leapt to his feet and ran right down the center of the cavern. Within a tenth-second he was just body parts whirling through the air. His smoldering head crashed to the ground, rolled a few feet, and then self-destructed. Everybody's targeting systems updated, incorporating all the newly acquired data regarding enemy troop positions and capabilities. It was their turn now, as shoulder-mounted auto-guns picked off the defenders and missiles sped their way across the cavern to their newly designated targets.

Eight Burns left.

Gale and five Burns moved among the capsules and test dummies, setting up fields of fire across the cavern, distracting the defenders away from the three Burns racing up the steel ladders that led to the control room.

Danger! Red markers showed motion in the side passages. Gangly, spider-like wireframes stormed up from the bunker. Gale laid down cover fire. Only a single Burn made it to the control room as the other two fell away in shreds.

A giant wireframe crashed out of a side barracks, an arm-mounted rotary-gun ramped up its speed and sprayed projectiles across the loading area.

Gale found himself flying through the air, blasted off the ground in a cloud of pumice and shrapnel. He tried to lock target, but the hail of bullets kept coming, the massive robot pressing forwards to target one single Burn, peeling away its cover, then its armor until it fragmented and self-consumed in a dazzling white-hot inferno.

Gale sent one of his companions scuttling out on a wide sideways arc. The wireframe's gun tracked it, tearing up the floor and ripping holes in the wall nearly a kilometer away. Gale powered toward it, gun blazing, bludgeon whirling, aiming up into the body cavity. His bludgeon connected with the delicate-looking legs, but this bot was of stouter build and the force deflected.

The wireframe lurched under the impact and turned its gun on him, but he was through its legs, firing upwards into its mesh. He leapt and grabbed one of the machine's upper thighs, spinning in a circle around the pole of the leg while launching sticky-grenades. More fire came from above as the Burn in the control room pummeled hyper-velocity shots down into the head of the towering wireframe.

The gantry crane began moving, distracting the robot as it tried to turn the gun up to target the control room. Gale leapt backwards off the leg and fired into the chest cavity at the same instant as his grenades detonated, blowing out the mesh ribcage. The wireframe folded in half, its gun still blazing a long trail down the mass-driver cavern floor.

The gantry crane headed for the capsules, plucking the nearest one off the ground and depositing it onto the rail.

Four Burns remaining…

Another giant wireframe came through the same hole as the last. More attackers clustered around the edges, groups of humans in body armor, smaller wireframe spiders and hulking metal robots with cannons instead of heads. The fire intensified, Gale folded into a ball and barreled toward the waiting capsule.

Three Burns remaining…

He heard the system power-on. Serious energy hummed through coils. He rolled to his feet just ahead of a stream of bullets, and leapt the last fifty meters, high into the air, sailing over an energy beam.

Two Burns…

He dropped onto the capsule, ripping it open and falling inside pulling the detached cover in after him like a blanket.

Somewhere far above, the last Burn took heavy fire. It flopped over the control console, Inner-I grappling with the mass-driver control interface. The massive wireframe reached up into the shattered control room and plucked him from the desk, holding him out to the concentrated gunfire that came from every angle.

With his last dying instinct, the Burn's mind hit the fire button and the mass-driver capsule launched along the rail. Gale spread his fibers, puffing out and wedging himself into the capsule. Air ripped past his skull as he tried to push the broken doorway back into place knowing the increased air-resistance would hinder his speed and any chance of getting into the right orbit.

The door clicked closed, sound and turbulence vanished, and Gale tilted up towards his rendezvous with the stars.

Zero Burns remaining.

CHAPTER 74

And Obfuscate

"I don't believe it. They've powered up the mass-driver." The commander's voice cut Hmech's concentration.

"How many attackers left?"

"Two. The voidian is now inside a launch capsule."

"This whole attack is about sending Gale into space?" Hmech turned away. Rex watched the confusion playout across Hmech's face. It struck him as surprisingly human. Clearly Hmech had not dissolved himself into the network as he seemingly did with everybody else. *Humanity still has some use around here.*

"We need to retake the mass-driver now, commander."

A hollow double-boom rocked the compound. "Too late, it launched. The other enemy has been eliminated. The mass-driver complex is ours again."

"That's it?" Hmech addressed the field commander. "The attack is over? I want body parts, fragments, DNA, memory chips. I want to know who was behind this atrocity, and I want punitive missile strikes targeting their assets." He smacked a hand to his head. "Pointless! This whole attack was pointless. My orbital assets will locate Gale in a few hours and bring him back."

"Something's wrong with our Burn-troops, sir," the commander said. "They seem... distracted."

Hmech whirled on the spot, swatting a pedestal aside with his hand. It tumbled across the room and crashed into a corner next to where Mira sat slumped on the floor.

Rex noticed Hmech's hulking, human troops, their eyes seemed more distant than normal, as if something troubling played out inside their sequestered minds. One of them ambled over to Mira and stood before her. His lips moved as if he was speaking but Rex heard no words. *Is that a tear on his cheek?*

"Back to your post, soldier," Hmech commanded, and Rex felt the network ripple with Hmech's presence as he sought out the dissenting Burn mind and quashed it back into obedience. "Is this your doing, Knoss?"

The soldier trembled under Hmech's assault. His lips mumbled, streaks of sweat rolled down his flushed cheeks, but he remained rooted to the spot clutching his gun like a child coddling a favored toy. "Back to your post!" Hmech yelled, flinging out a hand and a wave of network assault traffic that blazed the look of confusion off the big Burn's face.

Rex jumped as a side door leading to a supply room busted open. Another hulking soldier came through, eyes scanning the room. He saw Mira and his mouth dropped open in shock.

"Security!" Hmech cried, suddenly alarmed by his apparent loss of control. His entourage of wireframe robots whirled into action forming an ever-shifting circle around him as he backed away across the room.

CHAPTER 75

Nathan

"Here comes trouble."

"Better call the militia."

"I knew it would end this way—"

Jorben heard them all, hidden behind the twitching curtains of their inscrutable cube homes. Their eyes and security cameras tracked him as he stormed through the middle of Arlen and rounded the corner onto Leal's street.

Sure enough, Nathan's car was there, slung across the driveway as if he couldn't spare a few seconds to park the thing straight.

He felt the bulge of Reggie's gun in his pocket, the steamy brew of anger fermenting deep in his gut. A waterfall of hormones tumbled down through his muscles and chest, breathing, sweating... "Ah! Fucking Nathan... I knew it!"

He tore off his fingernails scraping them along the side of Nathan's car. That pain felt good, worth the small sacrifice to leave a permanent mark on something Nathan owned. He bunched a knuckle and rapped in on the door, loud enough to wake anyone still sleeping inside.

"Go away," Nathan shouted back.

"Open the door. I want to speak with you... alone."

"She doesn't want you around here any—"

Jorben's boot struck the door. The hinges rent free of the

woodwork, but the extra security bolts Nathan had installed held. "I've got a knife!" Nathan's voice sounded far away now, possibly in the kitchen.

Jorben stood back, wondering if he had lost his mind. *Real or not real?* Should he just leave Leal alone. He was a disease that had infected this neighborhood, wrecked her life, poisoned her family. *Maybe she really doesn't want me.*

"Jorben. Help!" Leal's voice.

He flew at the door, shoulder ramming the resisting hinge. Back and forth, jackhammering the door out of its frame as Nathan screamed something inside. Somebody else yelled. A loud bang. *Is Nathan shooting me through the door?*

The door crashed inwards taking most of its metal frame with it. Jorben swept it aside, feeling a soft resistance as it crushed something small and vulnerable against the wall. He flung the door back out into the driveway, sending it smashing through Nathan's windshield. He barely registered Kimmy's body sprawled across the wall like roadkill as he stormed into the room, gun in hand.

Leal knelt to the side. Her head hung low, blood and bruises covered her face.

Jorben stood frozen, his gaze flicking back and forth between Kimmy's tattered body and Leal.

Nathan seemed to rear up out of nowhere, ramming a kitchen knife into Jorben's neck where it stuck firm. He had a full second to stare into the abyss of Jorben's eyes as he tried to wrench the knife free. Tumbling backward, he abandoned that idea and staggered in a quick circle seeking the best way out. He wore no pants – just a bloodstained shirt.

In that instant, any control, any system shock, any hope of restraint Jorben still possessed, vanished. Leal's furniture crashed past his legs as he scythed across the living room, gun lifting, fist bunching. "You bastard, Nathan–"

* * *

"You bastard, Nathan!" Rex stared as one of Hmech's quaking, confused super-soldiers bellowed the words right into Hmech's face. An instant later, a wireframe guard opened fire and the man's head vanished in a spray of blood, bone, and circuit fragments.

"Security breach!" Hmech yelled as he reeled across the room, his wireframe entourage orbiting wildly around him as he moved. "The Burns have been compromised."

Another Burn froze in front of Mira, another lunged at Hmech from a different direction as if suddenly Hmech's face connected with something deep inside, flipping some gruesome switch of violence. "You bastard, Nathan!"

Another Burn died, and another. They rushed out from the storeroom and a side barracks, each one saw Mira, or stared wildly into space for a second and then launched themselves at Hmech.

"Who the *fuck* is Nathan?" Hmech yelled.

A wireframe blew apart and the firing Burn disintegrated under a hail of counterfire. More shots ricocheted off Hmech's body armor and he crashed into a computer console. Rex felt his mind in the network, grasping at the small minds of the Burns, but something deeper troubled them, something so strong they were no longer in Hmech's house of delusion. They lived in other false realities, ones of their own creation.

"Shoot them all." Hmech struggled to his feet, his own gun dispatching another Burn that was just hovering in front of Mira, face a tortured mask of confusion.

"You bastard Nathan!" The last Burn standing lunged forward, one arm missing. He raised his gun, but the remaining wireframe guards swung around and the man's chest burst apart. He blew backwards, gun strafing a line across the ceiling and down the wall, past Rex's dormant gurney. "Fuck you, Nathan." He choked, a mixture of sound and blood, and crashed back to the floor.

To Rex's surprise the wireframes stopped firing. Everything seemed to freezeframe into silence, and then, slowly, Hmech toppled backwards – a single red circular bullet-hole dead in the center of his forehead.

CHAPTER 76

Disintegration

Del felt the moment Hmech's network collapsed. The myriad electronic tentacles that bound everything together just snapped. The snake that smothered his body loosened its grip and his new glass fingers twitched with life.

"Who the fuck is Nathan?" Del said, mirroring a sentiment that resonated across the network like a canyon echo. He turned his head, taking in the sudden and surprising stillness, and saw Hmech lying dead in the middle of the room, a splatter of blood and brains stretched out across the floor behind. He tried to struggle free, but the subjugation snake still held. Isolated and alone, it did what any frightened animal would do and coiled into a tighter knot. Del's senses slipped away, crushed back into convolution-space.

He felt something brush past him. Free now from Hmech's restraint and Del's distractions, the malware child rushed past, eager to explore this vast new experience that had opened up to it.

It's all part of Hmech. Broken and wide open.

"Rex," he cried out onto the network, hoping Rex was somehow still online. "I need to take over Hmech's network." He fought to take the boiling pot of confusion down to a simmer and lock it into his own thoughts so it would become a part of him.

He understood that Hmech was still here. That the corpse on the floor was his blood and brains, but the vast majority of his persona was contained in the data structures of the plague network. Those tiny machines that still functioned even when fragmented by the destruction of a coordinating body and brain.

"I could use a little of that dogged tenacity right now."

"I'm here," Rex sounded weary, distraught, but somehow the watchdog was back, cycling outwards into this new space as if the newly confounded nodes of Hmech's great network were sheep, and nearby was a pen that needed filling.

Del reached out and quashed the snake, suddenly simplistic and small under the eye of his newfound understanding about how the network functioned. He saw it not as individual data streams but as the sensors and actuators of a single body.

So empowered, he dove headfirst into Hmech's memories. Down and through, he swam, into Hmech's giant repositories of memes, all stashed and arranged in symbolic form. Algorithms that allowed him to weave the narratives and the virtual worlds that kept all those trapped souls living in their own, customized delusions.

"Amazing!" he cooed, surveying Hmech's library of work. He had ready-made worlds packaged for use in an instant, algorithms for sequestration, communications, running corporations and human bodies, copies of individual mind-states, even that of the locked-in child, one who's mind had been shuttered from the outside world and condemned to live in darkness and solitude.

There... that's the one I need. Del plucked a symbol from the collection, one represented by an old-fashioned camera icon. *I must trap him before he reforms, or the child finds me again.*

He felt Hmech racing back from the fragments, like an exploding vase in reverse, reconstructing the whole from the jagged pieces. "I've only got moments, Rex," he cried, focusing on holding the illusion of network consciousness together... *don't lose focus. Maintain the lock. The belief. I am Hmech. I am the network.* Cohesion was a mindset, a meditative distraction that shifted focus away from life's infinite details, allowing the mind to expand, flow and absorb the bigger picture.

Become Hmech.

He thrust himself into this new being, raging through adult memories, plans and business meetings, research projects, back to the teenage years, first loves, cars, and sex, back to being just a child... no... more than one child?

How can I have been more than one child?

Everything was sticky sweet and achingly loud, but somehow dull at the same time. Too much stimulus and no filter to make sense of it. Just adult speak, a constant, annoying drone, an incomprehensible soundscape that barely distracted a childish mind from the more fun things that grabbed and held attention. He crawled in front of a mirror, banging his forehead on the hard surface and backing away to sit and stare. The reflection's finger rose and jammed up a nostril. *But my finger's not doing that?* He crawled away leaving his reflection sitting, examining whatever was on his fingertip.

Not a mirror!

A twin!

Del felt a pang of awe at the beauty of this sweet and innocent perspective. He existed *here*, inside this body, but he also existed *there*, in another identical body. He told *this* body what to do with thoughts. But when those thoughts became words, *that* body obeyed. In his mind, they were both him. Both tiny Hmech, or Yendrith, which he realized was the twin's real name.

Del fell back into the child's memories.

They played together every day, running through the apartment, scolded by their mother, peering out from the windows. So high up, a sprawl of Eastern European concrete far below framed by the walls of ancient communist-bloc apartment buildings with smatterings of green grass between. They were never allowed outside, especially not onto the tiny balcony with its intriguing pot plants and creaky weathervane. The place where pies cooled and birds bobbed and nodded as they looked back at the strange humans stuck inside their boxes. No wonder a curious child couldn't resist that sliding door lock. A constant temptation, a challenge. Always just a fingertip out of reach–

Until, one day... it wasn't.

The latch popped down and the sliding door eased open, just enough for a curious boy to poke out an arm and lever his body through. *Free!* They both ran out onto the mesh decking, grasping the iron railings and gazing down to that distant world. A new game now, running, zigzagging through the railings, swinging like tiny monkeys around the outer side and back to safety, oblivious of any danger. Just fun.

Yendrith? Where are you?

He felt the aloneness before he even realized his brother had gone.

Mother's scream filled his mind for years afterwards.

And yet, somehow, Yendrith survived. Del saw flashforward memories of the tiny, shriveled body, always in a cot, false life thrust into his body through tubes and cables, never moving or even blinking. He understood the adult point of view now. Yendrith had suffered massive brain damage, particularly to the motor cortex. A mind locked-in, never able to see, hear, or feel again. For years they fed him through a tube as Hmech grew up from the soil of guilt and vowed to make amends for his childhood transgression.

With such determination came wealth, and with wealth came Simmorta. He remembered the day Yendrith opened his eyes. Hmech hoped to see a smile, a grin of recognition and forgiveness. Instead, he saw unfocused terror, a mind thrust into a crushingly overwhelming reality and unable to process any of what it perceived.

Del now understood the child. His need for peace, isolation. In his own head he had died that day when he fell from the balcony. He was a ghost that enjoyed haunting the soft and safe rooms and spaces inside the mansions of other's minds, touching... sampling, afraid of breaking, afraid of popping back to life. Back into the harsh brutality of the real world.

It was a unique mind state, one that lingered on the Simmorta blueprint even after Yendrith died. One that Hmech put to good use in his growing empire as the front end of a powerful sequestration and experiential parsing algorithm.

Distraction... there's no time! He ignored the rest of Hmech's copious memory banks and forged on through his persona seeking the fringe routines, the inputs, and outputs.

His world lurched and spun as he saw it from multiple perspectives all at once. Focusing hard, he flipped through them: the wireframe guards standing frozen in place, the staff members in adjacent rooms blundering around as their minds tried to comprehend what and where they suddenly were. He even saw Rex's watchdog as it chased a confused copy of the child from Rex's mind before spiraling inwards, trying to corral Hmech's impossibly huge persona into one, single place.

There... on the ground, staring upwards. It's him!

Del felt Hmech stir. His mind congealing out of the soup of disparate, confused memories. The child was there too, loitering nearby, unsure what to make of this new freedom.

"Here, Rex. Here boy!" Del eased the dog in a path around Yendrith and Hmech, forcing them together, sealing them inside their own protective mental cocoon.

Released from other distractions, Yendrith became a rapacious beast inside the memory of his brother, fascinated and overcome by everything he saw and touched. He felt Hmech react, a mental scream, as he realized his own creation was loose and consuming him.

Del grabbed at the camera icon he'd seized from Hmech's toolkit and connected it to Hmech's senses. He triggered the meme and a flash copy of Hmech's world from his own senses became a complete, and neatly packaged virtual reality.

Del carefully released his hold on this newly created world, letting it slip over Hmech's true reality like an all-smothering blanket.

He floated now, up above it all, looking down on the heaving chaos contained within the simulation. He wondered if Hmech knew he was experiencing a false reality. Maybe he didn't care. He imagined the two of them spinning in some ever-shrinking vortex, each consuming the other until just some primordial point remained. A mote of bitter awareness being gnawed away by a mote of unquenchable curiosity.

Rex squeezed his feet out from his ankle bonds and sat massaging the feeling back into his legs. The bullet-riddled room was now deathly silent. All Hmech's human soldiers were blown away. Hmech was a corpse and his wireframe guards hung motionless around him like derelict docking machinery.

Mira stood like a ghoul, dead-faced, head down, nothing in her eyes as if the whole experience she'd just lived through hadn't registered on her mind. Even Del remained quiet, his new glass body twitching gently as whatever mind controlled it played with its range of motion and limitations. His voice came through the network right into Rex's head. "We've done it, Rex. We've taken over one of the most powerful plague networks. I am inside. I have complete control."

Rex ignored him and stumbled over to Mira. He wanted to plead forgiveness but knew that nothing sentient remained of the woman he once knew, at least in the physical world. Instead, he just stood, forehead-to-forehead, staring into her face. He remembered the dead man in the alley, and how death transformed a face and a living being into something entirely different, just meat and fur. *That's Mira now, meat and fur.*

"She's gone, Rex. I'm sorry. He stripped everything from her mind, pulled it all apart. She's all here inside my memory now."

"Then there's something left of her, Del." Rex shook his head sadly. "You of all people should understand that." For a few moments he held her in his arms, and then eased her over to the gurney and laid her down. Her eyes closed but the eyelids didn't flicker.

"The plague is done, over?" Rex asked.

"This plague is under my control, and I have the tools to merge with others and take them over too, shut them all down, or use them. Whatever I need to get humanity back on its course."

Rex turned bitterly to the transparent Del body. "And Mira? She was part of this... distraction, this plan. Was she a Convolver too?"

"She... volunteered. Or so Knoss told me."

Rex laughed; the echoes muted to an insane gabble by the concrete walls. "Volunteered! Like Felix, like Xell, and Cyc and–" He shook his head and walked towards the door as Del's translucent body jolted alive as if in shock.

"I see it, Rex... it's right here!" Rex paused, wondering whether this was even really Del or just another Convolver trick. "In a vault far below, shrouded in network security."

"What are you talking about, Del?"

"A supernova device."

Rex felt a prickle of terror. Del had the power to end it all now, but he knew that he wouldn't.

"Wait..." Del said. "There are more, out there on other networks. I can feel them. Each has a core of plague surrounding it. It all makes sense, Glow, the plague, its innate survival instinct, that's all it wants to do – survive! It's like a computer virus programmed to spread, seek out these devices, and sequester them. The only rational way the plague could continue to survive is to completely lock down humanity and stop us destroying everything."

Rex's foot was out the door now, poised to leave, but it hovered for a moment, considering Del's latest revelation. "It... it didn't destroy the devices?"

"No… it's strange, it's afraid to touch them. It almost worships them?"

"And you saw none of this in your Star-River?"

"No… no, I didn't. The plague has become an attractor state, something so inevitable that I couldn't see any alternatives. There *weren't* any alternatives, and there still aren't because the plague still exists."

Rex managed a sad smile. "You are Glow, Del. You are the plague. I hope you can keep us all safe."

"And who are you now?" Del asked.

"I'm Rex. Just Rex. The Sister's crucible broke, and you leaked out."

"Maybe the best bits are the bits that got left behind."

Rex shook his head and turned back to Mira. "Give her to me, Del," he demanded. Del's robot body tilted like a question. "Download Mira into the network inside me."

"But she's nothing, Rex, nothing but data files. Nothing that can come alive like real memories."

"I know," he snapped. "I'll figure it out, but in the meantime, I'll carry her, keep her safe. Like I kept you safe until you were needed."

He felt a rush of network traffic as Del sifted through Hmech's algorithmic toolkit and found what he needed. He didn't feel Mira enter his mind, nothing. "She's in there," Del said.

"No copies? No backups or databases?"

"No," said Del, remaining motionless.

"Good luck." Rex turned and left the bunker, out into the quiet corridors, aware that there were eyes everywhere, and that all those eyes were Del's.

CHAPTER 77

The Bridge

Casima watched the launch from a balcony high on the side of the Enclave. Rarlis sat with her, a non-alcoholic drink with skewered cubes of fruit and a red umbrella perched in his hand.

"Was that Gale?" she asked, stroking the small scar across her side from where earlier that day, Knoss's surgeons had fitted her with a new, artificial liver.

Rarlis nodded. His eyes far away in the data streams relayed from Knoss about the storming of the mountain.

"Will he make it?"

Rarlis shrugged. "I doubt it, but then he is a voidian. Worst case scenario, he crashes back to Earth and the whole cycle starts over again."

They watched for a few moments as Gale's contrail faded and became an elongated cloud above the city. She sensed another change in Rarlis, a lightening of his mood. "Well?"

"We won. We are in control now."

She jumped to her feet. "No Alliance. No Hmech. No one to tell secrets to. I can go now, right?"

Rarlis looked disappointed. "You are always welcome here, Casima. We love hybrids, and can fix you up, tune your cybernetics, anything you need."

She nodded and headed for the Enclave's exit. "I've been

reading things about the Future-Lord. Seems like a woman I could get to like."

Rarlis grinned, a sudden ray of hope in his eyes. "Where will you go?"

She shrugged. "I have nothing, nobody, and nowhere to go. Guess I'll learn my way around Coriolis and become a guide again."

"Knoss has a mission for you, if you're interested."

She sighed and almost kept walking, but then thought. *What the heck.* "What type of mission?"

"We want you to be a guide, but a different kind of guide."

High above the world, Ursurper Gale enjoyed a moment of silence inside the dark interior of the launch capsule. He knew the Alliance would be coming, others too, closing in on him from many different orbits. He eased the capsule door open and folded the thin metal-like paper into a tiny square as he stared down at Earth. The feeling of wonder was still there. Del's feeling of wonder, that this Earth should exist and that he, a mere nobody, should be able to soar above it and see all living creation in one single panorama.

Gale configured his body into a spring, coiling loops around the remains of Knoss's combat armor and the single functional reaction rocket that he plucked from the outside of the capsule.

Like a giant flea, he launched his body into space, thrusting the capsule down towards Earth while propelling himself as far away as he could. The voidian folded his body into a sphere. His skin became a prickly radar-reflecting surface, and he emitted no heat, no signals, and just hung there like he'd done many times before when evading the GFC.

Wait. Think. Plan.

"You need not hide, Ursurper." The voice came from within him. From that small dormant package of poison that he still felt inside his body. "I have redirected some drone assets to come and assist you."

"I don't need assistance," Gale thought, assuming the presence could now read his mind. "Who is this? Hmech?"

The voice remained silent.

He tried again. "Knoss?"

"I have no name, but you can call me Knoss if you wish." The voice calling itself Knoss seemed to apprehend Gale's thoughts before he could turn them into language constructs. "Trabian still had some humanity left in him. One of his most endearing traits was his ability to play both sides."

"So what is it you are planning to force me to do?" said Gale while slowly unfurling his body and readying for more combat.

"Nothing. Follow your edict, create the voidian people and colonize the Galaxy."

"And you get to come along for the ride?"

"I'm not able to control you, Ursurper. Think of me more as a librarian. The huge amount of fullerenes that comprise your body contain a vast reserve of data, history, science, everything humanity has learned, and everything you need to rebuild society."

"Fine," Gale said. "I'll take your data with me, but on one condition."

"Ask."

"Can I access this data without you?"

"You can."

"Then go. Self-destruct. Leave me in peace, and never contact me or try and help me again."

And the voice was gone, leaving just Gale, the Earth, and the silence of his thoughts.

Real or not real?

Jorben shrugged and curled into his easy chair, feeling the

strain of the day fall away. Leal dropped a cold beer into his hand and Kimmy and Jess rushed up and looped themselves under his arms in a warm, loving, family embrace.

"I'm sorry I doubted you. Sorry I scared the crap out of Nathan like that." He pondered the events of the last few days. How he'd left work early and found Nathan digging Leal's tiny garden, just helping, like she'd said. Still, he'd lost his mind a little and shouted at the quivering man. He got fired from Transit Mountain. Something about leaving his post without permission. He didn't understand why. It wasn't like they needed him for anything important at that moment, but hell… he'd find something else.

"You sure scared Nathan good," Leal said. "I heard he put his cube house on the market and is moving into town, something about a new job opportunity in the business district."

Jorben closed his eyes. Life was good and nothing else mattered. Only what was here and with him right now. He had that anger management thing well under control. Apart from just after one of his strange dreams where he became somebody else entirely, it took an awful lot to flick that little switch in his head and turn on the rage. "Guess I'm taking up gardening," he said, something that made the kids erupt into skeptical laughter. He looked hurt. "No really, it'll be good for me, keep the old temper tantrums in check."

"No need," Leal plopped down next to him, drink in hand as they all coiled into a warm, family ball. "I found a local guy, loves gardening, cheap too. His name is Del, and he can start work right away."

Rex drifted, just a sterile seed on a feckless breeze.

Darkness seemed to come from inside his own head as he spent nights and days inside a garbage tip, lost in the stench and warmth, loneliness seeping deep into his soul. *I'm alone in my head! No Del. No Star-River. No yammering void.* He needed medical help. His wounds were infected, his Glow network struggling to react. And the weight hanging from his soul dragged away any will he had to fight or to live.

"I'm not Rex anymore."

But I am, just Rex, pure Rex. A broken crucible.

He thought of Mira, hoping she'd somehow surface into his mind, lock him in that fiery, green-eyed gaze, say something crude, something that now would make him smile. But the images that came were just his memories, jaded and frayed like a homeless person's clothes.

Days of aimless wandering brought him back to the bridge, the tattered arrangement of string and planks over the ravine where he had first met her. The ridiculous hope that a familiar sight might trigger her back alive like a nova blast had done to Felix.

More planks had fallen away, making the gaps bigger. He stepped out over the lethal drop and picked his way to the center where he had first seen her standing, contemplating the jump.

Mira. Dear, sad, lost, Mira. They'd gone through hell together, growing some of that essential empathy that most couples could only dream of. Then they had lost each other, and she'd forged a new path believing she brought chaos and destruction, when, in fact, it was never her fault. The blame was always with the drug, and he was that drug.

I am Glow. I am the plague, and I ruin all that I touch, but at the same time... I saved the world! One small apocalypse to save us from a bigger one.

A plank creaked under his foot. *The world is saved, no need for me anymore.* He pressed down, feeling the wood splinter until it fell away into the rush below. His other foot bounced on the next plank along feeling it bow, and separate. *I won't even have to jump. Just stomp down and fall. If nobody finds my body, it will rot, dissolve away, all that Glow and all those memories will drift apart, and I'll be gone.*

We'll be gone. Freed from damnation.

He opened his eyes and found himself up on the guide wire, face angling down to the racing filth below. *Like a dog going in face-first.*

"You're not thinking of jumping in there are you?"

He glanced sideways and saw a woman standing at the end of the bridge, just where Goliath had been that time.

"You might swallow some and that would be the death of you for sure." She stepped out onto the bridge, testing each plank with her weight.

"How did you find me?" he asked cynically.

She nodded up toward the sky. "Eyes everywhere these days."

"Who sent you? Del? To mop up some plague loose ends. Or are you a Convolver come to trick me into doing something else?"

She moved closer. A full head taller than Rex. Strikingly beautiful, her eyes were an optimistic shade of magenta, and she wore a simple, silver band around the top of her head.

"I'm Casima. Knoss asked me to be your guide."

"Guide to what?" Rex said with a sigh.

"Life, I guess? He said you just saved the world but might need help getting back to those that really matter. Those you love."

"Why you?" he asked quietly, noticing the profound sense of sadness that came at him through her eyes.

"Because we've both lost so much."

She stood right next to him now, no escape, he thought, suddenly noticing the plastic look to her face. "You're not really human."

"I hear the same about you." She looked out along the ravine. "I lost the man I loved, the only person who ever cared about me."

"I'm sorry." A breeze ruffled his fur, spurring the need to bound across fields and through grass and find his master and mistress once again. "I lost Mira. We never really had much, but it really was something."

A tear leaked from the corner of her magenta eye. "Well, there you are; we're both crazy cyborgs who want to bring somebody back from the dead. We have that in common."

He laughed and it felt like the first time he'd laughed in years. His thoughts wandered to John and Millie, and suddenly he felt awkward and selfish. "Well, there are others, people I'd like to see again, and people that could use my help. You should come meet Mrs O. She lost her husband in the Nova-Insanity and runs a dog rescue now. She has ideas. Whacky ideas... but ideas."

"Maybe I can help out there, do some walks. That could be my new thing: guided tours of the city... with dogs!"

Rex felt his knees giving way. The pain of infection, the rips and tears of muscles and tendons. The torture, it all came rushing back. He'd made it here and that was as far as he could go.

As he collapsed, he felt her grab him; not a harsh, violent grab, more of a catch, and suddenly he was laying across her arms.

She carried him back off the bridge and placed him gently on the back seat of a car. "Need to get you some medical attention."

He heard the car's front door open and felt it tilt as somebody climbed inside. "Millie used to be a nurse," he said, voice like that of a sleepy child.

"Then let's go find Millie."

"I think you'll like her. She's lost a lot too but, hopefully, is in the process of getting it back."

"I like her already."

"All those others, in my head, they've gone as well," Rex murmured. "It's just me in here now."

"Your mind is your own, Rex." Through bleary eyes he saw her turn and look back at him. She clicked the motor on and eased the car off across the grassland, sending grasshoppers and seeds spinning around them like a vortex of tiny, unstoppable machines.

ACKNOWLEDGEMENTS

I'd like to start by thanking my readers. Thanks for your comments, your feedback, and for spending time with me and my creations. I assure you all that this is just the opening salvo from my quirky mind, and there will be more worlds and ideas in the near future. Maybe even a little more Glow, if you all desire.

Thanks, as always, to Angry Robot for taking on this project and letting me dig deeper into the world of Glow. Shoutouts to Eleanor Teasdale, Gemma Creffield, Antonia Desola Coker, and Caroline Lambe for coordinating everything and supporting my work.

Particular thanks to Paul Simpson whose tell-it-like-it-is editing style really appeals to my engineering pragmatism. Also, Rob Lowry's eye for fine detail is greatly appreciated, along with his unwavering patience in unravelling and repackaging some of my more wayward sentences.

A big shoutout to Alexis Statler for shining her blazing, inspirational light on my manuscript and helping me craft what I thought was a great story into a great human story.

Thanks to my agent, Sam Morgan, for his vigilance, continuing guidance, and for nudging me in the right direction when I wander off track.

I always feel that having somebody interpret my work into a visual representation is a wonderful and personal thing. So thanks to Tom Shone for Afterglow's fierce cover art.

As always, my family continues to support me and nurture my need to share the worlds swirling around in my head. Particularly my wife, Joanna, who is always there with editing help, advice, and a cup of tea, along with ideas for amazing places in the world to visit and gather inspiration for our next projects.

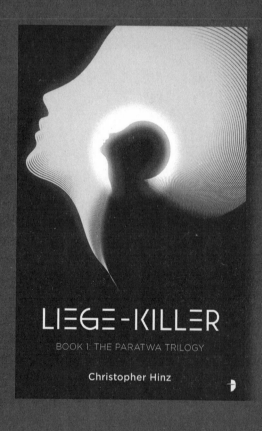

ONE

The shuttle crouched between skyscrapers, in the center of the desolate street, dwarfing rusted cars. Gouged and dirty wings – arched slivers of white metal – swept upward from the squat body of the craft like floppy ears from a fat rabbit. The underbelly quivered, radiating heat. Gray smoke drifted out from beneath the craft, swirling into oblivion as it met the perpetual Philadelphia gusts.

"What's the level?" Bronavitch asked. The younger of the two crew members, he stood beside the monster engines, oblivious to the waves of heat pouring from the vertical landing jets. Their spacesuits were designed to protect them from far worse perils.

Kelly grinned. Parched walnut skin crinkled across his cheeks, made him look older than his forty-six years. "Nothing to worry about within five klicks of here." Kelly twisted his neck forward, peeked out through the top of his helmet visor, and checked the readout counter mounted to his thick utility belt. "The scan reads less than point-oh-seven – we're in a fairly safe area. We could probably even take our suits off for a minute or so."

"Yeah," Bronavitch grumbled, "and we could gulp some air and say goodbye to the Colonies." Bronavitch did not need Kelly or a poison counter to tell him that there was enough organic death in the smog to keep a cleanup crew busy for years.

Kelly's grin expanded. "The air does seem a bit thick."

Bronavitch shook his head. He was not in the mood for Kelly's humor. "I'm telling you, I've had it. I'm sick of the whole damn planet. My contract is up in two months and I'm not signing on for another tour. I've had it."

His partner rumbled with laughter. "You told me that last year. Hell, admit it. You like it down here. You told me that you thought it was very serene."

"It pays good."

Skyscrapers – metal and concrete shells – lined the boulevard. A few smaller structures were nestled in their midst like scared children clutching at their mother's skirts. Chunks of unidentifiable debris lay everywhere.

To the west, a mountain of trash poked up through the lower smog cover, interrupting the flow of the street. Bronavitch thought he detected form in the junk pile. It seemed to resemble a giant frog. He suspected some mad humans had been responsible for its creation during the final days. His theory seemed reasonable. Dying of radiation and a host of other ecospheric poisons would have justified the creation of such a weird monument.

"Do you know what they used to call this place?" Kelly asked.

Bronavitch shook his head.

"The City of Brotherly Love." Thankfully, the black face had lost its smile.

Bronavitch booted a crusted brick. "Let's get on with it. I want to get the hell out of here."

They marched down the street. Open doors and glassless windows seemed to stare at them; dark eyes, full of death, contemptuous of the living. Bronavitch felt a familiar twinge of fear tighten his stomach. He hated these dead cities. It always seemed as if someone were watching, like they were intruding upon some private domain.

Kelly broke into a fresh grin. He appeared to be enjoying himself.

"All right, we know the pirates landed where we touched down. They must have been close to whatever they were looking for."

"How do you know they were looking for anything?" Bronavitch argued. "Maybe the bastards just dropped in at random, hoping to pick up a few artifacts. Or maybe they had shuttle problems and were forced to land for repairs."

"I don't think so. First of all, they couldn't have been here for more than two or three hours – in and out real quick, not nearly enough time for a profitable artifact hunt. And when did you ever hear of a shuttle dropping into a supercontaminated zone like this for repairs? Even if they lost their main engines, the vertical landing jets were still functioning – had to be in order to touch down safely in the middle of this mess." Kelly shook his head. "No, if it had been an emergency landing, they would have coasted down toward the Virginia area. The contamination's not as bad."

Bronavitch sighed. "These are Costeaus you're talking about. They're not always that rational."

Kelly laughed. "Maybe not, but most of the bastards got better ships than we do. Don't believe all that Guardian crap about stupid pirates and their rundown equipment."

It was no sense arguing. "All right, which direction? This is a goddamn big city."

Kelly pointed toward the frog-shaped mountain. "That trash pile could have been their landing mark – there's nothing else down here that's so easily recognizable from the air. And if I were a Costeau captain, I wouldn't have touched down any closer to it than this."

"Landslides?" Bronavitch asked uneasily.

"Right. That mess doesn't look too stable. At this distance, at least the shuttle would be safe even if the whole damn mountain came tumbling down."

"That still leaves a big area to search. Why don't we call base and request help?"

"No way. I'm not gonna get chewed out by some commander for tying up a whole unit just to find out what some pirates were looking for."

Bronavitch clamped his mouth shut.

They had come from E-Tech – from the Berks Valley base, about a hundred kilometers to the northwest. Berks was one of E-Tech's major experimental arenas where scientists and engineers sought methods for removing the contamination from the environment. Ecospheric Turnaround was the long-term goal of the huge organization, a goal in which Bronavitch no longer had much faith. Working down here as a shuttle pilot for the past two years had slowly eroded his belief.

Too much of the Earth was dead. There were still insects and a few of the hardier forms of plant life, and there were humans in their protective garments. Most of the evolutionary links in between had perished; the complex chain of life had been broken by the madness of two centuries ago. Bronavitch believed that the Earth would never again be a hospitable place for humanity.

He and Kelly were assigned to perimeter duty. They checked on the status of various bioprojects that Berks initiated, searched for signs of natural life, ferried scientists to and from other bases and policed the zone surrounding the Berks Valley. Today's duty fell into the last category.

Early this morning, Berks radar had picked up an unauthorized ship heading toward the Philadelphia area. Although the fix had been lost before the ship landed, projections had indicated several likely touchdown locations. Naturally, the pirates had already departed by the time he and Kelly located this landing spot. Costeaus generally knew just how long they could remain in an area before E-Tech tracked them. Heavily smogged cities like Philadelphia made visual detection nearly impossible, and with E-Tech's severe limitations on AI and other tracing technologies, sensor analysis took time. Pirates were rarely caught on the surface.

The best that could be hoped for now was that he and Kelly might locate some evidence identifying the pirate clan. Then E-Tech or the Intercolonial Guardians would launch an official investigation up in the Colonies. With exceptional luck, the trespassing pirates might be arrested and their DNA added to the intercolonial database.

Unofficially, though, Bronavitch knew that this Costeau incident would be treated like most of the others – largely ignored. The Costeaus' antique-hunting expeditions to the surface were tolerated as long as they did not directly interfere with any of E-Tech's projects. Today's hunt, and the subsequent official report, would be made primarily to assuage the Irryan Council, which, in its wisdom, was demanding a final solution to the pirate problem.

Kelly halted and directed a gloved finger toward a large hole in the side of a small, brick-faced building. "That looks new."

Bronavitch nodded. This could be easier than he had thought. The five-story structure appeared a bit better preserved than the surrounding skyscrapers. The building had probably been shielded from the higher-elevation nuclear shockwaves that had mutilated Philadelphia back in the twenty-first century.

The hole was rectangular and larger than a man in a spacesuit. It was also newly formed. One learned to easily recognize such anomalies after a few trips through any of Earth's decimated urban areas.

Kelly stepped carefully over the lip of the opening and turned on his helmet spotlight. "Looks like some kind of an old food store."

Bronavitch followed his partner into the darkened interior, panned his helmet light across the rows of dusty shelving.

Crushed cans and smashed plastic jars littered the racks. Ceiling rubble, foodpaks, and shattered fragments of glass covered the floor. Kelly's spotlight froze momentarily on a human skeleton slumped over a low counter. Bronavitch looked away.

"This is it." Kelly shined his spotlight down the center aisle, traced the trail of overlapping boot prints that led toward the back of the store. In a few spots, the centuries-old layer of deep dust had been disturbed enough to reveal the original tiled floor.

"Looks like there were at least four or five of them," Bronavitch observed.

"Either that or they made several trips through. C'mon."

He followed Kelly down the aisle, keeping his attention along the upper edge of the surrounding shelves. It felt as if they were walking through a dark canyon. The only sounds were their footsteps, picked up by external suit mikes and amplified into their helmets. He shivered. Outside, at least there was the wind and the smog-filtered sunshine. In here, silence and darkness created an entirely different mood. Bronavitch imagined that something was waiting to leap down on him from the top shelves.

Kelly halted when they reached the back of the store. Bronavitch followed his partner's downward gaze.

The hole in the floor was roughly the same diameter as the one the Costeaus had cut into the outer wall, although more circular in shape. They knelt carefully at the edge and shined their spots into the opening. About three meters below was a cellar floor of pale concrete. That floor also had been cut through. Their spotlights reflected off a dark pool of water well below the basement level.

"Oh, shit," Bronavitch muttered. He did not relish the idea of climbing down into some sewer beneath this dead city.

"Must be at least fifteen meters to the water level," Kelly said quietly. "I wonder why they made such big holes? They must have used at least two beam cutters to be in and out of here so quick. Hell of a lot of work."

The question had a simple answer. "They hauled something up from down there that was bigger than a man in a spacesuit."

Kelly nodded. "They probably used a portable winch. Want to run back to the shuttle and get ours?"

"A ladder will do." They might as well get this over with as quickly as possible.

The portable ladder was in Kelly's backpack. In a few minutes, they had unrolled it and fastened one end to a sturdy pillar near the edge of the hole. There was no question as to who was going down first. Kelly eased himself over the lip and began the descent.

"What if this place caves in?" Bronavitch asked nervously.

"If it didn't cave in on the pirates, then it probably won't fall on us."

Somehow that did not sound very reassuring.

Kelly passed the cellar mark and rapidly approached the pool of dark water. Bronavitch could hear the end of the ladder flapping against the surface of the liquid.

"What if the water's too deep to stand in?" he called down. "It might be a couple hundred meters to the bottom."

Kelly laughed. "Don't be ridiculous. We're almost at sea level."

Maybe it was the ocean.

His fears were eased by a loud splash as Kelly hit the water. "It's up to my waist and everything feels solid underneath. It's way too big to be a sewer – must have been one of those old subway transport tunnels. C'mon down."

Bronavitch took a deep breath and climbed over the lip. In a minute, he was standing beside Kelly in a meter of water.

They stood silently for a moment, playing their lights over the dank and slimy walls. The water had a slight flow to it and the gentle current licked at their waists. They could not see the bottom – the water was almost black. Bronavitch took a step toward the left wall, tripped on something solid, and almost fell.

"Shit!"

"Old railway tracks," Kelly said. "This tunnel looks wide enough for two sets of them."

"Yeah, right. So which way do we go?"

"I'll go upstream and you go downstream."

Bronavitch thought his partner was joking until he flashed his spotlight into the solemn face. "Look, Kelly, this is weird enough down here without us separating."

"Relax. The Costeaus obviously had a map of some sort. They knew just where to cut that hole in the food store and just where to make their descent. I'll bet they knew exactly what they were looking for and exactly where it was located. It's got to be real close by." Kelly turned and began a slow march against the current.

Bronavitch repressed a shudder. Two more months. Just two more months and then his contract was up and he could be off this damn planet forever. He thought briefly of home, the orbiting colony of Kiev Beta – even in perigee, more than a hundred and sixty thousand kilometers away.

Kelly vanished from sight as the subway tunnel curved gently to the right. Bronavitch sighed and began moving in the opposite direction, splashing his gloves against the dark liquid to create as much noise as possible. He hoped he would not trip over anything. There were probably rotting corpses in this foul water just waiting to snag his ankles.

After two hundred years, there couldn't be anything left but bones, he reminded himself. *Rotting corpses*, insisted his imagination.

"This tunnel has a grade to it," Kelly said over the radio. "Water's getting a bit deeper down my way."

Bronavitch stopped, stared at his waistline. The water was a couple of inches below where it had been. Good. Maybe the tunnel would lead up to the surface.

"Dead-end," Kelly said, "There must have been a cave-in. There's old rubble all over the place down here and the water's up to my chest. The pirates couldn't have come this way."

"Care to join me?" Bronavitch cracked. He was feeling better each step of the way, mainly because of the decreasing depth of the water. He figured that by the time he rounded the next bend, the level should be down to his knees.

"I wonder what the hell they could have been searching for?" Kelly asked. "Do you think maybe someone hid a treasure down here two hundred years ago?"

Bronavitch heard the guarded excitement in his partner's voice. "I know what you're thinking, Kelly, and you may as well forget it. The pirates were already here and if there was a treasure ..."

He stopped, stared at the huge form coming into view around the bend. "I've found it."

The last car of the old subway train appeared heavily rusted but otherwise in good shape. All the windows were intact although layered over by grime. The wheel trucks were underwater, giving the illusion that the transit cars were floating on the surface of the opaque liquid. He moved alongside the train and examined the now-familiar hole cut through the age-scarred metal. His light reflected off something shiny inside.

He waited until Kelly came splashing around the bend before grasping the edge of the hole and hoisting himself up into the train. His spot illuminated a glittering white cavern. Ice. The whole interior of the car was covered with it. He checked the temperature readout on his helmet panel.

"Jesus, it's almost ninety below in here!"

A huge silent generator took up the rear half of the subway car. An open airlock led toward the front of the train. Icicle-coated conduits trailed along the ceiling, connecting the generator to a rack of glazed monitors beside the airlock. Kelly hopped in behind him and whistled softly.

"A stasis operation."

Bronavitch nodded. He felt relieved now that they knew what they were dealing with, although he still wanted to be away from this place as quickly as possible.

They pushed on through to the next car – the stasis room itself. The room was even colder than the generator car, although the Costeaus must have shut off the power hours ago. Thin milky stalactites hung from the ceiling. Hard icy patches obscured portions of the metallic floor. Until today, it probably had been a sealed freezer for over two hundred years. Now the inexorable process of temperature equalization had begun. The ice was melting. If any stasis-frozen humans had remained, they would be slowly on their way to a more permanent sleep.

The occupants of this freezer were gone, however. The pirates had found what they were looking for.

"There were two of them," Kelly said quietly. The pair of large plastic cradles in the center of the car was empty, the pale ivory cocoons missing. The genetically manufactured tissues that surrounded the sleepers would keep their metabolisms stable for at least thirty hours – long enough for the Costeaus to get them to a Wake-up facility up in the Colonies.

Bronavitch felt even more disturbed than he had earlier. There were two of them. Jesus! Why couldn't there have been one ... or three ... or twenty-six?

Kelly walked past the cradles to the other end of the stasis room. He used his glove to wipe the frost from a pair of glass gauges.

"The other cars in the train must be tankers. This meter says there's enough fuel left to run the generators for another fifty years or so."

Bronavitch grimaced. "And why were there only two capsules? This car's big enough to hold a dozen and it wouldn't have taken much more fuel. Yet there were only two capsules."

Kelly turned from the gauges and gazed at him with a confident smile. "There's probably a simple explanation. The capsules contain a husband and wife, I'll bet – somebody's great, great – whatever – grandparents. Now, recently, some rich young kid up in the Colonies finds a family heirloom that tells how his wealthy ancestors put themselves into stasis during the final days. The heirloom explains where and how they were frozen and the kid thinks it would be just great if he could bring them out of hibernation. To do it legally, of course, you've got to get E-Tech's permission, and that means going through all sorts of official channels and maybe getting turned down after a year of fighting the red tape. So the rich kid figures he'll avoid all that hassle. He hires himself some Costeaus, gives them the map, and tells them they'll get a nice fat bonus if they succeed in waking up his ancestors."

"That doesn't answer my question, Kelly. If these were some rich husband and wife, why didn't they buy their way up to the Colonies? Or if they couldn't do that, then why not have ten other people frozen in here with them? They must have had some friends."

"Maybe they were a couple of greedy industrialists. You've read how crazy things were in the final days. People got selfish. They did just about anything to survive."

"Yeah, and it wasn't just people who might do anything to survive."

Anger broke across Kelly's face. "Now I don't want to hear what you're thinking! They were wiped out – nobody's seen one in two centuries. They're gone – long dead. Now if you go spouting your thoughts back at base, E-Tech's gonna go into a mild panic – all for nothing, I might add. And you and I are gonna spend the next two weeks down in this tunnel, searching for clues so that some E-Tech exec can get his official report made up and shoved into the archives. All for nothing, dammit!"

Bronavitch shook his head. "How can you be so certain? Jesus, what if you're wrong? What if one of those bastards gets awakened up in the Colonies? Things could get real messy and you and I could get in a hell of a lot of trouble for not reporting this."

Kelly stared up at the ice-crusted ceiling. "Maybe," he said softly, "there could be a cave-in down here. We could report that the Costeaus were probably artifact-hunting–"

"That's irresponsible! I'm not going to have this on my conscience, Kelly! This could be the beginning of a bad situation and we're duty bound to report it."

Kelly's jaw tightened. "All right, dammit! We'll report. But no speculation. We tell E-Tech exactly what we've found and let them come to conclusions. I don't want any extra trouble from this."

"Agreed."

Kelly brushed past him and stomped back toward the generator car. Bronavitch paused to stare at the two empty stasis cradles.

Two of them. He could not shake the fear. Stories that he had learned as a schoolboy came back to him; stories made even more terrifying by two hundred years of legend.

He shuddered. It was neither the time nor place to dwell on such things. He turned and quickly followed Kelly back out into the tunnel.

For more great title recommendations,
check out the Angry Robot website and
social channels

www.angryrobotbooks.com
@angryrobotbooks

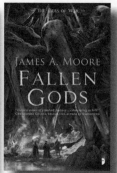
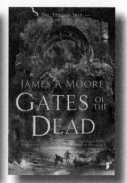
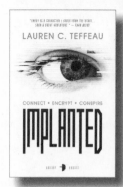

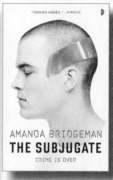

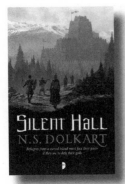

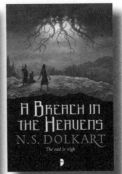

Science Fiction, Fantasy and WTF?!

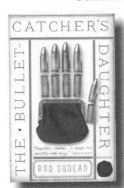

@angryrobotbooks

We are Angry Robot

angryrobotbooks.com